Together Again, Together Forever

by

Doreen Alsen

Together Again, Together Forever

Contact Information: info@thewildrosepress.com

Cover Art by *Tina Lynn Stout*

The Wild Rose Press, Inc.
PO Box 708
Adams Basin, NY 14410-0708

Visit us at www.thewildrosepress.com

Publishing History
First Scarlet Rose Edition, 2022
Print ISBN 978-1-5092-3907-8
Digital ISBN 978-1-5092-3908-5

Published in the United States of America

**Sometimes you are lucky
and get a second chance at love.**

He stood. "Thank you for dinner."

Laughing, she wiped her hands on her jeans as she got out of her chair. "Such as it was."

"I'll talk to my mother about the cooking thing."

"I appreciate it. I need all the help I can get."

They walked to her front door, close enough for Tony's skin to prickle in awareness of the woman who had tossed him away so many years before.

He wanted to kiss her, damn her.

Damn him.

As if she knew what he was fighting, Pearl faced him, studying him with those shiny, bright-blue eyes. She opened her mouth as if to say something, but she didn't. She just stared at him, her dazzling, plump, soft lips apart, like an invitation to kiss her.

His hands trembled as he reached over to cup her beautiful face. Consigning himself to hell, he leaned in and brushed his lips across Pearl's, soft as a whisper.

Dedication

To Donna Janoplis-Hough for
believing in me. Old friends are the best.
To the Thistle Dew group for all the times you
listened to me reading bits of it. This book was born
there, and I thank you for all the help and support!
As always, love to Eberhard, Emilia, and Louisa.

Chapter One

"Pearl. You okay?"

Pearl Marlowe turned and looked at her brother, Sterling. He appeared so dignified with his perfectly cut and groomed hair and dark pin-striped designer suit. An American flag pin glinted from his lapel. She smiled for his sake. "I'm as good as it gets, given the situation."

Pearl, Sterling, and their two sisters, Ruby and Opal, were back at their childhood home in Provincetown, Massachusetts, to bury and memorialize their grandmother, the great Camille Marlowe.

Camille's funeral was absolutely the only way Pearl would ever come back to P-town. She'd burned too many bridges back in the day. She shouldn't be here. She should be somewhere else, rebuilding her life. She needed to leave as soon as she could, someplace where no one knew her.

"Yeah. How about you?"

Sterling quirked up one perfect eyebrow. "I'm okay. Grandmother left very complete instructions on how to manage her whole final arrangements."

"No doubt." Camille Marlowe's commitment to detail bordered on the terrifying. Pearl touched his arm. "How do you feel?"

"I'm numb, to tell the truth. Camille had been doing well after the stroke. Ruby kept saying she was okay. I should have done more."

"I should have been here more often." Pearl had avoided coming home for all sorts of reasons. Bitter regret weighed heavy on her shoulders.

"You were fighting to stay out of jail. Thank God Henry came clean."

"I'm grateful to him for that." And only that.

"It's the least he could do after he tried to make you take the fall. He was the one guilty of embezzlement and fraud, not you." Sterling looked at his watch and sighed. "The car should be here soon. Robert's going to meet us at the mortuary."

She nodded. Robert was their grandmother's general lackey and Pearl's personal pain in the ass. "Is Amy here?" Amy was Sterling's very capable campaign manager.

"To handle the press, yes."

"Good." Pearl hated the members of the third estate with a passion, with good reason. They'd made her life a circus and given her no privacy when she and Henry had been arrested. Shivering, she turned to gaze out the window again. She rested her forehead against the smooth, cold glass.

Gray sky met with gray sea, except for the white caps that frothed along the churning water. Small boats bobbed on their moorings, trying to stay anchored in the midst of the spray from the waves and the pelting rain from the sky.

"The car's here," Opal said.

Pearl turned to see Opal and her other sister, Ruby, standing in the doorway.

"Thanks," Sterling said as he straightened his cuffs. "Coming, Pearl?"

Pearl nodded. "Let's get this over with."

****

Tony Cabral leaned on the bar and swirled the scotch on the rocks in his glass and wondered what the hell he was doing at Camille Marlowe's memorial service. As far as he knew, she had appreciated his ability to bring her lobsters straight from the sea but not much else.

She certainly hadn't liked him hanging out with her princess granddaughter, Pearl, way back in the day.

So how had he managed to get invited to the memorial service for Camille Marlowe, the most exclusive gathering in the literary world?

He sipped his scotch and studied the room. Pictures of Camille lined the rose-colored dining room walls of her favorite restaurant, Bradford Street Seafood. Professor-type people from all over gathered in clumps to share stories about La Grande Dame Marlowe over cocktails and fancy appetizers.

Classical music wafted softly and sweetly into the room, punctuated with low murmurs of conversations and ice clinking in highball glasses. The air carried the scents of delicious spices coming from the kitchen. Each table featured a flickering candle in a hurricane lamp while the overhead lights were set to dim.

Tony wanted to leave in the worst way but resigned himself to staying until Pearl and her family got there.

Before he could stop himself, he looked around the room to see if she had arrived, the woman who had shattered his heart into a million pieces when she'd left him without a backward glance.

Ancient history. Water under the bridge. He didn't think about Pearl at all anymore, at least not much and not often.

He grimaced, not convinced of his own lie. Since she'd been in the news, she'd been on his mind. He'd fought long and hard against the urge to jump into a car and go to Manhattan to save her, like some crazy superhero. Captain Lobsterman.

"Hey, Tony. You need a refill?"

He turned his head at the sound of his girlfriend Jenny's voice. She was working the event. He didn't know why. Jenny had never liked Pearl, nor had she ever had any use for the Marlowe family. "No, thanks. I'm good for now."

"Well, give me a holler if you need anything." Jenny bit her lower lip. "Word in the kitchen is that the family is going to show up any minute now."

Good. He could pay his condolences and get the hell out of there.

"I'm getting a summons from Christie," Jenny said. "Duty calls. I'll see you later, yes?"

"Maybe. I've got an early morning tomorrow."

She gave him a little hip check and a pout. "You always have an early morning."

"It's called making a living."

Her pout turned from playful to annoyed. "Make sure you kiss me good-bye before you take off."

"Of course."

The air in the room changed, sparking electric, and Tony didn't need to look to know what was happening. Pearl Marlowe was in the house.

He looked in spite of himself. His world spun and narrowed until there was only one person in the room.

Pearl Marlowe. His first love.

He gulped the rest of his scotch while he studied her.

She'd always been small, fit, and lean. In high school she'd worn her red hair long and in a perky ponytail, but now it was short and pixie like. She'd chosen a form-fitting black dress and mile-high heels, all big-city polish and style.

She was pale, almost translucent. Delicate. Well, he guessed she'd been through a bad time of it if the newspapers were to be believed. Whatever his feelings were about how she'd left him, he knew she wasn't a thief. Apparently the federal court system knew that as well, as they'd sent her boyfriend to prison and released her and proclaimed her innocent.

There was zero doubt in his mind she would blow out of town as fast as she blew in. She'd turned running away into an art form.

Pearl's sisters, Opal and Ruby, towered over her, Opal with long, straight locks of red hair, Ruby with red curls tumbling down her back. Her brother, Sterling, was a member of the United States House of Representatives from the Ninth US Congressional District, Barney Franks' old position.

Sterling bent down to whisper something into Pearl's ear, and she nodded. Like a beacon searching the night, those blue eyes of hers immediately homed in on Tony.

He felt a jolt, and by the rounding of her eyes, she felt it too. Her mouth opened, a little O of stunned surprise.

What? She hadn't known he'd be there?

Unless she just hadn't cared about the guest list and never expected Tony to make the cut.

Damn, he had to get his sorry ass out of there before he made a total fool of himself. He set his scotch glass aside and made a beeline for the exit, paying his respects be damned.

****

Tony Cabral? No one had told her about Tony.

"Steady," Sterling said as he gripped her elbow.

Steady? When the man she'd loved and abandoned so many years ago was across the room? No way could Pearl manage steady. "Why is Tony here?" she whispered over the broken glass of her vocal cords.

"It was in Grandmother's instructions on whom to invite." He tightened his grip on her elbow, like he was afraid she was going to run away.

"And you didn't think to warn me?" Her voice cracked at the end of the sentence. She'd been prepared for everyone to stare at her and wonder if she really was guilty of those financial crimes. She hated the idea of Tony looking at her and judging whether she was guilty or not.

"I didn't think it was that big a deal."

Not a big deal? She should have hit him harder with that tennis racquet back in elementary school. Might have knocked some sense into him. At the time she had settled for a bloody lip, which had been very satisfying, seeing as he had given her favorite Barbie a Mohawk. A puke green Mohawk. She settled for jabbing her pointy elbow into his rib cage. He made a very satisfactory *oof* of pain.

She watched Tony walk across the room. "I need air." She slipped outside before any of her family could stop her.

"Pearl." Tony's baritone rumbled as he stood in front of her for the first time in seventeen years. His voice was a lot deeper than she remembered. She trembled at the sound. She couldn't still be attracted to him, could she? It was her grandmother's memorial after all.

Damn, she was sick.

"Tony," she said as she looked into his face. God, he still had those deep chocolate-brown eyes and those outrageous eyelashes. "Thank you for coming."

"Yeah." He pressed his lips together. "How are you doing? You look great."

That was as smooth a lie as she'd ever heard. "I've been better."

He cleared his throat. "I'm really sorry for your loss."

"Thank you." His cologne was woodsy, and she stepped to one side, out of range. She didn't need to remember how good Tony smelled.

Tony stared at her face and made something flutter in her stomach. He shouldn't have this effect on her anymore. No, no, no, no.

"It's good seeing you, Pearl. You take care," he said, those amazing brown eyes of his cool and unreadable.

Once upon a time she could read his mind. "You too," she answered.

He looked like he wanted to say something more, but he didn't. He just turned and headed for the parking lot. She watched as one of the servers rushed out of the kitchen door and made a beeline for Tony. Was that Jenny Silva? How could Tony date Jenny Silva, the girl who had made her life miserable in high school? Her breath caught in her throat when Tony leaned down and kissed Jenny. He got into his truck, and the woman turned and smirked at Pearl.

Trust Jenny to be Jenny.

Pearl shook her head. She didn't need to borrow trouble. Whomever Tony dated shouldn't be any of her business.

"Pearl?" Ruby came up to her and touched her shoulder. "We really need you to be in there with us."

"I'm ready," she lied.

Chapter Two

"I think that was the worst two hours of my life," Ruby said as she flopped down on a chair in the parlor.

Pearl had to agree. Their grandmother's memorial service had been a nightmare. Never mind being in the same room with Tony since she'd broken his heart. Her face muscles nearly cramped from forcing a smile as she listened to the literary elite wax rhapsodic about Camille.

Sure, Camille had taken in her orphaned grandchildren. It was all for show.

Pearl sat in one of the cushy leather chairs near the fireplace and took in the familiar scents of her grandmother's home, lemon furniture polish and a hideous potpourri mix her grandmother had loved. Camille's lawyer had a video from her to play for them after the memorial. In true Camille Marlowe fashion, she'd orchestrated her passing right down to how many cocktail napkins they'd need.

Now she was going to lay down the law from the grave.

Just another day in the life and death of La Marlowe.

Pearl sighed.

Sterling came into the room with Camille's lawyer, the ever helpful Robert Harrison. "We're all set to see the video." He looked around, a frown on his face.

"Where's Opal?"

"Right here." Opal slouched over to the sofa, already changed out of her funeral clothes and into a pair of sweatpants and an oversized tee.

Robert rubbed his hands together. "Let's get started, shall we?"

"Might as well," Ruby muttered.

"Go ahead, Robert," Sterling said as he perched on the arm of the bottle-green velveteen loveseat.

He'd taken his jacket off, rolled up the sleeves of his custom-made dress shirt, and loosened his tie. He looked so natural and solid. Dependable. He'd been the one constant in Pearl's life for as long as she could remember, at least when he wasn't scalping her Barbies. Love for him rolled over her.

He frowned when he caught her looking at him. "What?"

She smiled. "You're just as ugly as always."

He winked. "Back at you, Pearlie."

"Are you ready?" Robert's voice held a tiny note of asperity.

"Yes." Sterling cleared his throat. "Sorry."

Robert cleared his throat, pointed the remote at the TV, and clicked.

Camille's face filled the television screen, larger than life, as usual. Her champagne-colored hair was perfectly coiffed in a style that belonged to the 1950s rather than the twenty-first century. A white and black patterned Chanel silk scarf, immaculately knotted, hung around her neck. Diamond studs the size of hubcaps winked from her ears.

The great Camille Marlowe, never a hair out of place, facial expression as implacable as ever, a veritable force of nature, commanded the room, just like always. Pearl didn't know whether to cry or laugh.

She did what she always did when confronted by her grandmother. She kept quiet and waited for disapproval to rain down on her.

Because there was always another shoe to drop when Camille was concerned.

As Pearl studied the suspended image of her grandmother on the television screen, she saw numerous cracks in her well and carefully executed façade. Makeup caked over lines in her face couldn't quite hide her parchment-fragile, gray skin. One side of Camille's mouth drooped, a result of the stroke that had led to her swift decline in health.

"Ah, my loving family," Camille said from the screen. "At the risk of ending up a cliché, you are all viewing this because I have shuffled off this mortal coil."

"Gah!" Opal rolled her eyes.

"Shhhh!" Ruby jabbed Opal hard in the ribs.

"Ruby, I saw that." Camille shook her head, the picture of sorrow. "And Opal, use your words. Now, if you'll all pay attention, I'll get on with it. It's no surprise to you children that I was not prepared to become your parent when your father and mother died. I had already raised my son, your father, and I did not want a house full of teens and preteens in my home. Be that as it may, I did my duty to the best of my ability, and I don't think you suffered for it."

Pearl cleared her throat. If only her grandmother knew—

"I have some things to say," Camille continued, "important things, and I'm going to make sure you hear

me. But first, I have a few words to say to each of you."
She sighed. "Sterling."

"Yes, ma'am," he murmured.

"Of all my son's children, you are the most like
him and not just because you're a man. You have taken
to heart the motto of 'to whom much is given, much is
asked.' You have devoted yourself to a life of service,
unlike your sisters."

Now that was a familiar refrain. Don't be so
selfish, girls. Be more like Sterling. Pearl shook her
head.

Grandmother hadn't always known what Saint
Sterling had been up to. Pearl shot him a dirty look,
which he ignored, like the brat he was.

"To the end of getting you elected to the Senate of
the United States of America, I have set aside money
for your campaign in a trust. While it is my dearest
hope that you win your election, I have made some
stipulations regarding the use of the money. Robert has
a letter for you and will be available, of course, to
answer all your questions.

"I'll go out of order with you girls. Ruby, you
stayed with me when I needed you, and I wish to
reward that. I, more than anybody else, know and
appreciate what you have given up to take care of me,
putting your dreams on hold. Here is your reward: all
the jewelry with the proviso that you keep the
collection intact. They are all heirlooms passed down
from generation to generation. Now"—Camille
smiled—"as with Sterling, there are stipulations. I must
insist that you stay on your medications and keep
seeing your counselor to keep your bipolar disorder in
check."

Pearl leaned back in her seat. Ruby had stayed behind when she and Opal left town as fast as they could. Ruby deserved anything good she got from Camille. To be honest, Pearl was a bit stunned their grandmother had noticed. For once she agreed with Camille about Ruby's meds. Ruby was doing so well. Pearl glanced sideways at Opal, who looked like a cat about to hack up a hairball.

"On to you, Opal. I had such plans for you, my girl, and how you've disappointed me."

Opal made a noise that sounded like she'd swallowed that hairball.

"Of all of your siblings, you were the one to follow my heart the closest." Camille closed her eyes for a brief second. "Words, and how to craft them into art, I truly thought you understood the power you had. But you turned your back on your gift and decided to write trash, books with trite plots, happy-ever-after endings, catering to popular taste instead of laboring to uplift the human condition.

"You have talent, and you have a responsibility to use it for good. Therefore, I'm giving you a huge task, with the hope that you learn your lesson and take up the Marlowe literary mantle. I hired a man named Benjamin Wallace to write a book about my life. He is to have full access to all my papers, both published and unpublished, and you are to work at his side and make sure the project turns out right. As with your brother and sister, Robert has instructions for you, about which he'll tell you in private. You are to follow my stipulations to the letter. I will not tolerate any deviations."

Pearl almost laughed but didn't out of loyalty to

Opal. If anyone thought she could call the shots from the grave, it was her grandmother.

Camille's high-handedness was the single most important reason Pearl had left town.

"Pearl. My poor, deluded girl." Her grandmother's voice sluiced through the room like a river of ice water. "Life would have been so much easier for you if you had listened to me and explored your creative side instead of becoming a bean counter." Camille waved. "Yes, yes, I know. An investment banker is not a bean counter. Spare me the details. While I pushed you to leave Provincetown for your own good, you stayed away too long and trusted the wrong people, as usual."

Each word punched Pearl in the gut. Even in death, her grandmother was telling her to explore a side of her, some kind of magic creativity, that Pearl just didn't have. Nothing in her life had ever been magic.

She refused to listen to the voice in her head that whispered, "Tony was magic."

He might have been a long time ago but not anymore.

Never again.

"I am aware you are quite penniless after all the fines and lawyers' fees that you accrued defending yourself against those trumped-up charges. If anyone had taken the time to look, they would have plainly seen you didn't have it in you to arrange such a scheme." Camille waved a hand. "You just don't have the mind for it. No matter. Your life needs fixing, and I'm the one who needs to do it."

Pearl felt the blood leave her face and a bitter cold leach out and grab hold of every molecule of her body. She knew, because how could she not know, how little

Camille thought of her, but damn, she had no idea her grandmother's opinion of her was that low.

Robert paused the video. "Do you want to take a minute?"

Pearl blinked and realized he was talking to her. "No. Let's keep going. I can't wait to hear what else she has to say."

"As you wish." Robert flicked the remote again.

"Really, Pearl, I don't mean to be so hard on you, but I feel it is my duty. I want you to remain here in town for at least a year and rebuild your life. Live here in the house. I'm adamant about that. I'm sure, after a nice rest, you can find any number of creative pursuits and become the person you were meant to be, which includes being loyal to your family. Robert knows my wishes in this matter, and he will counsel you in the way to move forward."

Pearl shook her head. Being subservient to her grandmother had cost her Tony.

"There is a penalty if the four of you disappoint me. And trust me, if one of you breaks the rules I've set down, all of you will face the consequences. To whit: all of my money and assets will go to the Fine Arts Work Center should any of you fall short of my expectations." Camille waved a pale, bony hand in front of her. "Now I can hear each of you protesting about how unfair I am, but I assure you, I still have my eyes on the big picture. Meeting my wishes is not a race with each of you running for the finish line in competition with each other. You will only have to meet with Robert every now and again to check in with regard to your progress on the tasks I've laid out for you." She sighed. "I have done my best in my duty to your parents and only hope for your health and happiness. I've loved you as best as I could. That should be enough."

Robert stopped the video. Opal jumped out of her chair and left.

"Opal." Ruby followed her.

Pearl wished she could leave the room, like Ruby and Opal, but she remained frozen solid, stuck to her seat.

Really, what did she have to offer in the way of comfort to Opal?

Nothing. Nothing at all.

"Are there any questions I can answer for you right now?" Robert straightened his shirt cuffs.

"You bet." Sterling's mouth stretched stern and unrelenting across his face. "I want a good look at that letter."

"I anticipated that and have it here."

Sterling looked at Pearl, who shrugged. "You should go read it."

"Let's go to the library," Sterling said. "We won't have any distractions there."

"I can leave," Pearl offered.

"No, you stay here. Robert and I will go to the library." Sterling nodded at the lawyer and gestured him out of the room.

Alone for a few blessed minutes, Pearl took several silent, deep breaths to calm her nerves and concentrate.

Standing, she dropped her chin to her chest. The sound of the surf breaking on the beach caught her attention, and she walked over to the french doors looking out over the gray, churning water of Provincetown harbor.

The warm air in the room pressed in on her,

making it hard to breathe. Without thinking, she opened the door to the deck and stepped out into the wild weather.

The gale-force winds whipped her hair, pulling strands every which way. Spray from the waves spit and bit at her face, and the roar of the surf and wind wreaked havoc on her hearing.

The ghosts of the past year swirled round her, tossed by the storm, like Camille had sent them down on purpose to torture her. No matter. She would defeat them all, including Granny Dearest.

She'd manage to stay here on her own terms, then get the hell out again as fast as she could.

****

Sterling made a conscious effort to slow down both his breathing and his footsteps as he led Robert to the Marlowe House library. He had a hunch he knew what was in the damn letter Camille'd left with her lawyer, and he didn't like it.

Not one bit.

They reached the library, and Sterling held the door open for Robert.

"Thank you."

"No problem," Sterling muttered.

Robert placed his briefcase on an authentic Louis Quatorze table and opened it. He pulled out a cream-colored envelope and held it out to Sterling. "Here you go."

"You know what's in there, don't you."

Robert shrugged. "Of course. But don't worry about it. It's covered by attorney-client privilege."

"Right." He took the letter.

"Do you want me to stay in case you have any

questions?"

God, no. "I don't think so. I'll give you a call if something occurs to me."

"Right. I'll see about the girls now."

Sterling snorted. "I'd stay away from Opal if it looks like she has something sharp and pointy in her hands."

Robert smiled. It looked unpracticed. "Sounds like good advice. I'll be in touch." He left.

Sterling sat in one of the brown leather library chairs and stared at the message from his grandmother. His hands shook as he opened it and studied the spidery old-fashioned handwriting.

Dear Sterling, I won't insult you by beating around the bush. As you have just found out, I have put aside a considerable amount of money for your Senate run. You are also smart enough to know the money comes with strings and conditions. To that end, I'm putting in a morals clause. In other words, you will remain scandal free for the time of the election. I must say this to you. The day you came out was the worst day of my life. So this clause means you must give up your little boyfriends for that period of time or else the money goes to your opponent. You may find this harsh, but it's for the best.

Sterling felt a slow burn rise up his face. The worst damn day of her life was when he came out? Not when her son and wife died leaving their children orphans? Not when her husband died? And when had he ever been indiscreet? Never. He took a deep breath and turned his attention back to the letter.

I really think you should give some thought to consider finding a woman to marry, a marriage of convenience for the good of your career. Yes, I mean a sham marriage. Most of my friends have been very happy in a similar situation, like I was, and I think you will, too. I'm sure any woman would consider you a catch and would love to stand by your side when you finally run for the White House. I'm sure she'd turn a blind eye to any discreet affairs you might indulge in, as I'm sure you would on her behalf. In fact, I've given Robert a list of names. It would be lovely if you could begin dating soon. In fact, I insist upon it. I've groomed you all your life for the job of President of the United States, and you owe it to me to repay my investment in you.

How will I know? Darling, I know everything! I have a private investigation firm tailing you. I have for some time. You won't know they're there, and they will report directly to Robert. It's for your own good, Senator Marlowe, and for the good of the country.

I truly believe you will be President of the United States one day and that you'll be a good one. It is your legacy. I make these conditions to assure that future for you and for the country. Some day you will thank me.

Not likely, Sterling thought as he carefully refolded the vellum paper in his hand. Not likely at all.

Jesus. Not that he had time to look for romance what with the business of the Congress of the United States and this Senate run. He also had no problem with celibacy. He was a fanatic about his privacy and had always run his relationships with discretion just because that was how he was hardwired.

His temples throbbed and pounded in cut time, syncopated like a drummer with ADHD had taken up residence in his head. He flung himself into the chair, hitting his head hard against the leather-covered back.

Damn Camille. It was always her way or the highway. Why couldn't she just accept him and trust him to do what was right? She thought he had enough sense to run the free world but not enough sense to run his love life.

Whatever. Maybe he should just throw in the towel and run a frozen yogurt stand out of Camille's kitchen, grubby-fingered, snot-faced tourist children running roughshod all over her rose garden. He'd use her beloved French antiques to serve Froyo. He smiled. That would show her.

He leaned forward and braced his elbows on his knees. He shouldn't make any decisions in anger. He needed to think logically, not emotionally. That was his strength, what made him a good leader, a man able to find a position and defend it, and to bring others to embrace that position. He couldn't let his grandmother's bigotry get in the way of his mission.

In this day and age, being gay was not an impediment to running for national office, especially in Massachusetts.

And did he want to hold the highest office in the land?

Yes. Yes, he did. He also wanted it on his own terms.

He had to figure out a way around Camille's idiotic conditions.

The biggest problem would be getting rid of the private investigators following him. He'd put his campaign manager, Amy, on it.

There. He had a plan. Things always looked better when you had a plan.

Feathers unruffled, he took his first unburdened breath of the day. Pulling his phone out of his breast pocket, he punched in his assistant Amy's number and got going on the next day of his life.

Chapter Three

"So what are you going to do?"

Pearl looked up from the tub of pistachio ice cream she was eating while standing in Camille's kitchen to see Opal. "I thought I'd finish this off"—she gestured with the gallon of ice cream—"then start in on the chocolate cookies left over from the memorial."

Opal rolled her eyes. "No, about Camille's will. Are you going to challenge it?"

"I haven't thought about it. What about you?"

Opal shrugged. "Not on my own. But if we both went in on it—"

Pearl licked her spoon. "If we challenge the will, it might hold things up for Ruby, whom we owe. Big time."

"So you have given it some thought." Opal's gaze turned triumphant.

"Briefly." Very briefly. "According to Robert, we're good and stuck."

"So you're just going to give up and stay here? What will you do for work?"

Pearl had been giving it a lot of thought. "Would you call Camille a private person?"

Opal frowned. "Not so much private as picking and choosing the face she showed to the world. Why?"

"How do you think she'd react if she knew I want to turn the house into a bed and breakfast?" Pearl scooped up another spoonful of pistachio.

Opal blinked. "A bed and breakfast?" Her voice squeaked a little bit. "She'd have a cow just at the thought of all kinds of strangers pawing through her stuff."

"She'd have two cows."

"And a litter of kittens." Opal narrowed her eyes. "What do you know about running a bed and breakfast? And is the house really suitable as a B and B?"

"As is? No. And of course I can't do anything to renovate the house without you, Ruby, and Sterling on board." Pearl nodded. "Especially Ruby."

"Ruby wants to move out. She's looking at a building on Commercial Street where she could live upstairs and turn the downstairs into a gallery and workshop."

Sighing, Opal shrugged. "She feels like this house is a prison, and I don't blame her. I can't wait to get back to Dorset."

"Don't you need to be here to work on Camille's biography?"

"Don't remind me. Hopefully, I can get that business done with and return to my own life. I really don't need to do a play-by-play of the life of the great Camille Marlowe."

"Need it or not, you're stuck with it." Pearl lifted an eyebrow. "Who knows? Maybe when I start tearing down walls, we'll find a bunch of skeletons."

"Oh, my God. That would be awesome. Wouldn't she hate it?" Opal's eyes clouded. "That sounds very selfish."

"Yep," Pearl said. "But it's also honest. We owe her a lot, but she owed us love." Pearl knew that right down to her bones. "What we got were expectations that were sometimes too high to reach."

"You don't have to tell me." Opal sniffed.

Pearl suspected her sister fought tears, and she couldn't do anything about it. Camille had been just plain out cruel to Opal, more than she was to the rest of them. It nearly destroyed what diminished sense of family they'd had.

It had driven Opal away, first roaming all over Europe, finally settling down in Dorset England. Pearl could count on one hand all the times she'd seen her younger sister in the past seven years. Opal had made it abundantly clear she wanted to be left alone.

Time to change the subject. "I'd like to add on a bathroom to every bedroom, and I'll have to renovate the kitchen so it's up to date, and I can do the whole breakfast thing."

Opal's brow furrowed. "Do you really want to start a business?"

"I'm ready for something different. I'll have to do a lot of redecorating, which is going to be fun. I may have to live in this house, but that doesn't mean I have to keep it the way she liked."

"Can you even cook?"

Pearl put the ice cream and spoon into the sink. "Not really, but I can read a recipe and follow directions. How hard can it be?" Seriously. She had an MBA.

"Bwah!" Opal honked. "This is gonna be good. Maybe I should sell tickets."

"Oh, ye of little faith. I will make this work, just wait and see."

****

"Man, what a day." Tony's spine cracked as he lowered himself into a booth in Fred's Pizza. "I'm done." He winced as he watched his brother, Gabe, slip into the other side of the table.

"You can say that again." Gabe looked around. The place was deserted.

Ah, Tony thought. The joy of the off-season. If it had been during the summer, he'd have gotten his meatball grinder to go and would have chowed it down with a beer in front of a Red Sox game on the television.

"So you never said what it was like seeing Pearl again."

Tony shook his head. "What?"

"You obviously ran into Pearl at her grandmother's memorial."

"Yeah." Tony squinted at Gabe. "And your point is?"

"Just curious. I mean, come on. She went to jail for embezzling money. It had to have taken its toll."

Tony thought back to the memorial and his first glimpse of Pearl after all those years. At least three times he'd picked up his phone with the intention of calling her. Bad idea.

The sooner she left town, the better. He knew more than anyone else Pearl was not going to stick around. She ran away. It's what she did.

"Earth to Tony?"

Tony shook his head. "Yeah. She looked good. Real polished and classy."

Gabe grinned. "Total opposite of you."

"Hey, guys! Thought I'd find you here!" Jenny came up to their table. "Move over," she said to Gabe.

25

He slid across the booth and made room for her. "What's up? Why aren't you working?"

"I got the night off." Jenny slipped her jacket off and let it fall behind her. "Class reunion meeting. I got news."

"What? You decided to change the school colors from orange and black?"

Jenny sighed. "Gabe, you think you're funnier than you really are. Now, I'm not going to tell you."

"I give you ten seconds until you have to tell us." Gabe nudged her shoulder. "C'mon. You know you want to."

"You know me so well. Guess who's staying in town and turning her grandmother's house into a bed and breakfast?"

Tony froze midway bringing his beer to his mouth. No. It couldn't be. God couldn't hate him that much.

Gabe knocked his knuckles on the Formica tabletop. "It's either Pearl or Opal Marlowe."

Jenny wagged her eyebrows up and down. "Got it in one. I heard it from Molly Santos. They've hired her brother Evan to handle the renovations."

Gabe whistled. "Didn't see that coming. I can't quite picture her making up beds and cleaning toilets."

Okay. Gabe had no business saying things like that. "Pearl's no snob," Tony pointed out. "You know better."

"You're pretty quick to jump to her defense." Jenny glared at him.

"Just sayin' that the Pearl Marlowe I knew wasn't afraid of real work."

She sniffed. "I guess it's not real work to steal from the people you work for." She shrugged. "You'd think you wouldn't have a nice thing to say about her after she left you high and dry."

"That was a long time ago. Ancient history." He refused to admit, especially to Jenny, that it didn't feel so ancient now that Pearl was back in town.

"I hope so. I'm still not sure she was all that innocent of those things the government accused her of." Jenny examined her manicure.

"She was cleared of all the charges." Time to change the subject. "Who's on the reunion committee?"

"The usual. Vicky, Laura, and Josie. Me." Jenny licked her lips. "We want a guy on the committee, and I sort of volunteered you."

"What?" Tony shook his head. "I don't have time to be on any damn committee! What do I know about planning a party?"

Gabe snorted a laugh. "Sounds just like the job for you, Bro. You can be in charge of counting the cocktail weenies."

Tony snarled at him. Gabe only laughed harder.

"It'll be fun," Jenny said. "It's something we can do together."

"Jenny, I work nearly twelve hours every day on the water. I don't want to sit around in some group arguing about what type of appetizers to serve at a party full of people who haven't seen each other for seventeen years."

"Okay. If you really don't want to spend time with me and my friends, I guess I have to accept the fact that you don't like them."

"I like your friends. I just don't want to evaluate canapés with them after working all day." Now he really wished that he had gotten his sandwich to go.

Gabe snickered. "We're not fishing right now. You'll have plenty of time to volunteer."

Jenny turned her head away with an injured sniff.

Gabe grinned like the idiot he was. "Sounds like you're gonna be doing time on the class reunion committee, Tony. Make sure to match the wine selections with all the dinner courses."

To Tony's way of thinking, Gabe was just asking for a punch in the face. He told him so.

"No. I don't want him to anymore." Jenny pointed her chin in the air. "I don't know what I was thinking. Obviously, my boyfriend doesn't want to support me."

Tony swore under his breath in Portuguese. "Fine. I'll do the committee thing."

"No, no. You don't have to. I don't know what I was thinking."

"I said I'd do it," Tony gritted out between clenched teeth.

Jenny shrugged. "Only if you want to."

"I want to." Please make it stop.

"Only if you're sure."

Argghh! "I'm sure."

Jenny brightened as she scented success. "Awesome! It's gonna be so much fun!" She pulled out her phone and started to text.

The waitress brought Tony and Gabe's sandwiches to the table and saved Tony from saying anything more. He picked up the hot sandwich and savored the scent of spicy pizza sauce and dripping mozzarella before taking a big bite. He refused to pay any more attention to smiling, giggling Jenny joking around with Gabe.

Why did he think this whole reunion thing was going to come back and bite him in the butt?

****

"Pearl? Pearl Marlowe? Is that you?"

Looking up from the two wedges of smoked mozzarella she was comparing at the Stop and Shop, Pearl peered at the person calling her name. A smile spread across her face.

Laura Souza, probably the one person in P-town she wanted to see. "Laura!"

Laura enveloped her in a hug, smoked mozz and all. "It's so good to see you!" She stepped back. "When were you going to come see me?"

"I'm sorry. It's been crazy." Pearl drank in the sight of her best friend in the entire world. Bad perm, too much makeup, clothes more suited for someone ten pounds lighter, but Pearl hadn't seen a lovelier woman.

They didn't get together often, like maybe once or twice over the years, but when they did, it was as if no time had gone by at all.

"I'm sorry about your grandmother. I wish I could have talked to you at her memorial, but you were always surrounded by people." Laura shook her head. "I know your relationship was troubled, but it still had to hurt."

"Thank you. It's been unreal." She pulled her grocery cart out of the middle of the aisle. "She was always such a huge presence, and now she's gone." She shook her head. "Sometimes I think she's going to come out of her study yelling orders and expecting us to jump and run."

"And what's this I hear from Molly that you're turning the house into a bed and breakfast?"

"News travels fast."

"And don't you forget it. Well?"

"Yeah, we're turning the house into a bed and breakfast, probably calling it Marlowe House."

Laura's eyes widened. "Marlowe House? It's simple and to the point. Does that mean you're staying in town?"

Pearl nodded. "For at least a year. I'm going to try my hand at being an innkeeper."

Laura bobbed up and down on her tiptoes and gave her a little round of applause. "Yay! I'm so happy! It's going to be like old times again!"

"Not quite." She shook her head. "I've got a lot of work ahead of me. But what about you?" She smiled. "What's going on with you?"

Wrinkling her nose, Laura shrugged. "The usual. Ron is still working for the town." Smiling, her eyes turned warm. "Little Shannon is in second grade and getting all A's."

"She's smart and takes after her mommy." If Pearl had stayed in town after graduation, she and Tony would have a little girl or boy the same age as Laura's Shannon, maybe older. Her child and little Shannon could have been best friends. Her stomach fluttered with the ghosts of the babies she'd never had because no one had ever measured up to Tony.

"You know it. Hey! I've got an idea. We've got the class reunion coming up at the Portuguese Festival. Why don't you join us on the committee?"

"The committee? What committee?" She didn't have the time to join a committee of any shape or form.

Laura pushed her on the shoulder. "The reunion planning committee! It'll be fun! I know everyone is dying to see you and would love to have you on board."

"That's got to be an exaggeration. I haven't seen

anyone for years. Nobody would want me on that committee."

"Who better to know how to entice the people who are far-flung to make the trip?"

"That sounds a little far-fetched." Pearl knew that for a fact. Actually, she thought something else might be up. "Maybe they'll come to get a good look at Pearl Marlowe, criminal."

"No one is going to think that."

Pearl tried to laugh. "Trust me, they will. My picture and a whole laundry list of my bad choices have been in the papers for the last year. There are a lot of people who believe that Camille, via Sterling, bought Henry's testimony exonerating me." Pearl looked away. "Camille didn't lift a finger, never mind spend a dime, in my defense."

Laura put her hand on Pearl's shoulder. "No one who knew you believes a word of the gossip about you. You've got a lot of friends here, Pearl, whether you know it or not."

Pearl hadn't known about it. Ruby could have told her, she supposed, but her emails and private messages had been all about Camille's medical problems There hadn't been room for the latest P-town gossip. "I don't think I should be a part of it. I haven't been a part of the town for the last seventeen years. I don't know the first thing about planning this kind of party."

"Please say you'll come. The next meeting is on Wednesday at Vicky's house. You can come to my house early, eat dinner with us, and then go to the meeting."

"I don't know. There's so much to do with getting the house ready and all."

"You can't hide away forever. We're all your friends. Come on, it'll be fun!" Laura's mouth quirked up to one side. "You know you want to."

Fun? Highly unlikely. "I don't know any such thing, but okay, I'll think about it." Pearl wasn't going to promise more than that, not even to Laura.

"Fair enough, but I'm warning you. I'll hound you until you decide to come. I'll even storm your house and kidnap you." She pulled her phone out of her purse. "Is your phone number the same?"

"After you threaten to harass me, I'd be crazy to give you my number." Pearl held back a laugh while Laura sputtered. "All right, the house phone is the same, no worries."

"Come about six, okay? I'll see you then." Laura hugged Pearl again. "It's so good to have you home!" With that, Laura turned her cart and plowed her way back into the grocery store aisle.

Pearl smiled and turned her attention back to the smoked cheeses. She could always count on Laura to be her best friend. Always.

Now that she'd decided on the whole bed and breakfast thing and gotten her family to back her, things were finally looking up.

She'd seal the deal tonight when she made them an amazing gourmet meal. They'd have no doubt about her abilities to run a B and B after tonight.

****

"What did Pearl say she's cooking tonight?" Ruby poured a healthy portion of Merlot into her wine glass while she watched her sister Opal pace in front of the fireplace.

"New England pot roast," Opal replied, her tone

32

glum.

Ruby raised an eyebrow. "Has she ever made pot roast before?"

"Not to the best of my knowledge."

"It smells like burned tires."

Opal pinched the bridge of her nose. "That's one way to describe it. There're other ways, but they don't bear thinking about."

"Hmmmmm." Ruby sipped her wine. "Where's Sterling?"

"He escaped to New Bedford. He's doing a town meeting with a bunch of peeved fishermen."

"I like fish. I like men. I could have gone with him." And she would have if she had known ahead of time. She might have been able to sell them some jewelry.

Opal snorted. "If I'm stuck here eating Pearl's cooking, you are too."

Ruby dropped onto the couch, blew up at her bangs, and sent them fluttering.

A major bang and clattering, followed by the word "shit," burst out of the kitchen. Ruby and Opal exchanged winces.

"That room of angry fishermen is looking pretty good right now," Opal commented.

"No kidding." Ruby drained her glass and got up. "Want a refill?"

"Sounds good." Opal nodded. "Can't hurt."

"No it can't," Ruby agreed. "It absolutely cannot hurt." She poured generous amounts into both her and Opal's glasses. "Here."

Opal stopped pacing and fetched her glass. She held it up in a toast.

Ruby grinned and clinked it with enthusiasm against Opal's. "To Pearl's pot roast. May it be edible!"

"You know it's not."

"Hell, yeah. But she can always surprise us."

Opal shook her head. "I love my sister, but she can't cook, no matter how much she imagines she can."

Ruby swigged her wine. "We can always hope."

The clang of the kitchen smoke alarm broke into the room, causing both women to jump. Ruby slapped a hand over her heart. "I think dinner's going to be late."

Opal grimaced. "I think you're right."

****

Pearl frowned at the charcoal lumps of beef chuck, singed carrots and potatoes, and lumpy, pasty, gray gravy. Not the most appealing platter of food she'd ever seen, that was for sure.

She didn't get what went wrong. She'd followed the recipe exactly. Sighing, she watched her sisters push their food around on their plates.

Ruby swallowed hard, stabbed a hunk of meat, and shoved it in her mouth. She suppressed a grimace. Bringing her teeth together with what sure looked like a lot of force, she cracked a bite of the pot roast.

Opal tossed her fork onto the table and stared at Ruby in rapt fascination as her sister labored to chew her food.

Incredulous, Pearl shook her head. Ruby really was a saint. "I know it's terrible. You don't have to eat it." She didn't even think she could choke it down herself.

Ruby picked up her napkin and spit the contents of her mouth into it. "Thank God." She plucked her glass off the table and drank deep.

"I appreciate your efforts on my behalf." Pearl kept

her tone of voice dry as dust.

"I vote in favor of you hiring a cook," Opal stated.

"I don't have the money to hire a cook. All my cash is tied up in paying my lawyers and in the renovations," Pearl complained. "Not to mention the PR I need to do to get Marlowe House's name out there."

"You've got to spend money to make money," Ruby informed her.

"I know that! Who has the MBA, me or you?" Squirming in her seat, Pearl glared at Ruby. "I'll hire someone as soon as I get some business."

Pearl, that's who. She had the degree. Ruby hadn't even gone to school. She'd apprenticed with that jewelry maker up Cape.

Not that Pearl would throw that in Ruby's face. At least not now, after she'd tried to eat burned pot roast.

Opal pushed away from the table and stood. "I'm making a grilled cheese. Anybody else want one?"

"Please," Ruby said.

"There's some smoked mozzarella in the fridge." Pearl's stomach growled at the thought of a warm, crusty, melty cheese sandwich.

Opal shook her head. "I don't think so. No offense, but I've had enough of smoky food tonight."

"Fine. Whatever." Pearl harrumphed. As she well knew, everyone was a critic.

Chapter Four

"I still don't see why I have to go to this meeting," Tony grumbled as he steered his truck up Bradford hill, up along to the West End. He still hadn't figured out how to get out of being part of the class reunion planning committee. It was a total waste of his time. He had the Celtics game to watch on the TV.

"Don't you even think about trying to blow it off," Jenny said as she fluffed her hair. "You promised me, and I told everyone you'd be on board to give us the male point of view."

Hunh. In Tony's experience whenever a guy gave his opinion, women more than likely ignored it. "Is there going to be food at least?"

"Have you ever gone to a Portuguese meeting where there is no food?" Jenny shook her head.

So much truth. If he could keep his mouth busy eating, maybe he wouldn't have to talk. It was worth a try.

As long as the food wasn't too girly, like veggies and low-fat dip. He shuddered at the thought. There might be pie. Blueberry pie might make the whole thing worthwhile.

So would lemon meringue. Or key lime. Vicky Freeman made an awesome key lime pie. She'd gotten the recipe from a restaurant she'd worked in on Key West and—

"Are you paying attention to me?" Jenny's strident voice intruded into his happy pie thoughts.

Only one answer for that question. "Yes, of course I am."

"So what did I say?"

"Uh." He might as well come clean. "I might have been thinking about Vicky Freeman's key lime pie."

Jenny rolled her eyes. "Of course you were. I was telling you about Josie and Sammy getting engaged." She sighed. "I can't wait to see her ring tonight."

Raucous warning sounds clanged in his head. Jenny was always hinting at getting married.

Tony was never getting married, not after the way Pearl left town without a backward glance.

What a fool he'd been.

Well, never again. He'd told Jenny as much. Marriage wasn't for him, not now, not ever.

And why couldn't Jenny just be happy with the way things were? They had fun. She knew nearly as much about James Bond movies as he did. That impressed him.

Anyway, not knowing what to say about Josie and her new jewelry, he went to his default setting. He grunted and let Jenny make of that what she would.

"I've heard they've set a date already." She sniffed and looked out the passenger side window. "I guess we'll find out at the meeting."

"I guess so."

"I hope it's in the fall. The fall is such a nice time for a wedding." Jenny studied her manicure.

"I'm sure it is." He thanked God for finally getting them to Vicky's house and for the parking spot right in front of it, amen. "We're here."

Smiling in an overbright curve of her lips, Jenny reached for the door handle. "I can't wait to see Molly's ring," she repeated.

By Tony's math, that made one of them.

****

"So does everyone know I'm coming tonight?" Pearl fiddled with the strap of her purse as she walked up to Vicky's house with Laura.

"Nope. I wanted to surprise everyone."

So not the answer she wanted to hear. "Why?"

Pearl felt rather than saw Laura's eyes roll. "Because."

"You didn't tell them because you didn't want them to demand you not bring me."

"No! Everyone is excited to see you. They can't wait to see you. Except for Jenny, maybe."

Pearl thought there was no maybe about it. Jenny had made it very clear how she felt about her at Camille's memorial. Jenny hated her, plain and simple.

Tonight was shaping up to be a rip-roaring good time.

Yay.

"Maybe I should go home."

"No, absolutely not." Laura put her hand on Pearl's shoulder. "Jenny can suck it up." Laura had never been Jenny's biggest fan, to say the least. She leaned on the bell.

Pearl heard laughter leaking through the closed door. It jangled her already jittering nerves to their very last edges.

The door swung open, and who to her wondering eyes did appear?

Her worst nightmare. Tony Cabral, in all his very

muscular flesh, answered the bell. "Hey," he said.

Pearl wondered if her eyes looked as panicked as Tony's. Clearly he had not expected her to attend this meeting.

It looked like Laura had some 'splainin' to do.

Laura's lips turned up at the sides in a remarkably unrepentant grin. "Hey, Tony! Good to see you! Did you know Pearl was back in town?"

Subtlety, thy name was not Laura.

"Yeah, I saw her at Mrs. Marlowe's memorial." Tony turned those heart-meltingly gorgeous brown eyes Pearl's way. "Hey, Pearl."

Pearl nearly swallowed her tongue. "Hey, Tony."

"Tony! Let them in and close the door! You're letting out all the heat," someone yelled from the inner sanctum.

"Yeah, God forbid that happens," Tony muttered.

Pearl snorted. Tony'd always had a fine-tuned appreciation of the ridiculous. It was one of the things she loved about him.

She had loved about him. As in the past. The distant past.

So, so, sooooo past.

And here she saw him, standing right in front of her, all muscles and gorgeousness, taking her breath away.

No, no, no. That would never do.

"Hey, Tony!" Laura piped up. "I didn't know you were going to be here tonight."

Tony made a slight choking noise. "Sh'yeah. Right."

Pearl agreed with Tony.

Laura crossed her heart. "Honest to God, I had no

idea."

No one had ever accused Laura of being a good liar.

"Tony? Who's there?" Jenny came up behind him.

Laura grabbed Pearl's hand and pushed past Tony and Jenny. "Hey, everybody. Look who I dragged in."

A chorus of high-pitched omigawds erupted from Vicky's living room. Pearl grinned as Vicky, Molly, and Josie tackle hugged her. She had no choice but to join in on the squeal fest.

Josie pulled away first. "It's so good to see you." Her smile dimmed. "I'm sorry about your grandmother."

Pearl nodded. "Thank you."

"My brother told me you're turning her house into a bed and breakfast," Molly said. "Does that mean you're staying in town?"

"For the time being. A year at least."

Tony had closed the door and stood still as a statue. He stared at her, but she had lost her ability to read his eyes, coloring her clueless. She couldn't look away.

Tony cleared his throat. "Jenny told me there would be pie," he called out to the general public.

"Of course there's pie," Vicky huffed. "Jenny told me you were coming, and I know you love my key lime." She bustled out of the room.

Josie linked her arm through Pearl's and dragged her to the couch. "I'm so glad you're back, even if it's only for a little while."

Pearl patted Josie's arm. "I'm home for longer than that. I'm here to stay."

"Of course you are," Pearl heard Jenny mutter.

They sat. Still as skinny as Josie had been back on

the cheering squad, she wore tight jeans and a loose-fitting top. She tottered around on high stiletto shoes, trying to fool everyone into thinking she was four inches taller than her actual five-feet-one-inch stature. Blonde and perky, she embodied everyone's idea of the perfect cheerleader, which she had been.

"So tell us everything about your plans for the house." Josie steadied herself to face Pearl.

"Not much to tell yet. We're doing some renovations, like adding bathrooms and upgrading a few things, like the kitchen. Putting in a hot tub on the patio just above the beach." She looked up as Vicky stood before her bearing a glass of white wine. "Thank you," she told Vicky.

She took a sip and tried not to wince. A very inferior chardonnay. Hadn't anybody in the Commonwealth of Massachusetts ever heard of a Finger Lakes Riesling? Knowing better than to ask that question, she set the glass on the coffee table. "So what are we up to tonight?"

"Jenny brought some menu samples and price quotes for dinner for us to look over, which is why Tony's here. We want a man's input on the food." Vicky inclined her head toward Jenny who glowered from across the room.

Pearl and Jenny had never traveled in the same circles. While many of their activities had overlapped, they'd never been friends. Truth to tell, no one would have voted Jenny to be "most likely to succeed."

They'd voted Pearl for that. Look at how wrong they were.

Dear Lord, here Pearl sat, back in high school. She shuddered.

At that moment she glanced up to see Tony watching her, a huge slab of key lime pie in his hand.

She had to force herself to swallow around the boll weevil in her throat. Damn him! He had no right to be that handsome. Dressed as he was in faded jeans, an old, orange-and-black Provincetown Fishermen tee shirt, and scuffed, well-worn boat shoes, he still had the power to make her heart skip a beat.

Which was ridiculous. She'd dated other men, had been engaged to a man who'd been the epitome of style, education, and taste. He'd also been as crooked as the day is long, the total opposite of scrupulously blunt and honest Tony.

The honesty was a refreshing change, the bluntness not so much.

His stare made her wiggle in her seat. She tried flashing him a smile, but he scowled and looked away. Jenny sidled up to him, rose on her toes, and planted a kiss on his grim, rigid mouth.

Pearl remembered a time when that mouth always smiled, ready to laugh, ready to kiss her senseless. She shifted her gaze to her shoes and wondered if the floor could open up and swallow her.

"We should get going," Laura announced to the room at large. "We've got a lot to get through. Jenny, what did you find out about menus?"

Jenny, with what appeared to be the utmost reluctance, disentangled herself from Tony. "Let me get my purse," she mumbled.

Tony took his plate and sat in a chair as far away from them as possible. He might as well have been sitting in the dentist's reception room, waiting to be called in for a root canal. Why was he here instead of at home watching a game, any game, on TV? Pie or no pie, the Tony Pearl knew wouldn't have signed up for the reunion committee.

The answer to that question sat in a chair across from the sofa Pearl perched on. Jenny pulled a notebook and several brochures out of her bag and made a big deal of getting organized. "So"—she made a little bounce with her butt on the plush chair cushion— "here's the 4-1-1. Things are a little pricey because of the Portuguese Festival and the Blessing of the Fleet, no surprise there." She slapped some of the pamphlets onto the coffee table. "Pass 'em around and take a look." Shrugging, she said, "If we don't like what we see, we can always reserve a table under the tent for the dinner on Thursday evening."

"Under the tent?" Pearl had never heard of this.

Jenny rolled her eyes. "As part of the festival, on Thursday, there's a big tent in front of the Bas Relief with a dinner that's all Portuguese specialties."

Pearl felt her face heat and redden. How was she supposed to know?

Answer: she'd have known if she'd spent more time here after graduation.

Josie bit her lip and opened one of the flyers. "That's pretty pricey, though."

"I'd kind of like to be off someplace on our own," Laura said. Vicky nodded in what Pearl took to be agreement. "We can catch up with everybody else in town later. Or the next night at The Beach Club."

"What do you think, Tony?" Jenny demanded.

Tony stopped mid-bite, mouth full of pie, totally on the spot. Pearl winced as she watched him try to force the pastry down in one humongous gulp. A hunk of graham cracker crust must have gone down the wrong way because Tony started choking. He hacked and coughed while his face turned poppy red.

Without thinking, Pearl stood and got out of the way when Laura leaped up and slapped him on the back.

Pearl shook her head, then blew out a breath she hadn't even realized she'd been holding. She needed some distance before she got herself involved in trouble she couldn't afford.

****

"I'm fine. Quit hitting me," Tony growled at Laura, who kept thumping on his back. "I'm okay."

Jenny pushed Laura out of the way and shoved a glass of water into his hands. "No, you're not, baby. Drink this."

As if he had a choice. He did as he was told, mortified down to the tips of his toes.

Manly men did not almost choke to death on key lime pie because their ex-girlfriend was in the room, not even if she was watching him like she expected him to fall over and croak any second.

Pearl's eyes, the relentless blue of a cloudless summer sky, had rounded into large circles that seemed to swallow half her face. Her rosy lips parted in—what? Alarm? Concern for him?

Nah, he wasn't that stupid.

"You okay now, baby?" Jenny rubbed his back.

"Yeah, I'm fine." He shrugged out of her grasp. "Thanks. So what do you all want to know?"

The girls all started talking at once, except for Pearl, who studied one of the brochures like it contained a map to the fountain of youth. Her chest rose

44

and fell with her breathing, a laboring accordion pumping out an asthmatic melody.

Tony also realized his own breathing was none too steady. He stood. "I'll be right back."

"Where are you going?" Jenny wanted to know.

"Out. To get some air."

"Do you need to go home?"

Hell, yeah, but not for the reason Jenny thought. Which left him in a predicament. He could say yes and look like a wimp who couldn't handle his pastry, or say no and be horribly attracted to Pearl for the rest of the evening. Either way he was a punk-ass bitch.

The look on Jenny's face made up his mind. She'd put a lot of effort into getting all her ducks in a row for this meeting. He could leave and make sure that she got a ride home from someone else, but he knew she would insist on leaving with him, which would spoil her fun.

So that meant he'd suck it up and stay at the meeting, Pearl and all. "No, I just need some fresh air. Be right back." He kissed the top of Jenny's head and walked to the door.

He would have kept walking, running from the demons that nipped at his heels. Hell, he only had one demon, and her name was Pearl. But he'd made a promise to go back, and he'd keep it.

His sense of honor demanded it.

Chapter Five

Working at the Marlowe family homestead, Sterling reread a paragraph in a report on fishing conservation regulations for what had to have been the fifteenth time. The dull thud of the hammers and the whiz-thwip of the nail guns were driving him straight up the wall.

He understood and supported Pearl's vision and plans to turn the house into a bed and breakfast. That didn't mean he liked the upheaval required to make her dream turn into a reality.

He really should get back to Boston and his offices, but legal details involved in Camille's estate needed his attention. He hoped his sisters appreciated the sacrifices he was making on their behalf.

The biggest sacrifice was eating Pearl's cooking. He winced. She was making stuffed clams for dinner. He prayed to the god of fine cuisine that he didn't get ptomaine poisoning.

What he wouldn't give for an evening at his home in Fall River, with a glass of wine and dinner from his favorite restaurant, and Verdi's *La Traviata* from his playlist. He frowned. When was the last time he'd been able to go to the opera?

He couldn't remember. He'd have to remedy that soon.

A couple of clumps, the second louder than the

first one, rocked the ceiling above his desk. He ripped his glasses off his face and tossed them onto the desk. Exhaling in a huge gust, he marched out of the room to get the workmen to move to another part of the house.

Each step up the stairs added more steam to the temper he was building up. He felt it pulse with every heavy thud from above.

As Sterling reached the second floor, he surveyed the mayhem. Dusty drop cloths covered the floors, and filthy plastic draped all the open doors. Power tools topped benches made out of sawhorses and cheap pasteboard. Fresh sawdust circled in the air. Power tools created a syncopated cacophony of loud buzzes, whacks, slaps, and slams. It plain flat out drove him crazy as he narrowed his eyes against the noise. The scent of newly cut wood assaulted his sense of smell. Coughing, he rubbed the back of his hand across his nose.

All he needed was a break, a whole hour of quiet. For that to happen, he had to find the foreman. Mentally completing a short game of eeny, meeny, miny, moe, he chose door number three. Pushing the curtain aside, he stepped into what had been his bedroom in his teenage life.

A tall man in well-worn jeans and a sweat-stained tee shirt used a nail gun on the wall while he swiveled his hips to the music running from a boom box. The shoulders filling out the dark blue tee strained at the seams. The waistband of his jeans rode low on his hips, hinting at a spectacular ass.

Sterling thought, pretty for sure, but hardly appropriate. More's the pity.

Sterling exhaled and brought his wayward thoughts

under control. "Excuse me."

No answer, but no surprise. The music was too loud by polite society's standards. He cleared his throat and tried again.

No answer.

He had two choices. Check out another room or tap the hella-sexy man with the power tool on his very muscular shoulder to get his attention.

Sterling swallowed hard. Decisions, decisions.

And he made his. Turning to leave—

"Can I help you?"

Sterling stopped dead in his tracks. God, had the worker caught Sterling ogling him? Dear Lord, nothing would be worse. He turned to face the man who'd asked him a question.

And lost his mind right then and there.

No man had a right to be so handsome. Hair dark as midnight, eyes just as swoon worthy, skin as swarthy as the proverbial pirate. The tee shirt clung to his pecs in wet swatches. And the way he moved, graceful and powerful.

Sterling swallowed. "I'm looking for the boss."

The man of his dreams stared him straight in the eyes. "You found him."

Great. Here Sterling stood, a man who used and crafted words to persuade for a living, and he couldn't come up with something to say. "It's pretty loud up here."

"Yeah, well, it's a construction site." The guy held up his nail gun. "Noise is part of the package."

Sterling refused to check out Dreamboat's package, no matter how much he wanted to. Camille had taught him better manners than that. "I'd like you guys to take a break for about an hour. I've got some work to finish, and the noise is driving me nuts."

"Are you kidding me? You want me to just up and call a break because you're bothered by the noise? Here's a thought. Go to a coffee shop and do your work there."

Sterling bristled and brought his fantasies up short. Who was this guy to tell him what to do? "Do you know who I am?"

The man glared at him. "The man keeping me from doing my job."

"And I'm the man signing the checks. You guys need to clear out for an hour."

"Pearl is the one who hired us, so as far as I'm concerned, Mr. Signer-of-the-Checks, she's the boss. If Pearl tells us to take off, we will, but only when Pearl gives the word."

Sterling shook his head. Maybe his hearing was off because of the symphony of power tools making his life a misery. "Pardon me?"

"You heard me. I'm only taking orders from Pearl Marlowe." The man angled his chin up, clearly a gesture of defiance.

"Who are you?" Sterling was going to make sure this guy got fired on the spot and never work in Provincetown again.

The guy grinned. "Alex Tudor." He executed a bow with great flourish. "At your service."

Sterling fumed. "Apparently not, if you won't do what I ask."

"Go get Pearl. She's the boss." He motioned around the room. "Now, if you don't mind, please leave. I've got work to do." He turned around and put the nail gun back to work.

Dismissed? Alex Tudor had a big surprise in store for him. No one dismissed Sterling Marlowe and lived to tell about it.

He should head back to the peace and quiet of his apartment in Boston where he could think and figure out a plan to deal with Alex Tudor.

****

"Pearl."

Pearl closed her eyes and counted to ten as she heard Sterling bellow her name. What now, she wondered. Everyone and his auntie wanted her attention, and she just couldn't deal with it right now. She peered at the pot of gray goop she had simmering on the stove and frowned. "I'm here in the kitchen," she called.

She thought she heard him say God save me, but she couldn't be sure. She smiled. She thought the cooking thing was going better every day.

"Here you are," Sterling declared as he strode into the kitchen. "I know I said I'd be here for that meeting with Robert, but I'm heading back to Fall River tonight."

Pearl blinked. "What?"

"I need quiet. I can't get it here. Make the noise go away so I can get some work done."

Well, crap. "But I'm making chicken and biscuits. And you promised to deal with Robert."

Sterling ran his fingers through his hair as he glanced wide-eyed at the pot on the stove. "I need quiet to do my work. Your work crew won't take a break so I can do that."

She put down her oven mitts and leaned against the

kitchen counter, prepared to deny what he wanted. "I'm paying them to work. The sooner they're done, the sooner they're gone."

Sterling gawped at her. "I'm only asking for an hour here. I'll get Amy to help out."

Pearl sighed. What did Amy know about construction? She was his campaign manager, great at knowing policy and public relations but not contracting. "It'll take you at least two hours to drive to Fall River. Can't you just deal with a little noise for this little bit?"

"What?"

"Don't yell at me. I'm sorry, but I need these guys to get the bathrooms done so I can open on time." She shrugged. "Sorry."

"I can't believe this." He started to pace furiously. "I'm a freaking member of the House of Representatives. I've got important things to do."

"And your work should trump all?" Pearl itched to put him in his place. She hated when he got all government, all the time.

"Well, yeah." He blushed.

Which made her go all mushy inside, which would never do. "I'm sorry. I can't. You're going to have to find another place to read your papers."

Sterling goggled at her. "For real?" His voice kind of squeaked at the end of his question.

Sterling always had such perfect control so that when he lost it, well, what a show. "For real."

He picked up a coffee mug and threw it across the room. It didn't break.

She forced herself to stay still. "Tell me how you really feel."

"Pearl, please. I've got real serious things to take

care of. Dealing with Robert for instance."

Well, when he put it that way— "I'm sorry. I wasn't thinking."

"You know what? Never mind. I'll stick to my plan and just drive back to Boston today instead of tomorrow."

"I wish you'd stay for dinner. Like I said, I'm trying my hand at chicken and dumplings, one of your favorites."

He blanched. "Sorry, I'm going to have to pass."

"I'll save you some leftovers, freeze them for the next time you're home, so you can give me your opinion."

"Don't go to too much trouble on my account. For the record, I'm sorry about leaving you to deal with the renovations alone."

"I'm a grown woman, and I can look out for myself. For what it's worth, I really am sorry about the noise. I'm just under the gun." She realized she really hadn't ever paid attention to Sterling's workload. He was her big brother. She took him for granted, and maybe she needed to fix that.

He opened his mouth like he was going to say something but closed it and nodded in one jerky motion.

She went over to him, rose on her tiptoes, and pecked him on the cheek. "I love you."

He sighed. "I love you, too."

"Drive safely, okay?"

"I always do." He looked at his watch. "I'll call you when I get there."

"Be sure that you do."

A horrendous crash came from the second floor.

Pearl grimaced, and Sterling cast hot, annoyed eyes upward.

What was that about? Sterling must really hate noise.

Well, of course he did. He was Sterling, after all. The King of Law and Order.

Doink-doink.

"I've got to get out of here," Sterling said as he bolted out the door.

Pearl's heart thumped as she watched her brother run away. What the hell was that all about?

Chapter Six

Tony loved the whales as much as the next guy, but there had to be a better way to save them other than regulate the hell out of where you could lobster, when you could lobster, and how you could lobster.

Not that he was catching lobsters right now. He couldn't. The feds said that you couldn't lobster off the Outer Cape from February 1 to May 15, to protect the whales as they moved through those waters, because they got caught in the stationary lines attached to the traps.

So here he was, at Fred's Pizza, after spending the day on the boat repairing all the things that broke during the last season. It had been a very long, very boring day.

"Penny for your thoughts, Bro," his brother said.

Tony turned his attention to Gabe. "That we should be building a fish market instead of busting our asses fixing every last thing on the boat."

As usual, their day's work done, they sat across from each other at a table at Fred's Pizza. "Not again," Gabe groaned.

"Yep." Tony poured the end of his bottle of beer into the thick red plastic tumbler.

"Just give it up. The fam is never going to agree to it, especially Dad."

Their father had a head made of granite when it

came to anything he couldn't imagine. "You could be a little bit more helpful in the persuasion department."

Gabe snorted. "Yeah, I could if I thought you were right."

He slammed his hand onto the table. "I am right, damn it!"

"Whoa, Tony." Gabe held his hands out in front of him. "Dial it back a little. It's just a really bad idea, with a lot of risk for something that may never make money."

"I'm not just talking about a fish market. I'm talking wholesale, too. We can totally cut out the middleman." Tony leaned forward. "Every year they tell us we can grab less and less fish. Selling our own product wholesale to local businesses and retail to the public is the only way we can stay afloat." And stop killing ourselves in the process.

Not that Tony was afraid of hard work. Quite the opposite. He relished the physical challenge, the battle between man and nature he met day after day after day.

They simply had to change the way they did things in order to survive, but no one could tell his family that. He glared at his idiot brother.

"What?" Gabe was the picture of moronic bliss.

"Nothing." Ma must have dropped Gabe on his head when he was a baby. It was the only explanation.

The bell over the door rang, and Tony glanced over, and his stomach dropped to his feet. Three gorgeous redheads walked into the restaurant. The Marlowe sisters.

Just what his mood needed, a dose of breathing the same air as Pearl Marlowe. Hopefully, they were picking up a to-go order, as there were no empty tables, and the girls would be forced to leave.

Gabe swiveled in his seat to check out the new arrivals, and his eyebrows shot up clear to his hairline. "Hey, ladies," he called. "What you doin'?"

Ruby sauntered over. "Hunting up some pizza." She looked around. "Looks busy."

"Maybe we could just get a pizza to go."

Ruby sighed and threw her arm over Pearl's shoulder. "Sorry, Sis. We promised you a night out." She looked at Gabe. "Pearlie here has been slaving over a hot stove for weeks now, and we dragged her away kicking and screaming."

"I made chicken and dumplings. We don't need pizza."

"You cook?" Tony said without thinking.

Pearl gave him a haughty look obviously meant to put him in his place. "Of course I cook."

Damn, it still got to him when she went all prim. It had made the times she'd let go all the sweeter.

He shook his head and studied the chipped Formica tabletop. What the hell was he thinking?

"You can share our table with us," Gabe offered.

Oh no. Not in this century.

Tony gave him a vicious kick under the table, and Gabe oofed loud enough to give Tony some satisfaction.

"We'd love to," Ruby crooned. "Thank you." She pushed Pearl down into the chair next to Gabe's and sat next to Tony, while Gabe stood and grabbed a chair for Opal, who shifted her weight from one foot to the other. Gabe plonked the chair down on the other side of his. "There you go, Opal. Take a load off."

"After such a gracious invitation, how could I

refuse?" Opal sat.

Gabe pulled out his own seat, turned it around, and dropped into it. "So, girls. How's it hanging?"

Tony shook his head. "Gabe."

Pearl fidgeted. "You know, I'm not all that hungry." She moved to get up.

Tony encouraged her impulse.

"Sit down, Pearl," Ruby said in a stern voice. "We're getting pizza. You shall enjoy it."

Pearl said something under her breath, but Tony couldn't make it out. Probably for the best.

Cindy, their waitress, came over and took the Marlowes' pizza order, linguiça, mushrooms, and black olives, and a very uncomfortable cloud settled over the table.

At least Tony felt uncomfortable. He hoped Pearl was just as unsettled.

How many times had they come to Fred's after pep rallies, him in his football jersey and her in her orange-and-black cheerleader uniform? That enthusiastic, bubbly girl was a far cry from the cool, distant woman across from him.

He wanted to reach across the table and mess up her hair. The fingers on his right hand twitched.

Ruby reached over, took hold of Gabe's beer, and took a swig. "So. What shall we talk about?"

Gabe smiled. "I want to hear all about the family home turning into an inn."

Tony clenched his teeth as his brother turned his most charming smile Pearl's way.

"What are you up to, darling?" Gabe said, the consummate picture of innocence, right to Pearl. "And what is this I hear about chicken and dumplings?"

Opal waved a hand in front of her face. "Oh, you don't want to hear about that." Pearl snapped her head in Opal's direction.

"Well, he doesn't! He wants to hear about the plans for the bed and breakfast."

The waitress showed up with Tony's meatball grinder and Gabe's buffalo chicken grinder. She smiled as she put Tony's sandwich down in front of him. "So, Tony, is Jenny working tonight?"

Oh great. Just fucking great. "Yes," he replied between clenched teeth.

Now, as Tony well knew, Cindy was going to text Jenny about Pearl being here, and he'd get a totally undeserved scene involving temper and tears from Jenny.

He couldn't wait.

"Tell her I said hi." She smirked at Pearl. "Your pizza will be right up."

"Hey, it's my pizza, too!" Ruby tossed her hair back. "You can't have it all," she told Pearl.

Pearl glared at Ruby. "You're insane. I think Mom dropped you on your head when you were a baby."

Tony snorted. "I often think that about Gabe, too." His cheeks warmed when Pearl shot him a grateful smile.

Gabe sputtered, the picture of affront. "Hey! I resemble that remark. Ruby? Are we going to let them talk to us that way?"

"Absolutely not. We must bide our time. Our revenge will be unexpected, clever, and vicious."

"Will you two stop?" Opal whined. "I have my editor's deadline to meet, and I really don't need to be here."

"You have to eat, don't you?" Ruby's tone was silky smooth.

"She could have eaten at home. Maybe I need to remind you that I did make chicken and dumplings," Pearl complained. "From scratch."

Ruby shot Opal a lethal look and smiled a bit too cheerfully at Pearl. "We wanted to give you a vacation."

"I'm not working. I don't need a vacation," Pearl said.

"Of course you're working. You're turning the family estate into a business. That's a lot of work," Ruby said.

Gabe had been following the conversation like he'd been watching a Ping-Pong match. "Just like Tony here. He wants to diversify and open up a fish market."

Tony was about to take his foot and upend his stupid brother's chair, but then his gaze caught Pearl's and found common ground.

Here they both sat, trying to start new businesses and dealing with incredibly annoying siblings. He didn't want to have anything in common with her.

He picked up his sandwich and took a big bite. He could scarf it down and head home before this night ended up being more of a clusterfuck than it already was.

****

Why was she here? How did it happen that Pearl was in Fred's Pizza, for all intents and purposes ready to share a table with Tony Cabral?

Just like in their glory days, back in high school.

Except, not.

So very not.

59

It was all Ruby's fault. It was her idea to leave a perfectly good meal of chicken and dumplings on the stove and go get a pizza at the old high school hangout. When they got home, Pearl'd wait until Ruby went up to bed, then murder her in her sleep.

She started to smile at the picture forming in her mind of how it would play out.

As Ruby bantered back and forth with Gabe and Tony, Pearl sat back and imagined the flesh peeling off Ruby's face and her eyeballs melting, just like the Nazis in *Raiders of the Lost Ark*.

She shouldn't smile, but she couldn't help herself. Except then she looked up and saw Tony staring at her.

Her smile crumbled and disappeared. She shouldn't be here.

"Don't you dare."

Pearl shook her head. She couldn't quite believe what she was hearing. "You sound like Grandmother."

Opal opened her mouth, then shut it. Pearl hoped permanently.

She knew that comparing Opal to Grandmother was the worst possible insult you could give her.

"You bitch," Opal hissed.

"And I'm so very good at it," Pearl tossed back.

"Is there a problem, ladies?" Gabe just oozed charm.

Totally unlike his surly older brother.

Who was right now chomping down on a messy sandwich that had to be very hot, what with all the red sauce and melted mozzarella.

Like he cared about the burn. He'd always been too hungry to wait for his food to cool. The roof of his mouth must be shredded to bits. Before Pearl could stop it, she ran her tongue over the ridges of her very intact hard palate. A sudden memory, of making out with Tony, of his tongue gently stroking the roof of her mouth.

They might have even made out at the very table they were sitting at.

Except they might have made out in every booth and table in the place. Back in the day, they hadn't been able to keep their hands off each other.

Here was the reason she'd never set foot into Fred's Pizza the handful of times she'd been back to town. How galling to realize he came here all the time and didn't feel the sting of a single memory.

Stupid man.

Pearl shot him a look and saw that he was studying her. He stopped chewing. He just sat there holding his sandwich chest height and gazing at her. "What? Do I have something on my face?"

"No," he grunted and took another humongous bite of his supper.

Honest to God, he used to be a bit more eloquent.

And cheerful.

And friendly.

Pearl's mouth turned down at the corners. She supposed she'd gotten rid of all rights to the friendly back when she'd left him.

Cindy showed up with their pizza and plopped it down on the table, along with a stack of napkins and some paper plates. "Enjoy." She shot Pearl a dirty look.

What else was new? Both Cindy and Jenny hated her. Pearl never knew the reason why. She tuned back into the conversation around the table.

"So like I said, they're sure to lower quotas again,"

Gabe said.

"Only a matter of time. Politicians," Tony said, shaking his head. "Damn crooks."

Ruby crossed her arms across her middle and gave him a pointed glare.

"What?" Tony wanted to know.

"I think you just called their brother a crook," Gabe pointed out.

"Oh, I'm sorry. I didn't mean to say Sterling's a crook." Tony actually blushed. "He's a great guy. Really looks out for us fishermen."

Ruby snorted. "Good save."

"Tony here"—Gabe jerked his head in his brother's direction—"wants to cut out the middleman and open our own fish store."

"It makes sense." Tony bristled, clearly annoyed by Gabe's words. "We've got to have something else to fall back on when the fish aren't coming in. A fish market is it."

"That makes great business sense," Pearl heard herself say before she could stop the words from leaping out of her mouth.

A silence bomb dropped on them, rendering them all speechless.

"What do you mean?" Gabe narrowed his eyes at her.

"Well, you'd have some big initial setup costs, but eventually, you could control the prices you get for your lobsters, and I'm sure you'd make it all back in short order." Pearl warmed to the topic. There was her MBA at work for them. "I mean, you'd have to work up a business plan and all of the start-up details and income projections, but in light of the changing times and the diminishing number of fish you can catch and areas you can fish in." She shrugged. "It makes a whole lot of sense."

Tony's eyes shone as they lasered in on his brother. "I told you."

"This from the man who's terrified of heights." Gabe shook his head. "He still won't climb up the Monument. It's so sad," Gabe said as he turned his attention to Pearl. "Tell us about the bed and breakfast."

Pearl stopped midway through grabbing a slice of pizza and glanced at Tony. "You're still afraid of heights?" He'd always been terrified and did everything he could to avoid any situation in which he had to face them. School field trips to the Monument and the Museum were torture for him. He'd hide before he climbed up the 350 foot granite tower.

Tony crossed his arms across his chest. "Tell us about the bed and breakfast."

"There's not much to tell yet. Right now we're hip deep in renovations. But I want to be very hands on, making up the rooms and cooking all the food."

Pearl wasn't certain, but she thought she saw Ruby's eyes cross.

"Impressive," Gabe said. "That's a lot of work."

"I'm excited about it. I want to put a fire pit onto the stone patio and serve wine and cheese and such in the evening. Serve them food I've cooked myself. Make the beds every day." She felt Tony's gaze and turned her head to meet it. "What?"

He shook his head. "I just can't picture you as a chambermaid."

For a second she couldn't breathe. The gall of that man. She'd just defended his idea to his brother. Would it kill him to give her a little support? She counted to ten while she bit the inside of her cheek. "Well, I guess you're going to have to paint a whole new picture."

Tony stared back at her. The intensity in his eyes made her want to squirm in her seat. She squashed the urge down.

"Well, let me just run right out and buy a new box of crayons."

Pearl, usually articulate, was at a total loss for words. Staring back at Tony, she struggled to find something, anything, to say.

"We're trying to convince Pearl to hire a cook." Ruby to the rescue. "It's an awful lot to take on alone."

"I'm ready for a challenge." Pearl plucked a piece of linguiça off her slice and popped it into her mouth.

"Why don't you help her out, Ruby?" Gabe said.

"I've got enough on my hands getting my jewelry shop set up."

Pearl sighed as Ruby and Gabe talked about the particulars of Ruby's business. She felt, rather than saw, Tony watching her. She focused on the pizza in front of her as her skin prickled with awareness.

Great. Just what she needed.

Chapter Seven

"You know you were being the world's biggest asshole?" Gabe jammed the keys into his truck's ignition.

"I don't know what you mean." Tony peered out the front window. He was not going to have this conversation with his brother.

Yes, he'd been a total jerk. Yes, he felt bad about it.

No, he wasn't going to discuss it. He told Gabe the same thing.

"And the assholishness continues."

Gabe's phone blew up as he backed his truck out of the parking lot. "Grab that for me, will ya?"

Tony sighed and did what he was told. Looking at the display, his brows crashed together. "It's Jenny. Why is she calling you?"

He saw Gabe's jaw clench. "How the hell should I know? Either answer it or let it go to voicemail."

Tony took the coward's way out and let it go to voicemail. He didn't feel like talking to Jenny. No doubt, Cindy had called her and told her about Pearl. He was in no mood for a harangue.

But why would she call Gabe and not him? The thought tickled his brain. "It's weird, that's all."

Gabe put the car into gear. "Not my problem. Jenny's Jenny. You know that."

Yes, Jenny was definitely Jenny. But still— "I just don't get why she'd call you."

"I don't have a clue. Just drop it, okay?"

Whoa. Here was a trip into backward and upside-down world. Why was Jenny calling Gabe? He kind of thought Gabe might be looking in Ruby Marlowe's direction. But it hurt his brain to ponder the craziness. Really. His brother wouldn't be spying on him for his girlfriend. That was ridiculous. "Consider it dropped."

Still, Tony watched his brother's stony expression as they drove along Commercial Street. Something was wrong, and Jenny somehow was deep in the heart of it.

And that something had nothing to do with Pearl.

He hoped.

Tony'd nearly fallen off his chair when Pearl supported his idea of the fish market. He supposed that, what with her fancy degrees and all, she'd know good business sense when she heard it.

Heat rose up from his toes and wandered all the way up to his heart. Having a solid case of the warm fuzzies for Pearl Marlowe was the last damn thing he needed.

****

"That's an experience I never want to repeat, thank you very much." Pearl fumed from the back seat of Ruby's Volkswagen Golf, sitting with her knees practically stuck in her armpits. She missed her spacious and fully loaded Mercedes, the first casualty of the things she'd had to sell to pay her lawyers, along with several first editions of Camille's books and a few good pieces of the Art Deco jewelry she'd loved so much to collect.

"What? I had fun." Opal didn't turn in her seat to

talk to Pearl. "I haven't been to Fred's Pizza in ages."

"All you did was complain that you had a deadline and needed to go home and write," Pearl pointed out.

Opal cleared her throat. "I got into the spirit of the reunion."

"Me too." Ruby burbled from the driver's seat. "It was fun to catch up with Tony and Gabe."

Pearl snorted. Well, that was one way to put it.

"I was surprised you supported Tony's idea for a fish market," Opal said.

What? "Why?"

"It being Tony's idea." Opal fluffed her fingers through her hair.

Pearl bristled. "It's a good idea! If you're losing money by catching fish and selling it for a low price to the people who sell the fish, and they turn around and sell it for a ginormous price, then you should diversify and control the price you get for the fish you catch by selling it to the public yourself. It only makes sense. A first-year business major could tell you that."

"I suppose ginormous is an official Harvard MBA term." Opal yawned.

"Of course." In addition to killing Ruby in her sleep tonight, she could also kill Opal. Two birds for the price of one and all that.

"It was still nice of you to support Tony," Ruby added. "His family is fighting him tooth and nail about this whole fish market idea, and I agree with you that it's the best course of action for them."

Something, jealousy maybe, crushed in on her, all spiky and fierce. "And you know all this, how?"

"I stayed in town, and you didn't." Ruby shrugged like it was just that simple.

Maybe it was.

Time to deflect. "You and Gabe seem pretty cozy," she told Ruby.

"You know, you did." Opal nodded. "I agree with Pearl."

"And what do the two of you know about me and my life?" Ruby's voice burned like acid. "You were off having a couple of glorious lives while I stayed here and took care of Camille."

Pearl thought before she spoke. "I'm very grateful for you stepping up to take care of Camille. God knows I couldn't. My life was a shit storm."

Opal sat up straight. "And did Camille lift a finger to help you?"

She thought about it. "She might have if I had asked. I didn't ask."

Ruby sniffed. "She invented tough love. That was the only way she could show any kind of affection at all."

"Ain't that the truth," Opal said, only a little bit of sarcasm leaking through to tinge her voice. "I had to go to another continent to avoid her."

"She loved you more than you know, Opie," Ruby said.

Opal stared at Ruby. "I don't know any such thing. I'm a published best-selling author, and Grandmama waved her hand in front of her face, as if something smelled bad, whenever somebody mentioned my books." Opal sank into sulk position. "If she'd loved me, she would have supported my career. And don't call me Opie."

"She did support your career," Ruby maintained.

"She did not!" Opal's head looked ready to

explode. "You know full well that she dissed me publicly. In the *New York Times*, where she said my work was derivative and pallid, in *The New Yorker*, where she said I wrote foolish love stories for delusional women, and in the *Washington Post*, where she claimed me and my readers needed extensive therapy. Who knows what she told other papers and what she said in interviews on TV." Opal shook her head savagely. "You can kiss my ass, Ruby. Camille nearly ruined my career. Never mind my career. She nearly destroyed me."

Pearl hated the way Camille had treated Opal. They shared the same fire, the same passion, telling stories, spending their days in front of their computers making stuff up. They should have been close.

Instead Opal lived a world away from Camille.

Pearl really felt something was wrong with that picture. "Please stop. I've had enough tension for tonight." That was true. Dealing with Tony had drained her.

Opal and Ruby stared at each other. Pearl's gut hitched. "Watch where we're going, please. I really don't want to end up a stain on the road."

What she really ached to do right then was to go home, clean up the mess she'd made in the kitchen, read a little bit out of Opal's novel, *Time of Longing*, the latest installment in her Time of series. Truth to tell, Opal had a knack for telling a story.

Pearl loved a happy ending. Lord knew, she wasn't getting one of her own any time soon, so she had to read about them.

Chapter Eight

"What are you doing home?" Pearl demanded as she rubbed lemon-scented furniture polish into a Chippendale marquetry commode.

Sterling scowled at Pearl. "I'm here because Ruby asked me to come."

Pearl wiped her hands on her raggedy old jeans while she stood. "Why?"

"There's a property in the center of town that she wants to rent, and she wants me to take a look at it." Sterling wanted to check it out himself anyway. There was the fact that Baxter Oglethorpe owned the property, and he sure as hell didn't trust the man as far as he could throw him.

He wouldn't let Robert release any money to her without his approval. Ruby frequently jumped in with both feet without thinking about the consequences, and she very much wanted to have her own place. Sterling wanted to make sure her new home was perfect for her.

"Ruby didn't say anything about moving out." Pearl pursed her lips.

Sterling snorted. "Moving out is all Ruby ever talks about."

"Well, okay, yeah, but she didn't say she'd found an actual place to move to."

"So now you know." He loosened his tie. "Is she around?"

"I don't know. I don't keep track of her comings and goings." She smiled. "How did you get here? Are you hungry?"

"I flew in and took a cab from the airport. And I, uh, I ate before I came." He shifted his weight from one foot to the other. "I'll just go around and see if I can scare up Ruby."

Pearl nodded. "She's probably upstairs."

Sterling rolled his eyes upward as he took in the construction noise from the second floor.

"Or she could be in the temporary workroom she set up in the basement. She took a shipment of new supplies yesterday."

Sterling knew. He'd signed all the checks paying for them. Something crashed. He closed his eyes. Being in no mood to deal with construction workers, he'd look for Ruby anywhere but on the second floor. "I'll check her workroom first."

Pearl nodded. "Good luck!" She dropped to her knees and put fresh furniture polish on her cotton cloth before attacking the ornate commode once more.

Sterling slipped his jacket off his shoulders and hung it on the back of an intricately carved ladder-back chair. Things sometimes got ruined when Ruby used sharp and pointy tools that got really hot.

And he was really, really fond of this suit coat.

****

Ruby was not in the basement, which meant Sterling had to venture into the wonderful world o' construction. He ground his teeth together with each step he took.

He could look at the bright side. Perhaps Alex Tudor, king of the contractors, wasn't working today.

His nerves popped and hummed with both annoyance and anticipation.

Hell, they jumped up and sang every Verdi aria ever written at the tippy tops of their screechy little lungs.

Loosening his tie another notch, he cleared his throat with a rusty harrumph and trudged up the steps. Hoping he'd find Ruby right away, he plodded onward, every footstep heavier than the last.

The whiz and thwap of every power tool thudded in his ears, a heavy refrain. He had to laugh at himself. The average staircase lasted about thirteen steps. That wasn't a big distance to travel.

Blame it on the power tools.

He went weak in the knees over the thought of power tools. What man wouldn't be? And, for Sterling, apparently, when they were wielded by sexy men who didn't care a whit about whom they disturbed.

He'd not been able to scrub thoughts of the very attractive Alex Tudor from his mind since the last time he'd been in P-town. With the election coming up, he could not afford to be distracted, especially not by a sexy construction worker. It was bad enough that he had to traipse back to town to deal with details from Camille's estate and his sisters' drama.

He hit the second floor and didn't think the construction was any further along than the last time he'd seen it. He picked his way down the hall toward what was Ruby's old room. He couldn't imagine why she'd be in there, with all the noise going on. Reaching his goal, he pushed aside the dust-laden plastic cover over the threshold with ginger fingers. "Ruby?"

"Hey. Sterling." His sister's voice called from

within the room. "C'mon in."

He wanted to take a deep breath, but the air was chock-full of heavy spackle dust, so he checked the impulse. Ducking his head under the filthy plastic, he stepped into the room.

He immediately wished he hadn't.

Ruby was in there all right, but she wasn't alone. Alex Tudor was with her.

Ruby's curly red hair was piled on top of her head, held in a messy bun by a couple of hair ties. She wore a faded green plaid flannel shirt over a white tee, pulled down over the top of ancient, ripped blue jeans. She leaned against a table made of two wooden sawhorses and a long, paint-stained piece of plywood. Her eyes were a sparkling blue while she laughed with Alex as he grinned at her.

Alex dressed in the same fashion as the last time Sterling had seen him, sweat-stained tight tee shirt, jeans, and a tool belt. The waistband of the jeans dipped down just a tad, making Sterling wish, for one hot, sweaty second, it would slip down enough to give him a glimpse of the skin underneath.

He pulled his polite politician's mask down over his face. "Ruby, you ready to go? I've got to get to New Bedford for a meeting later on today."

Ruby pushed away from the table. "Sure thing." She grinned at Alex. "I'll catch up with you later."

Alex flashed her a flirtatious smile. "Sure thing." He turned a cheekier smirk to Sterling. "I'm going dancing with your sister later. Want to come?"

Sterling blinked. What the hell should he say to that? Was the guy making fun of him? "I have some meetings."

"That's too bad. See you, Congressman."

Sterling gave him a curt, dismissive nod and followed Ruby out of the room.

"I'll just be a minute. I want to change real quick before we go," Ruby informed him.

Now he did sigh. "There's no such thing as a quick change for you."

"Don't be silly. It's not like I'm Pearl and need to put on full makeup just to go to the Stop and Shop." She faced him. "Why don't you go wait for me in the kitchen? I heard she made a big batch of oatmeal raisin cookies."

"You're an evil woman." He'd seen that plate of cookies. They'd looked like hockey pucks, only harder and blacker.

"I'll be right back." She sashayed down to her basement studio.

Sterling stood, feet rooted to the floor, as he watched her walk away. Against his will, he gazed back to the room that held Alex Tudor. He shook his head, disgusted with himself, and went down to the kitchen to retrieve his jacket, shuddering at the thought of Pearl's oatmeal cookies and wondering about how he could avoid eating one.

****

It took Ruby twenty minutes to change into a pair of skinny jeans topped with a sapphire tunic and slouchy brown high-heel boots. She and Sterling stood in the center of what would eventually be her jewelry shop. "What do you think?"

Sterling paused and considered. "The location's great for a business, right smack dab in the middle of Commercial Street. But—"

"But what?"

Sterling knew he was picking a fight with this one. Ruby needed her downtime to stay whole. "Do you really think it's a good idea to live over the shop? Think of the noise. The town doesn't sleep…you'd never sleep. Would you have the peace and quiet to create your jewelry?"

Ruby tossed her head back in that way she had when you rained on her parade. "I like noise. I love the nightlife."

"And you like to boogie." He sang the old disco refrain. His voice cracked on the high notes. He wondered if her friend Alex Tudor was as fond of the night scene as Ruby seemed to be. "And Baxter Oglethorpe for a landlord?"

"Sterling," she said. "I've really got my heart set on this place, even with Baxter Oglethorpe attached to it." She twirled in a big circle, arms out wide like Mary Tyler Moore in that old '70s sitcom, totally confident that she was going to make it. "I can so see myself happy here."

"Then there are safety concerns. It's not always safe for a woman alone, and you'll have expensive supplies here for your jewelry."

Ruby waved his concerns away with one beringed hand. "I'll get the landlord to put in a state-of-the-art security system."

Of course she would. "Any determined thief can get past a security system."

"I'll get a gun."

His stomach froze at the thought of Ruby locked and loaded. "You'd have to learn to shoot one."

She shrugged. "Details. C'mon, Sterling. I really

want this place."

Sterling still couldn't sign off on it. "Ruby, maybe we could look at a couple of other sites."

She fisted her hands by her sides. "I want this place, and I deserve to get what I want after giving up my life all those years taking care of our grandmother." Her fingers turned white.

"Relax your hands, for Chrissake. Give me the lease, and I'll have my people look it over."

A new voice entered the room. "My leases aren't usually looked over by anyone's people."

Sterling turned to view the new arrival. Baxter Oglethorpe. Ruby's potential new landlord. He'd gone to school with Baxter. Back then he'd been, well, no other word for it but fat, and the kids teased him by calling him "Ogre." He'd shaped up over the years, losing weight and such. Sterling held out his hand. "Oglethorpe."

Baxter nodded and shook Sterling's hand. "Congressman. I've brought the lease here for you to look at."

"I'm here in the room, and I'm the one who's going to rent the building," Ruby said, her voice dripping stalactites.

Bax turned to Ruby as he reached into his jacket pocket and pulled out an envelope. "Here's the lease."

Ruby snatched it out of his hand. "Thanks."

"Any questions?" Bax looked at her, then at Sterling.

"I'm concerned about security, frankly." This from Sterling, the king of bluntness.

"Oh, for God's sake. Let me handle this. It's my business after all."

"I've installed the best of the best systems out there. It's solid gold." Bax gestured to a panel next to the front door.

"You'll send me the specs." It wasn't a question. It was an order. Sterling was very good at giving them. He considered it one of the best things his grandmother taught him. "We'll see if we have to upgrade. Ruby's safety is the most important thing to me."

"Again, I'm right here." Ruby tapped her stylishly boot-clad foot.

Sterling sighed. Sisters were so much work. Obstructionist politicians on the other side of the aisle were less trouble. "Ruby please let me bring some of my people in so they can evaluate the security system. Then you and Baxter can talk. That okay with you, Oglethorpe?" Sterling glanced at his watch. Time to finish up here. He didn't want to stay in Baxter Oglethorpe's presence any longer than he had to. Something about him made Sterling's teeth ache.

"Sure. Just have them stop by my office and get the keys."

"Great. Ready to roll, Ruby?"

She slipped her huge purse over her shoulder. "Might as well."

"Let's go." He looked at Baxter. "You'll be hearing from me."

Baxter watched Ruby. "I look forward to it."

Ruby grabbed Sterling's arm. "C'mon."

Sterling was glad it was a short ride home.

They drove in silence, but Sterling could feel Ruby fuming over in the passenger seat. "Why don't you want my lawyers to look at this lease? Or my guys to check out the security system? At the very least have

Doreen Alsen

Robert look at it."

"I don't care about any damn lawyers. You just waltzed in and made all these decisions without taking into account my opinions and wishes. You and Baxter just took over and left me out."

"Camille would want you to consult Robert." And tell the Oglethorpes they were not in charge. "All I want is what's best for you."

"This location is what's best for me. Speaking of Grandmother, don't forget you and Pearl and Opal owe me for staying and taking care of Camille. I'm really sorry to play that card, but there it is. That storefront is what I want."

For some strange reason, Alex Tudor's handsome face flashed across his mind. Ruby was meeting Alex at a club later that night for a little R and R. "I'm sure your date will take your mind off all the trouble I deal out to you."

"My date?" Ruby sounded puzzled.

"Yeah. Alex Tudor." His fingers tightened around the steering wheel.

A long beat of silence filled the car, then Ruby burst out laughing. "You think I'm dating Alex?"

He felt his face heat and redden. "I heard you making plans with him with my own two ears."

Ruby waved her hand in front of her face. "Sterling, we're friends, that's all. For a gay man, you have the world's worst gaydar. He plays for your team, not mine. Which is too damn bad because he's hotter than hell." She sighed. "Which is also good because of his job."

Sterling frowned. "Why does a person have to be drop-dead gorgeous to work construction?"

78

Ruby cracked up all over again. "He only works construction and other odd jobs in the winter. Once the season starts, he's a dancer."

"A dancer?"

"Yep. Of the exotic variety."

Dear Lord. "Are you telling me that—" He almost drove the car into someone's front hedge.

"That Alex is a stripper? Yeppers! That's exactly what I'm telling you."

Chapter Nine

"Are you sure you guys are okay on your own for dinner?" Pearl really hoped Ruby and Opal were going to stay so she had an excuse not to go out to dinner with the reunion committee to try out the menu options at Olivia's Bistro.

She didn't think she could choke down one bite of food sitting at a table with Tony and Jenny. Sharing a pizza with Tony and Gabe at Fred's had been difficult enough.

"We're good," Opal said. "You just go and have a good time. Let us know how the food is at Olivia's."

Ruby nodded from behind Opal. "Bring us dessert."

Pearl frowned. They didn't need more sweets in the house as she'd been in a baking frenzy all week. "Well, then. Okay." She grabbed her purse and hung it on her shoulder. "I shouldn't be out too long."

Ruby sighed. "You've been working all day, tied to the house. You deserve a night out and some fun."

Pearl didn't think fun was on the menu at Olivia's, at least not while Tony and Jenny were around. How had she let Laura talk her into this? If she'd known in advance that Tony was on the committee, she never in a million years would have said yes. "If you're sure."

"Pearlie." Opal picked up Pearl's jacket and pushed her to the door. "Go away."

Just like that Pearl found herself on the outside of the door Opal shut behind her with an audible and emphatic thud. She might as well go to this dinner from hell.

Olivia's sat on the beach side of Commercial Street. Since it was still off-season, there was plenty of parking nearby. She remembered back to when she was a child that the restaurant had a different name, and Camille had taken them to dinner there often. She smiled at the memory. It was one of the good ones. She had to admit there were a few.

Sighing, she pulled up the hand brake. It was time for dinner.

The inside of the restaurant had a definite European flair to it. Crisp white cloths covered the tabletops. Sparkling crystal vases held fresh flowers alongside two matching crystal candleholders. Classical music drifted from discreetly placed speakers. The air was filled with the glorious scents of clams, garlic, and red sauce.

Her mouth watered.

"Pearl! Over here!" Laura waved and caught her attention. The only other person at the table with her was Tony. A little thrill snuck up her spine. Sooner or later she'd stop getting these little frissons of attraction to him. She crossed her fingers in hope.

Tony stood and held a chair for her when she reached the table. He'd always had the best manners.

"Thank you," she said as she sat. "Where is everybody?"

"Vicky cancelled because her kids are throwing up, Josie went to Boston to look at wedding dresses, and Jenny had to work at the last minute. So," she said in a cheerful voice, "we're it!"

"Oh." She glanced at Tony. He didn't look too happy.

Tough. She picked up her menu. "What's good?"

"That's what we're here to find out. I hear you can't go wrong with anything pasta." Laura opened up her own menu. "Have you eaten here before, Tony?"

"Yeah. We took our parents here for their last anniversary."

"How are they?" Pearl hadn't thought of Tony's parents in years. They'd always been good to her, at least until she'd broken their son's heart.

"They're good. Both of them work too hard, but we can't do anything about it." He turned those heart-melting brown eyes to her. "You know how it is."

She did know. Pearl could have written the book on difficult parents. Not that Tony's mom and dad were difficult. They were angels sent from God above compared to Camille.

They most likely wanted nothing to do with her. Her throat clogged up at the thought. At one point in time, the Cabral home had been her refuge from Camille's constant criticism.

Their house had been filled with love and warmth and acceptance. Camille's house was more like a museum or a photo spread in a glossy magazine dedicated to the life of the rich and famous Camille Marlowe.

"Are you ready to order?" A waiter appeared at their table.

"Just a sec." Laura smiled at him. "Let's try this," she said. "Bring us one spaghetti with clam sauce, one chicken Parmesan, and one order of sole amandine. We can pass them around."

Sounded fine to Pearl. Her thoughts were all mushy, sharing the same oxygen as Tony, so she didn't mind Laura taking over.

"So how are the renovations going?" Laura frowned as her phone rang from inside her huge purse. "Oops, it's home. I've got to take this." She got up and went over to the hostess station.

Tony cleared his throat. "So, really, how are the renovations going?"

Good God, she had to make small talk with Tony. Back in high school they had talked all the time, intimate conversations where they shared their fears, their hopes, their dreams. They'd finished each other's sentences. After all of that, chatting about little, inconsequential things seemed almost obscene.

The waiter came around with their drinks just as Laura rushed back to the table. "I'm sorry. I've got to go." She frowned. "Shannon must have the same bug Vicky's kids got, because Ron says she's puking her guts up and wants her mommy."

"Do you want me to cancel your order?"

Laura looked at the waiter. "No, these two will stay here and enjoy them." She grabbed her coat. "Let me know what you think. Call me tomorrow, Pearl." With that, she left Pearl and Tony alone.

A huge fist plowed into Pearl's stomach. From the look on Tony's face, she could tell he felt the same way.

"What do you think we should do?"

Tony gave it some thought. "We've got food coming. We might as well stay." He shrugged. "We're grown-ups, after all. We can share a meal in spite of what happened in the past."

"What about Jenny?"

"I'll explain the situation. She'll understand."

Pearl doubted that. "You're sure she'll be okay with this?"

"Yeah. Why not? You and me"—he motioned between the two of them with his hand—"we've been over for years." He leaned back in his chair and crossed his arms over his chest, not exactly a picture of openness.

"Yes, we have." Seventeen years to be exact. Again she missed the easy intimacy of their teens. Now she just didn't know what to say. She wracked her brain. "Tell me about your plans for a fish market."

His eyes widened. "I don't really have anything specific yet. I just think we can do better by selling what we catch ourselves. Fishing is a gamble at the best of times. We're being regulated to death by the government because, you know, whales."

"I think it's an excellent idea."

"Tell that to my family. Gabe and my dad won't even discuss it."

"Maybe you could put together a business plan to present to them."

"A business plan?"

"Yeah. Get all the details together, along with cost and income projections, and show them how long it would take to be a success." Pearl shrugged. "You'd need to do that anyway to get money from the bank."

Tony tapped the index finger of his right hand against the tabletop. "That's their major gripe. They don't want to borrow money to get it off the ground."

"Sometimes you have to spend money to make

money."

"Is that what you told your big Wall Street clients?"

Was that a dig? "My clients thrived on risk. It was a given. They made a lot of money. They lost some money."

Shaking his head, he flashed her a lopsided smile. "I can't imagine living that way."

She smiled back. She couldn't help it. Why would she want to? "There were many nights I lost a lot of sleep."

"Being an innkeeper will be dead boring compared to that."

"I'm looking forward to it. I've had enough excitement to last me a lifetime."

Their waiter arrived with their food. The spaghetti with clams smelled garlicky and winey. Mozzarella cheese and tomato sauce dripped over crisp pan-fried chicken. The flounder appeared perfectly prepared, the delicate fish covered with almond slices sautéed in fresh butter. Pearl had thought she'd have trouble eating with Tony, but the food proved her a liar. She couldn't wait to dig in.

Truth to tell, it was a welcome relief from her own cooking.

"Looks good. What do you want to try first?" Tony slipped his napkin onto his lap.

"The clams!" She craved the spice of the dish and anything pasta. She was a slave to carbs.

She counted that as a point in her favor.

"I'll try the chicken parm." He slid his knife into the sauce-laden poultry and stuffed it into his mouth. "Mmmmmm." He chewed and swallowed. "Just like I remember it. Perfect."

Oh, that's how she remembered everything too. Perfect. Why had she blown it up to hell?

Food. He was talking about the food. She had yet to take a bite, pasta twirled around her fork, midway between the plate and her mouth. Speaking of which—

"You've got sauce on your chin."

He ducked his head, grabbed his napkin, and swiped at his chin. "Did I get it?"

"Yes." Such a shame. Her mouth went dry. She would love to lick the sauce off his chin, then nibble her way toward the hollow at the warm base of his neck and throat. She would rain kisses down, down, down his torso and not stop until he begged for mercy. Maybe not even then.

Her pulse raced, and she struggled to slow it down, hoping like hell she wasn't drooling. She must stop thinking about him that way. It did her no good.

"What should I do to come up with a business plan?"

Oh, God. Did he notice her staring at him? She shook her head to clear it. Yes, talk about business. That was way safer. "Well, you make a list of what your goals are for a few years out, like say, five years, and how you plan to get there."

"How I plan to get there?"

"What resources you'll use to reach your five-year goal."

"Oh." He forked up another piece of chicken parm and chewed slowly.

"There are templates you can get online. I'd be happy to take a look at it when you figure it out," she heard herself say.

He swallowed his chicken and narrowed his eyes. "Why?"

Good question. She had enough on her plate getting Marlowe House up and running. "I don't know. I guess I just think it's a really smart idea, and I want to help you."

"Hmmmmm." Tony picked up his beer. "That's nice of you."

"I can be nice."

"Yeah." He stared at her, and once more she regretted not being able to read his mind. "How is the pasta?"

Confused at his abrupt change of subject, Pearl looked at the clam-laden strands of spaghetti still entwined on her fork. She put it in her mouth, chewed, and swallowed. It was both garlicky and tangy, just the way she liked it. "It's good."

"Maybe we should try the sole."

"Maybe." She guessed keeping the conversation about their food was the safest course. Still disappointment stung her at him not wanting to accept her help. She should have anticipated it.

She was a big girl. She'd get over it.

****

Tony was insane. He had to be. Here was a real businessperson, an expert, sitting across the table from him, offering to help him convince his family to back his dream, and he'd nearly refused.

By the look on her face, he could tell Pearl thought he'd rejected her, when the truth was he needed time to think about it. He'd actually love to have professional help, even if it came from her.

But man. Jenny would blow a gasket. He'd lied

when he told Pearl that he could make tonight's little dinner right with Jenny. He knew he couldn't. So why didn't he leave? Good question. Very good question. He'd blame it on the chicken parm. Jenny might buy that.

Oh well. What was done was done. He really didn't have to explain anything to her. She wasn't his mother.

He knew that Jenny had weddings on the brain. He supposed it was the next logical step.

Maybe the word logical was be a big ol' honkin' clue.

There was only one woman Tony'd wanted to marry, and she was sitting across the table from him, trying to eat spaghetti and clams without making a mess.

She looked adorable doing it.

He'd have to think about the whole thing. Maybe he should get more information about her brush with the law. He'd ignored, on purpose, all the press surrounding the charges against her and her fiancé.

Especially the fiancé part.

"Are you okay?"

Tony looked across the table. Pearl watched him, her brows furrowed. "Yeah. Why wouldn't I be?"

"I don't know. You're just frowning really hard."

Shit. "Just thinking about work. Gabe and I set off tomorrow for a week scalloping with my uncle. I should probably call it an early night."

"You're going to leave me alone here with all this food?"

"No." His mother taught him better manners than that. "No, of course not. Laura's going to want a full report from both of us."

Pearl stared at him for a long second, then nodded. "That she will."

He forced himself to smile. "You need to try the chicken parm."

Her lips formed a tentative curl. "If you say so."

"I do."

****

"Are you freakin' kidding me?" Jenny waved her arms as she screamed at Tony.

Tony winced. He should have expected this. "It's no big deal. Pearl'd be doing me favor, that's all."

"Oh, she wants to do you a favor all right. I doubt a business plan is it."

Tony jammed his fingers through his hair. "You could have a little faith in me. I've never given you a reason to think I'd cheat."

That stopped her in her tracks. "You don't know how she works. She'll find another way to"—Jenny quirked her fingers into air quotes—"help you."

"Look, you know how much this fish market means to me. If she can get me a few steps closer, I'm going to take advantage of the offer from an expert."

"Some expert. Don't forget she went to jail."

"Jenny, get a grip. It's a fantastic offer, and I'm going to let her help me."

"Great. Just great." She grabbed her jacket. "I'm not going to fight with you about it anymore." Stuffing her arms through her sleeves, she stomped to his front door. "I still can't believe you didn't leave when Laura left."

"We'd already ordered food. We couldn't just leave."

She snorted. "There's a little thing called To Go.

You know. Order the food, box the food up, and take it home to eat. Speaking of which, I'm going home." She slammed the door behind her.

He flopped onto his couch and sprawled across it. His temples throbbed. Jenny'd get over it. She always did.

He didn't feel right leaving for a week with her in this mood. She'd most likely do her best to run into Pearl and make a scene. He wished Jenny would get over her insecurities about Pearl. She really should leave high school in the past. Standing, he grabbed his jacket to go after Jenny and fix this before it got all out of hand. Except for when he got to Jenny's, she wasn't home. That could only mean one thing. Jenny'd gone to have it out with Pearl.

While the thought of going to the Marlowe house brought back all kinds of bad memories, he forced them down. He had to intercept Jenny and put her anger on him where it belonged.

Not on Pearl.

Chapter Ten

Somebody pounded hard enough to rattle the windows at Pearl's front door. Had Ruby forgotten her damn key again? Sighing, Pearl set her cup of peppermint tea down on the table next to her comfy, overstuffed chair and rose to let Ruby in. Sometimes she couldn't wait until Ruby moved out into her own place. "Coming!"

She looked out the window in her door and groaned. It wasn't Ruby. It was Tony.

Certainly not dressed for a visitor of the hot male variety, in her baggy sweats, oversized and faded orange and black PHS Fisherman tee shirt, and thick socks, she didn't consider herself ready to entertain visitors.

Why the hell was he here? Only one way to answer that question.

She opened the door. "Tony. What's going on?"

He froze, his gaze darting around the hall, for the shortest of moments, exhaled, then stepped through the doorway. "Is everything okay?"

"Of course it is. Why would you think otherwise?" She closed the door behind him.

He met her gaze. "I told Jenny about dinner and about our business thing. She went ballistic."

Pearl's headache got worse, pain stabbing her right between her eyes. "Our business thing?"

"Yeah, your offer to help me. I thought I could convince her that it was a good idea, but she got really pissed. I just came over to see if she was here to pick on you and to, well, you know." He shook his head.

Tony's face darkened as Pearl watched him glance around the foyer. He was deeply embarrassed, she supposed. "I appreciate it, but she didn't come here. Now, I won't let her in if she does, so thanks for the warning."

"I would have called," he blurted out, "but I don't have your number."

"Let me give you my cell number, but we didn't disconnect Camille's land line. You must have that one."

"I do." He shook his head. "I didn't want to wake anybody up."

"Other than me." She laughed. "Of course, if Jenny had burst in here with guns blazing, nobody would be sleeping."

"I wasn't really thinking. I just wanted to keep track of Jenny. She's got that Portagee temper. She doesn't always think before she shoots."

"I appreciate that and your willingness to defend me." Something warm slinked up her spine. "I think we can be friends again, Tony. What do you think?"

He froze, no other word for it. Pearl couldn't even tell if he was breathing. That's how still he had become. Finally, "I'm not sure we're friends yet, but I think we might be able to get there." His hands shook, just a slight tremor. "I really appreciate your offer to help me with the business plan. Can I give you a call when I get back from my week away?"

"Of course." So happy to have this chance to help

Tony have a shot at making up for hurting him so many years before, Pearl felt lit from the inside, all warm and glowy. "Got your phone? I'll give you my number."

****

"You're late." Tony glared at his lazy-ass brother Gabe.

"Excuse the hell outta me," Gabe grumbled. "I overslept, okay?"

The sun had yet to rise, dawn a hazy golden smear on the eastern horizon. The longer the boat stayed at the dock, the smaller the catch.

Time meant money.

Still pissed, Tony studied Gabe. "Late night?"

"Back the fuck off."

Yep, someone had had one hell of a time last night. "Anybody I know?"

Gabe's head snapped toward Tony, and his eyes gleamed hotly at him. "You don't know shit about anything."

Tony held his hands up and took a step back. "Okay. Lighten up. We've got some scallops to gather. Uncle Manny's already checking the trawls and ready to get underway."

Gabe grunted, a disgusting and rude sound, and turned his back to Tony, who busied himself with coiling lines that really didn't need the attention.

They worked in hostile silence as Tony piloted the boat out of the harbor and around the backside of Long Point. Headed for the Race, the frigid, salty chop leaped over the bow and slapped them in the face as they toiled, hissing icy stones flung like a spoiled two-year-old tossed unwanted toys against a wall.

Scalloping was miserable, backbreaking work at

the best of times. Tony had a strong hunch that it was going to feel longer than one week.

A hell of a lot longer.

Might as well try to do something to alleviate the tension. "So what bug crawled up your ass?"

Gabe shot him a burning look. "Mind your own business."

If he kept this up, Tony was going to have to kill him and dump the body overboard. "You need an attitude adjustment, Bro."

"At the risk of repeating myself, fuck the hell off."

Great. Just great.

****

"So, Laura. How's Shannon?" Pearl was gunning for bear. The more she thought about it, the more she was sure Laura set her and Tony up, so she called her first thing.

"Home from school today, unfortunately." Laura sounded perturbed.

Good.

Might as well get it over with. "Is Shannon really sick, or did you make it up so that Tony and I would be alone together?"

Laura's breath of indignation gusted over the line. "Honey, come on over. You can clean up all the vomit."

Ew. "No, thank you. Poor baby. Is she okay?"

"For now. Honest to God, if I have to hear another song from Hamilton, I'm going to throw myself off the top of the Monument."

"What? You're actually throwing away your shot?"

Laura growled like a really hungry attack dog.

Still, it sounded like Shannon was sick, so Pearl cut

Laura some slack. "Do you want a report on last night's dinner?"

"Oh, God, yes! Details, please! Don't leave anything out, and I'm not talking about the food, if you catch my drift."

"There's not much to tell. We had dinner, and it was civil."

"Well, that's boring," Laura complained.

"What can I say? I'm boring."

"You are not." Laura was such a loyal friend, even after all these years. "I can't believe there was nothing between you."

"Again, sorry to disappoint."

"Not even one teensy, weensy spark?"

Might as well spill all. "Okay. If you must know, I offered to put together a business plan for him."

"Oooooh, a business plan. I'm fanning myself just thinking about how romantic that is."

Pearl laughed. "It can be hella sexy in the right hands."

"I'll take your word for it. Did he say yes?"

"He didn't say no."

"So you're going to see him again?"

"Just as friends." Which was a big deal, given what she'd done to him. "Nothing more."

"You know, I always thought you'd come back here and get together again." Laura sounded wistful.

Pearl refused to admit that she'd fantasized about that very thing herself. "You're a hopeless romantic."

"Yep. And proud of it." Laura sighed. "Are you sure there's no chance for you two?"

Oh dear. What to say? There was no choice. Pearl was sure of it. "There's too much water under the bridge, and besides, he's with Jenny." Why did her heart feel so heavy in her chest, like a boulder made of steel wool?

"I don't know about that. Lately I've gotten vibes that not all is well in paradise."

Pearl shook her head. "Doesn't matter to me one bit."

"Doesn't it?"

Enough. Time to end the conversation. "Look, I've got to go. I hope Shannon feels better soon."

"You and me both!"

They clicked off, and Pearl sat at her kitchen table, frozen in place. Memories of her and Tony floated around the edges of her brain, snapshots of him in his football jersey and her in her cheerleading uniform on a cold fall Friday night, riding around town in the back of a pickup truck drumming up school spirit. The two of them wrapped around each other on the dance floor as they swayed in time to music, so dizzy and stupid in love.

The scent of Ralph Lauren's Polo still made her pulse flutter.

Why had she let her grandmother convince her to break up with him? Why hadn't she stood up for what she wanted? Easy. At eighteen she'd stood no chance against Camille.

She remembered crying as she took off Tony's ring and left it on her dresser.

One thing was true. What she could do was help him get financing for his fish market and hope for the best. That would have to be enough.

Chapter Eleven

Tony huddled in his bunk on the boat, a hammock strung across the cabin. He was cold and wet, his clothes damp and scratchy against his skin. Even though it was his turn to sleep, he didn't think he could.

His mind raced back to being in the Marlowe house for the first time since he'd gone to pick up Pearl to drive her to Harvard, only to find she'd left already. Instead he'd faced Camille, and she'd handed him a very hard version of the truth.

"Is Pearl ready?" Tony looked past Camille, checking the room for his fiancée.

"She's already left."

What? "I'm here to drive her to Cambridge." Pearl had to be there. They'd made promises!

"Sterling has taken Pearl to school."

"Why?" His ears buzzed like killer bees had made his head their new home.

"Pearl has decided that considering marriage to you is unwise. She gave me this to give to you." Camille held out her hand, a small diamond ring in the center of her palm.

"No." He nearly staggered back.

"Pearl no longer wishes to be tied to you."

"What do you mean?"

"She sees no more usefulness in your association. Marriage to you will only hold her back in her career."

Camille sounded cold to Tony's ears. "As you children say, she's breaking up with you. Please take your ring and go."

"I don't get it."

"Please, Tony, spare us both the embarrassment of spelling the whole thing out. She doesn't want to marry you. If you love her, you'll leave her alone. Otherwise, you're just an albatross around her neck."

Though his heart had shattered into a million pieces, he took the ring, turned, and left.

Tony squirmed at the memory. Not his finest moment. He'd stolen a bottle of cheap blended whiskey from his father and headed out to the beach. He'd gotten totally shit-faced, staggering, falling-down drunk.

Even more embarrassing, Camille had called his house to tell his mother and father that he wasn't on his way to Cambridge. Since Gabe knew all Tony's go-to brooding places, it hadn't been hard to find him.

They'd sat on the sand, looking out onto the harbor, watching the lights twinkle in the distance, hearing the ding-dong sound of the bell buoys, the pinging slap of halyards against masts of sailboats moored close to the beach. A heavy mist had rolled in, and the foghorn blared out a warning.

Tony could have used a warning about Pearl Marlowe a long time ago, like from the get-go.

Jenny had come and picked their drunk asses up. Somehow she'd stuck around.

Now Pearl was back. He couldn't deny that he felt a pull toward her.

He just didn't know if he could trust her.

The upshot was that he couldn't stay with Jenny

while he felt this pull to Pearl. Making sure Jenny knew this was his first priority the minute he hit dry land.

Jenny had always been very clear about what she wanted. He'd just kind of floated along, taking her for granted and ignoring her. That was wrong.

Totally and completely wrong. It had to stop.

She deserved better than someone who was never going to give her what she wanted, so he had to let her go.

His temples throbbed. It wasn't going to be pretty. He probably shouldn't have let it go on as long as he did. But he had, so that was that.

He hadn't even noticed he was just existing, not living. Did he want Pearl back? He sure as hell didn't know. What he was sure of was that he needed to make a change, and that meant stop stringing Jenny along. He never meant to do that. He was ashamed that he had. He hadn't wanted to date anyone permanently, happy enough to hang out with the Eastern European girls here to work for the summer. Jenny had worn him down, and he'd started going out with her a couple of years ago.

However, Pearl was back, and he certainly didn't feel numb anymore. More truth? He felt as humiliated the other night in Pearl's foyer as he had been when he was eighteen and Camille had given him his ring back.

He still had the ring. He'd kept it in his pocket every day for a year, hoping against all hope that Pearl would come back to him.

Talk to him. Show an interest in him.

For a whole damn year. He'd walked around with that little diamond ring in his fucking pocket, until it became clear to his stupid brain that Pearl wasn't coming back.

Wasn't interested in him. Had left him long behind. Hadn't looked back.

He'd stuffed the tiny ring in his sock drawer, where he saw it every day. It reminded him to never, ever trust another woman ever, especially if her name was Pearl.

He stared at the ceiling, which lurched above him with each toss of the waves. Closing his eyes, he prayed for sleep. He had precious little time for it, and one wrong move could mean the difference between life and death.

He let the wind and the waves take away his worries. The weather, even bad weather, was always a comfort to him.

****

Pearl hadn't been able to get Tony off her mind since their dinner a week ago, try as she might.

Dreams. She'd had the most amazing and vivid dreams of her and Tony like they'd been back in the day. She dreamed about kissing him, locked in a tight embrace in the back seat of his car, parked at Race Point, watching the "submarine races," an excuse to make out.

She smiled and touched her mouth, remembering the passionate pull and tug of lips and tongues, the fever to touch and caress of hot skin. Had she really ever been that young? Had life really been that simple? Life had only been simple when Tony was around. Life with Camille had been very difficult.

She looked around Camille's inner sanctum and let time fade back to when she'd been in high school and Camille had ruled with an iron fist. Anything less than an A- was fodder for a dressing down. Marlowe House had been a pressure cooker just waiting to blow up, so she'd thrown away P-town and Tony in her desperation to get away from Camille.

She shook her head. Marlowe House was hers now. People might come to stay there because of Camille, but Pearl wanted them to come back because of her and the experience she provided them.

While she hadn't been raised to be an innkeeper, she was getting into it. Excited about it.

Thrilled to be living in the most beautiful place on earth. Forget Tony. She was here to stay, changing a once oppressive place into one run by her rules. She didn't need any damn person, man or grandmother, to define her. She'd done that far too long.

From now on she was living by her own rules. She would call the shots.

Sounded like a good plan.

****

"Man, am I beat." Tony rolled his shoulders forward, then back, wincing as his neck cracked. "I want a shower, a beer, then bed for about three days."

"No visit with Jenny?" Gabe leaned back against the door of Tony's truck.

That was the most Gabe had spoken the whole fishing trip. And no, he wasn't going to see Jenny. He needed time to formulate what he was going to say to her. "I think she's working. It'll wait until tomorrow."

Gabe grunted, staying true to his new man-of-no-words superpower.

"Bro, you really need to tell me what's going on with you."

"I really don't," Gabe said as he pushed himself away from the vehicle. "Good night." He clomped away.

Tony shrugged it off. Whatever had Gabe by the short hairs wasn't any of his business.

Chapter Twelve

"Let's go to Bradford Street Seafood for fish fry tonight," said Ruby as she walked into the kitchen.

Pearl looked up. "I was planning on making boiled dinner. I got a Daisy ham from the Stop and Shop."

"It'll be fun," Ruby said in a sunny, little-too-loud voice. "We haven't had much sister time lately, and I want your opinion on some new jewelry designs I made." Walking over to Pearl, she lightly butted her in the shoulder with her own shoulder. "Come on. You know you want to."

Pearl knew no such thing. Jenny worked at Bradford Street Seafood. So far Pearl had avoided Jenny, and that's the way she wanted to keep it. "Jenny works there. I'm trying to avoid her."

"She doesn't usually work fish fry night."

Pearl's bullshit meter pegged hard to the total-crap end of the scale. "Since when do you have Jenny's work schedule memorized?"

"I've got my finger on the pulse of P-town." Ruby shook her head. "Do you really think I'd ask you to go to anywhere Jenny was going to be?"

Well, put that way. "I don't know." She looked down at the work clothes she wore, all spattered with furniture polish and dust smudges. "I'm not exactly presentable."

"Just change your clothes, for Chrissakes. Nothing

a little makeup and a comb can't put right. C'mon. You've been working so hard. You deserve a break."

Sure, but going to the restaurant where a woman who hated her worked didn't constitute a break to Pearl's way of thinking. Plus she never went out without being dressed for success. "I really don't think I—"

"Don't you want to spend some sister time with me?" Ruby's face looked like Pearl had just kicked her favorite puppy.

However, Ruby was right. They were overdue for some sisterly bonding. Pearl was interested in Ruby's jewelry designs. If she still had money other than what she'd inherited, she'd invest in Ruby's business. "Of course I want to spend time with you. Do you want to make the reservation? Or better yet, eat somewhere else?"

"We won't need a reservation, not this time of year. And yes, please can we get fish fry? I've got a real craving."

Ugh. "Okay, have it your way."

"No, silly. That's Burger King, not Bradford Street Seafood." Ruby flashed her a cheeky grin.

"What?"

"Never mind. Be ready to leave around seven."

"Aye, aye, Captain." She gave Ruby a crisp salute.

"This is going to be fun!" Ruby grabbed a Granny Smith apple out of the wooden bowl on the kitchen table and polished it on her shirt as she left the room.

Pearl hoped Ruby would be right about the fun. You never knew what was going to happen, especially with Ruby around.

****

Tony sat at the Bradford Street Seafood's bar nursing a Sam Adams while he tried to formulate exactly what he was going to say to Jenny after she got off work. He usually would have gone to his brother for help, but not with the mood Gabe was in at the moment.

Tony liked his head right where it was. On his shoulders.

"So, Tony, did you decide what you want to eat?" Cheryl, the bartender, studied him while she washed a couple of glasses in steamy, soapy water.

He scraped at the moisture-beaded label of his beer bottle with his thumbnail. On Friday, at Bradford Street Seafood, you got fish fry, which was what he told her.

"Sole or haddock?"

"Haddock, please." He smiled at Cheryl. "Extra tartar sauce."

She rolled her eyes. "You think I don't remember you want extra tartar? Please. Give me a break." Eyeing his beer bottle, she said, "Need a refill?"

"No, I'm good for now."

"I'll just go to the kitchen and put in your order, then I'll be back." She winked at him. "You can tell me all the juicy details about that brother of yours."

Tony watched her go into the kitchen. He wished he knew juicy details about his brother.

Dollars to doughnuts, he bet the whole thing was about a woman. Tony shouldn't worry about Gabe's problem with some female. Tony had enough trouble with ladies all on his very own.

A burst of laughter caught his attention. He looked at the source and groaned. "Great," he muttered into his beer. What the hell were Pearl and Ruby doing there? They were walking right in the path of Hurricane Jenny.

Pearl glanced at him, then did a double take. Her eyes widened, and she grabbed Ruby's arm and whispered something to her. Ruby shook her head, lifted her hand, and waved at Tony. Dragging Pearl's arm in a death grip, she pulled her along behind her as they followed the hostess to their table.

Trust Ruby Marlowe to enjoy a scene, because Tony imagined there was going to be a doozy once Jenny got the news that Pearl Marlowe was in the house.

Cheryl reappeared carrying a platter of golden-brown fried fish, crisp french fries, and coleslaw made of shredded red and white cabbage and carrots, tossed in a light celery-seed dressing.

Any thought he had of running away to avoid the situation disappeared in the face of this huge plate of food. Cheryl plonked it onto the bar and reached underneath to pull out a bottle of ketchup. Thumping it down in front of him, she smiled. "Do you need another beer?"

"Yeah, thanks."

"Hey! Is that Pearl and Ruby Marlowe?" She wiped her hands on her apron. "I haven't seen Pearl in years." She spared him a look. "I have to go say hello. Give me a call, will you, if someone needs a drink." She took off.

"Absolutely," Tony said, watching Cheryl walk away. He picked up his fork and studied his food, determining where to dig in.

Through the metallic clatter of flatware against pottery, Tony heard Pearl laughing. Unable to help himself, he looked over at her. As if she felt his gaze, her lips parted, and she stared back at him. He toyed with the idea of picking up his food and going to sit with Pearl and Ruby. Maybe they could get rid of Ruby. Maybe they could—

"Hey! Cheryl told me you were here." Jenny sidled up to his seat on the barstool. She went on tiptoes and kissed his cheek. "You need a shave. How was your trip?"

He nearly jumped out of his seat. "Good. It was good." Please don't notice Pearl is in the dining room. Please don't notice Pearl is in the dining room. Please don't notice—

"What is she doing here?"

Too late. "Who?"

She turned and gestured into the room. "Pearl Marlowe. What's she doing here?"

"Uh, eating dinner?"

"She should know better than to show her face here."

He thought that was extreme. "Honestly, Jenny. It's a public place."

She turned to him, her eyes snapping with anger. "Did you come here tonight because you knew she was going to be here?"

His face flushed hot. "No. I came here to get dinner and to see you."

She blinked five times in a row. "Oh."

Just like that Tony knew he couldn't call things off with Jenny that night. He'd have to pick another time when she wasn't all up in arms about Pearl. "Why do you hate Pearl so much?"

"What?" She shook her head with a slight, barely there, wink-and-you-missed-it motion.

"Why do you hate Pearl so much?"

107

"It's just like back in school. She always got whatever she wanted and acted so entitled, like she was better than everybody because of her grandmother." Jenny hiked up one shoulder, then dropped it. "Everybody was so much happier before she came back to town. Now everything's turned upside down just because of her."

Tony knew better than anybody else that Pearl didn't get whatever she wanted and that her grandmother held her to impossibly high standards. "Come on. It wasn't like that. Besides, even if it was, that was high school. We're all different people now."

"I knew you wouldn't understand. I've got to go and pick up an order." Jenny left.

Looking at his now cold plate of food, Tony grimaced. Still hungry, he stabbed at a piece of fish, dunked it in tartar sauce, and shoved it into his mouth. For no reason at all, he looked across the room to Pearl.

She and Ruby still had their heads together over the tablet. They were smiling as Ruby pointed out things on the screen. The two sisters made a very pleasing picture.

They were as unalike in style as two women could be, with Ruby's long red curls and Bohemian style and Pearl's hair more tamed and subdued, her clothes conservative and polished. Still the resemblance between the two screamed that they were sisters.

They fought each other constantly and then turned around and had each other's backs. They were a real team. He knew all about that kind of connection because he and Gabe had the same thing. Well, just not lately.

Pearl shifted her attention from the tablet she and

Ruby were studying and caught him staring at her. He felt his face heat and turned his attention to his cold plate. He should probably get Cheryl to box it up so he could nuke it at home. He no longer wanted to talk to Jenny that night. It would have to wait.

He waited for a quiet moment to flag Jenny down to say good-bye. He'd claim tiredness, what with just being back from a week of scalloping.

He snuck one last glance at Pearl. She laughed at something Ruby said. While he didn't hear her, he remembered vividly the sound of her laugh, a light, bright chime. When she'd first left, the memory haunted him, and he'd worked hard to forget it.

He'd been unsuccessful.

Man, he had to get out of there. Too many ghosts.

He allowed himself one last glance at Pearl over his shoulder and cursed himself for wanting what he could never have again.

Chapter Thirteen

"These designs look good." Pearl tapped on Ruby's tablet with one finger. "I really like that one." A pendant made of hammered gold held a deep blue sapphire. It was simple and elegant, more her style than Ruby's usual fanciful, whimsical designs.

Ruby shot her a smug smile. "I knew you'd like that one. I had you in mind when I created it." She lifted her frosted beer mug. "Did you see Tony over there?"

"He's a big guy. It's kind of hard to miss him." She was totally working on ignoring him.

"He keeps looking over here." Ruby sipped her chardonnay and smiled. "Why don't we invite him over?"

Hell no. "That's the worst idea you've ever had."

"What'd be the harm?"

More than her sister could even imagine. "If you haven't noticed, Jenny's working even though you told me she wouldn't be. And in case you forgot, this is supposed to be sister time."

"Nothing wrong with saying hello."

"There's everything wrong with saying hello." Pearl wanted to shake Ruby. "Just drop it, okay?"

"Consider it dropped. But man, he looks fine tonight."

Pearl had to concede that point. He looked exactly

what he was, a man who spent the day fighting the sea and the wind. He'd barely tamed his wavy, thick black hair. Sporting a five-o'clock shadow, the sculpted planes of his face made him look dangerous. He'd shoved the sleeves of his work shirt up his arms, revealing sinewy, muscular arms. She knew for a fact that as a boy he had been all strength. She could imagine how much more Tony, the man, would be.

"I'm not interested," Pearl said as she picked up a french fry.

"You're such a liar."

Sighing, Pearl frowned at the now limp fry. "I need to focus on getting back on track and opening Marlowe House before the season starts."

Ruby scraped her thumbnail along the damp label on her beer bottle. "You're doing a great job, really. Camille would have a dozen kittens and drop another dozen puppies if she saw what you're doing with the house." She brought her gaze up to Pearl's. "I just remember how much you and Tony adored each other. Devotion, stop it," Ruby said when Pearl choked. "Devotion like that just doesn't go away overnight."

"It was hardly overnight. It's been seventeen years since I left town. I was engaged to another man, for the love of God."

"Henry does not qualify as a man. He's a loathsome troglodyte."

Pearl laughed. "That's a little bit dramatic, even for you."

"The man is pond scum, okay? He set you up to go to jail!" Ruby shook her head. "Thank God for Sterling and his magnificent lawyer skills."

Pearl needed to change the conversation. She

111

would not wallow in the past. She only looked forward these days. "What's the status of your shop? Are things on target?"

Sighing, Ruby puffed a breath toward her eyebrows. "A state-of-the-art security system is being installed tomorrow. Once Alex's crew is done working on Marlowe House, they're going to be handling the renovations at the shop." Her eyes sparkled. "I can't believe this is finally happening! I have to pinch myself sometimes to make sure it's real!"

"You deserve it. You really do. Sterling, Opal, and me, we all owe you for staying in town for Camille."

"And don't you forget it."

Pearl loved sister time. "Won't ever happen, Rubes. You won't let us forget."

Ruby snorted. "You got that right."

Swamped by a wave of love for her sister, Pearl put her hand over her heart. "Don't ever change, okay?"

"Why try to improve on perfection?"

"My thoughts exactly."

****

Two days later Tony found himself sitting at the bar, again, in Bradford Street Seafood, nursing a beer. One of these days they were going to put a plaque on his favorite barstool: "Here Tony Cabral planted his ass while he waited for Jenny Silva." What a legacy.

"I'm just waiting for my last table to pay, then I can go," Jenny said as she stood behind the bar. She bit her lower lip as she stuck her pencil in her ponytail.

Tony nodded. "I can wait."

She squinted at him. "I'll be right back."

He considered chugging down the rest of his beer but thought better of it. He was done, in more ways than one.

"Okay, I'm ready." Jenny showed up next to him, first pulling on her coat, then slinging her huge pocketbook over her shoulder. "Where are we going?"

He'd give her a choice: have this little chat in a quiet little corner of some bar or go to her apartment. Both options had their problems. Given the time of the year, their options of bars with quiet corners were really limited. Breaking up with her in her place would leave boatloads of bad vibes in her apartment.

Taking her to his house was not an option. Jenny could take control of the conversation without him being sure of how it happened. If things went south at her apartment, he could walk away.

Shit. How depressing was this?

Didn't matter. It had to be done.

"Hello? Tony?" Jenny waved a hand in front of his face. "Where do you want to go?"

"Um, I don't know. Someplace quiet." He lifted one shoulder in a shrug. "It's up to you."

She eyed him, her expression bland. So not Jenny. "How about the Provincetown Inn?"

"Great." His first choice. "I'll follow you."

"Of course you will." She examined her manicure. "I'll see you there." She hiked her bag over her shoulder once more, turned on her heel, and waltzed out.

"I'll be right behind you." Just in case she hadn't heard him the first time.

Jenny waved a hand. "Whatever."

Tony had more than an inkling that this was not going to go right. He watched Jenny sashay out.

What had been his first clue?

Chapter Fourteen

In a town where everything was trendy and innovative, the Provincetown Inn remained a bastion of old-school Cape Cod. The murals depicted life in a historical fishing town, the exposed beams were treated to look like charred wood, and the lounge had a quiet, dark charm.

It was deserted at midweek, so it was not difficult to find a private corner.

When Tony got there, Jenny was leaning against the bar chatting with the bartender. She knew everyone in town. She turned toward the entrance when he came into the bar. "Go find a table. I'll bring our drinks," she told him.

He nodded and scanned the place for the most concealed spot. He'd just sat down as Jenny brought him a beer and a chilled chardonnay for herself.

"Thanks," he said as she lowered herself into the seat opposite him.

"So. How was your trip?"

"Good. Exhausting." He studied her face, looking for any sign of temper. She actually appeared hopeful. Shit. His stomach clenched. He really didn't want to have this conversation. "How was your week?"

She shrugged. "It was okay. Just working, like usual. You said you wanted to talk."

"Yeah, I did." He took a breath. "I've been doing

some thinking about us."

She lifted an eyebrow. "You have."

"Yeah. See, here's the thing. Our…relationship…has been, I don't know—"

"You don't have to say any more." She clapped her hands together in front of her like a barking seal. "I say yes!"

Yes? What the hell? "Yes? You haven't even heard me out."

"I've been waiting for this moment since I saw you in first grade." She bounced up and down in her chair. "I've been in love with you for that long."

Oh no. He was toast. "If you'd just let me finish."

"Go ahead, then." She giggled. "I'd love to have this story to tell our grandchildren when they ask me how you asked me to marry you."

Tony thought he might throw up. "Slow down." He might as well just blurt it out. "You've got the wrong idea. I'm not proposing."

"What?" Her eyebrows scrunched together. "Come again?"

Damn. She looked like she might cry. "I'm not proposing."

"What?" She shook her head like she was trying to clear her ears.

He sighed. "I'm not proposing."

"You're kidding."

What the hell was he supposed to say? He'd never been any good with words. "I think that we haven't been on the same page for a long time. You want to get married, and I just don't see marriage in my future. I can't give you what you want."

"Of course you can give me what I want. I want to

get married. You want to get married. It's what people like us do."

Yes, people like them get married. Except there was only one person he'd ever imagined himself married to, and it wasn't Jenny. It shamed him. He didn't love Jenny enough, didn't love her the way she deserved to be loved. Again at a loss for words, he repeated, "I can't give you what you want, because I don't want to get married."

She froze up, except for her eyes, which snapped with fire. "Are you breaking up with me?" she spat through a clenched jaw.

"Not breaking up. Setting you free." He felt that reason was inspired. "I've been really selfish all these years, knowing what you wanted and never giving it to you. I'm just not the marrying kind. You deserve more than I can give you."

"You are breaking up with me."

"Jenny." Tony felt his face flush. "It's not you. It's me."

Her hands fisted at her sides. "What a fucking cliché." Jenny stared at him, eyes wide, jaw dropped. After a moment's silence, she slammed her hand down on the table. "You son of a bitch. It's not that you're not the marrying kind. You're breaking up with me because your precious Pearl Marlowe is back in town!"

"Pearl has nothing to do with it." Even though she'd been the catalyst for him making this decision, this was something he had to do. He owed it to Jenny. "I'm trying to do the right thing here. Would you rather I string you along for the next twenty years? I'm never going to be able to give you what you want. I just don't think marriage is in the cards for me."

"That's bull, and you know it. Pearl has every damn thing to do with it." Jenny fired back. "You wanted to marry her. God, you were so damn pathetic that night she broke up with you, drunk off your ass, crying over that stupid tiny diamond ring."

Tony felt his face heat, whether in anger or embarrassment he didn't know. Probably both. "Lay off, Jenny," he warned her. "Leave Pearl alone."

"Lay off. Lay off?" She snorted, the sound juicy and unpleasant. "You didn't think everyone knew that you were carrying that ring in that pocket. We were all laughing at you, pitiful fool, carrying a torch for the woman who ran away as fast as she could without a backward glance."

Tony couldn't say anything. It was true.

"It's always been about Pearl," Jenny spat at him. "You're sure as hell the marrying kind, only if the woman is Pearl Marlowe." She pushed away from the table and shot to her feet. "You've just made the biggest mistake of your life." She picked up her huge purse and swung it at his head, connecting with a clunk, turned on her heel, and beat feet out of there.

Tony sat there blinking while the bartender crossed the bar and handed him a bar towel with ice. "You should know better than to piss off Jenny."

Tony took the frozen towel. "Now you tell me."

****

Sterling loosened his tie as he punched up the volume to the music blaring from his car's speakers. His taste was usually opera, but tonight he wanted head-thumping rock. He could see the Monument spearing up out of Provincetown's landscape. The blue of the harbor winked and sparkled at him.

Usually the view calmed him, but not today. He was not fit for company.

Since he felt like punching someone, he decided to go to the gym before he went to Marlowe House and checked in with his sisters. He'd been burning the midnight oil fighting on the floor of the House for a bill putting regulations back into the EPA that had been stripped by the agency. Fierce resistance had come from across the aisle, in the form of the oil companies' best friend, Garrett Williams.

Sterling straddled a fine line when it came to the environment. All the regulations had made it very difficult for the fishermen, but there needed to be some protections in place for the health of the ocean and the preservation of the whale population.

So he was going to run a few miles, assault a heavy bag for a few rounds, and then shower off the rest of Garrett Williams' oily, toxic stink.

Williams had the gall to bring up Pearl's troubles, most likely thinking he was going to blackmail Sterling into giving up on the bill.

He'd worked his ass off to get all charges against his sister dismissed. No one was going to use Pearl again, especially not a manipulative snake like Williams.

Finally at the gym, as he changed for his workout, he thought about Pearl back when the trial was going on and got all hot under the collar again. He never wanted to see that haunted, defeated look in her eyes.

He liked the spark and the energy he saw in her now. He'd eat any number of bad meals if he had to, just to keep that gleam in her eyes. He changed, then put himself to work on the treadmill.

He ran as far and as fast as he could for thirty minutes, trying to defeat the demons set loose by Garrett. Moving on, he attacked the boxing bag.

After wrapping his wrists and shoving his fists into his gloves, he hauled off and pummeled the bag with blow after punishing blow. Power sang down his arms as he punched the bag and danced on the balls of his feet.

"Take it easy, Congressman. What did that poor bag ever do to you?"

Sterling jumped back and almost snarled at Alex Tudor, standing right there in the hot, sweat-slicked flesh, grinning at him. "Tudor. Why are you here and not creating a ruckus at my family homestead?"

"It's all done except for the cleanup. Then it's on to your other sister's shop."

What? "I didn't know that."

Alex lifted one shoulder in dismissal. "A boy's got to eat." He shifted his weight and leaned against the bag. "You need a workout buddy? I'll hold the bag while you destroy it."

Now there was an invitation, and back in his college days, Sterling would have grabbed it with both hands.

Ahem. Totally not appropriate. He was just sayin', only not out loud. He'd kept his thoughts to himself all his life. He was pretty damn good at it.

"Hello? Congressman?"

Sterling shook his head. Alex was looking at him with a small bit of expectation in his eyes. "Sorry. What?"

Alex turned his man-killer grin up to eleven. "Want me to steady the bag?"

Tempting, but… "No. I'm done."

"Maybe some other time."

Oh no. Too dangerous. Sterling's heart skipped a beat. "Maybe."

That enticing curl of his lips stayed in place. "See you around." Alex jogged off.

Sterling fought the urge to watch Alex walk away. Good thing work was going to keep him away for a while.

Chapter Fifteen

Pearl was up to her ears in hot, sudsy water as she swabbed the kitchen floor. She'd had a baking accident, and things had not gone well. Her nose and eyes stung and watered from the pine-scented disinfecting cleanser she liberally mopped on the floor and scrubbed the counters. She didn't know what smelled worse, the cleanser or the sour-dough starter.

She straightened and leaned on her weapon of choice, the mop. Stretching to one side and then the other while her lower back muscles screamed at her, she moaned.

Who knew bread dough could explode? Certainly not Pearl.

She glanced up to the ceiling where some gelatinous goop threatened to come raining down on top of her. Shuddering, she returned her attention to the task at hand.

She'd just put her shoulder back into it when the phone rang. Pulling her rubber gloves off, she slid on a wet section of floor, nearly falling on her butt. She slammed into the bread-dough-covered counter, breaking a nail to save her from knocking her face into the gloppy dough.

Yelping, she snatched the phone receiver and held it up to her ear. "Marlowe House."

"Pearl? It's Tony. You okay?"

Taking a deep breath, she said, "Tony, hey. I'm fine, thanks for asking. What can I do for you?"

"Um, I've been thinking of your offer to help me out. You know, like, why don't we go to dinner some night this week and talk about my business plan?"

What? Well, she had offered. "Um, that would be, uh, fine."

"What's a good night for you?"

Take your pick. A thought occurred to her.

Okay, dinner might fun, but not somewhere they might run into Jenny. Although, Jenny was Tony's girlfriend, she should know Tony was asking Pearl out to dinner. "Is it okay with Jenny?"

One beat of extremely uncomfortable silence. Then, "I broke up with Jenny."

What the wha? "Come again?"

This time the answer came right away. "Jenny's and my relationship was going nowhere fast. She wants things I can't give her, so it's time to cut bait and free her up to find someone else who can give her what she wants. What she deserves."

"Oh." Her knees went a little wobbly, probably because of her near face plant on the kitchen counter.

Yeah. That was it.

"Pearl, you still there?"

"Yeah, I'm here." As of now, she really didn't want to run into Jenny while having dinner with Tony. She swallowed back the sudden lump lodged in her throat. "Why don't you come here and let me make you dinner?"

"You want to cook for me?"

No, she didn't want to cook for him, at least not yet. But she didn't want to run into Jenny even more.

She'd lead with the truth. "Honestly? If we go to dinner right after you broke up with Jenny? People will say you broke up with her because of me, and I don't want that. I just can't."

More silence, then— "I get that. Whatever you want. When are you free?"

She gave her floor and ceiling the side eye. Probably a good idea to have him over after she finished hazmatting the kitchen. "Can I get back to you on that?"

"Sure. I'll give you a call."

"Do you have my number?"

"I'll call you in a couple of days. I've got some things around the house to take care of." Understatement her brain trilled in a singsongy voice.

"Great. I'll wait for your call."

"Yep. Bye."

"Uh-hunh. Bye." Tony hung up.

Pearl set the receiver back into the old-fashioned wall phone with great care. So Tony had broken up with Jenny. The devil perched on her left shoulder stood up and did a happy dance. The angel on her right shook her head and said, "Tony is not for you. You gave him up, remember?"

Like she could ever forget it. Still, she was sure that Tony breaking up with Jenny had nothing to do with her. She needed to keep that in mind.

A glob of raw bread dough picked that moment to disengage from the ceiling and land on the floor, splat! Right on her foot. At least it didn't land on her head.

What was she going to make for him? For the life of her, she couldn't remember eating anything other than pizza and burgers with him. No, that wasn't true.

123

He loved his mother's lasagna. She'd do a twist on that, a seafood lasagna with a béchamel sauce. She went right to her computer to find a recipe.

****

Tony stared at his phone like it was a rattlesnake. Something was definitely off with Pearl. He'd certainly hoped for a bigger reaction to his announcement about breaking things off with Jenny.

Not that he should expect Pearl to make a huge deal of it.

He might as well face it. He'd always been a sap when it came to all things Marlowe.

Especially Pearl Marlowe. The girl who got away.

She wasn't a girl anymore… She'd grown into the promise of that girl. She'd achieved her dream career, lost it, had nearly gone to prison, but here she was, back in town, preparing to open a bed and breakfast.

He wondered how long that would last, how long it would take before she got bored and moved back to the bright lights of the big city. Bottom line, she didn't have it in her to stay. He knew that better than anyone.

He went to his closet and pulled out a shoebox from the back. He slid his hand over the lid to get rid of the dust. Holding his breath, he opened the box.

It held the ghosts of his past. There were his old orange-and-black PHS athletic letters, a certificate or two proclaiming excellence in one thing or another. All his yearbooks, the Long Pointers. But most of all it contained pictures of him and Pearl when they'd been young, in love, and totally out of their minds.

There were tons of candid photos mostly with the two of them wrapped around each other, sporting ear-to-ear grins. No one could ever look as happy as they did then.

He picked up the formal portrait of them at the junior prom. Remembering how proud and grown-up he'd felt, he smiled in spite of himself. Pearl had been so beautiful in a green, blue, and purple dress with a lot of sequins. She'd looked like a mermaid, a siren straight out of the sea.

He ran his finger down the image of Pearl in the picture. Unwelcome feelings washed over him. Soft, sentimental sensations about Pearl weren't going to make anything better. He'd best shove them way down and ignore them.

Better to remember that she'd been engaged to another man, as much as that clawed at his stomach.

He and Pearl had a business relationship. That's all it could ever be.

Right.

No, all wrong.

He didn't know.

Crap.

Chapter Sixteen

"You know, you could make this easy on yourself and get some takeout." Opal leaned against the refrigerator.

"I want to cook. I invited Tony for a meal here, and I'm making it myself." Pearl reached up and behind her head to tighten her ponytail as she squinted at her recipe for seafood lasagna one more time. The béchamel sauce didn't seem to be thickening like it was supposed to. Had she skipped a step?

Opal shook her head. "But it's so stressful. You could relax and let someone else do all the work."

"Cooking relaxes me."

Opal looked dubious. "But don't you want to use the time to get all dressed up?"

Sighing, Pearl turned to face her younger sister. "I don't need to look nice," she lied. "This is just a business meeting."

"Puh-leez." Opal pushed away from the fridge. "Of course you want to look good for Tony. You hardly ever go around without some war paint."

Maybe a little bit. "I repeat. This is just business, not a date."

"You're having a man over, and you're cooking dinner for him. That's a date, sweetie."

"When do you go back to England, Opie?"

Opal hoisted herself up to sit on the counter. "Not

soon enough. I've got to meet with Camille's biographer to deal with some problems he's got with the manuscript. And don't call me Opie."

"What kind of problems?" Better to get Opal talking about herself than about Pearl dating Tony.

"Apparently he found some love letters, really juicy ones, that Camille wrote to this guy she supposedly had an affair with."

"Camille? An affair?" Inconceivable. "No way."

"Yes, way, if this guy is telling the truth. Not only has he found the letters, he found the guy who wrote them."

"He's still alive? He must be a real geezer by now."

"Here's another kick in the head. Lover boy was way younger than Camille." Opal shuddered. "I'd rather clean bathrooms on the Mass Pike rest areas with my toothbrush than read dirty letters our dear old granny wrote to some sweet young thing."

Pearl felt her jaw drop. Ewwww. "I don't blame you." The thought of Camille and sex with some young stud was just flat out icky. "I'd have to bleach my eyes if I read them." A cheerful thought jumped out at her. "Better you than me."

"Ugh." Opal leaped off the counter and landed on her feet with a solid thud. "I just know he's going to want to include all the gory, sordid details. I'm pretty sure that is not the way Camille wanted to be remembered. I don't get it."

"What don't you get?"

"Why Camille chose him to write the biography. He's known for being a sensationalist, totally the opposite of everything she admired in a writer."

"That is odd." Pearl dumped a cup full of flour into the watery béchamel and whisked it vigorously, wincing when drops of hot milk flew up and attacked her. Now it was still thin but had little pasty lumps floating around in it. She frowned. "Camille always put such a high price on image."

"I know, right? It makes no sense." Opal came behind Pearl and peered at the pot full of lumpy, bubbling sauce. "You know, it's not too late to call for takeout."

****

Tony parked in front of Marlowe House and took a deep breath. He'd spent all day wondering whether he should bring wine or flowers or both to his business dinner with Pearl.

He'd never been to a business dinner, so he had no idea what was protocol. Flowers had seemed too much like a date, so he'd gone with wine.

He knew absolutely jack shit about wine. Neither had the person manning the cash register at the package store. Since they'd both heard that French wine was the best, he went with a wine whose name he couldn't pronounce but looked impressive to his way of thinking.

He'd changed his damn shirt five times. Thank God, he'd stopped himself from slapping aftershave on his face.

What the hell was he doing here? He bet God didn't even know the answer to that question.

He had to get over himself. It was just dinner. A business dinner. It shouldn't be such a big deal.

He refused to let it be. Clearing his throat, ready, eager even, to get the job done, he got out of his car.

And he immediately regretted his action. Too late. He was going to have dinner with Pearl at Marlowe House, something that had never once happened the entire time he'd gone out with her in high school.

Camille hadn't allowed the kids to have anyone over for dinner. That was the time of day when they had to check in with their grandmother.

He'd never understood the pressure Camille had put on them. His parents were strict but loving. A family dinner had been a normal, happy thing. They'd asked about his and Gabe's day and their successes, their trials, if either boy wanted to talk about them.

Pearl had always referred to dinnertime as "The Inquisition." Truthfully, Tony had never been able to wrap his head around that. He walked a few more steps.

Oh, looky here. Tony stood in front of Pearl's front door. Might as well knock on it.

He sighed and gathered his courage to the sticking point. Wherever that was. He only knew he'd heard it once in English class. He hadn't thought a lot about it back then, but right now it made a lot of sense.

The universe was sticking it to him and probably laughing its ass off. His future was now in the hands of the woman who'd made it clear that she wanted nothing to do with the future he'd offered her seventeen years ago.

Yeehaw!

Would a time ever come when Pearl Marlowe didn't tie him up in knots?

Despite the intense, crawly feeling of impending disaster, he pushed the doorbell. Might as well get this over with.

He rolled his shoulders back and forward as he

heard movement on the other side of the door. Practicing a couple of what he hoped were friendly smiles, he braced himself for Pearl opening the door.

She threw the door wide, smiled at him, and he knew he was a goner. Every word just picked up and flew right out of his head. His tongue ballooned five sizes too thick.

"Tony. Come on in." She stepped aside and motioned for him to cross the threshold.

His feet turned into cinder blocks. All he could do was stand there and drink in the sight of her.

She cocked her head to the side as she smiled at him. Her red hair shone and looked so soft he had to stop himself from touching it and mussing it all up. Over a silky blue shirt, she wore a white chef's apron, which was stained with several different colored substances. "Don't just stand there. Come in!"

Since it sounded like a good idea, he managed to unlock his feet and step through the door. "I brought you some wine." He thrust the bottle at her.

"Oh. Thank you." She checked out the label. "It looks lovely. Shall I take your coat?"

"Sure."

Laughing, Pearl shook her head. "Listen to us, how polite and grown up we are!"

He grinned at her while he felt his face heat. "We were getting a little small talky there."

"We need to stop it now. C'mon, I'll get you a drink, and we can go over some things while dinner finishes cooking."

"Great. Since when do you cook?" From what he remembered, Pearl's best dish was ordering pizza. His mother had been concerned that he wanted to marry a woman who had no interest in cooking a meal.

"Since I decided to turn the house into a bed and breakfast. I like it a lot more than I thought I would. It's relaxing."

Pearl looked so happy. He saw her in a very different light. The girl he'd known was no domestic goddess. Had no interest in being one.

She gestured down the hall. "Go on to the living room, and I'll be right along with some drinks and hors d'oeuvres. Shall I open the wine?"

Why not? "Yeah, thanks."

"So go ahead." She waved her hand. "Shoo. I'll be right there."

He watched her go and steeled himself to deal with the ghosts of the past that lurked in Marlowe House's parlor. Turned out he didn't need to.

Pearl had done some serious redecorating. The room had always looked like an exhibit in a museum with delicate, spindly antiques, heavy upholstery and drapes, and a dark, so-old-you-shouldn't-walk-on-it oriental rug. She'd exchanged the curtains for filmy white sheers, the carpet for floral area rugs, and most of the fragile furniture for sturdy pieces that were made of bone-colored driftwood. Instead of the dark leather couch and chair cushions, she'd used a sea-hued fabric with large cream-colored sand dollars spread across it.

She'd put Camille's small and exclusive sculpture collection into any number of nooks and crannies she'd made by building various shelves at random heights along the walls. He didn't know much about this kind of thing, but he knew Pearl, and none of this had been left to chance. Pearl would be the one to mix the primitive with the high art.

"What do you think?"

He swiveled around to see Pearl standing there with a tray laden with two glasses of wine and a platter of something he couldn't identify from the distance. Her eyes were wide and her smile hopeful as she returned his gaze.

That look of hers was likely to bring him to his knees. Tony's breath caught in his throat. The last time he'd seen such hope, he'd been totally, madly in love.

Right before Pearl had broken his heart. Some ice started to creep up along his spine to his heart, trying to harden it before he fell back in love with her.

Which was a dangerously close possibility.

So he welcomed the ice. This dinner was about business. He'd best remember that. Still…what would it hurt him to acknowledge the changes she'd made here?

Pearl was doing something he was absolutely chicken about doing: breaking away from his family and their expectations. He imagined that if Camille were still alive, like his own parents were, Pearl'd still be embracing the status quo, even though she'd nearly gone to jail for a crime she didn't commit.

"It looks very different from what I remember."

She set the tray down on a low table in front of a love seat. "Different good or different bad?" Frowning, Pearl straightened. "I've pretty much thrown out Camille with the bathwater."

He snorted. Good thing she could joke about it now. "It looks good." He pointed to a chair. "I'm not afraid it's going to break if I sit on it."

She grinned. "That's the plan. I want people to feel comfortable. It's a house, not a museum."

Oh, Lord, that smile of hers. It zapped him right

between the eyes. "You're doing a good job. Maybe I can get a tour later?"

"Absolutely! It's not all done. I'm still picking out wallpaper and light fixtures for the bedrooms, but the bathrooms are roughed in. I think you can get a good idea of what they're going to be like." She practically wiggled with enthusiasm.

A quick bark of laughter burst out of him. This was the Pearl he remembered, exuberant and looking forward to the future. Of course back then much to his continued surprise, her future hadn't included him. He'd do well to remember that.

"Well, let me get you what I've been working on, and you can look at it while I put the finishing touches on dinner. Be right back." She wiped her hands on her jeans as she walked away.

Tony wandered to the double doors leading out to the deck, leaned against the doorframe, and studied the waning sunlight. Days were getting longer, he mused as he stared out at the sea he loved so well. A gold shaft of light speared down from a break in the cloud-spattered sky. It promised bad weather the next day. A storm. He appreciated the fact that he wouldn't be going out to fight it.

All kinds of storms were coming. He shuddered against a sudden chill.

"Tony?"

He turned to face his first big squall and nearly lost it in the sweetness of her smile. He swallowed. "Yeah."

"Here's a template of a business plan that might be helpful." She held out a file folder. "Let me know what you think."

Nodding, he took it from her. "Thanks."

"Take a look at it while I get dinner on the table." She flashed him another smile that twisted him in knots.

"Uh-hunh." He glanced at the file folder she'd handed him. Might as well look at it. After all, that's what he was there for. After about three pages in, his eyes started to cross. What was he thinking? His father and brother were right. Tony had no business opening a fish market.

"So what do you think?" Pearl's voice broke through his misery. "Are you okay? You look kind of pale."

"This is a mistake." He waved the papers in front of him. "I'm wasting your time."

"No, you're not. It's a bit overwhelming, even if you have done a business plan before." Her gentle voice broke through his embarrassment. "I'll walk you through it every step of the way."

"The reality is a lot more complicated than I imagined."

"It always is." She shook her head. "Dinner's on the table. Let's go eat."

Might as well. Plus, he wanted to understand her new commitment to domesticity. He still had trouble reconciling that side of the new Pearl with the Pearl he remembered. "Sounds good. I'm hungry."

She moved her hand toward his, then pulled it back. If he hadn't been looking, he wouldn't have seen it. "Come on," she said and gestured for him to follow her.

What else could he do? He followed her.

Chapter Seventeen

Pearl looked at the snot-colored lasagna she'd put on the table and tried not to grimace. Her food never looked like it did in the pictures on Pinterest. It also never tasted like she expected it to.

Not stupid, she didn't believe her family liked her food. Too bad. This was her circus and her monkeys, and she would make it work.

However, tonight it wasn't about her. She and Tony would eat and discuss his hopes and dreams for his new business. She'd show him around later, keeping all her monkeys in their fragile, golden cages. She fixed a cheerful smile on her face. "I hope you like seafood lasagna."

"I love it," Tony said. "It looks delicious."

It didn't, but it was nice of him to lie. He'd always had the loveliest manners. She cut into it and slid an oily slab onto his plate. "Here you go." Fortunately, she'd bought fresh Portuguese rolls and had made a big green salad. She wouldn't send him home hungry.

She got everything dished up and sat down. Picking up her fork, she watched Tony tuck into his food and take a big bite. He started to chew. And chew. And chew. Finally he swallowed with a loud gulp. "It's good," he said as he grabbed his wine glass.

Not Tony, too. "You don't have to pretend. It's not good."

He took another swig of wine. Pure panic winked in his eyes. "No, it's—"

"You don't have to lie, Tony. My family does enough of that, trying to spare my feelings. I'm a terrible cook."

He grabbed his napkin and swabbed it across his mouth. "You just need experience, that's all."

"I'm on my own and flying blind." Pearl sighed. "What I need is help."

Tony stared at her for a very long moment. She fought the urge to wiggle under his scrutiny. He cleared his throat. "Maybe my mother could help you."

"What?" His mother? No, no, no, no, no, no, no. "Tony, your mother hates me."

"No, she doesn't."

"You're such a liar."

He gave her a sheepish grin. "She might hate you a little bit. But listen. She's heard all about what you're doing here, and she's very curious."

That Pearl could believe. Everyone was very curious. She couldn't go to the Stop and Shop without having to answer a bazillion questions. "Define a little bit."

He sighed and tore a piece off his roll. Discomfort clung to him. "It was a bad time, okay? I did some things I'm not proud of, and she blamed you."

"Wonderful." Wasn't it just?

He shrugged. "What can I say? She's my mom. She loves me."

Of course it was as simple as that. Pearl waited a minute to speak around the huge lump in her throat. "Of course she does. Like you said, she's your mom." Pearl had known that kind of love for a very short time. She cherished every memory.

"She is." He tossed the hunk of bread onto his plate. "She'd also give her left pinkie finger to be the first to know what you're up to. She's also a very forgiving human being."

Pearl's heart clutched. She longed for forgiveness from Tony's parents, especially his mother. She'd gone to Tony's mother for approval for her prom dress, outfits to wear at college visits, just about everything she needed that she couldn't get from Camille.

Before Tony's mom? She remembered her grandmother's assistant, the hapless Mrs. Wolverton, taking her to Macy's in Hyannis to buy her first bra. Pearl had spared Ruby and Opal the Mrs. Wolverton experience and had taken them to Macy's herself.

That had been way more fun.

"Do you think she'd really want to work with me?" Pearl stabbed a limp shrimp, thought about putting it in her mouth, then put it back on the plate.

Tony pursed his lips. "Yeah, I think she would. I can ask, of course, if you want."

Her heart thumped hard. "You'd do that for me?" She held her breath, not daring to believe it.

"You're helping me with my business plans. Frankly, I'm not sure I can do it without you. And"— his eyes sparkled—"if you can bring her over to my side of the cause while you two are cooking, that would be great. She's the best chance I have at convincing my father and brother."

She found she could sit there and have him look at her like that forever. But he was here for business, so she'd best get to it. "I'll do my best. I don't have to work hard to generate enthusiasm for your project. It's a winner, Tony."

A warm, cozy cloak descended on them, again familiar, but still brand new. Pearl didn't dare breathe, not one breath in or out lest she break the spell. She kept her eyes shuttered because if she looked at him, she'd be lost.

She couldn't afford to get lost right now. She had so much to do.

Tony let loose a very noisy breath. "Let's give up on the seafood and eat salad and bread." He paused, studied her. "I trust there is dessert?"

She nodded. "Ice cream and Pepperidge Farm cookies."

He smiled, and his eyes warmed. "My favorites."

"You don't even know what kind of ice cream I have."

"I don't have to hear. You remember what kind of ice cream." His eyes glinted as he said this.

All her skin prickled and popped. She did. "Mocha chip."

"That's right."

"The cookies are Brussels?"

She nodded because she couldn't speak.

"Let's have dessert now." He stood.

She struggled up on her wobbly knees. "I'll get it. Go on out to the living room."

He grinned. "Let me help. I'm an expert at opening Pepperidge Farm bags."

"I bet you are." She knew he was. Pointing her head toward the kitchen, she said, "Follow me into my lair."

****

They sat at the kitchen table, armed with ice cream,

cookies, and white wine. Papers littered the table, the template for the business plan scattered over the top. "Yeah, so we're going to save the executive summary for last as it has to pull together all the other sections," Pearl told Tony.

"That makes sense." Tony looked at the list she'd given him. "So where do we start?"

"Let's start with a general description of your company. We know what business you want to start and what it will do."

"Well, yeah. I want to open a market to sell the lobsters we catch and cut out the middleman." He shook his head. "I mean, we could sell them off the boat, but I want it to be more than that. I want to sell to people who wouldn't even think about going to the boat."

"Hmmmmm. That's good for a start. Have you thought about a business philosophy?"

"Like what?"

Pearl gave him a patient smile. "Like what's important to you in business?"

"I want to make money." Score one for another, duh.

"Obviously, but dig a little deeper."

"Deeper?" he repeated like a dimwit. He hated it when he got tongue-tied.

"For example, you want to provide quality seafood, straight from the ocean, to an exclusive and discerning clientele."

Well, put that way, it sounded pretty fancy. "Okay. I like that."

Pearl tapped her pen on her yellow legal pad. "Is it a growth industry?"

Tony's stomach clenched. "Not really. There are all these regulations about where we can fish, and what with global warming and all, the lobsters aren't there like they used to be because of the water temperature." He shrugged. "Lobsters are still better than going for ground fish."

"That's what I suspected." Pursing her lips, she sat back in her chair. "So we have to expand your scope a little bit so it reflects a way toward growth."

"Off the top of my head, perhaps I could offer cooking the lobsters for people if they want. Lots of tourists want the lobster without the work."

"Have you ever thought about offering a clambake?"

"Clambake?"

"Yeah, the whole nine yards. Lobsters, steamers, linguiça, corn on the cob, those little salt potatoes, right down to the seaweed. It would be great! And then maybe make a deal with an ice cream shop downtown and add a store coupon into the package for dessert."

"That sounds pretty complicated." Tony rubbed his chin.

"Sure it does right now, but I do think that's where you'll be able to promise growth."

"Seriously?" Tony couldn't imagine it.

"It's an awesome idea and could make you a ton of money." She smiled, and he felt like Hercules. "Have you thought about what type of legal ownership you want to have?"

He'd googled it. "Ideally I'd like a partnership with my father and brother."

"That sounds best to me," Pearl said as she grabbed a cookie and broke it in half. "You said before that you

140

need help convincing them."

Sighing, Tony took a healthy slug of wine. "Ain't it the truth. Neither my dad nor Gabe is interested in this project. Mom sides with them."

"Will that be a problem when it comes to getting financing for the project?"

"What do you mean?"

"Unless you have a secret stash of cash, you're going to need a loan."

In the back of his mind, Tony had realized that. "Yeah."

"So do you have any assets you own by your lonesome?"

Galling to admit but… "No." He looked around at Pearl's expensive home, and the cloak of not being good enough covered him again.

"Unless you get someone from outside the family to invest."

"Who?" He didn't know anybody who had that kind of money lying around.

She toasted him with her wine. "Don't give up just yet. Let's finish your plan and then worry about getting them on board. It will be much easier if they see you've thought things all the way through."

Which was the exact reason he'd agreed to her help on this project. Already he'd confronted a bunch of things he would never have considered on his own. He just wouldn't have known.

"Do you have a location in mind for the market?"

He'd thought he'd run it from his parents' garage, but now he realized that wasn't going to work, not if they were talking about clambakes. "I have no idea."

"You want to keep it close to town, yes? But easy

to get to with parking?"

"Of course." Good luck finding anything with parking close to town.

"How about this?" She narrowed her eyes as she talked. "Go through the real estate listings and see if there's a place that seems like it would work. If not, think about buying land and building what you need."

"I can do that."

"Make a list of the equipment you'd need to make the space into your store. That way we'll have a much better idea of where to look and what to look for."

"Good idea." He had a list going he considered pretty complete, but he could look at it again now that Pearl had green lighted the clambake idea.

"You'll have to hire someone to man the cash register and sell the lobsters while you're out catching them," Pearl pointed out. "We'll have to add that to your list of expenses." She smiled and looked like an angel, all big blue eyes, generous mouth, and rich red hair. "We should stop here, but I think we've made a good start. Do you want some coffee?"

"Maybe." He had a question he had to ask, and there was no way to ask diplomatically. "How did you end up engaged to a man who stole from people and put the blame on you?"

The question landed like an active grenade between them. He'd expected the reaction, but he had to know.

She swallowed and patted her mouth very carefully. "You should know, especially if you're thinking of going into business with me."

It had nothing to do with business and everything to do with his heart. Why this asshole Henry and not him? He had to know.

"I didn't know what Henry was up to, obviously." She wouldn't look at him. "But he had access to my laptop and did all his illegal transactions on my computer when I didn't know about it. Pretty stupid, right?"

"Why did you trust him so much?" The Pearl he knew wasn't that stupid.

Unless she'd been madly in love with this Henry. The urge to break something had him seeing red and his hand itching to punch good ol' Henry in the face.

"In hindsight it looks pretty ridiculous. I just, I don't know, I let things happen." She took a healthy gulp of her wine, draining her glass. "My heart was, numb, I guess would be the best way to describe it. I'd gotten the right job, was on track for a corner office, had a boyfriend who was as ambitious as I was." She finally looked at him. "Everything seemed in sync, and Camille approved, or so I thought." She sighed. "I guess I didn't know as much as I thought I did."

"Did you love him?" The words left his lips before he could think about them.

She fixed a pointed look at him. "I guess as much as you love Jenny."

He figured that was true. It made him queasy. "I cared for her as best I could."

"There you go." She toasted him with the wine bottle. "Want some more?"

"No, thanks." More wine would make his stomach rebel even more than it already was. "Why were you with him?"

"Why were you with Jenny?"

"Good question." He wasn't proud of his answer. However, he had to tell the truth. More duh. "She wore

143

me down, and she was convenient. I'm not proud, but I'd given up on finding true love." Not like he'd been looking. True love was a crock of shit as far as he was concerned.

"I see." She caught his gaze and held it. "I also don't think I really loved Henry. We had the same goals in life, and a life together would have been comfortable. I guess that's the same."

"Maybe." It absolutely was. "Still no matter what you can say about Jenny, she was loyal. She wouldn't have made up anything to send me to jail."

"Greed is a powerful motivator." She gave a fake laugh. She still held his gaze. He wanted to look away, but he couldn't. "I let it all happen, no matter what he did. But I learned my lesson. Don't ever trust anyone ever again."

What? The woman he had loved and who left him could not trust, refused to trust anyone else ever again? Unbelievable. He blurted out as much.

Pearl's face turned sad. "I deserve that, but let's move on. I do want you to know that I know business, and I can help you with this plan. My arrest has nothing to do with my ability to do my job."

He chose his words carefully. "I never thought that." Which was true. "I trust you with my business hopes and dreams."

She gave a curt nod. "I get that. Really, I'm surprised you do."

His chin itched, and he rubbed his hand over it. "I do trust you." Did he believe that? He honestly didn't know, but it seemed like the right thing to say.

"You're being very generous." She glanced around the room. "Do you want some coffee?"

His head swam with all the honesty floating around the room. He knew he was telling the truth, against his better judgment. He had to get out of there. "I should probably go. I've got an early morning." He needed time to think about everything.

"You're sure?"

"Yeah. Do you need help cleaning up?"

She shook her head. "I've got it under control."

He stood. "Thank you for dinner."

Laughing, she wiped her hands on her jeans as she got out of her chair. "Such as it was."

"I'll talk to my mother about the cooking thing."

"I appreciate it. I need all the help I can get."

They walked to her front door, close enough for Tony's skin to prickle in awareness of the woman who had tossed him away so many years before.

He wanted to kiss her, damn her.

Damn him.

As if she knew what he was fighting, Pearl faced him, studying him with those shiny, bright-blue eyes. She opened her mouth as if to say something, but she didn't. She just stared at him, her dazzling, plump, soft lips apart, like an invitation to kiss her.

His hands trembled as he reached over to cup her beautiful face. Consigning himself to hell, he leaned in and brushed his lips across Pearl's, soft as a whisper.

She hummed and put her hands over his. Together they fell into each other, lips and tongues tangling like there were no years between them.

The sweet taste of her kisses, so familiar yet foreign. He'd never forgotten her, forgotten her power over him.

He knew her kiss, way down deep in his soul.

Something that had been coiled tightly in his heart tied itself loose and sank further into Pearl.

She melted against him. He brought both his arms around her and cupped the soft flesh of her bottom and flexed his fingers, lightly kneading the supple skin he found there.

Pearl moaned into his mouth and to Tony's mind a sure sign of her desire. He'd had enough sweaty dreams about those hot sexy noises she made. He'd hated those dreams since he knew they would never come true.

He felt her stiffen in his arms. The spell had broken.

They broke the kiss, and each took a step back, Pearl staring at him warily. His chest constricted. "I've got to go. Thanks for dinner." He grabbed his coat with jerky, uncooperative arms.

"That's for the best," Pearl said, looking exactly as unsteady as he felt. "Call me to set up another time to meet."

"Yeah, sure." He opened the door and barely escaped with his sanity and dignity.

Chapter Eighteen

"How did your meeting with the biographer go?" Pearl caught Opal making coffee in the kitchen. "Be careful with that. It's a brand new espresso machine, and it cost me a kidney and part of my liver."

"The biographer's name is Ben Wallace, and he's a pain in the butt."

"Are the letters real?"

"I'd love to say no, but they are real from one gory detail to the next. He had a handwriting expert check it out." Opal shivered. "Granny was a freak. I may need brain bleach."

"Uh, ewwwww. What was in those letters?" Both repelled and thrilled, Pearl had to know. "Tell me."

"You don't want to know. I wish I didn't know. There's just something squicky imagining Camille having sex. Here's the thing. He wants to include the letters in the biography, which I'm dead set against. I'm supposed to be praising Caesar, not burying her."

"I can't imagine Camille wanted those kinds of details out there for the general public to consume." Their grandmother had been all about appearances.

"It gets worse. He wants to track down the boy toy."

Pearl's eyebrows rose so high they nearly flew off her forehead. "No."

"Yes. I've got to find a way to stop him," Opal

wailed.

The two sisters looked at each other for a long moment. Then, "Sterling," they said at the same time.

Pearl laughed. "And Camille was worried about Sterling causing a scandal. He may be her only hope for stopping one."

"She's going to rotate in her grave." Opal grimaced. "I shouldn't say things like that. It's extremely disrespectful. Let's change the subject. How did dinner go with Tony last night?"

"Good. We've got a lot of work to do on the marketing plan, of course, but we made a good start." Pearl's eyes narrowed. "His mother is going to give me cooking lessons."

Opal lifted one eyebrow. "Delores? Really?"

"That's the plan. Tony said he'd talk to her when he couldn't help but notice that I really can't cook."

"He said that to you?" Opal squeaked.

"I told him, but it was pretty obvious when I tried to feed him a lasagna made of seafood and slime."

"Oh." Opal's face was blank for a second, then brightened. "I told you to get takeout."

Oh, what Pearl wouldn't give to have her largest cast-iron skillet within arm's reach. She'd conk Opal right over the head with it. "At least he didn't pretend to like food that was horrible like some people I know."

"At the risk of repeating myself, I told you to get takeout."

"So you did. He kissed me."

"What?" Opal squealed like a tween about to meet the heartthrob of the month. "Tell your favorite sister everything. Don't leave a single detail out."

"There's not a lot to tell. We were at the door as he

was leaving, and next thing I know we're locking lips."

"Wow, oh, wow, oh, wow! Was it any good?"

Pearl felt her face flush. "Better than I remembered."

"Hot damn!" Opal slapped her hand down onto the counter. "I bet he's learned a trick or two since you two were in high school."

Pearl didn't like the thought that Jenny had taught Tony to kiss. "It wasn't like we were making out. It was just one kiss."

Opal's eyes lit with disbelief, and her mouth curved into a snarky little half smile. "If you say so. When are you going to see him again?"

"I don't know. After we kissed he took off like a bat out of hell. I told him to call me, but—" She shrugged.

"Who'd you tell to call you?" Yawning, Ruby walked into the kitchen. "Damn, Opal, you said you were making coffee."

"I am. I got distracted. Tony kissed Pearl last night."

"Oooh, the plot thickens." Ruby rubbed her hands together in glee. "Word on the street is that he broke up with Jenny, which earns a thumbs up and an 'about time' from me."

"Stop it, both of you." Pearl's nasty little gremlins banged on tympani in her head. "I don't think either of us are in a position to embark on a relationship right now."

"You've got a relationship whether you want one or not," Opal said. "Tony's getting his mother over here to teach you to cook makes sure of that."

"Say what?" Ruby grinned. "Delores Cabral is

going to give Pearlie cooking lessons? Hallelujah!"

"If you didn't like my food, why didn't you just come out and say so?" Pearl grumbled.

"I didn't want to spoil your fun. You seemed to be having such a good time."

"I was," Pearl mumbled. "But I'd like to have more fun."

"Which brings us back to you kissing Tony." Ruby nodded. "Is something happening there?"

"No. Maybe." Sighing, Pearl sat at the kitchen table. "I can't trust my instincts when it comes to men anymore because of, you know, Henry."

Opal snorted. "I wish I didn't know Henry, but there you go." She went to Pearl and started to knead her shoulders. "Don't give up on finding love again just because of him."

"Says the romance novelist," Pearl's inner cynic said.

"True love is a beautiful thing," Opal said.

"Pffffft." Ruby waved a dismissive hand. "True love is a myth."

"I can't wait until it happens to you." Opal smirked.

"You're going to wait a long time." Ruby studied her manicure. "Besides, we're not talking about me. We're talking about Pearl and Tony."

"No, we're not," Pearl decided. "That conversation is over. Opal? Why isn't there coffee yet?"

"I've been too busy commenting on your love life." She thrust the pot under the sink's spigot and filled it.

Ruby started looking around in the cabinets. "What happened to all the Brussels cookies?"

"They were part of last night's dessert," Pearl said

and braced herself for Ruby's reaction.

Which was a shrug. "I'll get more from the store later."

"By the way, maybe Ruby knows." After opening the bag of whole coffee beans, grinding them into a very fine powder, and poured the water into the coffee maker, Opal went to the sink and washed her hands.

"Know what?"

"Camille's biography researcher found racy letters some guy wrote her. Any clue as to who lover boy might be?"

"Lover boy?" Ruby scrunched her nose. "Camille? Does not compute."

"Yeah, well, I've seen the letters, and they are, well"—Opal blushed bright red—"really sexy."

Ruby gasped. "Ew! No!"

"I'll get them for you so you can see for yourself," Opal, the ever helpful, said.

"No, thank you." Shuddering, Ruby sat at the table. "Are you sure they're Camille's?"

"No doubt about it, unfortunately. You were around. You remember any young guy hanging around Grandmother?"

Ruby pursed her lips. "I don't know. I really didn't pay attention to everyone coming and going out of the house."

"Rubes, Rubes, Rubes. Trust you to not be nosy when it really counts!"

Pearl smiled. Brewing coffee now scented the air, its nutty aroma pungent and comforting. Ruby and Opal started to argue the way they always did since they were children, also comforting. Some things didn't change.

Pearl touched her lips with her fingertips. Did that include her connection to Tony? She just didn't know.

****

"Hey, Ma. Can I talk to you for a second?" Tony found his mother splicing buoy line in their basement. The days between February 1st and May 15th were all about fixing equipment. Everyone in the Cabral family took part.

She put down the lines she was working on and smiled at him. "Of course, sweetie. You can always talk to me."

Tony hoped that would hold true after he told her what he wanted. "I had dinner at Pearl's last night."

Her face clouded. "I know. Did she do something to upset you?"

"No, just the opposite. She gave me a lot of help on this plan for the fish market."

"You know your father is never going to go for that. You should forget it."

"Maybe he will once he sees the nuts and bolts details all laid out for him, but that's not what I want to talk to you about."

"All right." Her face was suddenly blank, all emotion hidden.

She wasn't fooling him. She didn't think the market was a good idea. He hoped Pearl could change her mind. To that end—

"You know how Pearl is renovating Marlowe House to be a bed and breakfast."

His mother chuckled. "I'd have to have been living under a rock the past couple of months not to know that."

"Well, the renovations are going great guns. You

wouldn't believe the changes she's made." Tony saw a reluctant flicker of interest in his mother's gaze. "But there's one area she really needs help."

"And you're telling me this, why?"

Ah. Sarcasm. He ignored it. "Cooking. She's been trying to teach herself, but she just can't seem to improve."

"I imagine in the city she ate at restaurants all the time." She sniffed. "Or just gotten takeout."

"Something like that. But here's the thing," Tony cajoled. "She really needs to make this bed and breakfast thing happen, not just because of the conditions of Camille's will but because she's left her life in the city behind."

"Is that really true, or do you just want it to be true?"

Surprised, he realized that he really, really wanted it to be true. "I think it's the truth. She's working so hard. You wouldn't recognize the place."

Again curiosity shone in his mother's demeanor. "What's she done?"

"Honest, Ma, I can't describe it. It used to be so fussy, and you'd be afraid to sit on anything. She's changed all that. You have to see it to get the full effect."

"Humpf."

He smiled at her. "So I was wondering if maybe you could give Pearl a few pointers."

Her eyes narrowed. "Pointers on what?"

"How to cook."

"How to cook." His mother fixed him with her don't-mess-with-me stare. "Why should I help Pearl Marlowe learn to cook?"

153

The big question. He had an answer, though. He'd practiced it several times on the way to his parents' house so he had it down cold. "Because no matter what happened in the past, you don't need to hold a grudge against her anymore. You're a bigger person than that. Karma already kicked her butt and almost put her in jail."

He watched his mother digest that, then he went in for the kill. "You'd be the first person in town, besides the family and me, who will see the renovations firsthand."

He held back a smile as his mother silently argued with herself.

"I suppose I could see if I have the time to help her out."

Tony wanted to jump in the air and pump his fist in victory, but he knew Mom wouldn't be amused. "I'll give you her number so you can call her."

"You can't call her for me?"

"Don't be a wimp. Just call her."

"Brat," she grumbled.

"Ma. You're never afraid of anything. Call Pearl. Imagine how everyone will be jealous when you've got the inside scoop on Marlowe House."

"There is that." She sighed. "Okay. I'll call Pearl after I finish splicing this buoy line. But I warn you. If she breaks your heart again, I'm going to have to kill her dead. In the face."

"I knew I could count on you." Tony beamed at her.

He'd kept his promise to Pearl. Hopefully, this wouldn't blow up in his face.

****

Pearl rubbed her hands on her jeans as she took one last look around her home. She saw out the kitchen window that Tony's mother had just rung the doorbell, and an army of demented butterflies careened back and forth in her stomach. She sniffed, satisfied that at least the house smelled like bright lemons, and the wooden surfaces gleamed in the early spring sunlight.

She'd done her best. It had to do.

Nerves jingling and jangling, she pasted her version of a confident smile on her face and opened the door. "Mrs. Cabral. Hello."

Delores nodded her head. "Hello, Pearl."

Pearl motioned toward the hallway with her arm. "Please come in."

Heavy silence hung in the air as Delores stepped over the threshold and looked around. "Tony was right. You've made some changes."

Tony had talked about the changes to his mother. She ignored the warm feeling at the thought of Tony talking to his mother on her behalf. Pearl wasn't sure about a lot of things, but there was one thing she would bet money on: lie to Delores Cabral and you'd never, ever get back in her good graces.

Pearl ached to be in Delores Cabral's extremely good graces. "Let me take your coat. I'm trying to open things up, make it more into a home and not a museum."

Delores sniffed and handed over her jacket. "Well, it does look a whole lot brighter in here."

That sounded like a compliment. She'd take it. "Thank you!"

Pursing her lips, Delores cleared her throat. "So Tony says you need some cooking lessons."

Pearl nodded. "I do. I've been going on Pinterest and experimenting, but I never seem to get things right. My family is humoring me and eating my science projects, I guess you'd call them, but I'm a real terrible cook."

"Why don't you hire one?"

"Hire one? What? A cook?"

"Yes." Delores clasped her hands. "Hire someone. I can give you some names. Why not?"

Sighing, Pearl realized that she should have anticipated that question. Eventually everyone else asked it. "It's important to me that I do this all on my own." Delores knew, more than anybody besides Tony, what mistakes Pearl had made and how much she had to prove to everyone.

Delores nodded. "I can respect that." She rolled up her sleeves. "So what kinds of things have you tried making?"

"Let's go into the kitchen. I've got a fresh pot of coffee on." Pearl led the way. "So I've been trying a lot of things, everything from soup to nuts, just hoping something would stick."

"Maybe you should concentrate on the things you want to serve your guests. You're going to open as a bed and breakfast. Concentrate on breakfast foods."

Oh, my sweet Petunia! That made sense. "Sounds like a great idea."

Delores smiled for the first time since she came into the house. "I take it you haven't been very successful with breakfast."

Shaking her head, Pearl grabbed a couple of mugs and filled them with coffee. "I haven't even tried breakfast." She set one mug in front of Delores. "Do you want cream and sugar?"

"Both, please. What have you been trying to make?"

"Things I remember my mother making." She shrugged. "Chicken and biscuits. Pot roast."

Delores looked at her long and hard. "That's important to you."

"Well, yeah. Sterling and I remember, and I want to share the memories with him. I know that Ruby and Opal don't remember as much. Opal barely remembers anything at all."

"What do you remember about breakfast from when you were a child? Did your mom have any favorites?"

"The usual I guess. Blueberry muffins, chocolate chip pancakes? Kid stuff." Pearl frowned. "I can't serve kid stuff at an upscale bed and breakfast for grown-ups."

Delores laughed. "Lucky for you I watch a lot of shows on The Food Channel. We can update those kid favorites"—she snapped her fingers—"easy as pie."

"In my experience, pie isn't very easy." In her experience, pie was damn near impossible.

"Lucky you've got a Portagee to teach you," Delores said. "We don't accept defeat. Let's make a shopping list and decide where we're going to go from here. We're going to bake first."

Pearl remembered those times in high school when she'd go to Tony's house. Delores always had something scrumptious in the oven. Her mouth watered a little.

The Cabral house had been a home at its heart, and all the smells and sounds filled your soul with family.

A family that Pearl had longed to be a part of.

She remembered going there after school to do homework, and Delores always had fresh-baked chocolate chip cookies. If she stayed for dinner, it was a raucous affair with everyone talking at once and sharing the details of their days. It was a very far cry from the formal dinners at Camille's.

She had forced herself to forget Tony's family as she tried to achieve Camille's vision of success, even though her grandmother had changed her mind about that. Now she was back in Provincetown trying to turn Camille's house into a home like Delores Cabral had made.

She looked at this woman in her kitchen, the mother she'd imagined having. The mother she'd dreamed of being one day.

She'd thrown those needs away with both hands, ultimately for nothing. She studied Delores' head, bowed over the piece of paper at which she was mumbling out a list. "Thank you."

Delores glanced up. "Do you have enough vanilla?"

"I don't have any vanilla."

Shaking her head, Delores went back to her list while she mumbled, "Vanilla."

Warmth cascaded over Pearl, slow and wonderful, filling up places she hadn't noticed were empty. She had a family she loved, didn't she? Sterling, Ruby, and Opal should be enough, shouldn't they? Of course they were enough. But a small part of her needed more.

She watched Delores scribbling things on a piece of paper at the kitchen table and smiled. Nostalgia and her childhood dream of working in the kitchen with this woman swamped her. Just like that, a little piece of her heart snicked right back into place.

And poof, her world felt right, like a fairy godmother waved a wand and made everything back like it should be.

Chapter Nineteen

Pearl closed one eye as she inspected a measuring cup full of flour.

"Don't close your eye. Measuring ingredients is like aiming a gun. You need all your faculties up and ready to go."

Pearl lifted her closed eyelid. Maybe she needed to get glasses, but damn, she had to get things right. One eye wide open was, for now, the only way to go. "I think I need glasses."

"Then go get them. Don't waste time on the small stuff. Is that batter done yet?"

Pearl had forgotten that Delores always was blunt and got to the point. "I just want to make sure that I've got it right."

Looking over, Delores tapped her spoon on the bowl. "It looks good. Let's get it into the muffin cups."

Pearl set the ruffled papers into the muffin pan. "Can I ask you a question?"

"Sure." Delores leaned against the counter. "What about?"

"What do you think of Tony's idea for opening a fish market?" Pearl promised she'd talk to his mother about this, and she was going to keep that promise.

"Well, it's complicated, that's for sure. Theo and Gabe are against it, and I usually side with Theo when it comes to the business. They want things to go along the way they've always gone. Tony, now, he's after something else, and they're fighting him tooth and nail."

Pearl gritted her teeth. She already knew that. "He's very serious about it."

"I know. I haven't seen him this interested in anything in a very long time." Delores put the spoon she was holding over the sink and rinsed it.

"We've been talking about it a little, and I think it's a great idea. An awesome idea."

"I suppose you would."

What did that mean? "I've got a little business experience, you know. I think I know a good idea when I see one. That's the reason I'm helping him put together a business plan. Once Mr. Cabral and Gabe see the details, I'm sure they'll change their minds."

Chuckling, Delores shook her head. "Not those two stubborn Portagees. One's got a head harder than the other."

"I think Tony needs this."

"What do you know about what Tony needs? You were gone an awful long time." Frost coated every word.

Taking a deep breath, Pearl finished filling the muffin cups with batter and sprinkled sugar on top of them. She'd expected the attitude and didn't blame Tony's mother one bit. "He's opened up to me about this. He's right about so many things. Regulations are making fishing harder. The fish are getting scarcer. And don't get me started about how allowing offshore drilling for oil is going to affect the fishing grounds. The people who are making money are the ones who are buying the catch for peanuts, then turning around and charging a lot more to the tourists and restaurants who want the fish. If you all sold what you caught yourself, both wholesale and retail, you'd make a lot more money and have more control over your business."

"That's what Tony says."

Time to cut to the chase. "I've been crunching numbers and putting something specific together, leaving nothing to chance. A real plan. It would be especially helpful for Tony if you would back him on this."

"And at the risk of repeating myself, what do you know about what Tony needs?"

"We've been talking. He knows I'm talking to you. He asked me to talk to you. He's told me that he'd love your support. Apparently you're the only one who can get Mr. Cabral to do anything."

"Hmmmmm." Delores tapped a finger against her lips. "That's true. I'd have to see this plan before I talk to Theo about anything."

Pearl picked up the muffin pan. "Should these go in now?"

"Yes. Set the timer for twenty-five minutes." Delores sat at the table. "I just don't want Tony to get his hopes up and have them all come tumbling down around his ears. It will kill him if it happens again."

Her stomach felt a little oily around the edges. "Is that a warning for me?"

"Maybe. I don't think he was ever in love with Jenny, no matter what she thought. But I could see him tumbling back into love with you in a heartbeat. So if you're not sure, this business plan better stay all about business."

Message received. Pearl nodded and gestured around the kitchen. "I have all this to fix up. It's got to be business for me, too."

"Make sure that it is. Tony never got over you. I don't want to see my son in that much pain again."

Tears welled in Pearl's eyes, sharp, hot, and bitter. "I never meant to hurt him. At the time, Camille, well, was Camille. She made it clear that I had to live up to her expectations. I was so confused. I thought I could do what she wanted, then come back here." Pearl swallowed around the lump of steel wool in her throat. "To Tony. To be honest, I was afraid of her."

"It certainly didn't work out that way."

"I want to make it up to him now by helping him start up this new business. It's the least I can do."

"And if it blows up in his face? He'll be worse off, and it'll be all your fault."

Cold icy fingers crawled up Pearl's spine. "It won't blow up in his face. He's smart, and he works hard."

"We agree about that. But hard work and smarts aren't going to get the job done. He's going to need some money to get the whole thing started. Where's he going to get that?"

Pearl had given the idea a lot of thought. "If he can't take out a big enough loan to cover the opening costs, he can get investors."

"Who? You?"

"Not necessarily. I know several people who would love to get in on an investment opportunity like this."

"Really."

"Yes. Maybe even Sterling. He and Camille's lawyer control the money. I'm sure Sterling's backing would bring in other investors." Why hadn't she thought about Sterling in the first place? It was a brilliant idea.

"I'm worried that if things get tense between you and Tony?" She shrugged. "He'll be beholden to the Marlowe family."

"I'll make sure things don't get tense."

"I'm sure you'll try. He's a grown man now, not the boy you left behind. He's got pride in spades."

"I know that." Annoyance flared up, and she tamped it down. Of course she knew that Tony had pride. Delores didn't need to remind her. Still it wouldn't be a good thing to snarl at someone who was doing you a favor. "I don't even know if Sterling would be interested."

"Well, don't say anything to Tony before you're sure."

"I'll have to convince him as well." Pearl wiped her hands on a tea towel.

"Look, I want to support Tony in this, but I can only do so much. I have to consider Theo and Gabe to keep peace in the family. None of my men know the first thing about compromising."

The oven timer went off, and Delores sniffed the air. "Check and see if those muffins need more time."

"How will I know?" Grateful for the change in subject, Pearl opened the oven door and peered in.

"You need to test them." She got up and fetched a thin, bamboo shish kebob stick. "With this. Stick it in. If it comes out clean, they're done."

"They smell good." It was a miracle to her that anything coming out of her oven smelled that great.

"Of course they do. It's my recipe."

Pearl tested and shoved the pastries back in the

oven for more time. Turning around, she looked Delores in the eyes. "I hope you can find it in you to support Tony on this project."

"Just business, between you and him, right?"

"Just business." That much was clear enough. It had to stay just business between her and Tony. No more good-night kisses, no matter what.

Chapter Twenty

The more Pearl thought about getting some of her old clients, at least the ones who believed she didn't try to steal from them, to invest in Tony's business, the better she liked the idea. Of course they might not be taking her calls anymore. Frowning, she guessed she'd start with Sterling. He held Camille's purse strings along with Robert. Camille's money should be invested in Tony's fish market.

Of course, Camille would not have liked any such thing.

All the more reason to do it.

Sterling would be showing up any minute now before he headed downtown to check out the renovations going on at Ruby's shop. She'd broach the subject when she saw him.

Dipping the paint roller into the paint tray, she loaded it up with the apricot hue she'd chosen for one of the new bedroom suites and applied it to the wall in front of her. She'd been at it for hours, and her arms were screaming at her. Her lower back creaked and groaned every time she straightened to move the roller up and down the wall.

Still, she wanted to do this part of the job herself, not just to save money but also to make more of this house her own. So she was covering her walls in sherbet and beachy colors, like warm apricot, sea-foam green, sun-kissed yellow, rosy watermelon, and pale aqua. She'd been spending time in local galleries and artist studios, picking out art for the walls, to sell on commission to her guests, getting money into the hands of the artists who made the magic.

At one time she'd toyed with the idea of becoming a painter. She'd create art and care for their children while Tony was out all day catching fish. Camille had squashed that idea right out of her head.

Maybe she'd sign up for lessons at the Art Association. It might be therapeutic.

It might keep her mind off Tony.

She'd replayed the conversation with his mother and replayed that amazing kiss she and Tony had shared a couple of days ago. When she'd first left town, she'd dreamed of Tony's kisses, but back then she'd pushed them as far out of her head as she possibly could.

Now the dreams were back with the added bonus that he'd learned a thing or two about kissing in the years they'd been apart. Not that they were together now. Even though Jenny was out of the picture, Delores had been right. Pearl needed to keep her distance from Tony so she didn't hurt him again.

Her heart still ached over the pain she'd caused him years ago. She wished with all her soul she'd never listened to Camille. But she couldn't change what she'd done. She had to own it and do what she could to make Tony's life better now.

Maybe kissing him wasn't the best way to achieve that goal. And wasn't that a damn shame.

She'd liked kissing Tony. Her lips had buzzed for days. Truth to tell, they still sent off very distracting aftershocks.

"Looks good in here."

Pearl turned at the sound of Sterling's voice. "Hey! I was wondering when you'd get here."

He'd already taken his suit jacket off and was rolling up his shirtsleeves. "I can't stay as long as I'd like. I've got to get back to DC to vote on yet another health-care reform bill."

Pearl shuddered. "Better you than me. You always had more patience and actually enjoyed arguing."

He smiled. "Still do. Enjoy arguing that is." He looked around. "God, I miss the ocean when I'm gone. Even though I should be choking on paint fumes, those open windows let all that fresh air in." He took a deep breath. "Nothing in the world smells better."

"It's low tide and smells like dying clams," Pearl pointed out.

"Doesn't matter. It smells like home and not like paint." He gestured randomly around the room. "Nice color. Better than that old wallpaper. It opens up the space."

"That's the plan." Tonight would be the perfect time to have an investment discussion with her sibs, as all of them were in town. "Can we have an informal dinner tonight? A family meeting?"

Sterling's mouth stiffened. "Sure. What's wrong?"

"Nothing's wrong. I just have a proposition I want to run by the three of you. We can get takeout if that's what you're worried about. Pizza and Greek salad."

"Sounds good. Do Ruby and Opal know what's going on?"

"No, I don't think so." How could they? "I'll call them to set it up."

"Just call Opal." He looked at his watch. "I've got to get downtown to check in with Ruby. Any insights as to how that whole situation is going?"

Pearl shrugged. "She's happy, so I guess it's going well."

"Good. I hope so." He studied a point on the wall above Pearl's head. "Baxter Oglethorpe isn't making things difficult for her?"

"Not that I know of."

"And she's okay with the work Evan's crew is doing?"

"Seems that way." Something was going on with Sterling. "You got a problem with Evan? He did a good job here."

"Not Evan."

What? Very puzzling. "Okay." Something clicked. "Alex ran the crew here. He's probably overseeing the crew at Ruby's. Is it Alex?"

Sterling's jaw tightened. "No, it's not Alex."

"Okay," she repeated. "Well, he did a good job for me here. He'll do a good job for Ruby. He's a good guy, Ster."

"Of course he is." He glanced out the windows. "Looks good in here. I'll be back for dinner. Make it early." He turned around and left.

What the hell was that all about?

****

Sterling fidgeted his fingers on the steering wheel of his BMW as he sped along Commercial Street from Marlowe House to downtown. He shouldn't be in P-town. His ass should be in DC, doing the nation's business.

He had to check in on Ruby. He owed it to her.

He was the worst type of coward. He loved Ruby, and he didn't mind controlling her purse strings. Lord knew what would happen if she had an extended manic episode. Even a small swing could derail her start-up. It was the reason Camille had put him and Robert in charge of Ruby's money.

No, he didn't dread this because he had doubts about Ruby. He felt too much of an attraction to Alex Tudor, the foreman in charge of the renovations to Ruby's shop.

He thought about Alex Tudor way too much, especially after he'd googled Alex and watched some videos of Alex's exotic dance routines.

Sterling swore. There was nothing routine about Alex's dancing. Not one gesture, not one step, not one hip swivel, not one pelvis pump.

He flushed. The pelvis pumps moved him more than he would even admit to himself. If he defined it, then it would be true.

No labels, no truth. A philosophy to believe in.

His stomach churned at the thought of a family meeting. He could see no reason to call one. Opal and Pearl were doing fine. So was Ruby for the time being.

With Ruby you always worried about when the other shoe would drop. Because another shoe always dropped. Sometimes it was like Ruby was a centipede. So many shoes, so little time.

Still, Ruby had stuck it out with Camille while neither he nor his other sisters could manage it. He owed her. They all did. So he'd walk into this project ready to back her up, whatever she wanted. But he surreptitiously checked out what was going on to make sure she was on the right track. Starting with the foreman of her renovation crew, Alex Tudor.

Sterling realized he was grinding his teeth into paste and cracked his jaw. Just the thought of Alex Tudor raised his hackles, whatever hackles were. He would not admit, even to himself, that the thought of Alex Tudor raised more than his hackles.

Ahem. He shifted in his seat and refused to think about it.

He walked from the wharf parking lot and stopped in front of Ruby's shop before he walked in. Through the windows, he noticed a lot was going on inside. He gritted his teeth and opened the door.

The crew was very busy. The newspaper-covered floor was dusty and splattered with eggshell-colored paint. The man of the hour, Alex Tudor, busied himself with putting together glass display cases, and he was looking better than any man had a right to. Dressed in a tight black tee and well-worn jeans that clung to him like a lover would, his sweaty muscles bunched and rippled as he lifted the heavy shelves into place. He looked up as Sterling got his bearings. "Congressman. What can I do you for?"

The word congressman caused heat to rise through his body, and not in a good way. Just the same way the two words "do you" did. Sterling had a couple of suggestions.

Damn.

In Provincetown he could be just Sterling. Just a guy you'd known forever, a guy you'd gone to school with, played basketball with. A congressman was something other than that.

He certainly shouldn't be blushing like a schoolboy because of attention from a totally unsuitable man. "Is

Ruby around?"

Alex leaned against the wall. "Yeah, she's in the back. Hey, Ruby," he yelled over his shoulder, "your brother's here to check up on you!"

"What?" Ruby hollered from the back room.

Alex tried again, even louder. "Your brother's here to check up on you!"

"Of course he is! I'll be right out!"

Alex grinned at Sterling. "She'll be right out."

For the love of— "Yeah, I got that."

Taking a water bottle and uncapping it, he toasted Sterling. "No flies on you, Congressman." He took a giant swig of his water.

Sterling, a lawyer and lawmaker with a tremendous command of the English, French, Russian, and Spanish languages, stood at a loss for words as he watched Alex Tudor's throat work swallowing the cold water.

"Sterling. I didn't expect you yet."

Saved by Ruby. He nearly sighed with relief. "There was less traffic than I expected."

She walked to him, stood on tiptoes, and pressed a kiss to his cheek. "You need a shave. Come on, let's get out of the dust, and I'll show you the new workroom and the new apartment so far."

"Sounds good." He did breathe that sigh of relief as he followed Ruby back to her workroom. The tools of her trade surrounded them. Gold and silver wire covered her workbench, as well as small cases filled with various precious and semi-precious stones encased in tiny plastic bags. Ruby was in it to win it as a jewelry designer. Off the chart creative, she had a good chance to pull it off. Her pieces were one of a kind and very expensive.

It was one of the reasons he insisted on her having the best security system money could buy. Nothing was more precious to him than Ruby. Not even Pearl or Opal. Pearl might be the closest to him, but it was Ruby he protected and worried about the most.

The one he lost sleep over.

She turned and grinned. Wearing a white, men's button-up shirt tucked into baggy khakis, safety goggles holding her curly hair back off her face, she looked more like a mad scientist than a jewelry designer. "What do you think?"

"It looks like a very busy artist works here. Where's the safe?"

She chuffed out a breath. "You never change. Don't you want to see what I'm working on?"

"After I see the safe."

"You and your one-track mind. It's over here." She marched over to the wall opposite the workbench, a sturdy metal door hanging open in the middle of it.

Of course Sterling had to inspect it. "This is the model Oglethorpe talked about?"

"Yes, this is the one you and Baxter talked about. I swear the only thing it needs to be safer is to demand a retina scan to open it."

"Did they have one with that option?" Sterling wanted it for Ruby. Pearl could probably use one, too.

"Sterling, this place is tighter than Fort Knox." She shook her head. "Don't think I haven't noticed the extra police patrols slowing down when they pass the shop." She put her hand on his arm. "Come see my new designs."

"I'd love to." Eager to see them, he let her lead him to the fruits of her labor.

She pulled out a velvet-lined box from under the glass display counter and placed it in front of Sterling. "I showed Pearl some of these designs when they were still just sketches. Here's a ring I designed with her in mind. This is one she hasn't seen."

Sterling reached out to touch it but pulled his hand back, feeling as if it would be sacrilege to touch Pearl's ring. No diamonds, they were too cold for Pearl. No pearls. They were too obvious. No, a concoction of highly polished rubies, emeralds, and sapphires, a veritable rainbow of a ring, the stones caught mid-dance in a setting of thin gold filigree. Sterling thought it the most beautiful thing Ruby had ever created and something totally representative of Pearl.

Pearl wasn't the flashiest woman in the room but made up of determination and strength of will that shone bright. And love, as shiny as the most brilliant star in the sky. "Damn, Ruby. You've caught the heart of her."

"She hides it, but you, me, and Opal know her right down to the ground. She's stronger than she thinks she is."

"I know I've said this before, but you are a genius. What else do you have to show me?"

She pulled a thick, bold ring made of hammered gold out of a velvet bag and rolled it onto the fabric-lined tray. "A wedding ring, I think. For a man."

Yeah, he knew that. How could he not? "It's a beautiful piece. You need to make a second one just like it."

"I already have." She plucked up a fiery garnet and diamond brooch. "This one is spoken for."

"I just bet. Who bought it?"

She wrinkled her nose. "Baxter Oglethorpe, if you must know. He invaded my shop to check up on your precious security system right when I had just finished the brooch. He grabbed it for his mother."

"How much did you charge?" Someone had to make sure Ruby didn't give her jewelry away. And Sterling was always ready for someone to stick it to Baxter Oglethorpe.

She laughed. "An arm and a leg. He blinked a couple of times, swallowed hard, then ponied up a check for the asking price." She danced a little boogie. "I am so a businesswoman!"

He laughed. "Yes you are. You very much are."

Ruby cocked an eyebrow at him. "Does that mean you're going to trust me and leave me alone?"

"Never." He resisted the urge to grab her and give her noogies.

"I'm on my meds, Sterling. I'm seeing a therapist and keeping my appointments with my psychiatrist." Ruby grimaced. "He wouldn't give me my meds if I didn't go to see him once a month. I'm doing everything I'm supposed to do." She placed a hand over her heart. "I want this shop more than I want to take my next breath. I'm not going to screw it up by not taking my damn meds."

He put his hands up in front of him, surrendering, in a way. Not that he'd ever really leave the field where Ruby was concerned. "Okay. I believe you." He ran his hand through his hair. "I have to ask, if for no other reason than I love you, and I want what's best for you."

"Okay. I also have a small fortune in gold and gemstones hidden away here. I get it, Sterling." Ruby gentled her tone. "I get it. I messed up a lot when I was a kid. But really, I thought I had proved everything to you guys."

"Of course, I believe in you. I just want to make sure you're safe."

"I know that. Let me show you how the upstairs is coming along. Do you want anything to drink?"

He followed her to the inside stairs going up to the loft over the shop. It had one big room, a combined living room and kitchen, with a curtained off area for her bed and a tiny bathroom off to the other side.

Typical Ruby, she had every window in the place open, letting cold air in. The french door to the outside porch was closed, but Ruby rectified that by flinging it wide open. "There. Now we can breathe."

Ruby had obsessive-compulsive disorder about opening windows. It went hand in hand with her bipolar disorder. Even if it was the middle of winter with a damn blizzard, she had to have at least one window cracked open. It had driven Camille nuts, making her scream about spending too much money to heat the outside. Yet Ruby persisted, as she really had no power over the OCD.

"So what do you think?"

Sterling took in the bohemian mix of styles and fabrics, none of which should go together but worked in a Ruby kind of way. "I think it's great. Really reflects your personality."

"So you think it's crazy."

"No, not at all. Don't put words in my mouth, especially the 'C' word. It's fun and whimsical and imaginative."

She smiled. "Come see the view off the back porch." Grabbing his hand, she pulled him outside with her.

The scenery was pretty spectacular with its panoramic vista of Provincetown Harbor. Seagulls darted hither and yon, following en masse the fishing boats coming around the breakwater that protected Macmillan Pier from the weather. The weather was mild for April, but he got the sense that the waterfront was waiting to break free once May came around and they could go lobstering and put out the shellfish cages again. "What a great view."

"Now you know why I was so stubborn about wanting to live here."

Sterling smiled. "Yes, I do. I still reserve the right to worry about you."

"Of course you do, and I love you for it." She patted his cheek. "But I'm a big girl now. I'm staying in therapy, and I'm on my meds, so it's all good."

"You're really working hard. I'm proud of you, Rubes."

His sister blushed. "Just doing what I have to do to make this whole adulting thing happen."

Sterling cleared his throat. "Do you have plans for dinner tonight?"

"No, I'm free. Why?" Ruby looked suspicious.

"Pearl has something she wants to run by us in a family meeting."

"She's not cooking, is she?"

"I heard that pizza and Greek salad from Provincetown Celestial Pizza will be on the menu."

"Okay then, I'm in. Do you know what she wants to talk to us about?"

"Not a clue." He eyed the stairs leading down to the street. He did not want to run into Alex Tudor again. "I don't know when she wants us there."

"I'll just pick up a six pack and mosey on over when the crew leaves."

"Sounds good." He grabbed his sister around the waist and pulled her in and kissed her on her forehead. "I love you, Ruby."

"Of course you do. You're my brother. You have to love me." She playfully pushed him away.

"I'll see you later."

"Not if I see you first."

"You're such a brat," he teased.

"It's my greatest gift."

Chapter Twenty-One

"So why do we have to have a family meeting?" Opal wanted to know as she pulled a piece of linguiça and mushroom pizza from one of the boxes on the table.

"I have a business proposition I want you guys to think about," Pearl explained for the third time that night, once to Sterling, once to Ruby, and now to Opal.

Opal piled Greek salad onto a plate. As usual, she hogged all the feta cheese. "This sounds pretty boring. Just get to the point."

Yeah, that's all Pearl had to do. Ask the sibs to financially back Tony without telling them that her feelings for him were coming back. "You all know Tony wants to build a fish market to sell what his family catches."

"Yeah," Ruby said, holding a fork loaded down with a dolma. "Who in town doesn't know that?"

"People don't know the plans he has for the market. It's going to be upscale and offer all kinds of things other than lobster, like gourmet clambakes ready-made for people to buy, like seasonal produce from locally sourced farms, that kind of thing."

"It sounds pretty ambitious," Opal said around a mouthful of pizza.

"Ewwww. Gross," Ruby complained as she threw a napkin at Opal. "Close your mouth!"

"God. Are you two or what?" Sterling shook his head.

Opal pointed at Ruby. "She started it."

Pearl took a deep breath and let it out. "What would you all think about investing in it?"

Silence. Pearl didn't dare look at any of them.

Sterling was the first to speak. "I think we need a few more details here, Pearl. How much money are we talking about?"

"I don't know," she confessed. "We have yet to complete the business plan."

"We? As in you and Tony?" He raised his eyebrows. "This conversation is really premature without a complete plan," Sterling said.

"Okay, maybe, but here's the thing. Would you be willing, in principle, to back Tony, especially if he can't get his father and brother on board?" Pearl crossed her fingers underneath the table.

"Hypothetically, yes," Opal said. "I still think we need more details."

"I know we need more details," Sterling added.

"I'm down for it," Ruby said. "Tony's a good guy, and this is his dream. It's not like he's some stranger coming in to steal profits from the locals. If we can help him out, we should."

Opal narrowed her eyes at Pearl. "Does this have anything to do with Tony kissing you the other night?"

"Wait, wait, wait." Sterling sat up in his chair. "Tony kissed you?"

"We kissed each other." Pearl waved a hand dismissing him. "It was a team effort."

"Goooo, team Pony!" Ruby cheered.

"Team Pony?" Opal looked amused and dubious at

the same time.

"Yeah, it's their 'ship name. 'P' for Pearl, 'ony' for Tony. Pony."

Pearl pinched the space between her eyes. This was not going the way she'd planned. She should have known better.

"I'm not sure about this, not one bit," Sterling complained. "You've got enough to do opening the B and B without complicating things with Tony."

"I'm not complicating things with Tony," Pearl griped. "I just think, in my professional capacity as an investment guru, that we could see a return by investing in Tony's project. The potential for expansion is exponential."

"How exponential?" God, Sterling was like a dog with a bone.

"I don't know, not yet. But I know we can have a plan nailed down soon. It's not like I'm asking you for money tonight. I'm only asking you to think about it. Tony is not a risk. He's going to work hard to make this dream come true." Since Pearl hadn't been able to make one dream of his come true, the least she could do was help him make this plan a reality.

"Come on, Ster." Ruby stabbed some feta-covered lettuce. "It's Tony. You could at least think about it."

"I'll think about it when I have more facts." He picked up a slice of pepperoni and onion pizza. "Until then, I'm withholding judgment. And I need to hear more about the team-Pony kiss."

"Oh, for the love of God." Pearl slapped her hand down on the table. "It was just a kiss between two consenting adults."

"Both of whom should know better." He took a

bite out of his slice.

"Sterling, you're not Camille. You don't get a vote in deciding who I kiss and who I don't."

"You're my sister, and I love you, and I don't want you making any more mistakes."

"Any more mistakes?" Okay, she should concede that point, but she wouldn't, just on principle.

"Ster, you need to back off," Ruby warned. "If Pearl and Tony lock lips, it's their business."

"I agree," added Opal.

"I disagree," Sterling said. He turned to Pearl. "I can't watch you go through such terrible pain all over again."

The sad look in Sterling's eyes just about broke Pearl's heart and her resolve. "If I promise to not kiss Tony again, will you at least keep an open mind about investing in the fish market?"

He swallowed his mouthful of pepperoni, cheese, and onions. "Yes."

"She's not going to be able to keep that promise. You know that, Sterling. You're asking for something she just can't give." Ruby reached for her beer.

"Honestly, Sterling. When did you get to be such a prude?" Opal shook her head.

"I'm not a prude." Sterling bristled.

"You are if you're getting this exercised about a simple kiss," Opal said.

"There was nothing simple about Pearl and Tony kissing, and you three know it." Sterling's jaw locked into stubborn position.

"Let it go, please," Pearl begged her siblings. She just couldn't deal with the conversation anymore. She looked at Ruby and Opal. "I appreciate your support of

Tony." She turned to Sterling. "I understand where you're coming from. I get the message. Nothing will pass between me and Tony that will get in the way of business."

"I hope you mean that." Sterling was relentless. Pearl had to give him that. It was one of the traits that made him a good congressman and an even better brother.

"I do." She stood. "Anyone up for coffee and blueberry muffins?"

"Who made the muffins?" Opal wanted to know.

"Delores Cabral gave me a baking lesson. They're her recipe, made under her supervision."

"Delores Cabral's blueberry muffins?" Ruby licked her lips. "I'll take one right now and a couple more to bring home with me for tomorrow's breakfast."

Opal rolled her eyes. "You are such a muffin whore."

"You say that like it's a bad thing."

Pearl caught Sterling's gaze. "What?"

"Tony's mother is giving you baking lessons."

"It's not a big deal."

"From where I sit, it's a very big deal," Ruby said. "Baked goods that won't kill your customers. Totally made of awesomeness."

"Is this the reason you're asking us to back Tony? His mother gives you cooking lessons while we invest in his project?" Sterling crossed his arms over his chest.

"No," Pearl said. "Tony has no idea I'm approaching you for financial backing." No, Tony thought she was asking strangers who didn't know him from Adam.

"That's good, then." Sterling nodded. "Where are

183

these legendary blueberry muffins? And did I hear something about coffee? I've got to get back to DC, and I'm catching the red eye out of Logan."

Pearl stood. "Coming right up."

****

"So I heard you had dinner with Pearl Marlowe."

Tony watched Gabe casually inspect the wood on the lobster pots they were fixing. "Yeah. I did. She's helping me put together a business plan."

Gabe groaned. "Don't tell me it's about that fish market thing."

"It was about the fish market thing."

"I told you not to tell me."

"I don't understand why you're so against this."

"It just doesn't make sense. We do well enough as it is."

"We could do better."

Gabe stood and stretched his back. "I hear you broke up with Jenny."

"Where'd you hear that?" Tony sure as hell hadn't told him yet.

"I, uh, ran into her at Fred's Pizza the other night. She was pretty upset."

"What did she say?" He really didn't want to know but couldn't stop himself from asking the question.

"She cried a lot and had some choice words about Pearl being the reason you broke up with her."

Tony rubbed a finger across his chin. "I suppose she would say that. It's easier to blame Pearl than to just admit that we weren't going anywhere."

"That's not the way Jenny sees it."

"I can't help what she thinks."

Gabe shook his head. "That's pretty cold. And to

remind you, Bro, you are doing some kind of dance with Pearl."

"It's just business."

Gabe snorted. "Right."

Tony put his hands up. He might as well move the conversation to the real subject he wanted to talk to his brother about. "Pearl thinks she might get some of her former clients to invest in our fish market. I'm psyched about it."

Gabe shook his head. "Of course you are. Why would some fancy millionaires want to invest in a rinky-dink fish market that doesn't exist yet?"

"I don't know, but Pearl seems to think it could work. And it's not a rinky-dink fish market. I have to say that it's really good to have someone who's in my corner and supports my idea."

"Yeah, yeah, yeah, cry me a river. Dad and I are just practical. This whole fish market thing is crazy."

"It's not, and I won't let you bring me down. Whatever you think of Pearl personally, she knows all about business and how to get this to work."

"Okay." Gabe finally looked Tony in the eyes. "Are you sure you can trust her?"

Was he? He guessed he did. "In this, yes, I know. I feel it in my bones."

"Are you sure you don't just want to jump Pearl's bones?"

Tony's fingers itched to punch his brother in the face. "If I do or I don't, that's none of your damn business."

"You do." Gabe smirked like it was his job.

Tony wanted to punch him and wipe that stupid smile off his stupid face. "Like I said, it's none of your damn business."

"Just like the fish market. If we want to sell our lobsters ourselves, we'll sell them off the boat."

"You'll miss all the tourist trade. No visitor is going to know about going down to the wharf to the boats. Where would they find parking? And you won't have the capability to cook the lobsters for them. We'd be able to do that in our market, as well as selling things like a clambake to go."

"A clambake to go? You've lost it, Bro."

"Can't you at least admit that cooking the lobsters for the tourists is a good idea? And that we can't offer that option on the boat?"

"Okay, yeah, we can't do that on the boat. But what are you gonna sell when the tourists are gone or, for that matter, when we can't fish? Are you going to close for those three months?"

"I suppose I'll close up from February to May." He hadn't really thought that far. He'd ask Pearl what to do.

"Who's going to take your place on the boat?"

"No one. We'll hire someone to man the market."

"We, huh? If you get this crazy idea up and running, it's all your baby."

Tony's phone buzzed in his pocket. He pulled it out and saw it was Pearl calling. "I have to take this," he told Gabe. As he walked away, he put the phone to his ear. "Pearl. What's up?"

"I'm wondering when you can break free so we can go scout out locations for the market. I did some investigating and found several promising locations."

"You did?" At least one person believed in him.

"Yeah. I went through the real estate listings for

buildings that already exist and for land that you could build on. How does Wednesday sound?"

"Wednesday sounds good. What time do you want me to pick you up?"

"How about ten? We can look at the properties and then talk about them over lunch."

"Sounds like a plan. I'll see you then."

"See you then."

Tony clicked off the phone and looked up to see Gabe staring at him. "What?"

"That was Pearl?"

"Yep. We're going to look at possible locations for the fish market. Want to come?" Please say no.

"No, thanks. These lobster pots aren't going to fix themselves while you go gallivanting around with Pearl Marlowe."

"We're not gallivanting. This is business."

"Sure it is. Since when does 'business' put such a goofy look on your face?"

"Shut up." The buzz Tony had gotten during Pearl's call disappeared without a trace. "At least she believes in me."

"Does she? You were wrong about her before."

"This is different."

"If you say so." Gabe chuffed out a laugh.

Tony'd had enough. "You know, there are all kinds of power tools lying around here. I could easily use one of them to kill you, then bury your body where no one would ever find it."

"Oh, I'm so scared."

"Just wait. I'll get you when you least expect it."

"I'm shaking in my boots."

"You should be. Asshole." Tony went back to

Doreen Alsen

fixing the lobster pot. He'd figure out how to get Gabe on his side. In the meantime, he had Pearl.

****

Pearl couldn't wait for Wednesday. She thought she was pretty darn clever researching locations.

All in the name of business of course.

She hoped he'd made some headway with the info for the strategic plan. She needed to show it to Sterling so he'd consider investing in Tony's project. Sterling was a reasonable guy. Once he saw the numbers, he'd see what a good investment opportunity this was.

God, if she could make this work for Tony, it would go a long way in alleviating her conscience.

Now, if only she could decide what to wear. Business casual was probably the way to go. She didn't want to make it feel like a date by getting really dressed up.

A blazer and tailored slacks would send the right message and help keep her promise to Delores. She and Tony had business between them but not monkey business.

She touched her lips and remembered that kiss the other night. It couldn't happen again, more's the pity. And daydreaming about the possibility of a relationship with Tony was counterproductive.

She could keep things on the up and up and still enjoy spending time with Tony. When all was said and done, that was the only real plan of action.

She needed to thank him for asking his mother to help her out on the cooking front. Delores was going to show her how to make bread that was edible.

She'd always wanted to bake her own bread. It smelled so nice and homey. Delores' house always smelled like the home she'd always dreamed of having.

Camille wouldn't have known a lump of dough even if it had been thrown in her face.

Well, no use in crying about the past. She guessed that meant Tony, too.

Chapter Twenty-Two

Pearl checked her makeup one last time. Tony would be there any minute. Anticipation skittered up her spine. Get a grip, she told herself. They were only going to look at properties, not exactly a most romantic thing to do together.

No, even though they were going to lunch, romance was not on the menu.

She heard his truck pull into her driveway. Grabbing her purse, she hurried to the door and pulled it open. Tony was right there.

"Hey," he said as he gifted her with one of his brilliant smiles. "You ready to go?"

"Yep. Let's go."

"Don't you want to get a jacket? It's going to rain later."

Pearl looked up at the clear blue sky. "Rain? Really?"

"Really."

She went to the hall closet. "How can you tell?"

"I make my living reading the weather. I can smell rain in the air. Let's go." He touched her elbow and led her out of the house to his truck.

She shivered at his touch, that innocent connection of his hand to her elbow. Business, just business, she reminded herself as her heart stuttered loud in her chest and her fingers itched to touch him, to skim along his warm skin. She shivered.

"Are you cold?" Tony held open the passenger side door for her.

"No." Who could be cold standing close to Tony?

He helped her into his truck. "Buckle up."

She saluted him. "Yes, sir."

Laughing, Tony shut the door.

****

A couple of hours later, they sat in the Speedwell Café looking at menus and sipping coffee.

It felt a lot like a date for Tony. Given the looks they were getting from the other patrons, they'd have a hard time convincing people it wasn't a date.

Would that be so bad? Taking Pearl to a restaurant on a date?

He'd have to think about it.

"I think I'll get the chowder and a side salad," Pearl said as she folded up her menu.

"What is it with women and salad? It's like you're afraid to eat real food."

She grinned. "A salad is real food."

"No, a cheeseburger is real food." He folded up his menu.

"That's what you're having? A cheeseburger?"

"And fries."

"Of course. So what are your favorites out of all the properties we saw today?"

He scratched the side of his nose. "I didn't like the big houses. It's not going to be a large-scale operation. We just need enough room to build a couple of tanks to hold the lobsters and a couple of steam cookers and room for a counter."

"Hmmm. I'm not so sure. I think you're going to

want the space." She took a pen and a small notebook out of her bag. "So with regard to smaller options, which ones flicked your bic?"

"Flicked my bic?" What bic would that be, gorgeous?

"In terms of image. Streamlined and modern or quaint and charming?"

He scowled at the question. What did he know about image? "What do you think would be the best one to pick?"

"I'd go for quaint and charming myself. It will mesh well with your family-business branding."

"Branding?" He could feel a headache coming on.

"Well, yes. How we present your product to the consumers. I think a lot of tourists come to the Cape looking for old-school New England charm. Those will be the people who will feel much more comfortable spending their money at places like yours."

Jesus. All he wanted was to sell the lobsters his family caught and the occasional clambake, although Gabe had made him reconsider the whole clambake thing. "I don't know. That all sounds really complicated."

The waitress came and took their order, giving them speculative looks.

"We're giving the gossips a real gift by eating here in town. Maybe we should have gone up Cape."

Tony shook his head. "We should have gone off Cape. Plymouth would be far enough away. Maybe."

Pearl bit her lower lip. "If you're hanging with me, you better get used to people looking at us funny. Everyone wants a good look at the local girl turned criminal."

He reached across the table and touched her hand. Her hand felt so small and delicate. It trembled beneath his, making him feel like Superman and Batman all rolled up into one amazing superhero. He was Captain Lobster after all. "You were cleared of all crimes. That's all people need to know."

Her face fell. "It can't be helped. People will always believe what they want to believe."

He remembered a conversation with Jenny who had totally believed Pearl was guilty. But that was Jenny being Jenny. He shook his head. "It won't always be that way."

She gifted him with a tremulous smile. "Most of the time I can fool myself into thinking that nothing had ever happened, that Marlowe House is just a career change and not something Camille foisted on me. Let's talk about branding the fish market. Do you have a name in mind yet?"

He ignored the thought that Pearl was only sitting across from him because her grandmother was punishing her and pulled back his hand. "My first thought was Cabral Family Seafood, but most of my family doesn't want any part of it. If they don't come around, it won't be Cabral Family Seafood at all."

"Don't worry about that. I think it's a great name. And your family will come around once you begin to show a profit. I had your mother more than halfway convinced when she helped me the other day. I learned how to make her blueberry and cranberry muffins, and they were good." Pearl positively beamed. "They didn't come out hard as rocks."

"Of course they weren't. My mother has never baked a rock in her life. She told me you had a good talk."

"She was very kind to me." Pearl tapped a finger on top of the table.

"My mother is a fair person."

"Yes, she is. She was always wonderful to me." Pearl put her hands in her lap.

The waitress came by, dropped off Pearl's salad, and topped up their coffees.

Pearl smiled, and his heart turned over in his chest. Time to change the subject. "Maybe we should get back to the business at hand."

She stabbed her fork into a ranch-covered tomato wedge and studied it. "As you know, I think that once you get the business established, you should branch out into selling fresh local produce."

"I want it to be a fish market, not a farmer's market." He had no idea where she came up with these ideas.

"The two aren't mutually exclusive. But if people can buy salad fixings to have with the lobsters you're steaming for them, getting the veggies in the same place they get their lobsters, it is much more convenient for them. Let's face it. The Stop and Shop is a zoo in the summer."

As Tony made it a point to avoid the grocery store in the summer for that very reason, he had to agree. "I'll think about it. That's so far in the future. I'm still trying to figure out how I'm going to come up with capital without putting the boat up for collateral."

"I wanted to talk to you about that. I've broached the subject with my brother and sisters, and I think I can get them to invest in this project."

"What?"

She smiled. "I asked my brother and sisters to think about investing in the fish market project."

What Pearl considered a project, an investment opportunity, was Tony's life's dream. Gabe's words from the other day played across his mind. Unknown investors were one thing. Being beholden to Pearl's family was quite another. He tapped his finger on the red Formica tabletop. "I don't know how I feel about that."

"Oh." She frowned. "I thought you'd be pleased. Well, of course you can always refuse."

He could, and he would, but his mother had tried to teach him manners, so he wouldn't jump down her throat. "I'm glad they're interested, but I want to see how much money I need first."

"Okay. We should probably wait until we have all the financial needs worked out. So I think the fifth property we looked at, the one in North Truro, would work best in my opinion. Did you like it?"

"Yeah. It had room for limited parking around it and could have the store I want."

The waitress showed up with his cheeseburger and her chowder. He welcomed the distraction.

"Thank you." Pearl smiled at the waitress. "So let's talk to the real estate agent and put in a bid for it," she said to him.

He picked up his burger and held it like it was a shield protecting him from her allure. "I don't think I have enough money put by to make a down payment." Not yet he didn't, but he would by the end of the summer. He hoped.

"You would if you let my family invest in the market. You could use that money to get a mortgage from the bank."

"I'll think about it." No, he wouldn't. His pride wouldn't let him do it. Besides, what if Gabe was right, and he shouldn't trust Pearl and her family?

"Don't think too long. Somebody else may snatch that property up."

Damn, she moved fast. Even if he bought the building now, there was no way he'd have the market up and running by this summer, not with May coming around the corner and him getting back on the water.

He suddenly felt very small. Not worthy of Pearl. Again.

"What's wrong?" Pearl stared at him from across the booth.

"Nothing. Nothing at all."

"Obviously, something is. It's your turn to confess." Her eyes held the light of kindness and understanding. He wasn't going to fall for it.

"Never mind. I don't want your family to help me out. I don't need your pity."

"No one in my family pities you. In fact, every one of them admires you."

"Your grandmother hated me. I was the servant who brought her the lobsters."

"You are nobody's servant. Me and my sisters and Sterling are nothing like her. This is a genuine offer, and it shows our faith in you."

Faith in him? He was taken back to the moment he learned the cold hard truth that Pearl had left him. All a game. Nothing faithful about it.

Suddenly his cheeseburger didn't taste so good. "I just remembered I have an appointment. I have to cut this short. Are you ready to go?" He pulled his wallet out of his pocket, liberated a couple of bills, and threw them on the table.

She looked at her half-eaten bowl of chowder, then back to him. She blinked her eyes a couple of times. "I guess so." After pulling her napkin off her lap, she tossed it onto the table.

He scooted across the bench of the booth and stood. "Let's go."

He saw how disappointed she was but didn't let himself care. He reminded himself to remember the lessons of the past. The kiss the other night had fooled him into thinking everything was okay.

Gabe was right. Nothing was okay.

****

Confused, Pearl looked out the passenger side window as Tony barreled down Bradford Street in an obvious hurry to get rid of her.

What had she said to upset Tony? While she longed to ask him, she knew better.

She'd come on too strong. She knew it. She'd just been so excited about his project. "I'm sorry if I pushed you too hard."

He kept his eyes relentlessly ahead. "Don't mention it."

"But I want to—"

"I said don't mention it."

"Okay." She got the point.

Silence rose up between them, thick and full, tangible as a brick wall. She couldn't talk, even if she wanted to. And as of right now? She did not want to talk to the man next to her in the truck.

They pulled into her driveway. "I'm going to be pretty busy the next couple of weeks getting the boat

Doreen Alsen

ready to go out. I'll take care of answering the other questions on that business plan when I can." Tony finally looked at her. "Thanks for showing me these places today. I really appreciate it." He leaned over and gave her a hard peck on the cheek. "I'll call you."

What the hell?

"Don't mention it." She reached for the door handle and jerked it open. "Thank you for lunch."

He cleared his throat. "No problem."

She dropped out of the truck. "Thanks anyway. See you around." Slamming the door, she turned on her heel and marched to her front door.

Pearl fought the urge to watch Tony back out of the driveway. She wouldn't give him the satisfaction. She was stupid, stupid, stupid to think that she and Tony could be together again. It was a total nonstarter, just like everyone had told her.

Chapter Twenty-Three

"So how'd it go? Are we going into the fish business?" Ruby took an apple out of the bowl on the kitchen table and polished it on her shirt.

Pearl glowered at her sister. "I think it's safe to say that we're not going into the fish business. As usual, I made a total mess of everything."

"Tony doesn't want our help?" Ruby took a bite out of her Granny Smith.

"Tony doesn't want our help."

"Really." Ruby said around a mouthful of fruit. "I'm not surprised."

"No?" Surprised, Pearl sat down and glared at Ruby. "Why didn't you say so when we had the family meeting?"

She shrugged and swallowed. "It didn't seem to be the right time."

"So you set me up to make a fool of myself?"

"No." Ruby shook her head. "You were so excited. I didn't want to rain on your parade. However"—she shrugged—"he had a rough time when you left, so it's not a stretch to believe he doesn't want our money, no matter what it's for."

"Why? You could have warned me," Pearl grumbled.

"It didn't even occur to me to warn you." Ruby toasted her with her apple. "I mean, you and Tony were already kissing buddies again, which I thought was a good sign."

"Apparently not. What do I do next, Ruby? I don't want there to be bad blood between me and Tony." Her temples throbbed to the raucous beat of an out-of-sync drum circle.

"I don't know. Maybe it's for the best if you don't resurrect your centuries-ago romance."

"What do you mean?"

"That it's overwhelming how the chemistry feels right now. Maybe it'll blow over."

Pearl's internal chem lab sure didn't feel like it was going to blow over. Ever.

She might as well admit it. She wasn't over Tony. She wanted a relationship with him. Perhaps they could find a common ground beyond the fish market.

The phone rang, and her heart jumped up into her throat. Maybe it was Tony.

"Oh, let me get it! I want to use the new official greeting."

Since Pearl didn't think she could say anything coherent, she told her sister, "Go for it."

Ruby danced over to answer the phone. "Marlowe House. Ruby speaking." She cocked her head to one side as she listened. "Let me hand you over to the boss, my sister Pearl." She held the phone out for Pearl to take.

Pearl released the breath she'd been holding. Not Tony on the line. She took the phone from Ruby. "Hello, this is Pearl Marlowe. How may I help you?"

****

"Ow!" Tony stabbed his thumb with the needle nose pliers he was using to work on the boat's cables.

"Hey, Son. Take it easy with the pliers."

Tony nearly groaned when he heard his father's gravel-scarred voice. He did not need to talk to his father right now.

By now Gabe would have told their father that Tony was taking up with Pearl again, so Theo was here to tell him how stupid he was. "Dad." He tossed the pliers onto the workbench and prepared to be lectured.

His father, Theo, stood in the doorway, looking just like he always did; skin lined and tough as leather, a beard that would make Santa envious, all topped by a Red Sox cap pulled low so as to shield his eyes.

Solid. Predictable. A port in any storm.

Except when it came to Pearl. He saw Pearl's leaving town without a word to be an even bigger betrayal than Judas selling out Jesus.

"I heard you and Pearl are going around looking at places to build a damn fish market."

Tony picked up a rag and wiped at the grease on his hands. "Gabe's been telling tales out of school."

"Someone has to be sensible in this family, and it sure as hell ain't you."

Wasn't that the truth? Tony wondered about his sanity every damn day. "Do you want something, Dad?"

"Do I need an excuse to visit my own workshop?" He grabbed a metal stool and slumped on it.

"Of course not." Maybe his father wasn't here to put him down. Maybe he didn't want to tell him what a fool he'd been over Pearl.

"So about this thing with Pearl," his father said, "I don't want her help or her family's help with you and this damn idea you got."

"Not to worry. I'm reconsidering her offer." He ignored the anger bristling inside him.

"Good," his father said, nodding. "I'm glad to hear you say that. Put Pearl Marlowe in the past, right where she belongs."

If only Tony could. "Yep."

"You can't trust that girl as far as you can throw her."

"I know that, Dad."

"Good. Got any beer left in the fridge?"

Tony looked at his watch and decided it was Miller time. He might need one himself. "Yep." He and Gabe always kept the fridge loaded with Miller Lite for their dad. Both he and Gabe went for Sam Adams. He pulled out a can of beer and held it out. "Here you go." After they both had beers, Tony decided it was time to cut to the chase. "What do you want, Dad?"

"What? I can't check up on what's going on around here?"

Tony rolled his eyes. "You know what's going on here. You don't miss a trick."

"Did you sell us out to the Marlowes or not?"

"Not," Tony said, with as much don't-ask-me in his voice as he could muster. "I told you that I was reconsidering Pearl's offer."

"Good," Dad said. "Pearl really seemed sweet, right up to the moment she left you." He flushed. "Your mother disagrees with me, so let's keep this little talk just between you and me." He planted both hands on his thighs and pushed himself up from the chair. "You might have some ideas I don't agree with, but you know who your family is." Lowering his eyes to half-mast, which didn't in the least make his gaze less dangerous, he said, "Don't disappoint me, boy."

"I'll do my best."

"You're going to drop this whole fish market thing and stay away from anyone named Marlowe?"

"I'll stay away from Pearl." He would not give up on the fish market. His father didn't have to know that. But he agreed about staying away from any backing Pearl and her family might offer. The whole casualness about the offer of money made him feel like he was some kind of peasant getting a boon from the royal family.

He still had the templates and the guidelines for the business plan Pearl had given him. He'd muddle through it himself, without her. "I'll stay away from Pearl," he repeated.

Chapter Twenty-Four

Pearl pulled her car next to the curb in front of Josie's house. She tried to get out of going to the class reunion meeting tonight, but Laura wouldn't let her wiggle out of it.

She didn't want to be in the same room with Tony and Jenny, but she figured she'd pull up her big-girl panties and deal. Laura was going to owe her for this.

Even though Tony had said he'd call her, he obviously hadn't meant it. It was probably for the best. She needed to focus on her own problems. The first of which was to get through this meeting. Better get on with it. She knocked on Josie's front door.

"Thank God you're here!" Josie pulled Pearl into the room. "I think I might commit murder."

"Who are you going to kill? I can give you a suggestion," Pearl said.

"Jenny." Josie's face was grim.

"Do it, and I'll help you hide the body."

"I'm sorry she and Tony broke up and all, but she's being extreme, even by Jenny standards."

"What's she doing?" Pearl slipped off her coat and handed it to Josie.

"Just disagreeing and arguing about every idea anybody else has. We're not getting anything done. It's so frustrating."

"I don't think me being here is going to help with

that. Unless it's to take her attention off you guys and focus it all on me." She craned her neck to see past Josie. "Is Tony here yet?"

"Tony called. He can't come tonight."

"Oh." Why did she feel so disappointed? "That's too bad."

"I think we can't count on Tony anymore because of, you know—" Josie lowered her voice to a harsh whisper. "—Jenny."

Possible. But Pearl suspected Tony was avoiding her as well. Regret poked at her, but she ignored it. It was for the best, she supposed. "I guess."

"Come on. I'll get you a glass of wine." She led Pearl into the living room.

Pearl sucked in a hard breath to gather her courage. "I'll probably need it."

Josie chuckled. "You and me both."

Josie's sense of style looked like a squirrel with ADHD had designed her living room. Flea market chic, Pearl thought. Whimsical. Totally random. Totally Josie.

She once wished she'd been as comfortable in her own skin as Josie was. In spite of the economic differences, Pearl knew that all of her friends were happier than she was. How sad. Pushing away the very unattractive self-pity, she grinned at Josie. "Let's get this over with."

They walked into the living room, and conversation stopped. Great. Just great. "Hello."

"Hey!" Laura patted a nearby space on the couch. "Sit here."

"Where's Tony?" Jenny spoke a little too loud in a really snotty voice. "I'd've thought he'd come with

Doreen Alsen

you."

"I don't know where Tony is. I haven't seen him in days."

"Sh'yeah. Right." Jenny examined her manicure, resentment oozing out of her.

Josie showed up with Pearl's wine. "Thank you."

"So let's get down to business." Josie pulled over a monster-sized floor cushion. It looked like My Little Pony had thrown up glitter all over it. She pulled out a legal pad and tapped her pen against it.

While the group chattered on about menus, deejays, and whether they should have party favors—right now the consensus was no to the party favors—Jenny kept shooting Pearl hostile looks.

So. Much. Fun. She counted the minutes until she could politely leave.

"What do you think, Pearl?"

She blinked only to find the rest of the women in the meeting staring at her. "What?"

"Which of these two menus do you like better?" Josie said, her voice filled with patience.

"What restaurants?"

"Bradford Street Seafood, Olivia's, or The Scepter and Throne?" Jenny huffed, like she was personally offended. Most likely she was winding up to being exponentially offended.

Oh. "May I see them again?"

"For the love of God," Jenny snapped.

Pearl took the three menus Josie held out. "Parking's better at Bradford Street Seafood."

"That's what I said," Laura chimed in. "Both menus are equally good. I think we have to take parking into consideration."

"Bradford Street it is, then," Josie said.

"Fine," Jenny said, in her best pissed-off voice. "Are we done here?"

"Sure, I guess." Josie opened the question to the whole group.

"Do you have anything else you need me for?"

A chorus of "no" responded.

"Okay," Josie rubbed the back of her hand over her forehead. "Let's set a date for the next meeting."

That task accomplished, Jenny slung her huge purse over her right shoulder and stomped out of the room.

"Well, that was fun," Josie concluded. "Who's up for another glass of wine?"

Pearl didn't refuse.

****

As Pearl walked to her car, she saw Jenny waiting for her. Wasn't that just fine and dandy? "What do you want, Jenny?"

"You and me need to talk."

Pearl sighed. "I don't think we have anything to talk about."

"I think we do."

Pearl decided that arguing her was futile. "Jenny. Just say what you have to say and be done with it."

"Why did you have to come back? Why couldn't you just stay gone?" She sniffed like she was keeping back tears.

"My grandmother died." Pearl sputtered. Jenny was freaking insane.

"Then why do you have to stay? Why did you have to break me and Tony up?" Jenny whined.

"I did not break you and Tony up." Truth. "I had

nothing to do with it."

"You had everything to do with it!" Jenny turned red in the face. "You always ruin everything for me!"

Oh, for crying out loud. "The world does not revolve around you. I don't sit up at night thinking of ways to ruin your life."

"Why don't you just go away? Back to the city. Aren't you bored here yet?"

"I'm not leaving. I made promises to my family, and I won't let them down."

Jenny knuckled a tear out of her eye. "You're such a liar. You're here because you want Tony back. You just want to ruin my life."

"Like I said, it's not all about you." Pearl'd had enough. "I'm going home." She pulled out her key fob and beeped her car door open. "You should, too."

"You're just mean and stuck up." Jenny curled her lips into a nasty imitation of a smile. "Don't get out the bridal magazines just yet. You never know what's going to happen."

"God! Are we still in middle school?" Pearl slid into her car. "I'm not a threat to you. I never was. Just leave me the hell alone!" She closed the door, stuck the key into the ignition, and shoved it into first gear. Pulling away from the curb, she shook her head about Jenny. She'd do best to just stop going to reunion meetings. The rest of the committee would understand. She crossed her fingers.

Other than that, she'd steer clear of both Jenny and Tony.

But she didn't want to steer clear of Tony. She wanted to make him laugh, to talk about his hopes and dreams. She wanted him to hold her close in his arms and kiss her senseless. While she was being honest with herself, she wanted him to love her again. Because after all these years, she still loved him. Damn him.

Damn her.

She pulled over to the side of the road, laid her throbbing head on the steering wheel, and grieved.

Chapter Twenty-Five

Sterling managed to get into the house and slip out again without any of his too-nosy-for-their-own-good sisters seeing him. He was headed out to the Scepter and Throne for a few drinks in a place where no one would recognize him, and the ones who did wouldn't care.

So he'd actually colored his light red hair a deep shade of brown and stuffed it all up in a cap. He toyed with the idea of a fake mustache but thought it might be a bit much. But a pair of glasses with dark heavy frames, frayed jeans, and a black leather bomber jacket.

He must be crazy, but work just hadn't let up, and he needed to cut loose, or he'd lose his mind. He didn't dare go anywhere in Boston or Fall River. Here, among his own, in his home, no one would blink twice. It had the bonus of being the off-season, and he wouldn't have to dodge tourists.

Clear skies, bright stars, and moon hanging low, it was a good night for a walk. He pushed his way through the front of the restaurant, then hesitated as he stood at the door of the Scepter and Throne's back bar.

The inside dark and private, even with the people crowding the bar and the dance floor, the air heavy and yeasty, the light dim, it seemed to be the place where all the cool kids were. He spotted a free stool at the bar and made a beeline for it.

All he wanted was a couple of drinks without being Sterling Marlowe. Was that too much to ask?

He ordered a dirty martini with three olives. As the bartender set it down on the cocktail napkin in front of him, a cool, solid presence brought the fresh smells of the evening in with him. Sterling slid a glance over to the newcomer, and his stomach plunged to his knees.

Alex Tudor was his brand-new barstool neighbor. Every nerve ending in his body stood up at attention. He both hoped that Alex would and wouldn't recognize him.

"Well, look who's here. That you, Congressman?"

Sterling sighed. "Keep your voice down. What gave me away?"

Alex rubbed a hand across his chin. "I don't know. I just knew. That's a real bad dye job, by the way."

"I'm a lawyer, not a cosmetician."

"The usual, Alex?" The bartender wiped the counter in front of them.

"Yeah, thanks." Alex turned his attention back to Sterling. "So I've got to be curious. What are you doing down here with us peasants?"

"Give me a break. I'm just trying to have a quiet drink."

Alex looked around. "If it's any consolation, I think I'm the only one who recognizes you."

Sterling didn't dare look around. His skin crackled and prickled. Alex Tudor sat too close to him, even though there was room enough between the two barstools. "Let's keep it that way." He hunched his shoulders over his martini.

"No one will hear it from me. So, Counselor, what's the story?"

"There's no story. I had some precious free time, and I wanted it just for myself."

Alex sipped his beer. "I guess there're a lot of moving parts in your job."

Wasn't that the truth? "Yes."

"Anything you want to talk about?"

Sterling finally turned to look at Alex. Could he confide? Even a little bit? Wouldn't that be glorious? Things he couldn't even confide in his sisters because they were a huge part of what kept him awake at night.

Damn Camille and her will.

But sitting there right next to him was a friendly face, one so handsome it should be illegal. Tudor was always turning up in his path. Maybe there was a reason for that.

No. His stuff was private, and it had to stay that way. One wrong word to the wrong person and he could wave good-bye to the Senate and fail his grandmother. "No. Everything's going exactly the way it should."

"Bullshit. You're sitting here in a bar with your hair dyed brown, wearing Buddy Holly glasses and an outfit that would make Tim Gunn drop dead of a heart attack. I'm a good listener." Alex gave him a beautiful, sweet smile, one so at odds with the Alex Tudor he thought he knew.

Sterling just bet he was a good listener. Could Alex keep a secret? Discretion topped the list of qualities he looked for in a friend, or in this case, an acquaintance.

Especially an acquaintance who attracted him like crazy. "Just needed a couple of hours to myself."

"Is that a hint for me to go take a lap?"

No! "You don't have to leave on my account. I can

ask you some questions."

Alex turned sideways and rested his elbow on the bar. "Ask away. My life is an open book."

Sterling realized there were so many things he wanted to know. "How'd you end up in Provincetown?"

"My family wanted me to go to college. Whose parents don't, right? I talked them into a gap year, trying to buy some time. Got here with some friends and knew there was no place else I'd rather be. Told the 'rents, and they pretty much cut me off." He sipped his beer. "No college, no money. But that was cool. No chains on me, you know what I'm saying?"

Sterling wished with all his heart that he could have said that to Camille, but he'd had Pearl, Ruby, and Opal to worry about. He sighed. He wanted to ask Alex if he was out yet, but thought it was too personal for the length of time he'd known him. "What did you do?"

"The usual. Waited on tables, got into construction, then the opportunity to dance came up for the summer. I tried it and got a huge kick out of it." He shrugged. "It's only taking your clothes off in front of people, no big deal."

Sterling would rather take a wooden stake and shove it through his eyeball than strip in front of strangers. His face must have been comical because Alex laughed.

Dear Lord, the man was beautiful, an angel's face with eyes full of the devil. Sterling longed to kiss those firm masculine lips, just a taste. That would be enough to get him past his desire for Alex Tudor. But that would never do, of course. It would rank right up at the top of things Sterling Marlowe could ever do.

"You okay?" Alex placed a hand on Sterling's forearm.

"Yeah." His skin nearly shuddered at that unexpected touch.

"For a minute I thought you were gonna faint or something." Alex's eyes looked kind and interested. "Your turn. What happens in a day in the life of a house representative?"

"Short story?"

Alex nodded. "Tell me all about it. Especially the juicy parts."

Snorting, Sterling almost laughed. "Trust me, there are no juicy parts. It's all dry as dust."

"But we see fights and all on the TV. That doesn't happen every day?"

He shook his head. "Only when the cameras are rolling. Behind the scenes we keep our disagreements civilized and above the belt. There's a lot of paperwork and reading and meetings with people who can't wait to tell you what an idiot and a bum you are."

"You lost me at paperwork."

"So that's why I need this little vacation from my life to recharge the old batteries." Sterling ate one of the olives from his martini.

"Makes sense." Alex looked around. "Do you want to go somewhere quieter?"

Oh, he did, he really did. But, the eternal word ruling his life, told him not to. He probably should go home before anyone recognized him, especially him speaking to a male stripper, of all things. There'd go all Camille's money to the Fine Arts Work Center. Regret filled him, thudding stronger with each beat of his heart. "No, thanks. I think I need to go home before anyone else recognizes me."

Alex's eyes snapped light. "What? Are you afraid of being recognized, or are you afraid of being seen with me? Never mind. I don't want to know. It doesn't matter anyway." He slapped a twenty on top of the bar. "Enjoy the rest of your night."

Sterling held his breath and didn't watch him leave. Why waste time looking at something he couldn't have?

He paid for his martini, followed Alex's example, and left head down, shoulders hunched.

****

Tony grinned as he inspected the repairs to the boat and its gear. May was coming up fast, and he couldn't wait to get out on the water, work hard, and fall in bed so exhausted he wouldn't dream of Pearl.

Pearl clinging to him, under him, on top of him, open to his mouth while she screamed out with pleasure, on her knees in front of him while he screamed with pleasure.

No, no, no. Just stop.

His dad clapped a huge mitt of a hand on Tony's shoulder, and he nearly leaped twelve feet in the air. "Lookin' pretty good, boy. You and Gabe did a fine job getting her fit for the season."

"Teamwork."

"Of course! I'd expect nothing less from the two of you."

Actually, at the moment the two of them couldn't stand the sight of each other, and Tony didn't know how to fix it. He didn't know what he'd done in the first place to make Gabe so pissed off. Each day it got worse, and Tony had enough. Gabe would have to either fish or cut bait. They couldn't go out every day into the ocean with Gabe having a goddamn hair across his ass.

One second of not paying attention and working together could be a matter of life or death. Bottom line, Tony wouldn't do anything to put his and Gabe's lives in danger, and he was pretty sure Gabe wouldn't either.

His brother might be an asshole, but he was a professional lobsterman. He'd do the job like the pro he was.

"Gabe, whaddaya think?" his father boomed. "Is this boat shipshape and ready to go out early tomorrow morning, or what?"

"It looks great, Papa," Gabe said, a grin on his face. "We're gonna have a great season. Make lots of money." He glanced at Tony. "Lots of money selling our catch to the middlemen who get us the best prices for our catch."

Fat chance, Gabe. Still he had this skin-cringing feeling that something was about to go terribly wrong. He couldn't shake it.

He looked over at his father and brother yukking it up and being all jokey, and he couldn't help but think all this was going to hell really soon.

He forced himself to shake it off. It was the start of a new season, a new beginning. Even if he were no closer to achieving his dream of a fish market, he'd be out on the water doing what he was born to do.

Thoughts of Pearl flitted across his vision, and he pushed them brutally away. Pearl had no place out on the water with him. She'd pull him away from his tasks just as sure as Gabe's anger would.

No. He tamped his thoughts of Pearl deep, deep

down where they couldn't bother him.

There was something between them, but he'd rather have a root canal without anesthesia than confront it. He'd left things badly with Pearl, and she needed an explanation, but damn him if he knew what the explanation was.

Again. Pearl had no place in his thoughts and on this boat. He started when his father's beefy hand nearly knocked him on his ass.

"My boys," Dad said. "Two better sons no man ever had."

Tony caught Gabe's eye. Gabe flushed bright red and looked away.

"We learned from the best, Papa," Tony said. The hell with Gabe.

"You know it, Papa." Gabe flung his arm around Theo's shoulders. "We got it covered."

"Just keep your attention on catching lobsters and not on building something that's not gonna work and will cost us more money."

"I'll keep things on track," Gabe said with a smug smirk.

Tony's jaw clenched so hard he might've crushed a tooth. Another dig from his father and brother about his pet project.

He had to get out of there, but he didn't know where to go. "I forgot about an appointment I have. I've got to leave."

Against his better judgment, he got in his truck and headed to Marlowe House.

Headed to Pearl, which made no damn sense.

Except that it did, as she was the only person on God's green earth who believed in him.

Chapter Twenty-Six

Pearl yawned and looked around her world. She'd stayed up most of the night doing the final painting of the last room. Her back, arms, and head ached to beat the band. She desperately needed a shower. Her stomach rumbled, as she hadn't eaten in twenty-four hours. The drive to finish had ridden her hard.

She'd never felt prouder in her entire life. She'd done it. She'd finished the renovations of her childhood home and was about to go into business for herself. Every pain, every cramp, every pang was worth it.

She'd beaten her grandmother. She'd won. Freedom swirled around her, and she laughed out loud for the sheer joy of it.

Camille'd thought that Pearl wouldn't stick, wouldn't stay. That she was a coward of the worst sort. Well, she'd proven Granny wrong. Pearl had beaten Camille.

The windows of the room faced the harbor, so Pearl opened them to let the sea breeze cleanse the room of all traces of the past. Sheer white curtains danced on the wind. Delighted, she threw out her arms and twirled in a wide, dizzy circle.

"Celebrating?"

Pearl stopped dead in mid-turn to see Tony standing in the doorway of the room. "Tony! You scared me half to death!" Just her luck he was in time to see her messy and smelly.

He took a step in, his presence filling the room. Rumpled dark hair framed a face too handsome for its own good. His dark eyes riveted on her face, and she couldn't look away even if she wanted to. She so didn't want to. What she wanted, right on down to her tippy toes, was to stand there and drink in the sight of him. "What are you doing here?"

He ducked his head and rubbed the back of his neck. "I came to see you."

What the what? "Has something happened? Something wrong with your mother or father?"

"No," he said. "I just need to talk to you."

She needed to do something to keep her hands busy so she wouldn't grab him and kiss the daylights out of him. "Come on, let's go downstairs, and I'll make us some coffee, and you can tell me all about it."

He followed her down the stairs. "It's what I came to do." His voice got husky.

"I don't mind." Which was so very, very true.

After they got to the kitchen, Pearl got out the things to make coffee.

"Need any help?"

She laughed. "No, thank you. I can manage making coffee that's drinkable."

He leaned against the doorframe. "I didn't mean it that way. I'll like it any way you make it." His face flushed red.

"Are you blushing?" Was he cute or what? He was handsome seventeen years ago and still rang every single nerve she possessed.

He gave her a lopsided smile. "No. I'm a manly man. I never blush."

"I'll try to remember that." Coffee brewing, Pearl wiped her hands on a tea towel and gestured for him to sit.

He walked to the table in the middle of the room and held out a chair for her. "You first."

The small gesture charmed her. "Thank you."

"Any time." He grinned and sat in the chair across from her and drummed his fingers on the tabletop.

"So what did you want to talk about?"

He ducked his head and rubbed his hand across the back of his neck. "The fish market. Gabe and my dad won't even listen to me."

"Still?"

"Yeah. I shouldn't let it get under my skin, but today it did." He shrugged. "I can't say anything right to Gabe. He's mad about something. I'm not looking forward to getting up before dawn and spending a day hauling lobster pots and dealing with his crappy mood. I hate being a whiner. So"—he put his elbows on the table and leaned forward—"I'm really impressed by the work you've done here."

"Oh." She didn't know what to say. "Thank you. It's been a revelation to me. I like it. I never thought I'd be happy staying in town and running a rooming house."

Silent, he stared at her. Then, "So you're not going to run away after you've done your time."

"Done my time?"

He sat up straight. "Yeah. From what Ruby told me, you only have to stay here one year to get your money."

The look on his face could turn a person to stone, but she was made of sterner stuff. "I'm not leaving.

This is my life now, and I'm enjoying it."

More silence. She squirmed under his gaze.

"Seeing is believing," he finally said.

She took a deep breath. "I know you don't believe me after what happened back in the day, but I'm here now. I'm committed to staying here and making this work."

Another uncomfortable stare. "Damn, Pearl, I want to believe you."

"You can believe me. I'm staying in town. I'm not going anywhere." She had to make him believe in her. "Like it or not, I'm here to stay."

"I don't know what to do about this, Pearl."

"About what?"

"You and me." He ran his hand through his hair. "Whatever is going on between us."

Hoo boy. She took the coward's way out. "We're old friends who used to be close." That was a very tepid description of what they had been.

"That's bullshit." He stood, hands clenched. "We weren't close. We were everything to each other, or at least I thought so."

She pulled her hands to her lap and worried her fingers. "We were. God, we were. I thought I'd die when I had to leave you behind."

Tony snorted. "You had to leave me behind? You did leave me behind, and you didn't look back."

"You could have followed me." Where had that come from?

But yeah. She'd wanted him to prove he loved her, to come after her.

He hadn't.

She ventured a look at him. To quote Benjamin

Franklin, he resembled a pig poisoned.

"Your grandmother convinced me that you didn't want me to follow you. That you didn't want me to go get you." He shook his head. "I only had your grandmother's word, and she was pretty clear that I needed to let you go and leave you alone."

She shook her head. "You didn't trust that I loved you." Profound sadness swamped all over her.

"You didn't give me any reason to trust you."

"I did what Camille told me to. I thought because we loved each other so much you would trust me. All those days and nights up against just one day. And dammit! I'm tired of apologizing and feeling guilty about the whole thing."

"One day was all it took," he said in a hoarse whisper.

The regret pricked at her with small, sharp needles. "I waited for you." She swallowed. "And you never came."

"You could have called me. Written a letter. Sent me a postcard. Dropped me a line." He shook his head.

Stunned speechless, she could only goggle at him.

Tony swallowed hard and turned his gaze to the side, seemingly studying the painting on the wall.

She found her voice. "Camille told me not to. That if I contacted you, she'd cut off the money for my college." Pearl angled her head. "I just thought you'd know."

"You thought wrong," he snapped.

She only had one thing to say. "Like I said, I'm really tired of being sorry."

He clenched his jaw. "So going to college was more important than me."

"No! That's not what I meant! I was so confused. I felt caught between my grandmother and you."

"And it was easier for you to just do what the old bat said."

She flinched. "Ouch. I guess I deserve that, because that's what I did." She put her heart on her sleeve. "Can't we just get past all that and talk about where we go from here?"

A heavy silence dropped over the room while she waited for him to answer.

"Yeah. I want that." His gaze warmed. "Right now, you're the only person in the world who believes in me and my dream. I don't want to lose that."

Relief swamped her. "Me, too."

They stared at each other, and she saw desire in his eyes. At least she hoped it was the same kind of desire she knew was in her eyes.

He cleared his throat, breaking the spell. She turned around and busied her hands with setting out cups, cream, and sugar. That done, she filled the white stoneware mugs with coffee. "Do you still take your coffee black?"

"Yes, please."

Making short shrift of putting it all together, she sighed and took the tray to the table. She sat and fixed her coffee with cream and six spoonsful of sugar.

Tony took one glance at her cup and chuckled. "Is that coffee or dessert?"

"So sue me. I've got a sweet tooth."

"I remember. I was always buying bags of Hershey's Kisses for you."

Kisses. Lots and lots of kisses. They'd shared kisses that had nothing to do with her love of chocolate and had everything to do with how much she loved Tony. Totally tongue-tied, she didn't know what to say.

He wrapped his big hands around his mug. "Did I say something wrong? I guess I shouldn't have brought up the past."

A ball of rusty nails lodged in her throat, and she swallowed around it. "No, it's okay." She would die before she told him about the steamy dreams she'd been having about him every night. Chocolate loomed large in some of them, as in Tony first painting her body with it and then licking it off her. "That's a good memory."

Tony took a swig of his coffee. "One of the best."

"There were a lot of good ones."

He gifted her with a sad smile. "There were." He stood. "Well—" He cleared his throat. "—I should probably get out of your way."

She also stood. "Thanks for dropping by."

"My pleasure," he said, "I'll see myself out."

Pearl followed him to the door anyway. "Don't be a stranger."

He nodded and stepped onto the porch. Before he went down the stairs to the front walk, he turned back to her. "Maybe you'd like to go to dinner with me some night?"

"I would love to go to dinner with you some night." Delight at the prospect wiggled up her spine.

"Is Sunday okay? Around seven?"

"That's great." So much more than great.

"I'll pick you up." He grinned. "See you Sunday." Opening his car door, he started to get in. "Oh, hell." He pushed away from the car and marched back up her front stairs. "Can't leave without doing this."

He cradled her face in his hands and bent his head

to brush his lips across hers once, twice, three times before he settled in and deepened the kiss. She clung to his forearms for support, as her legs were about to buckle.

He tasted of coffee and all her dreams come true. She trembled at the sheer fact of being in Tony's arms again. Their lips broke apart, came together, broke apart again. Tony rested his forehead on top of Pearl's hair. She felt him take deep breath and sigh.

Too soon, way too soon, he released her. Smiling, he ran whisper-soft thumbs over her cheeks. "I'll see you Sunday." He left.

Pearl gently touched her lips and waited for her heart to slow down. She felt something she hadn't felt about Tony for a long time. Something awfully close to hope.

Chapter Twenty-Seven

Tony and Gabe worked efficiently, due to a lifetime dedicated to the routine of baiting pots, dropping them, then hauling them back up, grabbing the lobsters, re-baiting the traps, and dropping them down again to catch more lobsters. Tony thought it might be engraved on his family's DNA.

Tony and Gabe also worked without saying one word to each other. Tony enthusiastically thanked St. Peter, the patron saint of fishermen, for that. He had no interest at all about listening to anything his brother had to say.

Sniffing the cold air, plowing the boat through the waves, salt spray in his face was Tony's idea of heaven. Then he remembered kissing Pearl the other day.

Her lips were so soft, so sweet. That kiss had brought more memories flooding back, all those steamy, sexy clinches in the back seat of his father's car when they couldn't get enough of each other. The time when they'd lost their virginities together, both of them as nervous as a cat with two tails in a room filled with rocking chairs.

Driven crazy by hormones, the two of them had lost their minds.

Pearl sniffled, then burst into tears. Undone, Tony pulled her into his arms and cradled her head right over his heart. A horrible thought occurred to him. "Did I hurt you?" He'd only had a general idea of what to do.

"No." Pearl sniffed. "I just…feel so much." She raised her eyes to his. "Too much."

"Are you sorry we did this?" He didn't know what he would do if she said yes.

"No! I wanted to be with you this way!" She pulled out of his arms, just enough to look at him. "I just didn't expect to be so, so blown away about it."

Relieved, he said, "I feel the same way." He kissed her on the forehead.

"I'm glad it was you," Pearl whispered. "Only you. I will love you forever."

"Me, too. I can't even imagine doing this with someone who's not you."

"God, Tony, I love you so much!"

"I love you more."

And, as it turned out, he did love Pearl more than she loved him, as she ran away from him at the first opportunity.

After their conversation the other day, he wasn't so sure about that anymore. How could he have known she wanted him to come for her? That she expected him to go to Boston and fetch her back to P-town. She could have damn well given him a clue because he wasn't a freakin' mind reader.

Her grandmother had done her job well. The Marlowe princess would not be married to a local fisherman. Something insistent and impatient niggled at him. Maybe he should have pushed the issue and gone to Boston, but Camille had destroyed him.

"So you got anything planned for your day off?"

Startled, Tony turned his head to look at Gabe. There was no way he was going to tell Gabe he was taking Pearl out to dinner. He didn't need the aggravation. "Nothing much. Sleep some, I guess."

"Bro, you need a social life." Gabe didn't look at Tony. "Maybe you should get back with Jenny."

Tony shook his head. "That ship has sailed. I can never make her happy."

"You could if you tried."

"I don't want to try. We're good and over."

"Jenny doesn't think so."

"Yeah, well, Jenny will just have to get used to it." When had Gabe gotten so chatty with Jenny?

"What if she doesn't get used to it?" Tony saw that his brother's mouth was puckered up like he'd been sucking on rotten lemons. He really didn't know Gabe anymore.

But since Gabe seemed to be in tune with Jenny, he could tell her this. "She has to. I'm not changing my mind."

"Any of this has to do with Pearl?"

No, it was about Tony and Jenny. Pearl had nothing to do with it. "I've already told you it doesn't, and I meant it. Jenny wants to get married, and I don't want that anytime soon. It's for Jenny's own good. She has to find a man who really appreciates her."

"Humpf."

"What does that mean?" Tony often didn't know what Gabe was talking about. This had to be one of those times.

Gabe exhaled long and hard. "Nothing. It means absolutely nothing."

Time to make this bullshit with his brother go away. "Do we have a problem here? You've been really pissed off lately."

Gabe looked out to the horizon. "You could fix that by giving up on the fish market idea."

Tony resisted the urge to punch his brother in the face. "Yeah, I got that loud and clear." He crossed his arms over his chest. "You could cut me a little slack."

"Can't, Bro. Dad can't take the stress."

Ah, the rancid smell of manipulation in the morning. "Dad'll be fine. Absolutely nothing would change, except we'd have another outlet to sell our lobsters and maybe attract an upscale clientele who would likely spend more money buying our lobsters. But you don't want to hear anything I have to say, so whatever." He was so over his brother and his father's resistance.

"Dad won't be—"

"Shut up! I'm done turning myself into a pretzel to please you two. You constantly insult me, call me stupid and unrealistic, and I'm done with it. So back off." Tony turned away from his now-silent-as-a-tomb brother and moved to the other end of the boat.

He had absolutely no one to tell about his renewed feelings toward Pearl. Lord knew he could only talk to Pearl about his career dreams. His world was narrowing to the point where Pearl was the only thing left in it.

He'd been there before and had his heart handed back to him in tatters. He chose to forget that now. He and Pearl were in a new place, and he planned to enjoy it. Because who knew if she was in for the long haul?

Did he want her back? Maybe. More than that, he wanted to enjoy whatever time he had with her while keeping his heart whole.

****

"Sterling? Robert Marshall is in the waiting room.

229

He says he has to speak with you immediately." Amy, Sterling's campaign manager, stood in the doorway of his Fall River office.

Sterling looked up from the document he was poring over and tossed his reading glasses on his desk. "Robert? Here?" His stomach dropped to his feet. This couldn't be good. Was everything all right with his sisters? "Let him in, please. Thanks, Amy."

She nodded and turned to Robert who stood just outside the door. "Mr. Marshall, you can go inside."

Robert nodded, walked into the office, and closed the door behind him. Sterling stood and offered Robert his hand to shake. "Robert, is everything all right with the girls?"

Robert shook Sterling's hand and sat in one of the dark leather chairs in front of Sterling's desk. "Your sisters are fine. It's you that has me worried."

"Me?" Sterling lowered himself into the chair behind his desk and unbuttoned his suit jacket.

"I'll get right down to business. I got a report about you from the private detectives. You remember that one of the conditions of your grandmother's will is that your conduct would be watched scrupulously. I'm aware that you've been in town and going out to bars and hanging out with unsuitable people. Don't bother to deny it."

Bristling in anger, Sterling said, "What? I can't go out for a drink? I can't go out and spend time with my constituents?"

Robert pulled a stack of photos from his briefcase. "In disguise?" He plopped them onto Sterling's desk.

He picked up the stack and ruffled through it. Cold dread tentacles spread through his body. Photo after photo showed him and Alex talking and laughing at the bar that one night. "I don't see why these are a problem."

"Do you know who the man sitting next to you and laughing with you is?"

"He works for the contractor doing the renovations to Marlowe House and to Ruby's shop."

"Alex Tudor is a homosexual stripper. He's exactly the sort of person your grandmother wanted you to stay away from."

"It was a public bar. I can't help who sits next to me."

Robert pinched the bridge of his nose. "Don't split hairs, Sterling. Look at those photos again. The two of you appear very intimate."

"Intimate?" Sterling snorted. "That's ridiculous." But true, regrettably. He saw the obvious connection between him and Alex.

Damn.

"You know politics. It doesn't matter if something is not true. The other side can spin every kind of scandal on one chance encounter. Stay away from Alex Tudor. Your future in the Senate, and the money to get there, is in jeopardy. I must abide by the conditions of the will." He stood. "I'll see myself out."

Standing himself, Sterling nodded and watched Robert leave. When the door closed with a quiet snick, he turned to peer out his window.

He'd known he should have stayed away from Alex. Sure, a couple of innocent drinks were nothing to brag about.

But forgetting about Robert's detectives was just plain old stupid, but that's exactly what he had done.

He slammed his fist on top of his desk.

He'd known from the very start that Alex Tudor was trouble and to be avoided at all costs. He only had one relationship he had to invest in, and that was being elected to the United States Senate.

Chapter Twenty-Eight

Pearl was in the middle of an earring crisis. "What earrings go with this dress?" Pearl burst into Opal's room. "The sapphire studs or the dangly, sparkly ones?"

Opal closed her laptop lid and turned in her seat. "Let me see."

First Pearl held the dangly ones up to her right ear. "These?" Then the studs up to her other ear. "Or these?"

Opal squinted. "They both look great. Where's Tony taking you?"

"I don't know. He hasn't told me." She hated when men didn't mention the dress code for the evening.

"Wear the ones that make you feel the prettiest, that make you happy." Opal nodded. "Don't dress to please Tony. Dress to please yourself."

"Is that advice from my sister or a romance writer?"

"Both." Opal stood and put her hands on Pearl's shoulders. "Tony's going to swallow his tongue when he sees how beautiful you are, both inside and out."

"I'm overthinking things again, aren't I?"

"Yes. Look"—Opal let her arms drop from Pearl's shoulders and took a step back—"even if you don't get back together but become friends again, then it's worth it."

"I don't know why I'm so nervous."

"Don't you?" Opal said, her voice calm and soothing.

"I'm just going out for a meal with an old boyfriend."

Opal shook her head. "Don't try to kid a kidder. Tony is way much more than an old friend to you."

"Opal, please leave it alone." She held up the earrings again. "Which ones do you think I should wear?"

"The bangles. They look great with your dress and bring out your eyes."

Pearl couldn't have loved her sister more.

****

Pearl's pulse jumped a wee bit harder as she went to answer her door. Pausing, she smoothed down her skirt before she reached for the handle. She took one last look in the mirror and grinned. Happy there was no lipstick on her teeth, she opened the door.

The supremely gorgeous, incredibly sexy Tony Cabral stood on the other side of it. Dressed in a dark gray suit with a lighter gray silk tee underneath it, he made her shiver.

He always did clean up good.

He held one hand behind his back, and he smiled as she watched him. "Hello."

"Hi," she said. "Come on in."

He stepped over the threshold, brought the hand from behind his back, and presented her with one perfect candy-pink rose. "For you. I hope pink is still your favorite color."

It wasn't anymore, but how sweet of him to remember. She'd been all about the pink back in the day. She took the rose, sniffed it, and smiled. Was there any scent lovelier than that of a rose? "It's beautiful. Thank you."

"You're welcome." He curved his lips into that Tony smile she loved. "It's nowhere near as beautiful as you."

And when he said things like that? Totally swoon worthy. How to answer without sounding like a jerk? "That's nice of you to say."

"It's nothing but the truth." He flashed her that megawatt smile of his again. "Ready to go?"

"Let me get my jacket." The evening May breeze still carried an edge of cold on it. She felt him watching her as she opened the hall closet. As she turned to Tony, he took the lacy, hand-knit sweater and held it out for her to slip her arms into. "Thank you."

Tony knew all the right moves. He helped her down the stairs with his hand lightly touching the small of her back. Not only that, he guided her to his truck, opened the passenger door, and assisted her into her seat.

She nearly sighed. When was the last time anyone had been so solicitous about her wellbeing? When was the last time anyone had given her flowers? She couldn't remember. Way too long.

Tony got them out of the driveway and on the way out of town. That was okay with Pearl. Less fodder for the gossip mills.

"Do you want some music?"

"Music is always welcome."

He nodded and turned on the radio. The weeping strings of a Brahms symphony filled the cab. Pearl frowned. "When did you start liking classical music?"

He shrugged as he slid the clutch into fourth gear.

"I don't know. Just kind of happened."

"Well, it's beautiful. Brahms was one of my father's favorite composers." She hadn't thought of that in ages. It was funny how music could call up a memory. This was a good one.

"You didn't talk about him much," Tony said as he rested his hand on the stick shift.

She wanted to lay hers on top of his, so she tucked it into her lap where it wouldn't get her into trouble. "It was hard to talk about my parents back then. One day you're in a happy family. The next day a drunk driver takes it all away." She didn't want to talk about it, ruin the evening. "Where are we going?"

"A little place in Wellfleet that's new and off the beaten path. Good food, cozy atmosphere. I think you'll like it."

"I'm sure I will." Except maybe he'd taken Jenny there. She'd cut out her tongue with a rusty butter knife before she asked him about that. "How did you find it?"

"Remember Lou and Mil Radtke? They're sisters. They came every summer from Framingham? Lou went to culinary school, and Mil majored in music and minored in business."

Pearl grinned. "Yes, I do. Their dad was an avid sailor, right?"

"Oh, yeah. Paul raced sailboats. He really jonesed on it." He shifted into fifth gear as they merged onto Route 6 out of town. "The girls came back to the Cape a couple of years ago, bought this house, and turned it into a restaurant, called it Seasters. They're gaining followers. It's got a really special atmosphere." He slid his glance sideways. "Maybe you can make a deal with them to offer discounts at the restaurant for people who stay at Marlowes at the Sea."

"That's a good idea." Business was business, and that was a good plan to connect her into more of the community. "I'm looking forward to seeing them again."

"I think you'll like the restaurant. Lou has put some really interesting twists on traditional seafood recipes. She's a genius with salmon. And what she does with Brussels sprouts is life changing."

That was high praise from Tony, who, she knew, hated Brussels sprouts. "I'm looking forward to seeing them again and eating there."

She followed her instincts and patted the hand he rested on the stick shift. He took his gaze off the road to look where they touched.

Her skin sizzled with the heat of the connection between them. He cleared his throat and captured her gaze. She couldn't have looked away if she had wanted to.

She didn't want to. She could bathe in the warm light of Tony's eyes forever.

She wished with all her might he would give her a chance.

Chapter Twenty-Nine

Tony felt Pearl's hand move over his on the stick shift, and his heart thudded hard and heavy. Just the whisper of a touch from Pearl Marlowe could bring him to his knees.

The woman next to him was the only woman he'd ever wanted. Needed. The woman next to him was his downfall and his salvation. Damn her.

Damn him.

Pearl wore a pretty light-green lacy dress that frothed around her calves when she moved and the kind of high heels that made a grown man beg for mercy. He could eat her up in two big bites.

Actually, it would be better if he took little nibbles to make the feasting last longer.

"Is the restaurant a long way out?"

He rolled his thoughts back to PG-13. "No, just a little Victorian cottage off Main Street."

"It's so pretty here," Pearl commented as he turned the truck toward Wellfleet center.

Tony nodded in agreement. With its narrow streets that wound around quaint cottages with roses climbing on trellises and fences, Wellfleet had a sleepy, old world charm to it.

Pearl squeezed his hand. "It always feels like *Brigadoon* to me."

"Brigadoon?" He remembered there once was a

restaurant in town called the Bonnie Doone, but Brigadoon? A mystery.

"It's an old Broadway musical. There's a town in Scotland that's cursed and only appears one day in every one hundred years. When it appears, everything is how it was in the past."

"One day?" He tapped a finger against the steering wheel. "You're kidding."

"It's Broadway, silly. The people in the town have to stuff all their living into twenty-four hours before they go into another magic one-hundred-year sleep." She sighed and pulled her hand back into her lap. "It's very romantic."

"If you say so." Women were a mystery.

"Of course everyone sang and danced throughout the whole day."

"Of course."

"The movie with Gene Kelly in it is so romantic."

"That tap dancer you always liked so much?"

She gave him a pointed look. "He's on a hunting trip in Scotland, and the village of Brigadoon appears. He falls in love with a woman there and is willing to give up everything about his modern life to go back and live in Brigadoon, even with the one hundred years thing. His love for Fiona, that's the woman's name, is so strong that he breaks the spell and wakes the town up early."

"Do they stay awake?"

Pearl shook her head. "No. He knew when he went back to her that he was going to disappear with her and the town for the next hundred years. He goes to sleep with the rest of them or, more important, with his arms around his true love."

Sounded stupid to him, but then, he'd never gotten into musicals. Nobody just walked down the street, suddenly burst into song, and danced across a busy intersection. If you had something to say, you just said it, no tap-dancing involved.

The going to sleep with his true love safe in his arms, though, sounded pretty much like heaven, no song and dance there. Tony shrugged and downshifted into third. "So he leaves his life to go live in the past with a woman he just met."

She smacked him across his bicep. "Jerk." She sniffed. "A case could be made for the fact that his life sucked, and he gave it up for a life with his true love."

"So it was love at first sight?" He whistled. "That never works out."

Pearl frowned. "Who said anything about love at first sight?"

"It had to be. They only knew each other for about twenty-four hours. Hey"—he snapped his fingers—"it had to be love at first sight."

"Well, put that way, I suppose it was. I don't see anything wrong with that. To quote Lin-Manuel Miranda, 'love is love is love is love is love is love.' "

She had a point somewhere in all that love-is-love-is-love stuff. He could almost see it. Time to change the subject. "So when are you opening?"

"We've got our first guests booked for the last week in June, the Portuguese Festival. There are a lot of kids coming home for the reunions." A cloud passed over her face, and she frowned. "A lot of them, I'm sure, are ready to see me fail. We've got a full house through the middle of July." She wrinkled her nose. "We've also got a lot of English professor/critic/fan boy types who want to worship at the shrine devoted to Camille Marlowe." Her smile looked awfully sneaky. He loved and appreciated it. "They're going to be disappointed about the shrine thing."

"I have no doubt." He pulled into a parking space in front of a black sign that proclaimed in gold letters, *Seasters*.

Pearl started to unbuckle her seat belt, so he put his hand on hers to stop her. "Wait right here."

He got out of the truck and jogged around it to her side. Opening the door for her, he extended his hand to help her out of her seat. Pearl's ocean blue eyes widened, and she smiled as she took his hand. "Thank you," she murmured.

After she stood, he gave in to impulse, brought her hand up to his mouth, and kissed her hand. She trembled underneath his lips.

He entwined his fingers with hers and pulled her closer. "C'mon. I'm hungry." Which was exactly the truth, but he had no desire for food.

He wanted for Pearl.

Since he promised her a romantic evening, that was exactly the thing he would give her.

****

The skin of Pearl's hand still tingled where Tony had kissed it. So romantic, just like the rose. She hadn't known he had it in him. She had to face it. High school boys didn't know much about romance. Tony wasn't a boy anymore that was for sure.

He was a man with a capital M.

Well, she supposed, she wasn't the girl Tony remembered.

Never mind all that. She was on a date with a very

interesting, sexy, romantic man. She decided to go all in for whatever the night brought.

Tony let go of her hand to open the restaurant door for her. She smiled. "Thank you." Stepping inside, she gasped.

The décor was intimate, fanciful, and very romantic. The room was small with pale-blue-colored walls. They'd hung watercolors of undersea scenes. Little fairy lights twinkled around the room, like little clusters of stars. Topping each table was a small bottle holding one flower and a trio of candles at different heights. Quiet Renaissance instrumental music filled the room, and the exotic aroma of whatever was cooking in the kitchen tangled with the violins.

"This is so charming."

"The food is really good," Tony said.

She chuckled. Of course he'd be all about the food.

His brow furrowed. "What's so funny?"

She shook her head. "Nothing."

"Hey, Tony." The hostess walked to them, a big smile on her face. "You here for dinner?"

"Hey, Mil. Yeah."

"Just you two or are more people coming?"

"Just us two."

Mil nodded and picked up two handwritten menus. "Follow me."

Tony touched the small of Pearl's back as they managed their way to their table. His hand was toasty, warm enough for her to feel it through her clothes.

"Here you go." Mil put the menus onto the table. "I'll be right back."

Tony pulled out a chair for Pearl. "Thank you," she said as she sat.

He smiled, took his own seat, and picked up his menu. "Let's see what's for dinner tonight."

"I can't believe they change the menu every day." Pearl studied the handwritten sheet of paper.

"Lou's extremely creative and gets bored real easy. They do have some things they offer every night," Tony chuckled. "She cooks what she wants when she wants to cook it."

"I'm not sure how it works as a business plan." Pearl frowned.

"It works for the sisters."

"Then that's what counts." She picked up her own menu. "What's good?"

****

Tony could have sat there all night just watching Pearl breathe. She exuded enthusiasm, just like the girl she'd been back in high school.

"Here. Try this." He held out a fork filled with a slice of steak Diane covered with a brandy, mushroom, and cream sauce.

Pearl leaned forward in her seat and opened her mouth. Her pink tongue darted out as she took the proffered treat. He stared as she used her teeth to pull the meat and sauce off the fork tines. Closing her eyes, she chewed, swallowed, and sighed. "That's sinful. It was really cool when Mil set it on fire."

His breathing got a little ragged as he watched her flick her tongue and lick the sauce off her bottom lip. He tried not to imagine that tongue stroking his cock. "Food with a flair." He cut another sliver off his steak and ran it through the sauce on his plate. "I suppose you ate in restaurants in New York that served this kind of thing all the time."

Doreen Alsen

She shook her head. "It was rare for me to eat anywhere other than my desk. I did a lot of takeout. Chinese." She rested her arms on the table and leaned forward again. "I don't know if you've noticed. I can't cook," she confided in a conspiratorial whisper.

"No! Say it isn't so!" He upped the wattage on his smile. "I bet your talents lie in other directions."

"Maybe I can show you later."

"Maybe you can." He'd make sure of it.

She speared a seared scallop coated in pistachio and basil pesto and held it out to him. "Your turn."

He'd expected the bite to be overly sweet, but something in the pesto added a fresh taste. "It's good."

She gave him that smile of hers that made him feel like the king of the world. Her eyes sparkled, almost as bright as the long earrings hanging from her ears.

"What? Do I still have sauce on my lips?"

"No. Just admiring your earrings. They make your eyes sparkle."

Her eyes widened, and her mouth popped open in a little O of surprise. She touched them and sent the crystals spinning. Light danced with the stones. "Ruby made them."

"They're pretty. Not as pretty as the woman wearing them."

"Thank you," Pearl murmured. For a moment she looked like the shy teenage girl he'd known.

She lifted her head. Her gaze was seductive, and her mouth curved up in a smile worthy of Eve. Pearl Marlowe was no shy girl anymore, and he realized he didn't want her to be that girl. He wanted to know the woman she'd become.

He wanted to be the man she wanted.

"Did you like the scallop? It was good, wasn't it?" Pearl forked up rice pilaf. "It met all my expectations."

What did she expect from him? Were they on the same page?

He was banking on it. "It was very good. What do you think would make it better?"

"Hmmmmm. I need to think about that." Mischief danced in her eyes. "Do you have any ideas of your own?"

His pulse bumped up a notch. "I might. I'm thinking…dessert."

"Ooh, dessert." She fluttered her eyelids, such a non-Pearl thing to do. "What kind of dessert?"

"I don't know. Something sweet," Tony teased. "But not too sweet. It has to have a little…bite…to it."

Her eyebrows raised so high and so fast it was a wonder they didn't crash into her forehead. "A little bite?" She shivered visibly. "Sounds promising."

It totally revved his engine. "Count on it."

"Oh, I will." Her smile contained lots and lots of secrets. "Count on it, that is."

He stared at her for a couple of seconds, trying to figure out what to say. "Do you want any input into my plans?"

She laughed. "Of course I want input. A lot of input." She lowered her head. "Lots and lots of input."

He cleared his throat. "I can give you as much input as you…desire."

"I might desire a lot."

He grinned. "I'm up to the task."

"I just bet you are." Pearl sighed. "Okay. I'm done. I wish I had Opal's gift with words."

"I don't." He laid his hand palm up on the table,

gesturing for her to put her hand on his. She did, and he wrapped his fingers around hers. "I think you're perfect the way you are."

"That's the nicest thing anyone has ever said to me." A sweet smile bloomed on her face.

His heart stuttered, then thumped hard at the sight of that smile. It all became so clear. He loved Pearl. He'd never stopped loving her.

"Tony? Are you okay?"

"Yeah." He'd never felt better. The world slipped back into place for the first time since she'd left him. He wanted to jump up and sing and dance just like those people in *Brigadoon*.

Mil took that moment to come over to their table. "How are you doing? Ready for dessert?"

"How about we take dessert home?" Tony asked. He glanced at Pearl. "Is that okay?"

"As long as it's chocolate, I'm down with it."

"Do you have any of those chocolate lava bomb cakes tonight?"

"We do. You want me to wrap it up?"

"Yes, please." He slid his glance over to Pearl's dancing eyes. "Is that okay with you?"

"It is. It is very okay with me." She stood, and he stood with her. "I'm just going to check out the ladies' room."

He sat after she left, ready to move to the next part of the night.

Being with her after all these years would be epic. She didn't know it yet, but she was going to be adored.

Cherished. Her every breath worshipped.

He couldn't wait to get started.

Chapter Thirty

Pearl walked around Tony's small living room, marveling at the sparseness of it. The eggshell-colored walls held no paintings, but one wall did sport a large, flat-screen TV. Very few books sat on the black bookcase in one corner. A small stone fireplace took up part of the room. A lone large-framed photo of his family sat on the mantel.

A brown plaid-covered couch rested against another wall. A lobster trap that served as a coffee table was covered in copies of magazines called *National Fisherman*. She winced when she saw a battered floral recliner next to a small table that was home to a lamp made from a chianti bottle and the remote control for the television. She thought she remembered the chair as one from his parents' house. Anyway, she didn't think *Country Living* would show up to do an article on his decorating prowess.

Venetian blinds shaded the windows, but no curtains draped them. Either he hadn't gotten any or he just hadn't gotten around to putting them up. This was a place to sleep, hardly anything around to turn it into a home. She should have taken Tony at his word when he told her that he was saving every penny he could set aside for the fish market. The emptiness of his apartment was oddly endearing.

He came out of his kitchen with a bottle of

Doreen Alsen

champagne and two glasses. He looked at her with a sexy half smile on his face and heat in his eyes. Desire streaked through her, sharp and hot.

He set the bottle and glasses on an edge of the table. Sweeping off a pile of *National Fisherman* magazines, he said, "Now there's room."

She was about to pick up the magazines scattered on the floor, but he stopped her. "Don't worry about it. I'll pick them up later." Smiling, he kissed her on the tip of her nose, something that foolishly charmed her.

He tore open the foil and wire cage and twisted the cork and the bottle, one to the left, the other to the right. It popped out with a fizzy thip. "Well, look at this," he gloated, triumph in his tone. "Didn't lose a drop."

"I didn't think champagne was your drink of preference."

"It's not," he said as he poured the effervescent liquid. "But I promised myself I'd treat you to some romance." He winked. Both glasses hissed and foamed as he filled them. He added more when the bubbles subsided. Holding out a glass to her, he said, "Take it."

She took the glass, his fingers brushing over hers before he relinquished the drink. "Careful. I hear those bubbles are pretty potent."

Something was pretty potent, and she didn't think it had much to do with bubbles. She conjured up her inner sassy. "Doesn't champagne demand a toast?"

His eyes lit brighter as he nodded. "I do believe it does. What do you want to toast to?"

In for a penny, in for a pound. She'd put on Sassy Pearl for a reason. Might as well own it. "To you and me."

He held her gaze for several nuclear-powered

248

moments. "I think you're right about that. For now, it's just you and me. No crazy exes and evil grandmothers between us." He snapped his fingers. "Do you know what we are missing?"

Pearl shook her head. "No. I can't think of a thing."

"Chocolate lava bomb cake. Let me go get it."

As she sipped her champagne, Pearl watched Tony go to his kitchen to fetch super chocolaty goodness.

She didn't know what would be more compelling, the chocolate or Tony.

Pearl decided it was both. Chocolate and Tony together? With champagne? Simply irresistible.

"Here we go." He set the pastry down with a flourish and sat next to her. After cutting into it with a fork, he scooped up a bite of dark, fudgy cake with some of the molten chocolate center. Holding the fork to her, he said, "Take a bite."

The rich flavors of warm, gooey chocolate exploded in her mouth. "Mmmmmm." She closed her eyes as she chewed, savored, then swallowed. "Omigawd, that's incredible!"

He kissed her, enjoying the flavor of Pearl and chocolate together. "I agree. Try another one."

She watched as he loaded the fork with dense cake and chocolate and brandy-tinged filling. Diligent, she opened her mouth to catch the next bite.

He pulled it back. "How bad do you want it?"

She licked her lips. "Pretty bad. It's been a long time." And she knew that they were not talking about chocolate cake. She opened her mouth and leaned forward, waiting for him to feed her.

He pulled the fork away. "Maybe I'll make you work for it."

"Work for it? What do you suggest?"

"Maybe you should kiss me before every bite."

"Kiss you?"

He nodded. "No kiss, no cake."

"Ahh." She leaned in and kissed his cheek. "Cake, please."

"I'm going to need a little bit more than that tiny peck. Show me how much you want it."

Pearl knew a challenge when she heard one. "Buckle up, buttercup." She put her glass down and took the plate out of his hand. Leaning in, she twined her arms around his neck and pressed her lips to his.

Passion erupted between them, volcanic and consuming, like a wildfire ripping through a tinder-dry forest. So hot. So very, very hot. Their lips and tongues tangled and danced as they gave in to what they truly craved deep in their souls.

What they had craved for seventeen years.

What they would crave forever.

Tony slid his hands underneath her top and petted her skin with his calloused working man's hands. Her breath caught and held in her throat as frissons of pleasure ignited up and down along her spine.

"God, Pearl," he whispered. "Your skin is so soft. I'd forgotten how smooth and warm, how perfect it is."

He moaned as his hands roamed over her. She shivered under his touch. Her nerve endings exploded in pleasure.

She pulled her mouth away. "Tony—"

"Just let me make love with you, Pearl." His husky voice and beard stubble scraped along her jaw. "I've missed you so much."

"I've missed you," she said, her voice clogged with

such a mix of emotions all tangled up tight in one big lump. "I really have."

"Come to bed with me."

"Tony—"

"We deserve this, Pearl. You and me," he pleaded.

"Do you really think we can make it work?"

He smiled a very wicked smile. "I know it with all my heart. Just let me prove it to you."

She shivered in anticipation. "I can't believe I'm here with you like this."

He put a finger on her lips. "I don't want anything more than being here with you right now. Kissing you." He replaced his finger with his mouth, spreading a soft, achingly sweet kiss across her mouth. He cupped her face in his warm, rough hands. "Right now it's just us, no past, our whole future ahead of us." He pressed his lips to her forehead. "Please let me make love to you, one night at a time."

"But—"

"No buts. Tonight is for us."

Tonight. After all the lonely days and the lonelier nights, she had the promise of this night. Her heart lurched and she trembled. She whispered his name. "Tony."

He loosened his grip on her and ran his fingers through her hair. She whimpered as he massaged her scalp with gentle, patient hands.

He nuzzled her hair. He whispered, "It's going to be so good, Pearl."

She climbed onto his lap and straddled him, placing her head so that her mouth hovered over his, so she could kiss him the exact way she wanted to be kissed.

Doreen Alsen

Like a woman crazy in love.

****

Way back in the prehistoric days, when dinosaurs roamed the earth, Pearl had never really kissed him. She'd responded sweetly and shyly to his kisses but hadn't ever made a move on her own.

Her soft lips parted against his, inviting him in. Tony slid his tongue into her welcoming mouth, his head spinning over the magic of their kisses. He sank into her, each kiss hotter, more avid, more greedy than the one before. He felt her heart jackrabbit hard against his chest and reveled in the soft moans that came from her throat.

He pulled his mouth from hers. "I need more," he growled. Without waiting another beat, he gathered her into his arms and carried her into his bedroom. He made it to the bed and laid her on it as carefully as he could. Damn, she looked amazing, clothes rumpled by his hands, hair destroyed by his fingers, lips swollen by his kisses.

He had to have her, the love of his life, his soul mate. He toed off his shoes and stretched on his side next to her. Stroking her hair away from her face, he spread it on his pillow. "You are so beautiful." He dropped a kiss on the tip of her nose. "You can't begin to imagine how many times I dreamed of seeing you right here, in my bed."

"Tony," she whispered, her voice hot against her lips. The desperate sound both conspired to make him hard and aching to bury himself in her body. "I'm going to touch you now. I can't wait another minute."

Sitting up, she licked her lips. "Please."

"Oh, darlin', I was hoping you'd say that."

He nearly swallowed his tongue as she slipped the straps of her dress off her shoulders and worked on the tiny buttons running down the front, revealing a sheer bra the color of a ripe peach, trimmed with pretty pale-pink lace with a darker pink bow nestled between her breasts. He cupped one breast with his hand while he pressed his mouth against the other one, tonguing her nipple through the delicate fabric of her bra.

"Oh, God, yes!" She threaded her fingers through his hair and held him close to her breasts. Hooking his fingers in the cups of her bra, he slipped them down so he could feast on her bare flesh.

She gasped. "They're a little bigger than they were before."

"They're gorgeous." Curling his fingers, he pebbled one long pink nipple. Not satisfied, not by a long shot, he scraped his teeth along the other rose-colored stem, making her hum with pleasure.

She undulated over him, her pelvis arching forward and back, begging for his touch. He ran his hand down the soft skin of her stomach to where she churned. "Shh, darlin'. We've got all night."

She worked at the buttons of his shirt, her fingers clumsy.

"Let me take care of this." He rolled them over so that he was now on top. He maneuvered onto his knees, pulled his shirt out of his pants, and jerked it over his head.

Pearl kept her gaze locked with his.

Tony sucked in a sharp breath as he touched her soft, smooth skin. Her breasts were round, pale, and crowned with rosy stems surrounded by puffy areolas, so much more beautiful than he remembered. Needing

253

to taste her, he guided her back down on the bed and stretched out next to her.

He took one nipple into his mouth and sucked the stiff peak while he tweaked the other.

"Mmmmmm." She leaned into his touch. "So good."

"I can make you feel better," he murmured against her skin.

"Please—"

He didn't need to be asked twice. He undid the rest of the buttons of her dress, desperate to see all of her. "You are more lovely than I remember."

He nipped his teeth against each of her nipples, then ran his mouth down her torso, licking here, nipping there. He settled her legs over his shoulders and cupped her soft, sweet bottom. Lifting her, he nuzzled his face in her soft curls and opened her up to reveal all her pretty pink skin.

Wet. She was so wet and ready. Using the tip of tongue, he lathed and teased the hard little button of her clitoris. She nearly flew off the bed, and he was glad he had a good grip on her ass. "Do you like that?"

"Eep," she squeaked, the sound startled and helpless.

"What about this?" He smiled against her soft flesh and fluttered his tongue over her sensitive bud. "Like that, too?"

"Yessssss."

He lapped and nibbled on her clit, reveling in the spicy scent and taste of her while she trembled and squirmed in his hands. Craving more, he slipped first one finger, then another inside her and stroked. Pearl gasped and nearly jumped off the bed.

So responsive, his Pearl. So damn sensitive to his touch.

"Oh, oh, ohhhhhh," Pearl panted. He felt her start to shiver violently as she lifted her hips into his mouth. His cock ached, eager to be inside her.

He feasted on her soft, wet flesh as he took her closer to the edge. One more pass of his tongue, then another, then a slight scrape of his teeth.

She screamed as she came, and he chased every last tremor, every last sensation with his greedy mouth. When she finally relaxed, he moved up alongside her and held her close.

"You okay, baby?" He kissed her on the temple and rolled one hard, pebbled nipple between his thumb and forefinger.

"I didn't think it could be like that," she said, her voice shaky.

"Did you like it? 'Cause I gotta tell you there's a lot more where that came from."

"Any more might kill me."

"Nope, not gonna let that happen." If he didn't get inside her soon, he was the one who might die. "Are you ready for your second trip to heaven?"

"Oh, God."

He hopped off the bed and took off the rest of his clothes, easing them gently over his massive erection.

Her green eyes grew round as she licked her lips. "All for me?"

"It's all for you, Pearl." He liberated his painfully erect penis, desperation riding him to thrust into her hot, slick sheath. "Everything for you."

****

Pearl's heart thudded as she tried to catch her

breath. She couldn't tear her gaze away as Tony freed his shaft from his clothes. She didn't remember him being that big.

He fished around in the nightstand, flinging things out of it like a madman. "Gotcha." He pulled out several foil packets and tossed them onto the bed.

First he ripped one open, then rolled it down the hard length of him. "I need to be inside you, Pearl. I can't wait anymore."

Her inner muscles spasmed in anticipation. "Me either."

He lowered himself between her legs and covered her gently. "I'll try to go slow, but I can't promise anything. I've waited so long to be with you."

Tony kissed her hard on the mouth, and she wrapped her legs around his back and guided his erection into her soft, welcoming heat. She moaned when he pushed all the way inside.

Oh, this! This. This is what she had longed for, that moment when he thrust deep inside her all the way to her womb.

"Damn. You are so tight," he rasped, his voice sending shivers against her skin. "So damn tight. Am I hurting you?"

Tears welled behind her eyelids as she stretched to accept all of him, but not because he hurt her. The enormity of being with him again after all these years drenched her right through to her core. "No," she whispered. "I love how you fill me."

"Thank God." He started to move in slow shallow thrusts. She arched her pelvis, trying to pull him deeper. Every time he moved inside her, that wonderful long, hard column of his rubbed against that sensitive spot high inside her. Little whimpers escaped her mouth and blossomed into full-throated cries of pleasure.

His breath tore out his lungs, sharp and ragged and scraped her every nerve. Every relentless thrust of Tony's sent her up, up, up until she could fly no more. Reaching her breaking point, she flew over it and shattered into a million pieces, convulsing in wave after wave of exquisite orgasm.

"Me, too, baby," Tony groaned as he pushed into her deep, so deep. "Me, too." One last amazing push and he came, groaning as he jetted deep into her spasming pussy.

The sound of their hoarse, ragged breathing filled the room. Her inner muscles clutched and released around him, the aftershocks of incredible loving. He braced a forearm on each side of her head, then ducked down and claimed her mouth in a tender kiss.

"I'll get off you in a minute," he murmured.

"No hurry," she assured him. "I love being with you like this."

"I'm heavy." He rolled over next to her, took care of the condom, gathered her into his arms, and held her tight. "That was amazing. You"—he nibbled on her earlobe—"are amazing." He ran his hand up her body, cradled a hypersensitive breast, and rubbed his thumb over its still-hard pebbly rose stem.

She held her breath as both peaks of her breasts, even the one he wasn't stroking, hardened and lengthened. "Oh, God."

"You like that?"

She could only nod.

"I love how your body responds to my touch." He took a deep breath and gave her a long, intense look. "I just really love you."

Hope leaped inside her. "Do you really mean it? It's not just a bedroom promise?"

"I do. I mean it with all my heart."

Only one thing to do. "I love you, too, Tony."

He closed his eyes for a moment, then opened them. "That makes me so happy."

"Me, too." She couldn't help but smile. "So very, very happy." But... "Can you trust me? Because I'm not going anywhere, and it will kill me if you still don't trust me."

"I do trust you, Pearl. It feels right." He stole a kiss. "Just as right as being here with you like this."

Her heart melted into a big gooey mess. She'd wanted nothing more than this since she'd come back to town. She rolled onto her side and faced him. "Where do we go from here?"

"I think the first step is to enjoy the now." He kissed the tip of her nose. "And go public."

"People are going to talk," Pearl pointed out.

"Let them. It's nobody's business but ours."

"But what about your family? Your brother and father hate me."

"They don't even know you anymore. They're not going to change my mind. What about your family?"

"They already think you walk on water, so they'll be happy for us."

He smiled. "There's that. We'll start there." He reached over and pulled her to him. "I need to kiss you."

They made out like a couple of horny teenagers, only more intense than anything she'd ever felt before. They sipped and tasted and held on to each other, their embrace tight. They sighed and murmured endearments and made slow, sweet love into the wee hours of the morning.

Finally sated, Pearl melted into sleep with Tony spooned around her.

Chapter Thirty-One

"Pearl. Wake up." Tony hated to wake her, but he had to get to work. Fishermen kept crazy early hours like getting out of bed at three in the morning.

He'd only gotten a couple of hours sleep, but he felt more energized than when he'd had a full eight hours, obviously due to a big dose of Vitamin Pearl.

Blinking, Pearl grumbled, "Go away."

"Can't, baby." He had to get her out of bed because she was too much of a temptation, all cuddly warm in his bed. "Got to get you home and go to work."

She yawned. "Don't want to."

"The lobsters wait for no man," he told her.

"I hate lobsters." She rolled away and presented him with her back.

He sat on the bed and bounced on it. "Wake up, buttercup."

"I hate you."

"No, you don't." He shook her shoulder.

"Don't make me hurt you."

"As if you could." He went in for the kill. "I see a spider crawling on your face."

"Noooooo!" She leaped from the bed and rubbed both hands across her face. "Get rid of it! Brush it off!"

She shrieked loud enough to blow out an eardrum or two and danced around the room while she batted at her face. He just couldn't help it. He busted a gut laughing.

Pearl rounded on him. "It's not funny."

"It kinda is." He grabbed her arms before she could pummel him. "There's no spider."

She stopped fighting him and glared at him. "You think this is a joke?" Her voice was still a little high and spikey. "You are a monster!"

He hugged her. Pearl's body still held the warmth of sleep. "I've got to go to work, baby. I need to take you home."

"What time is it?" She slumped against him.

"Time to go to work." He dropped a kiss onto the top of her head. "Get dressed and let me take you home."

"You're insane, you know that?"

"Just a working slob who needs to get up before the lobsters do. C'mon. I've got coffee made. I'll get you a cup while you get dressed."

"I might forgive you."

"I'm a lucky, lucky man."

"And don't you forget it," she said over her shoulder as she hunted down her clothes.

Just a half an hour later, they left his house and made their way to where his truck was parked. "What the fuck?"

Someone had taken a sledgehammer or something heavy and slammed it into the hood and both doors of the truck and its windows. The haze of love and great sex totally dissipated.

He ran his hand over the biggest dent on the driver's side. "I'm going to kill someone."

Pearl came up beside him. "Oh, my God! Who would do something like this?"

"I don't know, but when I find them, I'm going to seriously hurt them." He ran his hand through his hair. This was freaking unbelievable.

"Should we call the police?"

"Yeah, we definitely should. I'll call Gabe, too, to give you a ride home."

She reached into her purse and hauled out her phone. "Do you want me to take some pictures of the damage?"

"Couldn't hurt." He looked at said destruction, shook his head, and got seriously pissed. Who the hell did this, he asked himself again.

"Okay, I got shots of all the damage." Pearl put her phone back into her bag. "I'll email or text them to you later." She put her hand on his shoulder. "Is there anything else I can do?"

He shook his head. Punching buttons on his phone, he tried to reach Gabe. His phone went straight to voicemail. "Damn."

Pearl laid a hand on his arm. "What's wrong?"

"Gabe's not picking up. I have no way to get you home." He rubbed his hand across the back of his neck. "I'd call my father, but I don't want to get him out of bed."

"Don't worry about it. I can call an Uber. I'll just wait with you until the police get here."

He reached out and touched the whisper-soft skin of her cheek. "Thank you." Pearl was a miracle to him.

"I'm here for you, Tony," she murmured. "Always."

He'd count on her to keep that promise.

****

Pearl figured it must be around four a.m. when she

finally got home and ransacked her bag to find her keys. Sunrise was still at least an hour away. She and Tony had kissed each other quite thoroughly before he dropped her off after they shared an Uber. Her lips still tingled.

She found her keys and was all set to unlock her door when Opal pulled it open. "Where have you been?"

"Out, obviously." She squinted at Opal. "What are you doing up so early?"

"I dreamed about some new scenes for my work in progress and needed to write them down. Was that Tony who dropped you off?"

"Sort of. We shared an Uber." She put her purse on the table next to the door.

"An Uber." She wrinkled her brow. "Was the evening a success?"

"Oh, yeah." Remembering, Pearl sighed. "Like something in one of your romance novels. Until we went to Tony's truck. Someone took a bat or something to it and totally trashed it."

"Who would do that?" Opal rolled up the sleeves of her Wellesley College sweatshirt. "That's nuts."

"I need coffee," Pearl said as she moved to the kitchen.

"Good thing for you I just made some."

"You are my favorite sister."

"I will lord it over Ruby 'til the day I die." Opal dropped into one of the kitchen chairs. Her laptop was open, and she closed it. "So spill! I know something went down, what with you coming home at the break of dawn with your hair all crazy and mascara smeared under your eyes. No detail is too small."

Pearl brought her mug over to the table and sat. "I love him, Ope. I never stopped loving him."

"That's not a surprise."

"He says he loves me."

"That's not a surprise either. Anyone with eyes could see it coming from miles away."

Pearl blew across the top of her mug, then took a sip. Shuddering, she put the mug down. "Jeez Louise, Opal. That's not coffee. It's jet fuel."

"Nectar of the gods. So are you two back together?"

Pearl took another sip. "Yes."

"That's awesome!" Opal leaped up from her chair, rounded the table, and gave Pearl a tackle hug. "I'm so happy for you!"

She returned Opal's hug. "Not everyone's going to be happy about it. Gabe and his father hate me."

"They'll come around once they see how ecstatic you two are."

"I hope so. I'm so happy, Opal. I can't remember the last time I felt like this." She figured she might just burst from it.

"Then it'll all work out." Opal went back to her seat. "Who does he think trashed his car?"

Pearl shrugged. "He didn't say. I don't think he has a clue."

"I hope they find who did it."

"Me, too." She yawned and rubbed her gritty eyes. "I should go up to bed and see if I can catch another couple hours sleep."

"Sweet dreams," Opal said.

Pearl thought of Tony naked in bed last night, all sleepy and warm, and smiled. "They will be."

****

"What happened to your truck?" Gabe sounded almost cheerful.

"Somebody used my vehicle for batting practice. Got any ideas who?"

"You make anybody mad lately?"

"Any number of people." And Gabe was one of them. He chose not to bring that up. "The cops came and took a look at it, so let's head out." He needed to be on the water and working hard.

Gabe just grunted.

They worked in concert with each other. Haul up the pots, grab the lobsters, rebait the pots, and toss them back in the water. Band the claws so the lobsters didn't kill each other.

The monotony of it left Tony free to reflect on his amazing night with Pearl. If you had told him six months ago they'd be back together, he'd have asked you what you'd been smoking. Now that it was true, it felt right, like a lost piece of his soul clicked back into place. How had he ever lived without her?

Not well.

He'd made a mess of things with Jenny and had ended up hurting her, something he'd never wanted to do. But could he help it if she made plans about things that weren't going to happen?

Jenny. She was pretty mad at him, and when she got mad, she didn't always think right. Would she be foolish enough to wreck his truck? Normally, no, but if she caught wind that he was with Pearl, she would go batshit.

Batshit enough to use his poor truck for batting practice? It was entirely possible.

Maybe Gabe knew where Jenny had been last night. No, that was too far-fetched. Whoever had wrecked his truck had to have done it in the middle of the night. No way Gabe was with her then.

Still… "Have you seen Jenny lately?"

Gabe's head snapped up. He glared at him. "Why?"

"I was just wondering about her, how she's doing?"

"What do you care? You dumped her, remember."

"Doesn't mean I don't worry about her."

Gabe's hands fisted at his side. "You lost any right to worry about her when you ditched her. Leave her alone."

Tony put up both hands in front of him. "All right. Nothing to get into a fight about."

"You have no idea how much you hurt her. All she ever wanted was for you to love her."

"So I should have stayed with her even though I couldn't give her what she wanted? How would that have made anyone happy?"

"Never mind. I've said way too much already."

Interesting. "Do you know something I don't know?"

"I know lots of things you don't."

Tony just had to ask. "Do you know where she was last night?"

Gabe's eyebrows crashed together. "What? Why?"

Tony stared at him and knew when dawn broke at Marblehead. Gabe's face turned a vivid red, and his jaw clenched. "You're going to blame Jenny for messing up your truck."

Whoa. He needed to talk it back. "I'm not blaming

anybody."

"Yes, you are, you little pansy ass bitch! You're blaming Jenny." Gabe pounded a fist against the side of a hydraulic lift. "I don't even know who you are anymore."

"The same goes for you. You've been pissed off for a while now, and you need to get your stupid ass over it!"

"Fuck. You're just not worth it. You threw away the best thing you ever had just to crawl back up Pearl Marlowe's butt. Don't come moping around when she leaves you high and dry again."

Tony stopped from jumping over and strangling Gabe with his bare hands. "You shut your damn mouth about Pearl. You don't know anything about her."

Gabe's eyes narrowed. "You're fucking her again, aren't you?"

Tony's jaw nearly cracked. "You don't get to use that kind of language when you're talking about Pearl."

"So you don't deny it. You are fucking Pearl." Gabe's eyes glittered in triumph. "Pathetic. I bet you think you're in love with her again."

Tony counted to ten in his head so he wouldn't go over, punch Gabe in his ugly-ass nose, and then throw him overboard. "I don't think I'm in love with her. I know I'm in love with her again. So watch your mouth."

"Shit." Apparently, that was all Gabe had to say.

Good thing. Now, if only he could keep his mouth shut, everything would be hunky-dory.

Nobody talked about Pearl that way, especially not his brother.

Chapter Thirty-Two

"The word around town is that you and Tony are back together." Laura made herself at home on one of the porches of Marlowe House that looked out over the water. It was one of Pearl's favorite spots, with garden pots loaded with flowers and a cool breeze off the harbor. Maybe a little too cool. Pearl had to wear a sweater and Laura a jacket.

Laura'd invited herself over for lunch. Pearl was happy that Laura had brought lunch. While her cooking was getting better, she still had trouble whipping up something with the wave of a hand. "The word is correct and accurate. We are back together." Pearl could hardly believe it herself.

Laura stomped her feet and rubbed her hands together. "I knew it. When did it happen?"

Pearl sat across from Laura and tucked her feet underneath her. "About a week ago. We had a really serious conversation and worked a bunch of things out. He asked me to dinner and took me home afterward. Laura," she sighed, "my feet haven't touched the ground since."

"I'm so happy for you. You two were meant to be, you know." She tapped the side of her head. "I know these things."

"It was all so wonderful until someone trashed his truck."

"Some people are saying Jenny did it."

"Jenny? Why would she do that to Tony?" Pearl was totally perplexed.

Laura leaned forward. "Rumor has it that she got word that you and Tony were getting pretty chummy at Seasters in Wellfleet, and she went ballistic."

"Are you kidding me?"

"Nope, and there's more. Apparently she got a call in the middle of her shift at Bradford Street Seafood and just took off. Said she had a family emergency, but get this. She didn't go home. She just kind of disappeared."

"Maybe the family emergency was out of town. I mean, the hospital is in Hyannis."

"All her family was having dinner at her sister's house. Then someone said they thought they saw her sitting in her car across the street from Tony's house."

Pearl waved it away. "We'd have seen her."

"Probably not with all those stars in your eyes."

Pearl's heart thumped hard. "If that's the case, then I really feel sorry for her. I know she's hurt, but she isn't trying to get over it. She practically attacked me after the last reunion committee meeting. Remember how she left early?"

Laura wrinkled her forehead. "Yeah."

"Well, she was waiting for me outside and tried to scare me away from Tony. She was pretty unreasonable."

"Do you think she's headed toward boiled-bunny territory?" Laura's eyes rounded and practically bugged out of her head.

"I have no idea where she's headed. I'm truly sorry she's so hurt and upset. I'm sorry that my happiness comes at her expense."

"But not sorry enough to give up Tony."

Pearl shook her head. "I left him once, and it was the worst decision of my life. I'm not giving Tony up for anything or anyone. And I will tell him about Jenny." A laugh burbled out of her. "I'm so happy, Laura. I feel like the heroine at the end of a fairy tale."

"If only you could get a fleet of servants to do your housework for you."

Pearl laughed. Laura could always make her laugh. "Around here, I'd have to train clams and lobsters to swab my floors."

"There you go." Laura looked out over the harbor. "Just watch out for Jenny. If she was the one to do this to Tony's truck, then she's freaking dangerous." She turned back to Pearl. "She tried like crazy to get him into her bed after you left. It took her a long time."

"That's sad."

"You're telling me. He kept to himself and didn't date for years. He just went out here and there with summer girls. You know, the ones who come from Bulgaria on a workers' visa. Jenny just wore him down. They've only been together for a couple of years."

"I see."

"I can't believe this about Jenny. She's always been a pain in the butt, but she was never crazy. She never did anything unhinged. But then again, that's when she was with Tony and before you came back to town."

"Well, I'm not going anywhere, so she needs to throttle it back and settle down." Pearl stood. "I'm starved. Let's get into that pasta salad you brought over."

"Good idea. Iced tea will go great with it."

"You got it."

Pearl made sure to take one more look up and down the beach before she followed Laura into the house. Who knew who was watching?

****

"Mom, can I talk to you?" Tony walked into his mother's kitchen.

She stirred the vat of kale soup she was making. The savory smell of the linguiça, the bite of the kale, and intoxicating mix of exotic spices always spelled comfort food for him. Called Portagee Penicillin, it cured whatever ailed you. "Tony. Is this about Gabe?"

"You know about the fight I had with Gabe." How did his mother find out about everything before he had a chance to tell her? She was spooky that way.

Mom gave the pot one last stir, then turned the heat down. "He might have said something to your father who of course told me. You're back together with Pearl."

"Please don't yell at me about it because I've got to tell you I'm really happy, and I'm determined to make it work with her."

She crossed to him, stood on her tiptoes, grabbed his face, and gave him a smacking kiss on each cheek. "I'm glad you're happy. That's all I've ever wanted for you, and it's made me unhappy to see you unhappy, but—

"I've been spending time with Pearl, and I believe her when she says she's here to stay. She's got a lot of pride and has done a great job turning that house into a bed and breakfast. She's not walking away from that or from you."

Tony closed his eyes in relief. "You don't know how good it is to hear you say that."

"It's only the truth. I'm working on your father, and he's coming around about Pearl but not the fish market yet." She put a finger up. "He's a stubborn Portagee. It'll take some time."

"Gabe's totally unreasonable about this. He won't listen to a word I say, and he's all up in my grill, saying horrible things about Pearl."

"Come. Sit down." She grabbed his hand and led him to the table. "Gabe's got himself tied all up in knots, and he can't see beyond that. He's just not in a good place." She patted his hand. "You? You're in a very good place, and you need to cut him some slack."

"What's going on with Gabe?"

Frowning, she shook her head. "That's not my story to tell."

"Something's got to happen because the tension on the boat is thick enough to cut with a knife. He's like this ticking time bomb about to blow up."

"It might come to that." Sadness crept into his mother's gaze. "We can't save him from himself."

"Well, working with him is a pain in the...it's really hard."

"Be patient. What's the story on your truck?"

"The insurance will cover the repairs, up to a point. It's not too bad since they're paying for my rental car." He rubbed the back of his neck.

"Do you have any idea who did it?"

Tony waited a minute before he answered. "I might." That's all he was going to say on the subject until he had a come-to-Jesus moment with Jenny. He wasn't looking forward to it, to say the least.

"What are you going to do?"

"I'll figure it out."

She stood and patted him on the head. "You will. Want some soup?"

He never passed up his mother's kale soup. "Please." He looked up at the kitchen clock. "I've got to meet Pearl in about an hour."

"Here," Delores said, "take enough for the both of you to go."

He thought of Pearl's cooking versus his mother's cooking. "Thanks, Mom. You're the best."

"Of course I am. Why are you surprised?" She sighed. "Just be careful."

He thought about his truck again. "I will be."

****

Pearl checked her reflection in the shiny part of the toaster one more time. Anticipation pricked and pulled at her whole body. Excitement zapped from nerve ending to nerve ending while she fussed and waited for Tony. He'd called her and told her not to worry about food, which was a relief.

She'd fussed with absolutely everything, candles, music, lingerie, his favorite beer, the whole nine yards.

It would be an early night, as Tony had to get up at the butt crack of dawn to battle with the sea. She'd always known fishing was a dangerous business. It was not a career you chose lightly. Tony didn't choose to become a fisherman. It was in his DNA.

She'd have to get used to the fact that fishing was pretty darn dangerous. She remembered tragic events when a boat would go down and a whole crew was lost. All the legendary stories of shipwrecks on Peaked Hill Bars had gone into history, but the fact remained that you took your life into your hands when you went out to harvest the sea.

She went cold at the thought of sending Tony out to work in the morning and of him not coming back at night.

Tonight, though, he was safe on dry land and coming over to be with her, which was plenty amazing to her on its own.

She heard the clamshells paving her driveway crunch, and her heart stuttered. It had to be Tony. Her mouth stretched into a huge smile as she went to the door. She opened it before he could knock.

There he stood, all dark wavy hair and dark eyes, wearing pressed khakis and a black polo shirt, holding a cooler in one hand and a cotton-candy-colored rose in the other. "Hey," he said.

She smiled. "Hey back."

He held out the rose as he stepped across the threshold. Taking it from him, she brought it to her nose and sniffed. Always thoughtful, he'd removed the thorns. Though the color was gaudy, it smelled divine. "Thank you." She shut the door behind him.

He held up the cooler. "My mother made kale soup. I begged her to give me some. Hope that's okay."

Her mouth watered because of the soup and the man who held it. "It's more than okay. I wonder if she'll give me the recipe."

"Only if you give her a kidney or something. That recipe is going with her to the grave."

"Are you hungry right now? We should heat it up."

He put the cooler on the floor, then straightened. "I'm hungry for this." Pulling her into his arms, he kissed her and stole her breath.

She could die in the sweetness of Tony's kiss. It coaxed and teased while he savored and treasured.

His strong arms wrapped around her, and his hands landed on her butt and squeezed. Heat poured off him, and she sizzled with the intimacy of it. She looped her arms around his neck and let herself be carried away.

They eventually had to come up for air. Tony looked around. "Where's your family?"

"Not here," she said, her voice breathy. "Ruby's at her own place now, Opal's gone somewhere on a research trip, and Sterling's in Boston."

"Then I've got you all to myself."

"Looks like it." She went back up on her tiptoes and gave him a brief smack of a kiss on his mouth. "Whatever are we going to do?"

Tony chuckled. "I might be able to come up with an idea or two."

"I just bet you can."

"But we need to eat first. I'm starved."

They worked together in the kitchen, adding the finishing touches to the meal. Intimate and homey, Pearl hoped for many more times in the future just like this one.

They could have this every day and every night forever if they wanted to. Right that minute Pearl yearned for it above all things.

They sat at the table in Marlowe House's airy kitchen as if they did it every day, with a tureen of fragrant, steaming soup and a loaf of warm Portuguese bread and a ceramic bud vase holding the pink rose between them. So ordinary, yet so special.

Pearl lifted a spoonful of soup, blew over it, and put it in her mouth. The rich, spicy taste of the linguiça transformed the little red round baby potatoes into a rich, buttery bite, which counterpointed well with the quiet tang of the kale. Little white pearl beans added texture. "This is so good! Your mother is a magician."

Tony paused while buttering a slice of bread. "She tells me that all the time."

"She's right, you know." Pearl paused. "Did you tell her about us?"

"I didn't have to. Gabe had already gotten to her." He grimaced. "My conversation with Gabe is another story, but Mom is happy if I'm happy."

"What happened with Gabe?"

"I might have suggested that Jenny was the person who wrecked my truck." He buttered a piece of the bread. "Gabe went ballistic."

Dear God. She dropped her spoon. "Do you really think Jenny did it?"

"I think she could have done it if she was mad enough, but I've got no proof. Who else hates me that much?"

"She doesn't hate you. She hates me." And, oh crap. "Do you think she knew we were together Sunday night?" She bit her lower lip. "I should tell you that she came after me after the last reunion committee meeting."

"What do you mean, came after you?"

"She confronted me about stealing you from her."

"Damn. You didn't pay any attention to her, right?"

"No." Pearl shook her head. "If anything, I pitied her."

"She'd hate that."

Pearl didn't think so. "I think she wanted me to

give in to her poor little old self-pity act. Laura told me some things about the night we were at Seasters. Jenny got a call at work and took off. She said it was a family emergency, but nobody knows where she went. It's very possible Jenny damaged your vehicle."

He took a deep breath, then flashed her a lopsided grin. "I don't want to talk about Jenny right now."

"What do you want to talk about?" She liked the naughty look in his eyes.

"Oh, I don't know. Maybe what I've got planned to do with you later on tonight."

"Really. Do tell."

"Well," he said as he leaned back in his chair, "I thought I'd start with kissing you all over."

"Hmmmmm. That sounds promising."

"There's more where that came from."

"Is there?"

"You bet."

"So send me a clue," she commanded.

"I might massage interesting places on your body."

"How interesting?"

He nodded his head. "Very interesting."

"Like where?" Little shivers ran through her. She had a good imagination.

"That's for me to know and you to find out."

"You're evil, you know that?"

He waggled his eyebrows. "And you love it."

Oh, she did. She really did. "I might."

"You know you do."

"I don't know. You might have to show me."

He smiled, stood, and extended his hand to her. Beckoned. "Challenge accepted."

She couldn't resist him. She didn't want to.

Standing, she placed her hand in his. "Let's go."

He brushed his lips across her knuckles and pressed a kiss into her palm. "Lead the way."

****

They walked hand in hand up to Pearl's suite at the top of the house. Tony's nerves twanged like harp strings. He wanted to take his time with her tonight, to give her slow wave upon wave of pleasure. He'd been too eager on Sunday, and he was going to make it up to her.

He'd hardly thought of anything else the past couple of days.

The door to her domain was already open. So were the windows, and sheer white curtains danced on the gentle sea breeze. The walls were painted a soft, fragile, spring-bud green. Framed photos of Pearl with her sisters and brother hung on the walls. Over the fireplace she'd placed old photos of Pearl and her family, including their parents. On top of an antique Peter Hunt decorated dresser stood a photo of her parents on their wedding day. He wandered over and picked it up for closer inspection.

"They were so happy," Pearl said as she came up behind him. Wrapping her arms around him, she sighed. He felt her soft breath flutter over his neck. "So much in love. Even as children we all knew that." She pressed her cheek against the space between his shoulders. "That's all I really ever wanted. To be in love like they were."

He turned to take her into his arms. "I love you like that." He kissed her. "I cherish you. I always have."

She snuggled against him. "I love you, Tony. I never stopped loving you."

"It's the same for me, Pearl. I never stopped loving you." Tony dropped a kiss on the top of her head.

She pulled his head down and angled her mouth over his. Her soft lips tasted so sweet, so familiar, yet so fresh and unknown, both his past and his future together at the same time.

He swung her up into his arms, walked the short distance to her bed, and laid her tenderly on the flowered quilt. He toed off his shoes and lay down on his side next to her. Smoothing her hair off her brow, he marveled at how soft and silky it was. He nuzzled her ear and breathed in the rose scent of her shampoo.

She squirmed. "That tickles."

He nipped at her earlobe. "Makes you a little wiggly?" He scraped his teeth across her earlobe again.

She turned on her side to face him and twined her arms around his neck. "Tony."

"Pearl."

"Make love with me," she whispered.

He chuckled. "I thought you'd never ask."

"Please," she whimpered. "Don't make me beg."

How he loved this woman. "Tonight is all for you."

She melted against him. "No. Tonight is for us."

He would have sighed, except he had a Y chromosome. "Let me love you."

She curved her lips into a smile that was as old as Eve. "Let me love you."

Kissing her soft, warm lips, he ran his hand down her torso, making sure his touch told her how much he adored her.

She hummed as he uncovered her, the sound as sweet as the music of the angels. When he finished he sat and feasted his eyes. "You are so beautiful."

Pearl blushed a pretty shade of pink. "One of us has too many clothes on."

"Let me see what I can do about that."

Tony wrangled with his own clothes. She welcomed him with open arms as he stretched out against her. "Just lay back and let me adore you."

Her eyes sparkled as she looked at him. "Yes, please."

****

Pearl sighed at every pass of Tony's hands. She squirmed as she threaded her hands through his heavy, dark hair, holding on for dear life as he kissed his way down her belly. He nuzzled her belly button, and she laughed, then moaned as he tracked open mouth kisses down to her thighs. He lifted first one knee, then the other and laved the sensitive skin behind them. Placing her knees on his shoulders, he kissed his way back up her thighs. The first pass of his tongue on her most sensitive spot made her yelp. Subsequent flicks, nibbles, and kisses had her moaning with pleasure.

"You are so beautiful here, so pink and pretty," he murmured as his mouth hovered over her, his warm breath fanning against her clit.

His big hands palmed her derriere as he lifted her to his mouth. It was magic, pure magic he was making, and she was helpless to do anything but go along for the ride. Sensations built, one upon the other, again and again, until with a cry she came apart against his mouth, drenching his lips with her cream.

And still he kept stroking her with his talented tongue, chasing those last elusive spasms until she was weak and breathless. She felt him smile against her. "Tony—"

"Shhhh," he rumbled. "I want you to come again."

She wiggled, but he held her steady against his mouth. Impossibly, the feelings roared through her again, and once more he made her fly.

"Oh, yeah," he murmured. His eyes were bright as he stared at her, his mouth wet from her juices. Her body still sang with the aftershocks of her two climaxes, and still she wanted more. But first of all, more than anything, she craved a taste of Tony. "My turn."

His grin was quick and wolfish. "Who am I to deny a lady what she wants?" He pressed hot, open-mouthed kisses back up her body, then reaching his destination, he took one of her painfully erect nipples into his mouth and nipped it. She jolted at the touch and then sighed as he soothed it with his tongue.

She held his head against her for a moment more, then pulled him up to kiss her. He tasted of her honey and the unforgettable essence of the man himself. Drunk on the flavor of his mouth, she craved more.

Wiggling out from under him, she slid down his torso, rubbing her breasts along his six-pack. Reaching her destination, she ran her hands along his long, thick erection and licked her lips. "You might want to hold on to something."

He barked out a laugh, and then he whimpered when she licked up and down his shaft. She palmed the root of him while she swirled her tongue around and over the bulbous head of his penis. Reveling in the impatient moisture that dewed the tip of his penis, she realized she wanted to be joined with him, to hold him deep within her core.

"Tony, we need a condom. They're in my

nightstand."

"You always did plan ahead," he whispered. Reaching over, he pulled the drawer nearly out of the nightstand and grabbed the condoms. He ripped open a plastic packet and held the rubber out to her. "You do it."

Laughing, she took it. "I'm glad I bought the extra-large size."

"Flattery will get you everywhere."

"This is the only place I want to be." She licked her lips as she rolled the condom down, down, down the hard length of his penis.

He held her so she couldn't lower herself onto him, then smiled a wicked smile as he positioned her so that he rubbed his erection against her wet, sensitive opening. Once, twice, he moved in long slow strokes against her. "Tony," she keened. "Now. Please." He locked his eyes with hers and let go. She pressed down on top of him, and he moved up into her with one sure, possessive thrust.

His girth and huge length stretched inside her, and she moved her hips to accommodate him. He seemed to like that because he made a very masculine, very aroused sound deep in his throat. Shifting his body, he rolled her over and began to thrust in earnest.

Her nerves singing with joy, she wrapped her legs over his ass as she met him stroke for stroke, totally thrilled by the sounds he made as he loved her. Changing his position slightly, he hunched into her while his mouth suckled her nipples.

Each pull of his mouth sent shivers in her body and moans of pleasure from her mouth. Her body began to race once more. "Tony!"

"Yeah, baby, I feel it," he managed around clenched teeth. "Let it go." His voice grated along her already overloaded nerves. "Come with me!"

They shifted again, Tony thrusting deeper, and Pearl wrapped her legs around his back, her heels digging in. He hammered into her, pumping high and hard. She was with him all the way.

It was glorious, and she gave herself to him once more. Her body came apart, squeezing around him with hard, powerful spasms, and she cried out as she came. Seconds later, he erupted inside her, over and over again, emptying as he pounded into her with three last thrusts. She took all he had to give, overwhelmed with the great joy of it.

****

"Damn, Pearl, you're amazing." Tony stared down with wonder at the woman who trembled beneath him. Making sure he was supporting his weight on his elbows, he relished the last few moments of being linked so intimately with her, of feeling her body shivering with the aftershocks of their shared pleasure.

"You're pretty amazing yourself." Her smile rocked his world. He would do anything to make her happy.

He separated from her and, after discarding the condom, came back to bed so he could wrap her up and protect her. She went so still and so silent he nearly died right there, staring straight into her eyes, trying to read her heart. The moment froze for him, and he knew he'd take it to his grave, the sight, the scent, the feel of her in his arms.

She hummed and slid her hand down his torso to cup him. He sucked in a breath while her small, delicate hand stroked his shaft, arousing him once more.

Their loving this time was slow and serious. She wept this time as she came, and he chased each tear with his tongue, tasting, then kissing them away.

The next time she moved down his body and loved him with her mouth and clever hands. She was going to kill him dead with her pretty lips wrapped around his cock. He gritted his teeth to hold on, to savor her. When he could not hold back anymore, he joined his body with hers, moving deep, skating along on the sharp edge of his climax. He toppled off that edge, bringing Pearl with him as they shattered into a million pieces.

Time had no meaning for them. They made love and dozed, only to rouse and make love again. They were voracious for each other until sleep claimed them.

She woke near dawn to find him getting dressed. The sky was already lit with the pinks and lavenders of the impending sunrise. He kissed her lightly to tell her he was going.

But she was a woman in love. She got up with him and made him coffee.

She wished she could wake up this way for the rest of her life.

Chapter Thirty-Three

Ruby stood in her shop, hands fisted on her hips, making sure everything was just perfect for her gala opening. Pearl and Opal showed up, arms full of boxes and trays of food. Ruby ran to the door. "Hey, thank you! Let me take some of that."

"There's more in the car," Opal said.

"I made some canapés," Pearl said.

"Uh, that's great," Ruby managed to say.

"I promise they are good." Pearl chuckled as she moved to the buffet table and listened to her sisters speak sotto voce.

"What did she make?" Ruby hissed.

"She's been very mysterious, so I don't have the first clue." Opal set down her boxes on a table covered by a white cloth decorated by bright hand-painted flowers. "Of course, it's all sunbeams and puppies and rainbows and kittens since she and Tony are back together. Oh, and the occasional unicorn covered in glitter."

Ruby's eyes widened to the size of dinner plates. "So the scuttlebutt is true?"

Opal nodded.

Pearl chuckled again.

Ruby slapped her hard against her arm. "And you didn't think to tell me?" Her voice squeaked at the end of her question. "What kind of sister are you?"

"A very busy one." Opal twirled around to take in all that Ruby had accomplished. "This is totally made of awesome," she cooed as she pulled Ruby into a quick little dance. "I'm so proud of you."

"What's going on here? I thought this was a serious establishment."

Both Ruby and Opal turned and squeed. "Sterling!" Ruby ran and tackle hugged him. "I didn't know if you were going to get here."

He hugged Ruby closer, then disentangled them. "Of course I'm here, squirt. I wouldn't miss it."

"My turn!" Opal pulled Ruby out of the way. "It's so good to see you!"

"It's not like I've been in Siberia or anything. You always know where to find me." Sterling smiled an indulgent smile. He kissed Opal's cheek. "Hey, Opie."

"Don't call me Opie."

"Come on. You've got red hair and freckles, and you're really little. All you need is a fishing pole. That's Opie for the win." Sterling leaned in and kissed her cheek.

"Gah," Opal said.

"And you have such a way with words."

Opal swatted him on the arm. "Stop it."

"Stop it, children." Ruby swept back into the main showroom. "We've got work to do."

"Yeah, Sterling." Opal smirked. "Get to work."

He flicked the tip of her nose, then turned to Ruby. "What do you want me to do?"

She pointed to a copper tub. "Put some ice in that, and chill the champagne."

He gave her a jaunty salute and went on his way to do her bidding.

"And you"—Ruby shoved glass cleaner and a roll of paper towels at Opal—"Get to cleaning the display cases."

Opal took the supplies from Ruby. "Damn, you're bossy."

"And I'm very proud of it." She clapped her hands. "Let's hustle, people. Time's a-wastin'. And where is Pearl?"

"Right here." Pearl juggled a couple platters full of food at the refreshment table. "Come check it out."

Pearl watched all three of her siblings stop what they were doing to gape at her. "What's wrong? Do I have mud on my skirt?"

They relaxed.

"What did you bring?" Ruby wanted to know.

"Tell me where to put these, and you can check it out yourself."

Ruby took one of the platters and sniffed. "These smell good."

"Wait 'til you taste one."

Pearl followed Ruby to the refreshments' table, and they both put the plates down. That done, Ruby lifted the foil off the one she carried and peeked. "These look amazing." She picked up one perfect golden-brown triangle of flaky pastry. "It's still warm. What's in it?"

"Oh, for God's sake, Ruby, just eat it." Pearl rolled her eyes. "Honest to God, I didn't fill it with poison."

Cautiously bringing it to her mouth, Ruby sniffed it once more, then took one tiny bite. Her eyes widened as she chewed. "Omigawd, Pearl! This is delicious!" She popped the rest of it into her mouth. "Mmmmmm. What is the filling?" she managed around the bite.

Pearl grinned with pride. "Brie and tomato

chutney."

Sterling and Opal hotfooted it to the buffet. "Let me try one," Opal demanded.

"I'm the oldest, so I should go first." Sterling reached over to pluck a pastry off the plate.

Laughing, Pearl picked up the platter and held it out to Sterling and Opal. It wasn't so long ago they'd run as fast and far away as they could from her food.

Oh, how the mighty had fallen. She sent mental thanks to Delores Cabral.

"Only take one," Ruby grumped. "They're for the opening."

Sterling and Opal each took one and clinked them together like they were making a toast. In unison, they each took a big bite.

"This is really good, Pearlie." Sterling polished it off.

Opal nodded, her mouth full.

Ruby clapped her hands. "Okay, everybody. Get back to work!"

"What do you want me to do?" Pearl rearranged the pastries on the platter to hide the empty places her family had filched from, smiling to herself. She'd worked long and hard to get these Brie bites exactly right, and she felt gratified that they were a hit.

"Help Opal, please." Ruby gave her a quick hug. "Congrats on the Brie things. They're really good."

Warmed by the praise, Brie things notwithstanding, Pearl smiled. "Thank you."

"Now." Ruby gave her a little push. "Go help Opal."

"Yes, ma'am. Ruby?"

"What?"

"This is going to be awesome. I'm so proud of you."

Ruby grinned. "Thank you. Now get to work."

Pearl did as she was told.

****

"Holy crap. There's a lot of people here," Tony told Pearl when he made it to the party. "I think the whole town is here."

Pearl twined her fingers with his. She loved the feel of that calloused, warm paw of his. "Isn't it great? I think Ruby's Jewelry Design is a success."

"The jewelry is very pretty. Shiny. Sparkly."

Pearl held her breath as Tony checked out the selection of rings. It was too soon, their reunion too new to be thinking about rings and such.

Wasn't it?

Tony squeezed her hand and gave her one of his warmest gazes, the kind that made her tingle all over. Was it working today?

Hell, yes. In spades.

He brought her hand to his lips and kissed it. He did that a lot lately. She never got tired of it. She never would.

She flashed him her most intimate smile and kissed his knuckles.

"Jeez, you two need to get a room," Opal interrupted them. "Pearlie, you need to mingle. Pass some hors d'oeuvres around." She hip checked Tony. "Grab a bottle of champagne and refill some glasses."

"Hey. I'm a guest!"

"Sure you are, so be a useful guest. Go make some people happy with more champagne so they'll be inclined to buy something with a huge price tag attached to it."

"Pearl, did you know your sister is really bossy?" Tony said, the picture of offended.

"Both of them are. It's my curse." But she smiled as she said it.

He pulled a bottle of champagne out of an ice-filled silver wine bucket. Camille had collected them like they were old postage stamps. Pearl was glad Ruby was putting them to good use.

She walked over to Sterling, who was in a heated conversation with Baxter Oglethorpe, Ruby's landlord. Baxter was pretty dishy now, but back in school he'd been overweight, and kids had teased him mercilessly. She'd gone out of her way to be nice to him, but Sterling and Ruby had not liked him one bit. It was so ironic that Baxter was now Ruby's landlord. "May I interest you in a canapé?"

"Hey, Pearl. Good to see you. Ruby's been telling me all about the changes you're making at Marlowe House. I can't wait to get a tour." His brows knit across his forehead. "Have you joined the chamber of commerce yet? Do you want to be a member of the Rotary Club?"

Chamber of commerce? Rotary Club? She could only handle the tour right now. "Give me a call, and I'll set you up for a tour. I'll get back to you about the other things." She held up the platter. "Hungry?"

Sterling shook his head. "I'm good." Then his eyes widened as he saw new arrivals come through Ruby's front door. "Excuse me." He fought his way over to them.

Pearl recognized one of them as Alex Tudor. She also knew that Sterling had some extremely negative feelings regarding Alex. "I've got a bad feeling about this," she whispered as she followed her brother through the room.

****

"What are you doing here?" Sterling demanded as he shook his head at Alex.

"Me?" Alex was the picture of innocence. "Ruby invited me."

The man with Alex came in. "I'm going to go socialize."

Sterling bristled.

He left Sterling and Alex alone with Pearl.

"I see some hungry people over there." Pearl left with her platter of goodies. "Duty calls."

"So, Congressman, how're things?" Alex said, his voice so cool and flippant, like there was nothing serious at stake because they were talking.

Sterling guessed that for Alex, that was true. And since he always told the truth, "I can't be seen with you."

Alex guffawed. "What are you afraid of?"

Everything. "I don't owe you an explanation."

"Well, let me put it to you like this." Alex got right in Sterling's face. "You came to me, not the other way around."

Sterling's jaw nearly snapped in half. He realized that he should not be having this conversation with Alex where anyone could hear. Robert's private eyes could be anywhere.

"And you're going to scare away all of Ruby's customers if you treat them like you treat me. So," Alex said as he put his hand on Sterling's shoulder, "I'm going to congratulate your sister." He left.

Sterling clenched his hands into fists as he watched Alex go schmooze Ruby, then he looked away. He had to keep his eye on the prize. First the Senate, then the presidency. He couldn't let either him or his grandmother down.

Chapter Thirty-Four

Tony leaned against a doorway and watched the people crowding into Ruby's shop. He'd done his duty pouring the bubbly, so now he was taking a minute to watch the show. And by the show, he meant Pearl. She was gorgeous in a black dress that clung to her curves, and she wore those spikey shoes that looked impossible to walk in. Pearl made it seem easy.

She smiled and took people around to check out the display cases, and he figured a bunch of the sales Ruby was racking up were because Pearl got the clients to open their wallets and whip out the plastic. She was smart, sexy, and most important of all, she was his.

He didn't want to waste another minute without his ring on her finger. Not the old ring. That had way too much bad luck attached to it. No, he'd been checking out Ruby's handcrafted rings. He didn't know much about jewelry, but he could tell Ruby's were something really special. And who better to know what suited Pearl than her sister?

He'd take Pearl to Race Point at sunset, surprise her with a fancy picnic, and when the time was right, he'd get down on one knee and pop the question. She'd say yes, fall into his arms, and they'd kiss to seal the deal.

He knew he was grinning like an idiot, but he couldn't help it. He got all turned on watching his girlfriend work the room.

The bell above the door rang, and Tony took his gaze off his best girl to see who the newcomer was.

Uh-oh. Hurricane Jenny had arrived. Why would Jenny, of all people, come to a Marlowe family function? She saw him right away, of course, and glared as she bulldozed her way through the packed shop right to him.

His stomach clenched. He knew that look on Jenny's face, and it didn't bode well for anybody in her crosshairs. Tightening his arms across his chest, he battened down all his emotional hatches.

"Tony." Jenny's voice was a sharp shard of ice cutting through the crowd. "I thought I'd find you here."

Her voice was loud enough to bring a hush to the room. Great.

Just great.

"What are you doing here? I can't believe you were invited."

"There are some things you need to know."

Okay, this should be good. "Let's go someplace that's not here, and you can tell me."

"I don't want to go someplace else. I think you should know right away. I'm pregnant, and you're the daddy."

His stomach plummeted to the floor and landed with a thunk. "What?" Maybe he hadn't heard her right.

"I'm pregnant, and you're the daddy," she repeated, only slower and louder.

His gaze slid right and left and found Pearl staring him, her eyes wide open and full of questions.

"As I said, this is not the place to talk about this.

Let's go someplace quiet where there aren't as many people around to overhear what we're saying."

"Fine." She whipped her huge bag over her shoulder. "Where do we go?"

His mind blanked. "Uh, how about the Provincetown Inn?" Where he'd actually broken up with her.

She nodded. "I'll meet you there." She stomped her way out.

Tony swallowed, his throat constricting painfully as he sought out Pearl. He wished he hadn't.

She stared at him, eyes wide with disbelief. He considered going over to her and reassuring her, but he didn't want any more scenes during Ruby's big moment. He'd talk to Pearl after he'd talked to Jenny.

Still he longed to reassure her. But then she looked away and turned her back to him.

Fine. One dumpster fire at a time. Pearl said she loved him. That meant she'd believe him once he got to her after talking to Jenny.

Jenny first.

****

"What just happened?"

Pearl flinched when Opal touched her back. "Damned if I know."

"Do you want me to take you home?"

"No." She shook her head. "This is Ruby's day. I'm not going to bail." She squared her shoulders and pasted a smile on her face.

Opal squeezed Pearl's shoulder. "That's my girl. Let's show them what Marlowe women are made of."

Pearl snorted. "Genetically, we do have a healthy dose of Camille in our backbones."

"That's what she told us. If it's true, it's the best Camille gift ever." Opal hip checked her. "Come on. Let's sell some jewelry."

Pearl was swallowed by the same numbness she felt when Henry had thrown her to the wolves. Today was not about her. It was about Ruby.

Tomorrow she could freak out about Jenny having Tony's baby. Right now? She couldn't, wouldn't even try to wrap her head around that possibility.

Why now? When everything was going well.

Why not now? She knew Tony had slept with Jenny, so the entire pregnant thing could be real.

And that? Totally sucktastic, having the truth of that brought home in a room full of people. She just couldn't think about it, deal with it, right now.

Ruby sashayed up to her. "You good?" Her face was full of concern.

"No, but I'll survive." Pearl hugged Ruby. "Point me toward the folks with the money."

Ruby kissed her cheek. "I love you. I'm super pissed at Jenny, though. How did she think ruining my grand opening would help her?"

"I love you, too. I'm also super pissed at Jenny." Pearl knew that for a fact. "It's just the kind of thing she would do. Now, let me go and do my job to salvage the afternoon by making you tons of money."

Ruby sniffed, her eyes watery, and slapped Pearl's butt. "Then you better get to it."

"Aye, aye, Captain." Overcome with love for her sister, she exclaimed, "I shall be the best seller of artisan jewelry you ever saw."

"Let me know if you need anything. I know some people who know some people. They can kill Jenny, and no one will ever find the body." Ruby checked out her manicure.

"Oh, you sweet talker, you." Pearl sighed. "I'll let you know."

Ruby frowned. "I'm sure Jenny's lying. Everyone in town knows that she kind of lost her mind when Tony broke up with her. And now that it's out that you and Tony are together again"—she shrugged—"she's even more squirrely."

"I'm sorry she's hurt, really, I am. But I can't pretend that I'm not thrilled Tony and I are together."

"It's all going to work out, you'll see. Karma has a huge present to give Jenny." Ruby gave her a quick hug. "Let's get back to work!"

"You're such a slave driver."

"All part of my charm, m'dear. All part of my charm."

Chapter Thirty-Five

"So do you want to tell me what the hell is going on?" Tony demanded as Jenny walked into the Pilgrim Room. He'd been sitting at the bar, fuming, while he waited for her to show up.

Pregnant? No way!

"Is that any way to speak to the mother of your child?"

He slid off the barstool. "Let's get a table. I don't want the whole bar to hear this conversation." Taking her elbow, he led her to the most private table in the bar.

He yanked out a chair. "Here. Sit."

Jenny sat.

"So. What are you up to?" Tony demanded, as if he didn't know. He was going to nip this thing in the bud.

She smiled. "I'm not up to anything. I just thought you should know that I'm pregnant, and you're the father."

"The hell I am. We haven't been together in a while now. You're on the pill."

"About that." She shrugged. "I kind of stopped taking it in January."

"Excuse me, what?" He shook his head to clear it. She couldn't have said what he heard her say. "You're lying."

"No, I really did. I just decided I wanted to get

298

pregnant so you'd marry me."

"You let me think you were using birth control, and you weren't?" What kind of person does that? He snorted. Jenny's type of person, that's who. "You don't look pregnant. How far along are you?"

"Probably about four months." She ticked off her fingers. "February, March, April, and now May."

He couldn't believe what he was hearing. "And you're just getting around to telling me now? At Ruby Marlowe's opening? Things just don't add up, Jenny. You picked today to cause a scene and embarrass Pearl and her family."

"Pearl, Pearl, Pearl. I'm so sick of everyone treating her like a princess." Jenny flicked a piece of lint off her sweater. "She's not a princess. She's a criminal."

He couldn't believe this. "Jenny," he snapped, "this isn't about Pearl. It's about a child, for Chrissakes." A child, which might or might not be real. He stabbed his fingers through his hair.

She smiled. If she'd been a cat, there would have been feathers coming out of her mouth. "Your child."

"I only have your word that you've been pregnant since February." How could she have stopped taking her pills and not tell him? Jenny was insane.

"I haven't been with anyone else but you. That makes you the father."

His breath sawed in and out of his nose. "I don't believe you. How do I know you're really pregnant? Just take you at your word?" He growled. "I don't think so."

"I figured you'd say that." She rummaged around in that massive purse of hers and pulled out a white plastic wand that kind of looked like a thermometer. "This is a home pregnancy test with a positive result. My test with a positive result." She held it out for him to take.

No way he was touching that thing. "Anybody could have peed on that stick. How do I know it's yours?"

"I knew you'd say that, too." She put the test stick back in her bag. "I'm willing to take another one."

He shook his head. She could easily cheat on another one. "I'll pick out the test, and you'll take it in front of my mother."

Her jaw dropped, turning her mouth into a little O. "That's embarrassing."

"No more embarrassing than you showing up at Ruby Marlowe's shop opening and announcing to the world that you're pregnant and I'm the father." His jaw clenched. "You did that on purpose to humiliate Pearl."

"That isn't fair. I went there to find you because I don't know where you keep yourself these days."

"You know where I live." And while he thought about it— "Do you know anything about my vehicle getting violated?"

"Violated?" She lifted an eyebrow. "That's kind of extreme, isn't it?"

"Someone took a heavy object and wrecked my truck. Did you do it?"

Her gaze shifted to the left. "And what if I did?"

God, she was one piece of work. "I'll press charges. Make you pay for the damage."

"You'd do that to the mother of your child?"

Fuck that. He stabbed his fingers through his hair. "I'm not the father of your child."

She smiled. "You'll see. And once you find out? You're going to marry me."

Tony's blood vessels popped, fizzled, and plain out exploded. "You need to listen to me. I'm not marrying you. Not now, not ever."

She turned hostile. "If you think I'm going to share my child with Pearl Marlowe, then you've got another thing coming to you."

Tony stared at this woman he'd once been fond of. "You leave Pearl out of this."

Jenny stood, fury in her eyes. "No. You leave Pearl out of this. She's not taking anything more away from me." She hitched her bag over her shoulder. "I'll call your mother to set a time to take another test."

Tony bounded to his feet. "Let me break it to her first."

"Whatever." Jenny turned on her heel and sashayed out of the bar.

He stayed there, rooted to the spot, his hands clenching and unclenching. If Jenny was pregnant, Tony was not the baby daddy. He knew this right down through his bones.

He had to get to Pearl and talk to her about this. He refused to let this mess with Jenny come between them, but it was probably too late. His heart sank.

No way he was the father of Jenny's baby. He pitied the guy who was.

Chapter Thirty-Six

"What a day." Opal dropped into a chair next to Pearl's. They sat enjoying the fuchsia-colored sunset over the harbor.

"You can say that again." Pearl took a sip of her chilled Riesling.

The sisters were alone in the main room on the first floor of Marlowe House sipping wine. Ruby had stayed at her shop, doing the bookkeeping for her fabulous first day in business. Sterling was in Camille's old office, taking care of the federal government's business.

"Have you heard from Tony?"

Shaking her head, Pearl said, "No."

"Are you worried?"

Good question. "Yes and no. Yes, I'm worried about Jenny maybe being pregnant. No, in that she's a big liar, hates me, and wants Tony to get back with her. I told you about Tony's truck."

"Yeah. Do you really think Jenny did the damage?"

Pearl sighed. "Tony does. Laura does."

"I haven't had much to do with Jenny. I wasn't here very often, and she was not in my circle of friends, but, man, she's way out of line."

"And maybe be pregnant with Tony's baby." God, that would be horrible, Jenny having Tony's first child. She hadn't thought about it before, but she realized now that she wanted very much to have Tony's child. If

Jenny really was pregnant, she'd be in Pearl's and Tony's lives forever.

"As you pointed out, she lies a lot." Opal shook her head.

"I'm really pissed that she cast a pall over Ruby's opening." Anger rose up anew at that factoid. "She used Ruby's opening to get at me. Pregnant or not, I won't forgive her for that. Ruby's probably the only one around who's defended Jenny."

Opal squeezed the bridge of her nose like she was trying to get rid of a headache. "What a mess."

"Ya think?" Pearl chugged her wine. She stood and waved her glass in Opal's direction. "There is too much air in this glass. Do you need a refill?"

Opal upended the contents of her wine goblet into her mouth, swallowed loudly, and handed it to Pearl. "Yes, please."

Pearl was about to take Opal's glass when someone with a very persistent fist knocked on the front door.

"Tony?" Opal raised her eyebrows.

Pearl's heart clenched. "Tony."

Opal leaped up and rescued the glasses from Pearl. "You go get the door. I'll hightail it out of here."

Pearl bit her tongue. She wasn't sure about Tony right now, and she didn't blame Opal for making herself scarce. "Thanks, Opal."

"No worries." She tilted her head toward the door. "You better let him in."

"I know." Pearl's legs forgot how to move. "Coming," she yelled. She was proud that she sounded a lot calmer than she felt.

She pulled the door open, and a very despondent Tony stood there. "You look terrible."

303

He stepped in and pulled her into his arms and just clung to her. "Jesus, Pearl. I need this."

"Come on in." She loosened his grip on her. "Tell me what's going on." After closing the door, she walked him over to the sofa and sat him down. "Do you want a drink?"

"Hell, yes." He forked his fingers through his hair.

"Beer or something stronger?"

"Something stronger, please."

Pearl poured two fingers of ancient single malt scotch into one of Camille's antique crystal glasses and brought it to him. "Here you go."

He took it and downed it in one big gulp. Hissing, he put the glass down with a big clunk.

"More?"

He shook his head no. "I need to talk to you."

She sat next to him and touched his arm. "What's going on?"

"She's crazy, Pearl. Batshit out of her mind. She insists she's pregnant, and I'm the father. I'm pretty sure I can't be, but Jenny? She's certain about it."

"Is she even pregnant?" She put her hand over her mouth. "Never mind. I shouldn't have asked."

"I've got my doubts. She claims that she stopped taking the pill back in January."

Pearl gasped. "She stopped taking birth control and didn't tell you? Who does that?"

"Those were my exact words. She's still got to prove to me she's pregnant first."

"How will you find out for real?" Pearl wanted to know.

"I'm going to make her take another test under my mother's very watchful eye. If that one is positive, then we'll really have to come up with a plan."

Pearl's ears buzzed. "A plan?"

"Yeah. If she's pregnant, Jenny wants me to marry her."

"Marry her? Would you really marry her? Why?" Heartsick, Pearl could barely speak.

Tony stood, and started to pace. "I don't want to marry her."

"You sound like there's a chance you would marry her," Pearl said in a shaky whisper.

He stopped pacing. "Let's not get ahead of ourselves. Most likely Jenny isn't pregnant."

"A lot of people who make a child together don't necessarily get married. People co-parent," Pearl pointed out.

"Like I said, don't put the cart before the horse." He dropped down next to her. "I hope Jenny didn't ruin Ruby's opening."

Pearl cleared her throat and found her voice. "No, she didn't. Ruin Ruby's opening, that is. There were a few uncomfortable moments, though."

He touched a lock of her hair and twirled it in his fingers. "I'm so sorry."

"I've gone through worse." It didn't make it any less humiliating.

"She all but admitted that she was the one who messed up my truck."

"What are you going to do about that?"

"I don't know." He swallowed. "I really don't know."

Pearl sat there with Tony in the type of silence that made him itch. She had to do something. "Are you hungry?"

Doreen Alsen

Shaking his head, he said, "No. I should probably go to my parents' house and tell my mother what's going on. I want to get this thing over with as soon as possible."

He stood and pulled Pearl up and wrapped her in his arms. "It's all going to work out, I promise." He kissed her, warm, gentle, and comforting. God, how she loved him.

As she watched him leave, she hoped with all her heart that Tony was right. Their future depended on it.

****

"If Jenny's pregnant, you're going to marry her."

"Ma." He'd known she was going to say this. "Things are different today."

"Your child is going to have your name on it." She pointed at him. "My first grandchild won't be illegitimate. You will marry Jenny."

"I'm not in love with Jenny, and there are lots of ways people who are not married have a child and co-parent." He remembered what Pearl had said to him. He just didn't know how the idea of co-parenting would go over with his mother.

"That may be, but if Jenny is pregnant with your child, you will marry her."

His answer? It didn't go over well.

Tony had to get through to her. "Ma, I can't. I don't love her, and I won't accept anything less than what you and Dad have. I can have that with Pearl, but not with Jenny. What kind of home would it be to bring a child up in a house with no love between the father and the mother?"

"You loved her enough to make a baby with her."

Tony winced but was resolute. "I didn't make a

306

baby with Jenny."

"We raised you to take responsibility for your actions." His mother cocked her head to the side.

"If she's pregnant, and if I'm the father, I'll do right by the kid. I want to know beyond a shadow of a doubt that I'm not Jenny's baby daddy. But I'm not marrying her." He remembered what Pearl'd said. "It's the twenty-first century, not 1950."

His mother sighed. "We'll talk about it later. Should I call her tomorrow?"

He nodded. "I don't think she'll be in any hurry to call you." He looked at his watch. "I should go. Dawn comes early."

"I hope you'll think about what I said."

"I will."

As he tossed and turned in his bed that night, Tony could only think of one thing. No matter what happened with Jenny, he was not going to give up Pearl. He'd lost her once, and it'd nearly killed him. He had her back, and he wasn't going to let her go.

Chapter Thirty-Seven

"I told you." Jenny smiled smugly at Tony. "I'm pregnant. You have to marry me."

"The hell I do," Tony growled.

"Is that any way to talk to the mother of your child?"

"I really wish you'd stop saying that. You aren't the mother of my child. I won't believe it without a paternity test."

"You can't always get what you want," Jenny said, a smile on her face and malice in her eyes.

Tony couldn't. He just couldn't. A sense of disaster overwhelmed him. He'd been so sure Jenny wasn't pregnant. How was he going to tell Pearl?

He had no clue. No fucking clue.

Despair clung to him like wet cotton. His worst nightmare. He looked at Jenny, who was smirking and staring at him, all proud of herself.

Disaster just dropped its solid, suffocating mass down around his shoulders.

He looked at his mother, who had her arms linked across her chest and her right foot tapping the floor like she was Fred Astaire. Her lips were pursed tightly, and her eyes were blank and flat.

"We can't make any decisions now," Tony insisted. Sweat beaded up on his forehead. "I won't make any decisions now. Not until after the paternity test."

"I'm not going to take a paternity test. What do you think I am? A slut?"

Delores gave Jenny her hairiest eyeball. "Jenny. Have you seen a doctor yet?"

"No. I've got an appointment tomorrow. Do you want to come with me?" Jenny watched Tony.

Hell no. "Why would I? I'm not the father."

"I'll go with you," His mother told Jenny.

Great. "Thanks, Ma." Tony had to get out of there before the top of his head blew off. "I've got to go. I have some things to see to."

"Oh. Gotta go tell Pearl?" Jenny demanded.

"What I do with my time is none of your business, but if you must know, I'm checking with the body shop fixing the damage you caused."

"You can't prove I did anything to your truck," Jenny said with a smarmy smile.

Tony's ears buzzed like a whole hive and a half of bees had taken up residence there, and he was pretty sure there was smoke coming out of them. "Whatever. I'll talk to you later, Ma." He stomped off, his work boots thumping hard on the floor.

He had to see Pearl before he took his vehicle to the body shop. He'd talk to her when she picked him up. Maybe they could take a walk on the beach, and he'd give her the bad news.

It was not a conversation he looked forward to.

****

Pearl sang a hugely out of tune version of "I Feel Pretty" from *West Side Story* as she got ready to go with Tony to the body shop. He'd come and let her know that Jenny was lying about being pregnant, and then they'd go for a nice dinner and celebrate.

With Marlowe House all set to open on Memorial Day weekend, her life was very near perfect right now. She twirled around in front of her mirror, happy to see her periwinkle blue dress float around her legs.

Her phone rang with the ringtone she had assigned to Tony, "She Will Be Loved" by Maroon 5. She boogied on over to answer it. "Hey, Tony!"

"Yeah, hey, Pearl. There's been a slight change in plans. Can you pick me up at the body shop in about a half an hour?"

She didn't like the way he sounded. "Uh, okay. Sure. Are you all right?"

"I will be once I see you." He coughed. "I've got to go. See you soon." He clicked off.

She blinked a couple of times as she looked at her phone. Somehow she got a clue that the night was not going to go the way she planned.

****

She pulled into Avellar's Garage and Body Shop forty-five minutes later. She took her time getting there, because if there was bad news? She didn't want to hear it.

So she procrastinated. Sighing, she put the car in park and pulled up the emergency brake. She got out of her car and found Tony talking to Manny Avellar. They didn't look at each other. They both looked at the ground. Tony rubbed his toe in the sand.

However, they made a deal.

Pearl pressed her fingers against her mouth. They were so serious. Her sense of dread ratcheted up a couple of notches.

In that moment, she knew, without a doubt, that

Jenny was pregnant. But since Tony hadn't confirmed it, it wasn't true.

Yet.

As if he sensed she was there, Tony turned to look at her. His bleak eyes nearly broke her heart.

Her stomach knotted into thousands of teeny tiny searing points. She pasted a smile on her face as she walked over to him. "Hey."

"Hey." His own smile was wan, and his face was pale under his tan. "Thanks for coming to get me." Placing his hand on her elbow, he led her to her car. Misery rolled off him in oily waves. "Let's go to the beach."

Pearl knew exactly which beach. When they were in high school, Race Point was their beach. They'd first made love there, he'd asked her to marry him there, and every time they'd needed to run away and be alone, they'd gone to Race Point.

They got into the car, Pearl in the driver's seat. She pulled out onto Route 6 and headed to the beach.

The sun had just begun to put itself to bed, the reds, pinks, and golds stretching across the horizon, putting on their best show. It increased Pearl's sense of melancholy and encroaching doom. Tony took her hand and squeezed it.

They got out of the car, and Tony wrapped his arms around her and held her close. "God, Pearl. Jenny's a mess."

"Tell me what's going on."

He rested his forehead on the top of her head. "Jenny's pregnant. It can't be my kid, it just can't. The timing's all wrong."

Pearl was glad to hear it. "Who do you think she

311

slept with?"

He let her go and stepped away from her. "Who the hell knows? It wasn't me, and that's all I care about." His brow creased, and he squeezed her arms in those big hands of his. "You know that, right?"

"Yes." She did. She very much did. Going up on tiptoes, she pressed a kiss on his mouth. "I very much believe in you."

"Thank God." He kissed her again.

"I'll always believe in you." Tears pricked at her eyes.

"Jenny's a liar. I can't believe I didn't see it earlier." He hung his head. "I'm a moron."

"We'll figure it out," she whispered.

They took off their shoes. He rolled up the bottom of his jeans, grabbed her hand, and pulled her toward the water. If they looked really hard, they could see whales jumping and playing in the distance.

They walked to the left, toward Hatch's Harbor. A long walk, they wouldn't get there, but they'd be assured of privacy.

Pearl struggled to keep up with Tony as he marched resolutely up the beach. A physical man, he needed to work off the anger she knew he was holding on to.

She longed to soothe him, but she had her own messy feelings churning through her. Here they were, finally together after so many lonely years, and Hurricane Jenny attacked.

Tony would never turn his back on his child. Of course he wouldn't. He was hyper-responsible and loyal. If Jenny was truly pregnant with his child, he'd stand by her. It was the reason he couldn't turn his back on his father and brother and tell them to go to hell.

"Jenny's definitely pregnant." The cold foam of the waves tickled her toes. "She's going to use that baby to get everything she wants."

"Even if it is, we can deal with it."

He picked up a rock and tossed it out into the ocean. "My mother is demanding I marry Jenny."

Pearl took a deep breath and counted to ten. Twice. "It's the twenty-first century. Marrying Jenny is the worst idea ever. You'd hurt that child for life." She knew that for sure. She'd lived with Camille, a loveless home, a childhood full of duty and not much else.

He kicked a rock out of his way. "I told my mother that, but she'd made up her mind, just like I thought. No grandchild of hers will be illegitimate."

When Pearl thought this couldn't get worse, it did. Acid boiled in her stomach. She rested her hand on her belly. "Surely she'll come around once she sees you can be in your baby's life without marrying Jenny. A bad marriage between you two would be the worst thing for your child."

"Tell my mother that."

"I will if I get a chance."

He kicked another rock. "You won't get a chance as she's made her decision, and my father will back her." Tony shook his head. "Though I hope it won't come to that, I might have to do something to appease them."

"What?" She couldn't believe his words. "You'd marry Jenny to appease your parents? And I have nothing to say about it?"

"You have to understand." Desperation tinged his tone of voice. "My parents are very old-fashioned. You know that." He messed his hair up once again. "It's a fucking slippery slope, Pearl. Nothing I decide makes everyone happy."

He shook his head. The waves crashed to the shore, and she felt the sand relocate under her bare feet. The shore was cold and shifty.

Just like her life. "Maybe you don't have to make everyone happy. Maybe you only have to make me and your child happy."

He thought about that for a couple moments. It felt like forever. "I don't know what to tell you. I can't even figure it out in my own head, never mind my heart."

Pearl didn't know what to say as well. She told him as much. "I just don't know what this means for us."

He swallowed. "Me either." He reached out and caught her hand in his. "I can't do this without you, Pearl. I need you in my life."

"To keep me in your life, you can't marry Jenny. Get rid of that idea right now. Because, for the record? I am not going to be your piece on the side."

"No, no, no. That's not what I mean."

"Then what do you mean?" Confusion and frustration settled over her like a heavy, impenetrable fog.

"Damn it, Pearl! I can't even tell my ass from my elbow right now." He stopped, picked up a stone, and threw it out over the ocean. "I can't think."

"That's the first sensible thing you've said all evening. You need to think. And the first thought you should get out of your head is that wild hair about marrying Jenny. It's too bad that you have to disappoint your parents, but you can't marry Jenny." She crossed her arms across her chest.

He scrubbed his hands over his face and sat in the sand. Pearl sat next to him. Tony was so torn up, so miserable. Some of her frustration dissipated. Not all of it, but she knew throwing it at Tony wouldn't do any good. She put her hand on his shoulder. "Are you hungry? Want to get something to eat? We can go to my house."

"I'm not really up for eating anything. I should probably go home and, you know, try to figure things out."

Tony not hungry? Nothing got in the way of his appetite. Pearl wasn't all that hungry either. "You just want to come over and watch a movie or something?"

Rubbing his chin, he sighed. "Maybe you could take me home?" He tried to smile, but it was more of a grimace.

"Maybe I should." What else could she say? Nothing. "Let's go."

Neither spoke a single word as she took him home. He gave Pearl the kiss of her life, all lips and tongue and heartbreak before he got out of the car. "Thanks," he murmured. "I love you. Never forget that." Then he was gone.

Never forget that he loved her? What did that mean?

Dear Lord, what was she going to do? She had no clue.

Chapter Thirty-Eight

Pearl hadn't seen Tony in a couple of weeks. They'd talked on the phone, texted, and things were still up in the air. She kept herself busy, what with getting ready for Marlowe House's opening.

Tony had been very depressed. As usual, Jenny was flexing her I'm-difficult gene.

As Pearl'd been cleaning mirrors, she grimaced at her reflection. "I hate this."

The mirror didn't answer. Pearl was losing her marbles. They were dropping out of her ears and rolling across the floor.

Thump! Thump! Thump! Pearl blinked. Someone was knocking her door down.

"What the…" She put down her old newspapers and vinegar to answer the loud summons. Pearl pulled the door open and saw Jenny.

A very smug and smirky Jenny. She pushed herself into the hall, planted her hands on her hips, and turned to face Pearl.

"What are you doing here?" Pearl tapped her foot and wrapped her arms under her breasts.

"Oh, I'm just here to bring you up to speed." Jenny's grin would make a crocodile jealous.

"Just spit it out, Jenny." The sooner Jenny said her piece, the sooner Pearl could get rid of her.

That crocodile grin grew bigger. "You lost. Tony is

marrying me."

Pearl shook her head as a loud buzzing took over her hearing. "You're lying."

Shrugging, Jenny just smiled. "It's official. Tony and me are getting married." She held up her left hand, and yep, she wore a diamond ring. "Call him if you don't believe me."

She would, but not while Jenny was in her hallway, doing a pretty good imitation of the Town Crier. All she needed was a pilgrim costume and a big ass bell.

Then Pearl recognized the ring Jenny wore. It was the same ring Tony'd given her all those years ago. Tony had given her own damn ring to Jenny. Fury whipped through her. "I don't know what kind of game you're playing, but you need to get out of my house. Pronto."

"Oh, I'll go right away. I just wanted to tell you about the happy news." Jenny boosted her smile to one million watts. "Although it's probably not so good news for you."

Pearl snapped audibly, a huge, painful click of her spine. "Get the hell out of my house!"

"Really. Is that the kind of courtesy to show to your guests? You'll be out of business in less than a year."

Gritting her teeth, Pearl pointed to the door. "Get. The. Hell. Out. Of. My. House."

Opal showed up right then. "What's going on?"

"Ask her," A grinning Jenny told Opal.

"Go away," Pearl said. "I can't stand the sight of you."

Pearl stormed up to her bedroom suite. She needed to get out of town as fast as she could.

She jerked open drawers and ransacked them, throwing underwear and camisoles on the bed. Pulling her closet doors askew, she grabbed dresses and tops at random and tossed them on the bed as well. After finding the duffel bag she took to the gym, Pearl stuffed them in as fast as she could.

"Pearl?" Opal stood in her doorway. "Jenny's gone. What are you doing?"

"I've got to go away for a little bit." Pearl zipped the duffel closed. "Did she share her happy news?"

"That she and Tony are getting married? Of course she did."

"And did you see the ring she was wearing? Tony actually gave her my old ring!"

Opal gasped and covered her mouth. "That's beyond cruel."

"Then you know why I have to leave." She slung her bag over her shoulder.

"Where are you going?" Opal wanted to know.

"I don't know. Fall River I guess. To Sterling's house." She shook her head. "If Tony comes around, tell him I'm gone, but don't tell him where I am."

"Are you okay to drive? You're pretty upset."

That was an understatement. "I'll be fine."

"You pull over if you get overwhelmed."

Pearl sighed. "I will."

Opal pulled Pearl into a hug. "I love you."

"I love you, too." She had to get out of there before she started weeping.

"Let me know when you get there."

Pearl sniffed. "Absolutely."

And with that, she left her room, her new business, and Tony, along with his fiancée wearing her old ring and carrying his baby.

She'd be back in a bit, but for now? Pearl turned her car east and drove like hell away from all things Provincetown.

****

Tony swore as he pounded nails into lobster pots while attempting to fix them. He'd split the wood more often than not, but he needed to pound a few nails. It was better than punching someone, anyone, in the face.

He had to tell Pearl. He had to let her go. She wouldn't continue their relationship, not with him married to Jenny. He couldn't ask her to.

It was killing him. The jagged hole that opened in his soul was a million times more painful than when she'd left him seventeen years ago. Now he was leaving her.

Wiping the sweat out of his eyes with his sleeve, he still couldn't believe he'd been blackmailed into marrying Jenny. His mother and father's disappointment and insistence that he do so was bad enough, he could fight them, but Jenny's insistence that if he didn't marry her, she'd get an abortion had won the day.

Jenny was totally capable of doing it. How had he dated her, slept with her, and not known how unhinged she could be? To his shame, he guessed he really hadn't paid that much attention.

He hated Jenny with more ferocity than he'd ever hated anything or anyone, including Camille Marlowe.

The fact that Pearl was staying in town made everything even worse. He'd run into her. Given the size of the town, how could he not? At least when she'd moved away, he hadn't had to face his failure.

Misery seeped out of every pore he had. Drenched in it, he hadn't been able to sleep or eat. He would nod off on his couch, television on, beer bottle in hand. Pearl would sneak into his dreams, sometimes seductive, sometimes playful, and the worst of all, furious and yelling at him to stay the hell away from her. He'd awoken from that particular dream with tears in his eyes and a gaping tear in his heart.

Gabe walked into the workshop, all quiet and grim. "I have to talk to you."

"Too bad. I don't want to talk to you."

"It's important." Gabe studied him, his eyes sad.

"I don't care."

"You'll care about this."

"Fine." Tony tossed the hammer aside and crossed his arms over his chest. "Talk to me."

Gabe studied the concrete floor. Taking a deep breath, he lifted his head and locked his gaze onto Tony's. "Jenny's baby isn't yours."

Tony snorted. He couldn't deny the truth, no matter how much he loathed it. He owned his mistakes. "If not mine, then whose?"

Gabe gaze didn't waver. "Mine."

"What?" Tony shook his head. "Excuse me, but what?"

"It's exactly what I said. I'm the father of Jenny's baby."

"When did this happen?" Tony couldn't believe what his brother was telling him.

Gabe still didn't back down. "She showed up at my apartment one night in tears about how you were mistreating her and that you were breaking up with her because of Pearl. I tried to comfort her, and one thing led to another, and I guess you can figure out what happened next."

"She said that, and you believed her?" Tony could feel his blood splattering and popping. "I did not mistreat her."

"It wasn't the only time. She would show up at all hours, in tears, needing comfort because of Pearl. We've been sleeping together for a while now." Gabe chuffed out a tiny little laugh. "I'm pretty sure the baby's mine." He shrugged. "I kind of fell in love with her."

Tony seethed. Because of Pearl? Pearl had nothing to do with it. Jenny had played Gabe, and Gabe hadn't seen fit to let him know what was going on. He didn't trust himself to say anything right now. "You fell in love with her? Even though she was pushing me to marry her? That's not only pitiful. It's cruel."

Some brother. Right now he hated Gabe as much as he hated Jenny. He wanted to throat punch his brother. Multiple times. Visions of him hurting his brother danced like sugarplums in his head.

Gabe kept on. "It means that you don't have to marry Jenny. I will. And you can go back to Pearl."

"You're going to marry a woman who lied to you, used you, all to get back at me?" Tony said, dumbfounded. His ears buzzed. He couldn't think over the noise.

"It's not like Ma's going to let me get away with leaving Jenny to twist in the wind." Again he made that resigned chuckle. "And I don't want any kid of mine to run around town without my name on it. And like I said, I kind of fell in love with her."

"You are out of your ever-lovin' mind. You should

have told me about this," Tony spat out. "All those times you took off my head about being with Pearl, and all that time you were sleeping with Jenny."

Gabe shook his head. "I'm sorry. I was going on what Jenny told me." He coughed. "Obviously, I was wrong."

"Hell, yes, you were wrong! Do you know what you've done?" Tony's hands shook.

"I do." Gabe looked ready to break into two jagged halves. "I'm doing my best to make things right." Tony figured Gabe deserved it.

Tony'd had enough. "I really can't stand the sight of you right now. I've got to see Pearl."

He turned on his heel and marched out of the workshop. The most important thing in his world had narrowed down to seeing Pearl and telling her the news.

Chapter Thirty-Nine

"She's not here," Ruby told Tony as he stood on Marlowe House at the Sea's front porch.

"Where is she?" Tony demanded. She'd promised him she'd never leave him again. She'd promised him. The need to know where she was clambered all over his back.

"I'm not allowed to tell you."

"What?" The buzzing in Tony's ears increased exponentially, from head splitting to nuclear blast.

Opal joined Ruby at the door. "Jenny came to see her and brag about your engagement. She even showed her the engagement ring you gave Pearl back in the day." Opal looked so solemn. So sad.

Ruby? Not so much of the solemn, a whole bunch of the mad. "You need to leave, Tony. I love you, but we're not going to tell you anything."

Tony stabbed his fingers through his hair. "She promised me she'd never leave."

"And you told her you loved her and trusted her. Then Jenny showed up at our door and just came waltzing in, bold as brass, proclaiming that she won." Ruby's tone of voice held so much contempt.

Tony's world crumbled around him in teeny, tiny pieces. "I need to tell you—"

"We don't want to listen to anything you have to say," Ruby told him, her tone of voice glacial.

"Pearl doesn't want to listen to anything you have to say." Ice coated Opal's gaze. "I was here when Jenny showed up broadcasting the happy news. She just couldn't wait to rub it in."

Ruby's voice dripped as much frost as Opal's eyes did. "How could you have given Jenny the same exact ring you gave Pearl?"

"What?" He hadn't given Jenny any ring.

"Not only did she lord it over Pearl that she was pregnant with your child, but she made sure she flashed the engagement ring you gave to Pearl back when you were eighteen." Ruby made a noise that could only be considered as disgusted.

He had no idea how Jenny got Pearl's old ring. It didn't add up. He sure as hell hadn't given it to her. She must have taken it from his sock drawer when he wasn't looking, which meant she'd been planning this for a long time.

He felt anger bristle and snap along his nerves. "I didn't give it to her. I don't know how she got it."

Ruby exploded. "What are you? Stupid?"

"God, Tony. Wake up!" Opal weighed in. "Jenny wearing Pearl's ring was just too much. Really!"

He didn't know how to answer the question. He took a deep, deep, soul-searching breath. "I'm sorry." Which he was to the bottom of his soul. "I should have seen what Jenny was up to."

"Yes, this kind of thing is right in her wheelhouse."

"When Pearl is done figuring things out," Opal told him, "she'll call us when she's ready to come home."

Hope leaped in Tony's heart. "She's coming home, then."

"We don't know," Ruby said. "Marlowe House is

her dream, but?" She lifted a shoulder. "There's only so much Pearl can take. She's been through a lot this year. You need to give her some space, considering the situation."

Self-loathing lanced through him, sharp and unforgiving. How could he have added to Pearl's problems? He had to face facts, as much as he hated them. He was responsible for Pearl's new pain, the dead-last thing he'd ever wanted to do.

He had to find her and make this right, face-to-face.

Heart to heart.

What he didn't want was to tell Ruby and Opal about Jenny's threats and Gabe's being her baby daddy. They'd learn that soon enough, at least about Gabe, given the gossip factory in P-town. But he wanted to tell Pearl himself. "Look," he said when it looked like both women were going to murder him. He couldn't blame them. He deserved it. But he still needed to get what he came to Marlowe House for. "I really need to talk to Pearl."

"No, you really don't. What you really need to do is go away." Opal gestured at his rental car. "Now."

He wanted to pound his fist through a wall. "Fine. But I will talk to her at some point." He stomped off to his vehicle.

About to bust a blood vessel, Tony had to do something, anything, to get control of this situation. Top on the list was to find Jenny and have it out with her.

No, the first thing he had to do was text Pearl and beg her to come back. His fingers fumbled over his phone's keyboard. Never had they ever felt so thick.

****

"We probably should have told him that Pearl's coming back." Ruby worried her lower lip.

"You weren't here when Jenny came over. I want him to suffer and grovel." Opal loved a good grovel.

"You're evil. I really like that about you." Ruby grinned.

Opal grinned back. "It's a gift."

****

Tony caught up with Jenny at his parents' house. Looked like Gabe was there too. Good. He had bones to pick with both of them. Jenny he could understand. She was crazy. Gabe was his brother and had betrayed him, and that had cost him the woman he loved.

He let himself in and found his mother and father looking pretty grim, his mother on the sofa, his father pacing in circles around the room. Jenny sat in a chair, weeping. Gabe stood stoic behind her chair while he stared at some point on the other side of the room.

Clearing his throat, Tony got their attention. "Jenny. Just who I was looking for."

Gabe's head snapped around, and his father stopped pacing. Standing, his mother moved over to Tony and laid a hand on his arm. "This is not the time," she said in her most comforting mom voice.

It didn't work. There was no comfort to be had for him. Damn Gabe to hell.

"There's no better time. Jenny drove Pearl out of town, confronting her and throwing our engagement in Pearl's face." His hands fisted. "Was that the whole point? Making Pearl leave town?"

Jenny's face was bloated, her eyes red, her nose running. Her mouth opened and closed a couple of times, making her look like a demented guppy. She couldn't manage to say words that were coherent and burst into tears. Gabe put his hands on her shoulders.

"Don't you dare defend her, Gabe," Tony gritted out. If he clenched his jaw any harder, it would shatter into jagged pieces.

"Dude, she's pregnant. Too much stress isn't good for the baby." Gabe massaged Jenny's shoulder.

Stress? Gabe was an idiot. "As for Jenny, she rigged all this to force Pearl to leave town."

"I did not," Jenny snarfled. "I just…I just wanted to show her she can't have everything her way."

Tony shook his head, Jenny's words falling like bricks out of the sky to whomp them upside the head. "Gabe, are you hearing this? She's playing both of us. Are you going to be fool enough to marry her?"

"What I do—or don't do—is none of your business."

"Then you really are as stupid as you look." Disgusted, Tony wanted to leave his brother to it. If he was willing to take Jenny on after what she'd done to both of them, then he could have at it.

Then Jenny reached for another tissue, and Tony saw the glint of the tiny diamond on the ring on her left-hand ring finger. "Take it off."

"Take what off?" Gabe wanted to know.

"The ring, the damn ring I gave Pearl in high school. I didn't give it to Jenny. She must have stolen it." He took a step toward Jenny.

His father stepped in between Tony and Jenny. "Go talk to your mother in the kitchen. I'll take care of things out here."

He didn't want to go talk to his mother in the

kitchen. Nothing she would say could take care of all that was wrong with this. She tugged on his arm. "Come with me."

"Shit."

"You don't talk like that in my house. Let's go. There are some things you need to understand." His mother pulled him out of the room.

He let his mother lead him because right now his body was stiff, like the Tin Man in *The Wizard of Oz*. He couldn't trust his legs to work. Whatever she said would not make one bit of difference to him.

They got into the kitchen, and his mother pushed him down into a chair. "Sit. I'll get you a beer. Are you hungry?"

Hell no. He might not ever eat again. "No, thanks."

"When was the last time you ate?"

He shook his head. "I can't remember."

"I'll make you a sandwich. Do you want any chowder with it?"

Water welled up behind his eyes as he remembered his and Pearl's last time in bed. It had started with his mother's homemade soup. He definitely couldn't choke that down. "No, thanks, Ma."

"I've got some porco em pau left over from last night."

Grilled pork tenderloin, really spicy, really buttery, and broiled with onions? He couldn't. "I'm fine, Ma."

"No, you're not fine." She sat across the table from him. "I'm sorry for my part of it."

"Sorry? What do you have to be sorry about?"

"That I forced you into proposing to Jenny when she threatened to have an abortion. Especially when I wondered about her and Gabe."

Tony's head snapped up. "What?"

She sighed. "I couldn't prove anything, but I had a really strong feeling that Jenny was sinking her hooks into him."

Incredulous, Tony stared at her. "You knew?"

"I suspected and didn't want to say anything until I had proof. It's a mess, that's for sure."

"You knew, and you didn't say anything to me? How could you do that? You ruined my life!" His hands clenched into tight fists. "Pearl is gone, and no matter that her sisters say she's coming back, I don't know if I can trust it." He blinked back the tears forming in his eyes. "If you had told me something, my life wouldn't be falling apart."

"There's more."

More than knowing about Gabe and Jenny and not telling him? Tony didn't really want to know. "I don't care."

"You will about this." His mother sat at the table and folded her hands on top of the '50s era Formica-covered top.

Exhausted, Tony might as well get this over with. "What do you have to tell me?"

His mother sighed. "I'm the reason Jenny got her hands on that old ring."

Okay. He wasn't expecting that at all. Just like that, no longer weary, he gaped at the woman sitting across the table from him like she was a stranger. "You gave Jenny that ring? Why would you do a thing like that?"

"I didn't know what she was going to do." His mother's voice was steady and unemotional. "She said she needed to get some things of hers from your apartment, and since you were engaged, I saw no harm to it. That's when she probably stole the ring."

Okay, the anger was back, and his vision contracted and was peppered with black, popping spots. "When she probably stole the ring?" He lurched to his feet and stabbed his fingers through his hair. "Of course that was when she stole the damn ring. That one little detail was the final straw for Pearl. It's the reason she left town. Do you know what you've done?" He yelled that last part. "She may never come back!"

"You feel like that now, but I know deep down in my heart that Pearl is coming back. She has too much invested in Marlowe House right now."

Tony snorted. "So her grandmother's house is more important than me?"

"I didn't say that. I said she was invested into making something for herself to feel proud of." His mother nodded. "She'll come back."

"Maybe she won't." His father's low, gravelly voice entered the room. "Gabe and Jenny are gone." He opened his paw-like hand and dumped the tiny ring Jenny'd worn on the kitchen table.

The ring spun in circles before it flopped onto its side. "I don't want it. Give it away, pawn it, or put it in the collection basket at church. I don't care. I never want to see that thing again."

"Tony, I'm so sorry for my part in this." His mother stood. "Please forgive me."

Just like that the anger subsided, and misery cloaked him like a wet woolen coat. He slumped under the weight of it. "Just get rid of it, please. I never want to see it again. But I don't think I can forgive you."

His mother picked it up and stuffed it into the pocket of her slacks. "You'll never see it again. I'm very, very sorry."

His mother had picked his brother over him and didn't let him know what was going on. "You betrayed me."

His father bristled. "Don't talk to your mother like that."

"It's okay, Theo," his mother said. "You knew that if I wasn't sure about Gabe and Jenny, I wouldn't say anything. And I did give Jenny the opportunity to steal the ring from Tony's apartment."

"I need a beer." His father retreated to the fridge.

Defeated, Tony told his mother, "I've got to get out of here."

"Where are you going?"

"I don't know." Find Pearl. Beg Pearl to come back to him. Sell his soul to the devil. Enlist in the French Foreign Legion if she wouldn't listen to him and take him back.

His father slammed the fridge door shut. "Leave Gabe and Jenny alone."

Brand new fury raced through him. "With all due respect, Dad, I was played by both Jenny and Gabe. Yeah, that's a great plan you got. Let your son marry a woman who just used him to trap your other son into marriage. That's an awesome idea." He sneered at them. "I thought both of you would have my back. Apparently, I was wrong."

He turned on his heels and stomped out of the house, not sparing another glance at his brother and Jenny. Gabe stood. "Tony," he began.

Tony put his hand up. "Stop. I've got nothing to say to you, and you've got nothing I want to hear."

Tony's whole family could go straight to hell. If

Pearl wouldn't come home, Tony would be totally wrecked. She had to come back to him.

A life without her would simply not be worth living.

Chapter Forty

"It's not that I'm kicking you out, but when are you going home?" Sterling walked into his living room to find Pearl sprawled on his couch, wearing a ratty tee shirt and even rattier sweatpants. She stared at the television, watching the QVC channel, cell phone at the ready to buy more cheap jewelry, while shoveling chocolate brownie fudge ice cream right out of the container into her mouth.

Pearl didn't look at him. "Soon."

He sat on the couch next to her and put his hand on her arm. "Sweetie, you've got to go home. I got a call from Robert, and he's not happy about you coming to visit me. I got another call from Opal. Things are getting busy at Marlowe House, and she wants you to come home."

Pearl stabbed the spoon into her ice cream and sighed. "I know, I know. I'll leave tomorrow."

"You need to go today. You're strong. You can take whatever Jenny dishes out."

"Something I fought long and hard to achieve," Pearl said, remembering the counseling she'd gotten after getting out of jail. "I just don't want to breathe the same air as Jenny."

Sterling studied her. "There's more to this than Jenny."

Pearl rolled her eyes. "Of course there's more to

this than Jenny, as in Tony asking her to marry him without telling me first."

Sterling nodded. "That was not well done of him, but it doesn't negate the years of history between you two." Sterling decided to push her a little bit. "Are you going to throw that all away?"

"There's nothing between me and Tony, not anymore. I won't let there be."

"You're mad, and I don't blame you. But, Pearl, you've got to put your big-girl panties on and get back to your life. Opal also told me Tony's been to the house every day telling her that he has to talk to you. Maybe you should go back and hear what he has to say." Being an exceptional lawyer, Sterling went in for the kill. "If you don't go back, Camille wins."

"Sterling, you don't fight fair."

"And don't you forget it." He took the carton of ice cream away from her. "And no more of this. Now get off my couch, grab a shower, and go home."

Pearl sighed as she rose from the sofa. "You're right. I need to get back and face the music."

"It might be a good idea to get Opal some flowers for taking care of your business."

"Are you going to tell me what kind I should get?"

He chuckled. "No, I'll let you wing that one on your own."

"Thanks a lot." She turned to leave the room.

"Pearlie?"

"What?"

"I love you."

Facing him, she smiled. "I love you, too."

"Everything's going to be all right. You'll see."

"From your mouth to God's ears."

Sterling watched her go to his guest room. He so wanted to make her life happy.

He also hoped he wouldn't have to go back to P-town and beat up Tony. He was a lover, not a fighter.

****

"Thank God you're home." Opal hugged Pearl.

Pearl hugged Opal back and sighed. It felt right to be home. "Thank you, Opal, for everything you've done for me."

Opal pulled away and kissed Pearl's cheek. "Are you good?"

"Upright and forward, one foot in front of the other."

"That's my girl." Opal's face turned serious. "There's been a lot going on."

"I can imagine," Pearl murmured.

"Tony's been over every day, around five, demanding to know where you were, really anxious to talk to you. Of course we didn't tell him a thing."

"Thank you."

"Pearl, I think you should talk to him."

"Yes. Then I can put the whole thing behind me and move on."

"I've got to tell you, Pearl, there are some crazy rumors running around town."

"I just bet." She didn't want to hear them. "Don't tell me. I'll find out from Tony." And then she'd be done with him.

Sorrow punched her in the gut. She didn't want to be done with Tony. She wanted to spend the rest of her life with Tony. But she would not be his piece on the side. She deserved way more than that.

Opal looked at her watch. "It's going on five. I

imagine Tony'll be over here soon."

"I hope not." Pearl needed some time before she saw him. Like time to do her makeup and get her hair to look hella sexy.

She wanted him to know what he was giving up.

"He looks totally wrecked and totally desperate."

Pearl looked off in the distance. "That can't be my concern. I have to think about me. I promised myself in prison that I would never be another man's victim. That includes Tony."

"Your decision, obviously."

"It is." Pearl was as sure of this as she had been over anything else in her life. "Do I love Tony? Yes. Will loving Tony in this situation make me happy?" She rolled her shoulders back. "No. It will not."

Pearl had no idea what she owed to herself, except happiness.

Everyone deserved to be happy. She'd been so sad for too long, and she was tired of it. "I don't have anything to say to Tony. Jenny said it all for him."

Opal frowned. "He's been over every day and the look on his face?" She shook her head. "He's destroyed."

"Marrying Jenny will do that to a person."

Slinging her arm around Pearl's shoulder, Opal steered Pearl in the direction of the stairs going to the second and third floors of the house. "You know I'm on your side. So is Ruby. Here's what you'll do. You're going to take a bubble bath in that big ol' tub in your suite, and I'm going to fix you something to eat." She lifted one corner of her mouth in an amused half smile. "Five is coming up fast, so get a move on." Opal left.

Pearl took Opal's advice and did the whole

pampering routine. By the end of it, she looked damn good, if she did say so herself, from her artfully tousled hair, expertly smudged eyes, slick painted mouth, and her most killer little black dress. She'd added some skyscraper heels and even dusted a little glitter powder over her cleavage, which the LBD really showcased. She took one last look in the mirror and went down to her office.

She opened the door and stepped through it and sighed. Look how far she had come, from prison and failure to Marlowe House and hope for the future. Nothing that happened between Tony, Jenny, and her could take this away from her. She just needed to believe in herself and this new life she was building.

Determination cascaded through her. For once, she would stand up for herself. She would succeed here, and she would be able to cope with Tony and Jenny being together in one happy little family.

"Pearl?" Opal knocked at her office door. "Tony's here."

"Okay. I'll be right out."

Pearl stood, and her hands trembled. She clamped them together and took a deep breath. The sooner she got this over with, the better for all concerned.

She opened the door to see Tony waiting for her with a hopeful smile on his face. If he'd had a hat, he'd have held it in front of him, the peasant confronting the queen. The rest of him looked like hell. He had dark bags under his eyes, and he clearly hadn't shaved since the last time she'd seen him. His messy hair stuck out all over his head.

"Pearl," he murmured.

He took a step toward her. She put up a hand to

stop him and kept her voice and attitude super frosty. "Hello, Tony. Opal told me you have something to tell me."

"It's great news, Pearl." His words came out in a fast jumble like they tripped over each other on their way out of his mouth. "Gabe is Jenny's baby daddy."

Whatever Pearl expected Tony to say, this wasn't it. "Gabe is the father of Jenny's baby." Maybe. Jenny had lied before. She could be lying now.

"Gabe admitted it. The minute he told me, I ran right over here to tell you, but you had already left." Tony licked his lips. "Why didn't you answer my calls?"

"Pure survival. After all I've been through, I needed space to protect myself," she told him the truth. "The news was overwhelming me emotionally. I was drowning in it. So I did what my former therapist told me to do when things got to be too much. I got some distance from the situation."

Tony took another step into the house. Shame covered his face. "I'm so sorry about what Jenny did and about my part in it."

"Your part in it," Pearl repeated. She could feel her face turn tomato red. Tony had hurt her more than Jenny had. "What exactly was your part in it?"

"I don't know what you mean." Tony squinted. "If you mean that I should have checked in with you before I agreed to marry Jenny, then you're absolutely right. But I had no control of Jenny coming to tell you."

"Why did you give her that ring?"

Tony sighed. "I didn't. She stole it. If you'd listened to any of the messages I left you, you would have known that," he said, sounding all high and mighty and arrogant.

Oh no. He wasn't making any of this her fault. "I was too busy picking up the pieces of my life. I thought Henry had done so much damage I'd never dig out from under it. What you and Jenny did?" She shrugged. "I promised myself I'd never let another man tear my life apart."

"Don't you realize that we can be together like we planned?"

Tears gathered hot and sharp behind her eyes. She shook her head. "No, Tony. We can't."

"What do you mean we can't?" Tony's face flushed. "Of course we can. We love each other, and we deserve to be together."

Her heart shredded into painful, bloody strips. "I had to find out from Jenny that you decided to marry her." Pearl just couldn't get over that one thing in particular.

"But I didn't decide I was going to marry her. Yeah, it's what my mom wanted, but I was not on board. We can go back to the way things were."

Pearl shook her head. "We can't. There's too much to just forget. And as long as Jenny is in your life, she'll be in mine. I just can't have her toxicity in my life."

"She's not in my life, except as my brother's wife."

Pearl sighed and blinked back hot tears. "She's having your brother's baby."

"That's just an excuse. I can't believe you're doing this to us."

Tony's eyes were suspiciously moist, but Pearl wouldn't let herself be moved. "I thought I could trust you. Apparently I was wrong."

"You can't trust me? That's rich." Tony's voice

sounded gruff. Rusty. "You promised you wouldn't ever leave again, and at the first rough patch, you bailed."

"I did not bail. I took a couple of days for myself after Jenny oh so gently broke the happy news that you were marrying her and had given her my old ring. I'm the one who can't trust you, even though you promised you would trust me." The aloof coldness she'd counted on was now morphing into full on despair. "See, here's the thing. I once let my love for a man blind me to what was really going on, and I paid the price."

"What?" Tony's eyes narrowed. "I don't know what you mean."

"Henry. I'm talking about Henry."

"The asshole who got you arrested and ruined your career?" Tony snorted. "Yeah, I'm just like him. God, Pearl. You can't be serious."

"I am serious." She folded her hands primly in front of her. "I turned a blind eye to what Henry was doing until it was too late. I put my own happiness second to his. It turned into a disaster, right?"

"I don't see how this pertains to me."

"It's not so much you as it is me. I've fallen in love with you all over again, but like I said, I can't trust you anymore." She swallowed. "Just like I couldn't trust Henry. I was kept in the dark, used, and I won't let that happen to me ever again."

Tony tunneled his fingers through his hair. "And I've fallen back in love with you. We can have the future we planned all those years ago."

"See, I'm not so sure about that. Jenny will always be in the picture, reminding me that while you were telling me you loved me, you were ready to throw me over while you married Jenny and made a future with her." Tears pricked behind her eyes, but she refused to let them fall. "I just can't just forget everything."

"What do you mean?" Fear moved right across his face.

Pearl took a deep breath. "We're over, Tony. I don't think it will work, and I have to protect my heart from more heartbreak. I literally can't survive that kind of pain again."

Tony shook his head. "I can't believe this! You're really breaking up with me after all we've been through to be together."

"I was an afterthought in this whole marrying Jenny thing. As awful as this is"—she hitched up one shoulder—"we need to move on."

Tony stared at her, his gaze turning cold. "Good luck with the bed and breakfast." He left.

Pearl stood there swaying. Tony was gone. That was what she wanted, right?

No, she didn't want that at all.

But since things were never going back to where they were before, then the two of them had nothing but broken hearts.

****

"Tony. Can I talk to you?" Gabe stood in Tony's front doorway.

Gabe. Just what he needed. "No. Go the fuck away."

"I need to tell you that Jenny and I are getting married."

Tony refused to look at his traitor brother. "Congratulations. You two are meant for each other. Both of you are liars and cheaters."

"I deserve that," Gabe said. "Jenny and I both deserve that." He cleared his throat. "I heard Pearl is back in town."

"You heard right."

"So things are good for you again, now that Pearl knows that you're not the father of Jenny's baby?"

Tony wanted to choke the life out of his brother. His fingers itched to do it. He flexed them like he was playing a Bach concerto. Violently.

Very violently.

"Things are not okay. You and Jenny made sure of that."

"I'm sorry about that," Gabe said, a little too offhand for someone who'd just destroyed his brother's life. "I know you love her. Maybe she'll cool down in time."

Fury rushed through him, pricking at him with rusty little claws. "Don't talk about Pearl. Don't even say her name." He fisted his hands. "I hope you and Jenny will be as happy as you deserve to be." He slammed the door in Gabe's face.

Leaning against the door, he slid to the floor. Arms resting on bended knees, Tony bowed his head into his hands as he grieved. It had wrecked him the first time he lost Pearl. He didn't know how he was going to get through losing her a second time. And this time he couldn't blame Pearl's grandmother. He had screwed this up all on his own.

Chapter Forty-One

Pearl was totally involved in putting big pots of flowers along the walk to the front door and on the porch. She smiled at the riot of red and yellow blooms. She'd never thought of herself as a gardener but found she had a talent for it.

"Your flowers look wonderful."

Pearl closed her eyes. She knew that voice. Standing, she took off her muddy gloves. "Hello, Mrs. Cabral."

"Do you have a minute to talk?"

Delores looked terrible, her complexion gray and huge bruise-colored bags under her eyes. "Would you like to come in? I just made a big pitcher of iced tea."

"That sounds lovely." Delores followed Pearl into the house. "This is beautiful, Pearl. You've done such a good job with the house. It really feels light and airy."

"Thank you. I'm happy with the results." She led Delores into the kitchen. "Please have a seat while I get the tea ready."

Her hands shook a little as she got out the ice and the tea. "Would you like lemon?"

"Yes, please."

Pearl brought the tall, icy glasses of tea to the table. An extremely uncomfortable silence fell over the room.

Delores took a sip from her drink. "I suppose you know why I'm here. I'm a big part of why this whole thing with Jenny, Gabe, and Tony blew up. I need to make it up to him."

She wanted to cry. "Tony and I are over."

"I hope I can change your mind about that."

"Delores, please—"

"Let me tell you what happened. He fought tooth and nail to get out of marrying Jenny, but she had a trump card to play. She told him she would get an abortion if he didn't marry her, and he couldn't let that happen. He didn't agree to marry her until the day she came to you to tell you what was going on."

Pearl could barely believe what Delores told her. "I'm sorry, what?"

"Jenny threatened to terminate her pregnancy if Tony didn't marry her."

Aghast, Pearl said, "Who does that?"

"Apparently, Jenny does." Delores folded her hands in her lap. "It's a horrible thing, and I made it worse."

"I can't believe that." Really. Delores Cabral was one of the best women Pearl had ever known.

Delores pressed her lips together into two thin, white lines. "I'm the reason Jenny got the ring."

Pearl heard her jaw drop to the floor with a thump. "You're the reason? Why would you give Jenny that ring?"

Delores licked her lips and took a careful sip of her tea. "I didn't do it directly. She asked me for the key to Tony's apartment so she could get some things out of it. She used that opportunity to steal the ring."

"You're kidding," Pearl blurted without thinking.

"I wouldn't kid about this. Here's the thing. I now see that Jenny is a very damaged person."

Damaged? That was one way to describe Jenny, just not the word Pearl would have used.

"I don't even want her with Gabe, but he's decided to step up and do the right thing. As you can imagine, I'm not looking forward to any family gatherings. I think Tony will just stay away, and I'll lose my son. So that's the reason I've come to you. To ask you to give Tony a second chance."

"Thank you for letting me know." Pearl managed to keep her voice smooth so as to hide the turmoil that brewed in her stomach. "I'm sorry things have ended up this way."

"He's been so miserable since you broke things off with him. It's even worse than the time you went away and left him behind. He's not talking to his father and Gabe. He's thinking of trying to get work on another boat so he doesn't have to deal with Gabe and Theo. My family is torn apart." Delores swiped at the wetness that pooled in her eyes. "I don't know how we're going to survive this. Theo was on Gabe's side, but he's beginning to see the light regarding Jenny. He definitely wants to keep Tony on the boat, but he's said things to Tony that were awful. Things that will be very hard to forgive." She took a careful sip of her tea. "This is my worst nightmare, and you're the only one who can fix it." She pulled a white handkerchief embroidered with pansies out of her pocket and dabbed her eyes.

Pearl had never seen Delores so undone. "I don't know what you want me to do."

"Now that you know the whole story, you can take him back. That's all you have to do. I know you love him. He's never stopped loving you. Please give him another chance."

Acid rolled around in Pearl's gut. "I don't know. I mean, I can't see how that would work."

"Think about it. Think about what you'll be missing. If you can't have an open mind, you'll be throwing love away with both hands. While I never met your mother, I'm sure she'd be telling you the same thing." Delores stood. "Promise me you'll think about it. I'll see myself out."

Pearl nodded. She knew she wouldn't be thinking of anything else.

She needed her sisters. Taking her phone out of her jeans back pocket, she punched in Ruby's number. Ruby picked up on the first ring. "Pearl. What's up?"

"You available for dinner tonight?"

"Dinner?"

"I really need you and Opal right now."

"Do you want to go out or order pizza and eat at my apartment?"

"Pizza sounds great." Although she doubted she could choke down a bite.

"Do you want me to call Opal?"

"If you don't mind. I've still got some gardening to get done before dark."

"I'll call Opal." Ruby sounded decisive. "Want to give me a clue what this is about?"

"I had a visit from Delores Cabral." Pearl grimaced at the phone.

"Ah. Are we drinking martinis tonight?"

"The dirtier the better," Pearl confirmed.

"You got it. See you around seven? Sounds great. We love you, Pearl."

"I know. I love you all, too." Her voice cracked

because of the tears clogging her throat. She had to end the call and pull herself together. "I'll see you later." She clicked off.

Thank God, she had her family on her side. From what Delores had told her, Tony's father and brother had deserted him. Gabe's betrayal, as well as Theo's siding with Gabe, must be killing Tony. While she still wasn't sure that they should be together, she didn't want him to lose his family.

She'd best turn her attention to her posies. They were simple. Give them love, water, and sunshine, and they would flourish. She wished life was as simple.

She wanted to cling to her anger, but she knew what kind of pressure Jenny's threats put on him. She also knew that if he hadn't capitulated to Jenny's threats, his father and mother, staunch Catholics, would have disowned him.

She felt sorry for him, which was the very last thing she wanted.

She loved him as much as she always had, maybe more. This was also the very last thing she wanted.

She sighed and slumped. Her shoulders were as heavy as an Acme one ton weight. She could barely hold them up.

Opal and Ruby would help her out, set her straight.

She crossed her fingers and made a wish.

****

Several hours later, Pearl sat on one of Ruby's big pillows in front of her coffee table, drinking chianti and scarfing down a linguiça, black olive, and mushroom pizza. Tomatoey, cheesy, garlicky goodness. Yum.

With Dave Brubeck playing "Take Five" in the background, and in the company of her most excellent sisters, she felt more relaxed than she had since Jenny announced her pregnancy.

Ruby lounged on her overstuffed couch. "So. Why are we here tonight? Other than checking out that new bracelet, which is hideous by the way."

Pearl sighed and put her pizza down. "Like I said on the phone, I got a visit from Tony's mother today."

Opal poured herself some wine. "What did she want?"

Sighing, Pearl shook her head. "She came to tell me what really went on that week Tony decided to marry Jenny. What kind of pressure he was under."

"So spill. What happened?" Ruby sat up on the couch.

"Apparently, he fought Jenny about the whole thing until she threatened to have an abortion if he didn't marry her."

Ruby nodded. "That sounds like the Jenny we all know and don't love."

Pearl took a big sip of her wine. "Delores also told me that Jenny stole my old ring and couldn't wait to show it to me."

Shrugging, Ruby said, "Again, I wouldn't put it past Jenny."

"Why didn't you two tell me about Jenny and Gabe?"

"We thought it best if Tony told you himself." Opal helped herself to another piece of pizza.

"It really wasn't our story to tell," Ruby added.

"I could have used a little warning," Pearl grumbled.

"I did tell you that there were rumors going around town about Tony, Gabe, and Jenny," Opal pointed out.

"And I told you to hear him out."

"Gah!" Pearl threw herself back against the pillow. "That wasn't a warning. It was a puzzle."

"I think you should take him back," Ruby said around a bite of pizza. "He's totally miserable, and he totally adores you."

"I agree with Ruby," Opal said. "You know that he would crawl naked over broken glass to make you happy."

"And," Ruby chimed in, "you know you're madly in love with him. You always have been, and you always will be."

Grimacing, Pearl shook her head. "It's too late for that."

"Why are you so certain?" Opal wanted to know.

"I just am." Misery wrapped its bony arms around Pearl and held on tight.

"I think you should keep an open mind," Ruby replied.

"That's not what you said before."

Ruby shrugged. "I changed my mind."

Pearl groaned. "You're no help."

"Maybe you don't have to decide right now." Opal nodded her head. "You take some time."

Pearl lifted her hands to her temples and rubbed at the headache brewing there. All kinds of things whirled around her brain. So many possibilities, so little time.

She sent up a heartfelt wish for a clue. She just didn't know what to do.

****

Tony didn't know what to do. He wished with all his might he did. All he was sure of was that he wasn't giving up on Pearl without a fight.

He pondered his options. Somehow he didn't think flowers would do the trick.

So he found himself at the Speedwell Café nursing a coffee and wracking his brain for something he could do to get Pearl to take him back. It had to be something big. He knew that much. A gesture so huge she'd never doubt that he loved her and that she owned him, body and soul.

That he was the man of her dreams.

What did she dream about? He had to find out. What should he do to make her dreams come true?

"Hey, Tony. Here's your Monument Reuben, piled sky high." Mary, his waitress who had been two years behind him at school, put a plate on the table in front of him. She guffawed. "Although a really tall sandwich is about the only heights you can handle. Do you want something else? Do you want me to top up your coffee?"

"No, thanks." He didn't want anything except Pearl.

"Enjoy your lunch."

He studied the sandwich, which loomed large with hot pastrami, sauerkraut, and Swiss cheese. Russian dressing oozed down the sides a bit, promising a messy, savory lunch. He had to formulate a plan of attack, a way to wrap his hands around it and make sure he got all the flavors in the first bite.

It was a veritable Eiffel Tower of a sandwich, well deserving of the title Monument.

He maneuvered the Reuben midway to his mouth, and it hit him. Sky high. Monument. How could he have forgotten what her dream proposal would have been? Tony knew exactly what he had to do to convince

Pearl that she was his whole world. He signaled Mary, and she came right over.

"Is everything okay?" A frown creased her face.

He slid the plate across the table. "Can you wrap this up for me?" He reached into his back pocket for his wallet and pulled out a couple of twenties. Grinning at her, Tony said, "And as for okay? I'll let you know."

****

Tony smiled as he finished a phone call that put the final touches to his plan to win back Pearl. He'd been working on this idea for a few days, and now all he had to do was find her. To that end, he pointed his truck in the direction of Marlowe House.

He pulled into Pearl's driveway and bounded up the stairs to her front door. He knocked on the door with the hand that wasn't holding a bouquet of candy pink roses. His heart thumped hard against his ribcage, and he bit his lower lip. This had to work. He couldn't live without Pearl, end of story.

Opal opened the door. "What do you want?"

He would not be discombobulated by the look of cheerful murder in Opal's eyes. "I want to see Pearl."

"She's not here."

Well, shit. "Can you tell me where she is?"

"Yes."

Tony waited.

And waited.

And waited some more.

He shook his head. "Please tell me where Pearl is. I really need to talk to her."

"I'm not telling you anything unless you promise me you won't hurt her."

"I'm never going to hurt her ever again." He would

make her the happiest woman on earth or die trying.

Opal pursed her lips as she considered him. He fought the urge to squirm.

"If this goes badly for Pearl, I'm going to hunt you down and kill you slowly." She grinned, but there was no mirth in it. "With a smile on my face."

"Please, Opal, just tell me where she is."

"She's at Laura's at a class reunion meeting."

"Thank you, Opal!" He picked her up and gave her a big, smacking kiss on her cheek. "I owe you." He put her down.

"Just remember what I said. I meant every word."

He saluted and bounded off the porch to his truck. He had a woman to kidnap.

Chapter Forty-Two

"So Gabe and Jenny just up and eloped," Josie confided to the room at hand. "My mother said that Delores is fit to be tied. She wanted a 'real' wedding at St. Peter's and all."

If Pearl heard one more word about Jenny and Gabe, she was going to hurt someone. "Don't we have to make the final decision about the restaurant?"

She found herself being stared down by Josie, Molly, and Laura. They swooped their heads so fast to look at her that she felt the breeze fly across her face.

"You must be happy that Tony's off the hook," Josie said as she studied her manicure. "How could Jenny have lied about something like that?"

"Don't forget this is Jenny we're talking about." Molly shook her head. "You're getting back with Tony now, right, Pearl?"

Damn, she should have kept her mouth shut until they'd finish the postmortem on Jenny and Gabe. This was one conversation she didn't want to have, to even hear. "Um, no. That's not going to happen."

They all gasped like some inner choir conductor had lowered her arm in an emphatic downbeat. Josie recovered first. "You don't mean that, Pearl. Tony loves you so much."

Laura and Molly nodded.

Lord, give her strength. "It's not that easy. I really

don't want to talk about it, okay?" It was time to change the subject. "What do you all think about the package Bradford Street Seafood offered us?"

Pearl heard Laura's front door open. It couldn't be Jenny coming late. No way Jenny would show her face around here. Besides, if Josie was right, and she usually was, Jenny was on her honeymoon with Gabe.

"Hello, ladies."

Pearl blinked. That was Tony's voice. What was he doing here?

"Tony. We didn't expect you," Laura said.

"I'm not going to be here long. I came to get Pearl."

"What?" Pearl stood. "I'm not going anywhere with you."

"Please. Come with me." He came close to her and took her hand with one of his.

She tried to pull her hand back. "I'm not going with you," she repeated.

"Oh, just go with him, Pearl!" Laura stuck in her oar. "Listen to what he has to say."

"If you don't go, Jenny wins." Josie made that point, and it was a direct hit.

"Yep!" Molly agreed.

"Good grief." Pearl shook her head. "It's not a case of winning or losing. Tony's not a prize in a box of Cracker Jacks."

"But I'm a prize, right?" Tony wanted confirmation.

"Oh, yeah, you're a real prize. I just don't know what kind."

"Pearl, at the risk of repeating myself, go with Tony and listen to what he has to say. You owe it to yourself." Laura was adamant.

"Please, Pearl." Tony gifted her with his most charming smile. "Come with me."

Pearl could never refuse Tony when he flashed her that grin now. "Okay." She put her hand into his.

"You won't be sorry," he said as he tugged her gently. Tony's fingers sent electric jolts up and down her arm.

Tony helped her into his vehicle, rounded it, and slipped into the driver's seat.

"Where are we going?" She itched to know.

"You'll see." He jammed the truck into reverse. "You're going to love it."

"I doubt that," she grumbled.

"Maybe," he said, his voice cheerful.

"Come on!" She couldn't believe him. This was spontaneous, and her Tony was never spontaneous.

Scratch that. The man driving the car was not her Tony, not anymore. She'd pushed him away with both hands.

She did a double take when he turned left onto Winslow Street. "Where are we going?" She wiggled in her seat.

He just looked at her and grinned. "Soon."

The next thing she knew, they were parking in the lot for the Pilgrim Monument and Museum. This made zero sense. Zer-Oh. Tony hated the Monument. "We're going to the Museum?"

"Nope. Up the Monument."

"The Monument!" What the wha'? "You never go up the Monument! You hate it!" At least, as far as Pearl knew, Tony'd never made it to the top without tossing his cookies.

"There's a first time for everything. Let's go."

Stunned, she watched him round the truck and open the door. He lifted her off the seat and let her slide down the length of his body until she was on her feet. She wobbled a little because her legs felt like overcooked noodles, but Tony held her so she didn't fall.

He grabbed her hand. "C'mon." Pulling her along behind him, he charged up the steps to the entrance of the Museum.

She stumbled as she tried to keep up with him. "We don't have to do this."

"Yes, we do." He took a deep breath, squared his shoulders, and started to climb the stairs.

Pearl stopped fighting him. She knew Tony well enough to realize he wasn't going to give this up.

Oh, well. She could use the exercise.

Tony struggled to reach the top. He clung to the wall, taking a couple of deep breaths at each platform. He hyperventilated and had to stop for a moment to control his gasps for air.

"Are you sure you want to do this?" Pearl touched his hand and worried how cold and clammy it was.

"I have to do this." His chest heaved as he labored to speak. "It's important."

"Sure. Okay." She noticed he still glommed on to the wall. "Then we should get moving."

"Right." He nodded. "Let's do this." He scooched up the cold stone one hand at a time. He gulped. "It's not long from here."

They trudged up the next couple of ramps and finally reached the last set of stairs. "Just a few more steps," Tony muttered.

A stiff breeze flowed through the door leading to the top observation deck.

Against one wall stood an ice bucket with a bottle of champagne in it, two glasses, and a flashlight. Tony swayed and leaned against the wall.

She put her hand on his shoulder. "Are you okay? We don't have to do this."

His jaw tensed. "Yes, we do." He pushed off the wall and slowly walked to the railing facing the harbor.

She looked around. There were no other people there. "Where is everybody? There's no one up here."

"I called Baxter Oglethorpe and promised him endless lobsters if he got us the Monument for ourselves for a while."

She walked up behind him. "What are we doing here?"

Turning to face her, he wobbled a little. She put out a hand to support him.

"Remember how you used to dream about a romantic sunset proposal on top of the Monument?"

"I'd forgotten all about that." She shook her head, amazed that he remembered. "You were so afraid of heights. I'd given up that particular dream."

"I want you, no, I need you to know how much I love you. I'd do anything for you. Anything. Face my worst fear just to show you that you're the most important part of my world." He dropped to one knee. "Take me back. Please, Pearl. Take me back. Marry me. Let's make the life we were always meant to have."

"What?"

He reached for her, and his touch broke down all her defenses. "Please. Marry me."

"You brought me all the way up here to ask me to

marry you, even though you're terrified of heights."

"Yes."

Her giddy heart stuttered and skipped a beat. He had to stop looking at her like she hung the sun, moon, and stars. She wanted him to look at her like that forever. "Oh, Tony."

"Is that a yes?"

"I want it to be." She crossed her fingers behind her back for luck. "What about Jenny? She's still on the scene."

"Don't throw away our happiness because Jenny exists. I'm not going to let her keep us from being happy. We've overcome your grandmother. We've overcome you nearly going to prison. Jenny's nothing compared to that. We're meant to be, Pearl." He pulled one arm with his hand and held it to his chest, where his heart beat strong and true. "If you trust anything, trust this. Trust my heart."

He was right, Pearl realized. They had gotten beyond Camille and Henry's treachery. She really couldn't come up with one reason not to believe in him. She took the leap into the future. "Yes, Tony. I'll marry you!"

He stood, gathered her into his arms, and held her close. "Thank God. I haven't slept for more than two hours in the past three weeks." He rested his forehead against hers. "I couldn't stand to lose you again."

"You won't. You can't."

He stepped away from her but then turned her in his arms so they were both looking at the dusk fall on the town below.

The royal blue of the harbor reflected the waning day.

He turned her to face him, and she lifted her head and smiled. He was so handsome.

"I love you, Pearl. I've never loved anyone in my life like I love you." With that, Tony kissed her. She melted into him and kissed him back, pouring all her love into that soul-deep kiss. "I'll spend the rest of my life making you happy."

She caressed his cheek, her hand trembling. "I couldn't be happier than I am at this exact moment."

"Challenge accepted." He rested his cheek on the top of her head. "Look out over the harbor. The moon is coming up."

She turned to watch the moon glow over the water and sighed. "It's so beautiful."

She felt him nuzzle her hair. "Yes, you are. You ready for some champagne?"

"You thought of everything." Hmmmmm. "Did you bring those things up here ahead of time?"

"Um, no. Baxter did it for me."

Chuckling, she murmured, "I'd better remember to thank him." She turned once more in his arms and faced him. "It's pretty and all up here, but maybe we should take it down and to my house." She nuzzled his throat. "We can christen the new hot tub."

"New hot tub, eh?" He waggled his eyebrows up and down. "I think christening it sounds like an idea whose time has come." He shivered. "It's getting a little chilly out here anyway."

Together they picked up their things and hand in hand strolled down to the bottom of the Monument, following the pale beam from the flashlight Pearl carried, stopping every now and then to share a poignant kiss.

Doreen Alsen

They reached the bottom of the Monument. "Are you ready to go home?" Tony wanted to know.

"Home." She smiled. "There's no place I'd rather be."

About the Author

Doreen has wanted to be a writer all her life but took a brief, okay, it was a long detour into being an opera singer and conductor. She realized that maybe she should spend more time writing when creating the back stories for her operatic characters was more fun than actually singing. Plus, her romance lovin' heart couldn't take all the dead bodies littering the stage at the end of the performance. She is still an active conductor and is regularly found waving her arms around in front of singers. *Together Again, Together Forever* is her eighth book with The Wild Rose Press, Inc.

~*~

Visit Doreen at
www.doreenalsen.com

Numbers Game
By Desiree Holt & Liz Crowe

Former professional football player and coach Duncan "Hatch" Hatcher fumbled his career and marriage. Now divorced and ready to tackle his future, he has an opportunity to redeem himself as coach of his college alma mater's football team. But how can he turn the team's losing streak around and keep the secret of his downfall buried when the school agrees to a documentary that will allow a lovely journalist to dig her way into his past…and into his heart?

Olivia Grant's ex-husband almost wrecked her journalism career while he definitely did a number on her self-esteem. The documentary on Duncan Hatcher is the perfect way to rebuild both. As a freshman in college, she'd had a crush on the senior football hero, but he hadn't known she existed. She never expects the sparks that fly between them as they work on the project nor the struggles they must face if they both want to win.